Immaculate

By
Elizabeth Forkey

Published by Entrada Publishing.

Printed in the United States of America.

Contents

For Molly, Emma, Logan, Eli and Drevyn

To my sweet friends and fans... You have encouraged me and pushed me forward. When I second-guessed myself, when I doubted, you made me believe in Ivy's story and what God can do through her. Without you, this process of becoming an author would have been gray and lonely. Thank you!

And to my amazing husband, Ron... You are my Matt. Ours is a precious story of teenage romance that endured the tests and trials of young love to becoming something unspeakably great. The fires and pressures of life have only made this diamond love more sparkly. And perhaps, most importantly, you crack me up. You are—and have always been—my most supportive, most encouraging, dearest, handsomest friend. I love you!!!

Prologue

The young man walked with an air of confidence into the lion's den. Well rehearsed lies ran their lines in his head. A month of seedy dealings and questionable compromises had afforded him this one chance. For her sake, he would take it. With a slight tremble in his step he marched across the gray tiles and heard his footsteps echo around the room. A woman in white appraised him from her place at the front desk.

"I'm here for the interview," the young man stated with forced bravado.

His dry eyes itched and he blinked rapidly at the woman. She tilted her head and studied him, biting her cheek.

"How old are you?" she asked, skeptical.

"I am expected," the young man said, forcing an air of superiority and haughtiness into the first lie of many he would tell today.

The woman in white pursed her lips and pressed a red button on her desk. Unsure of what the red button did, the attractive young man wondered if he had already failed.

"Go on back, second door on the left," the woman said without looking up again.

The liar fought the urge to thank the woman. *Stay in character*, he lectured himself.

A set of oak doors buzzed from across the room and he made for them. He pushed against the doors and found them locked. The woman at the desk buzzed the doors again and he pushed through successfully into comfortable sterility.

He had always felt at home in a hospital. The white speckled floor tiles and eggshell colored walls didn't make him nervous at all. Wheelchairs and gurneys reminded him of who he was and where he came from. The smells that would bother most were recognizable and inoffensive in his nostrils. He knew the name of each instrument and fixture he passed. He found himself wanting the job he was faking for.

At the second door on the left, he collected himself and prayed a short internal prayer. Then, he knocked.

"What?" a woman called out from the other side of the gray door.

"I'm here for the Ultrasound Technician opening," the young man said and cursed himself because he knew his voice lacked conviction.

"Come."

The young man pushed down on the silver door handle and put his whole heart into making an entrance.

An older woman sat behind a plastic folding table that had been set up as a desk. She was heavily made up. Her orange hued makeup did a poor job of covering the scaly patches of LS on her cheeks and neck. Appraising her, he guessed she was nearing sixty. She made direct, unblinking eye contact. Despite his resolve, the young man looked away as though studying the room.

The office was small and cluttered, filled mostly with cardboard boxes overflowing with white, yellow and pink papers. The lighting was dismal and the young man wondered if the room had been a supply closet at one time. Still staring at him, the woman did not stand to greet him. Neither did she invite him to sit. He sat anyway in the metal folding chair adjacent her desk. The shrewd woman's penciled-on eyebrows raised appreciatively at him and she cracked a smile. There was red lipstick smeared on her teeth.

"Name?" she asked.

The young man wondered if the entire interview would be conducted in one word questions.

"Dr. Hale Shepherd, graduate of Harvard."

"What year?" she asked.

"Twenty-six," he knew it was his least believable lie. His beard helped a little.

"I graduated from Harvard in '02, it's a shame what's been happening there," the woman said, puckering her red lips.

"Mmm," the young man agreed, clueless.

"You look very young," she said seductively.

The young man fought the shiver that danced around his spine and dove into his next lie, "I finished my residency when I was twenty-one."

The pencil lines where her eyebrows should have been shot up in surprise.

"Genius?" she asked another one word question.

"That's what they said," the young man shrugged and played humble like Jesus at a foot-washing.

"Where did you do your residency?"

"Upstate New York," he went for vague and far away and hoped she wouldn't ask more. "They've been converted."

"Blood Centers are important, but it is a shame to see so many hospitals going under," she said.

He nodded.

"What brings you here to us? You're a long way from New York."

"I heard about the incredible work you're doing here with the carriers and I came to watch you heal the world," he stroked her ego and spouted his biggest lie of all.

"Let's see what you can do," she said standing up with an eager twinkle in her eye.

THREE MONTHS EARLIER

Chapter One

Sorry Doesn't Cut It

The junky station-wagon sounds about as trustworthy as a zombie politician. The decades old car is making an unhealthy whirring clunk as we drive slowly through the dark, our headlights off. Diluted moonlight illumines the potholed road before us. My town, my home, my life for the last four years is burning in the rearview mirror. The smell of smoke has filled the car. As I inhale the noxious fumes, I am hit with the morbid realization that I'm breathing the ashes of our home and our loved ones. My empty stomach turns upside-down and threatens to wring itself dry.

Images I didn't see, but can't stop envisioning, play in stop-motion at each blink of my eyes. Eyes open, I see smoke and darkness and too few survivors. Eyes closed, I see the screaming faces of friends and loved ones. Eyes open, pale moonlight behind winter-bare forest branches that hover over us as we creep away from the familiar and drive towards my nightmares. Eyes closed, fire! The Inn burning! The U.R. burning! Bodies burning!

Eyes open! Don't shut them! Don't blink!

We are escaping Toccoa in the middle of the night after witnessing the vicious attack on our compound. Our small band lives by some miracle, though I of all people should be dead. The horde came for *me* and ate through good people and sentimental places in its carnivorous search. So many casualties lay piled in the streets, a grievously imbalanced transaction for my freedom.

Harmony, my best friend, is twisted like a paperclip in her seat. She stares out the back windshield watching the fiery glow of home shrink from view. I can barely hear her crying over the metallic grind of the old engine. Her tears aren't loud or dramatic, but the sound is so heartbreaking, so forlorn, that I am overwhelmed with guilt and remorse.

All my fault!

Thump.

All my fault!

Whunk.

All my fault!

Thwunk.

My thoughts repeat the guilty message in cadence with the clunky car noises. I'll never be able to forgive myself for the death of all the people we loved. I should've gone back and turned myself in. My choices brought us to this calamitous night. Harmony's mom is most likely dead, either burned to ashes or murdered out on the street. Harmony didn't get to say goodbye to her mother, who was her hero and her only family. I hope she never forgives me. I don't want to be forgiven. It's too awful.

Matt, Thomas and Tim sit together on the open bench front seat, with Matt at the wheel. Matt's little brother, Thomas, is still recovering from a zombie attack that left him hanging on the edge of death only a few weeks ago. He lost most of his right hand - which is still healing beneath layers of bandaging - and he sustained many other deep wounds all over his body. My guilty thoughts find blessed distraction as I study the top of his shaved head in front of me. If I had turned myself in, Matt wouldn't have gotten Thomas out. Sweet Thomas would lay numbered among the dead. He's alive because I stayed.

Is that anywhere near enough?

Thomas' sniffles join in gut-wrenching chorus with Harmony's quiet keening. His adopted parents, Jose and Ellen, are probably in Heaven now, too. At the young age of eleven he's already said too many goodbyes. There were one hundred ninety-five people living within the supposed safety of our fenced-in utopia. Most of them lost their lives tonight because Pravda is hunting me. Even if some of our friends escaped, we'll never see them again. There wasn't a contingency for this. No place to meet up should evil descend and destroy. If any survived, they are on their own and we are on our own. Any survivors would follow wisdom's course and head in the opposite direction we are driving.

Our insane course?

Atlanta. Pravda's headquarters.

Thomas yelps as the car bounces through a deep pot hole. I see a grimace on Matt's rugged face as his eyes leave the road to glance down at his Tom. Thomas is the bravest, sweetest kid I've ever known. Since joining our community of the Living, Thomas has been an example of triumphant faith

- even in the hardest of circumstances. But tonight his head is hanging on his chest and swaying with each jolting pothole as he whimpers in heartbreak and pain. I'm afraid that all the hoop-jumping it took to get out of Toccoa - the ups and downs through Matt's secret tunnel - may have reopened his still healing wounds.

I lean forward and catch a glimpse of a ghost in the rearview mirror. No, not a ghost. A haunting version of myself. My curly hair is matted and flat. My brown eyes look black and empty. Horror, guilt, and sorrow have changed the landscape of my teenage face into something older and uglier. Tears have carved tribal lines like pagan tattoos in the dirt and ash on my cheeks.

How was this Your will? I ask the One who let this happen.

No answer. Just more weight added to the invisible burden crushing my lungs. My foolish romantic feelings for Matt must have pushed me off track. There's no way it was supposed to turn out like this.

I despise myself.

Thomas stifles a cry as the Station Wagon hits another bump and Matt hisses through his teeth. I'm not alone in my self-loathing. Matt blames himself for Thomas' horrible injuries. Not two weeks ago, Matt tried to take Thomas back home to Atlanta and they were attacked on the road.

The same road we're heading down now. And we have a larger, more conspicuous group. And two children. How will we ever make it? Matt couldn't keep his own brother safe and I've given him more unwanted charges. I am humbled - and well, shocked - that he took this on for me. He didn't want this responsibility, but he took it so I would come with him. If not for Matt and his tunnel, none of us would be here right now. We'd all be dead. Thomas included. That has to mean something. It has to. We owe this handsome, green-eyed zombie our lives.

Tim leans away from Thomas and Matt, his head against the cool window. He doesn't react to Thomas' whimpers. I can't see Tim's face and I don't think I want to. Every time I look into his warm brown eyes I feel lacking. Lacking courage, lacking wisdom, lacking moral fiber. Tim told me that he loved me tonight in front of everyone. I knew he cared about me. I knew he wanted me to be just his. But saying "I love you, Ivy" out loud in front of Matt and Harmony and begging me to choose a life somewhere safe with him was over the limit of what I could process. And he still came with me even though I chose Matt. Tim lost his family tonight because of me.

It isn't only guilt that I feel when I meet his gaze. His strange devotion makes me feel loved too, the way Aunty loved me. Loved like I could do everything wrong and the love would still be there. I lean against my window and try to catch a glimpse of him through the crack between the seat and the door. His eyes are closed. His tired, sad face makes me ache.

The ache is a concoction of eight parts guilt, one part confusion, and one part - feelings. Not the same as with Matt. Not the heart-thumping, excited attraction that Matt's emerald green eyes and crooked smile induce, but something small and deep-down that grows when I wish it would die. Tim is a good man. A man after God's heart. A man who would give his life for me, I have no doubt.

When all trace of Toccoa is erased by fog and distance, Harmony melts back into her seat. I stare silently as she lays her freckled cheek against the cracked leather cushion. Her auburn hair spills messily over her face like a mourning veil and hides her eyes from my sideways nervous glances. She must blame me. How could she not? She's only with us because there was nowhere else to go. Pravda would've found her and killed her if she had stayed behind.

Pravda. An organization of dead scientists and doctors who are trying to cure a curse from God with Band-Aids and delusions of grandeur. Pravda thinks my blood holds some secret to curing the disease that is killing the whole world. Chuck Fox said they found what they were looking for in the sample they took of my blood and that they'll hunt me to the ends of the earth. And the saddest thing is they are wrong. If it were true, I would turn myself in. If I could stop all the sickness and pain that the curse has caused, I would. But He is the only Cure to what they are dying from. Whatever they think they found in my blood is just more grasping at weak straws. More sick ignorance. Ignorance that our town - our loved ones - paid the price for.

Harmony is my best friend and she needs me now, but I feel ashamed to offer any words of comfort. God knows I'm acquainted with every agonizing emotion she's going through. I've just been through it myself. I lost my Aunty Coe this week to that unfair thief, Death. Aunty was my mother for the last four years and the most important person in my life. Losing her tore me apart. But I got to say goodbye, got to bury her. She died because it was her time to go home. And, when I thought I had no family left, Matt told me that my dad and Aunty Betty are still alive. Harmony has no one. With no family left and nowhere safe to go, she's been forced to come along on this suicidal quest to rescue *my* family. The utter unfairness of it all lays its full weight on my already guilt-ridden spirit.

Little Rosa, an innocent who was rescued by one of our missionaries, sits quietly between Harmony and I. Her too big Mickey Mouse hat hangs so low that her long dark eyelashes flutter against it when she looks up at me. She has been through terrible suffering in her short life - I'm not even sure how old she is - and she seems to find empathy more natural than speaking. In the few days that I've had her she has been more of a comfort to me than I've been to her. Looking up at me expectantly, Rosa's big brown eyes are asking me for something that she can't voice herself. She glances back and forth between me and Harmony. I nod, understanding her unspoken request.

Rosa smiles at me and turns away from me, confident in my permission. She pats Harmony's thin hands and scoots closer to her. I watch Rosa as she becomes comfort. Her empathetic little face fills with sorrow and concern. She nestles herself into the crook of Harmony's bent body and pulls Harmony's limp arm around her. Rosa's chubby hands were the same comfort for me last week when I lost Aunty. Harmony pulls Rosa close, holding her like teddy bear. I can only pray for my friend that she'll find comfort in that hug. I didn't mean for any of this to happen.

Chapter Two

The Enemy Of My Enemy Is My Significant Other

We've only gone a few miles when Matt turns left onto the old college campus. He took me here just a few days ago. It was a romantic date - my first date - in the midst of my deteriorating life. Like a trip out of reality. I remember laying next to him looking up at the grandeur of the beautiful waterfall under the sunset sky. I was happy, really happy, in that place out of time.

"Why are we here?" I ask leaning forward over the front seat to whisper to Matt.

Pravda's angry mob is only a mile or two behind us. We should put more distance between us and them. I had expected we'd drive through the night, straight to Atlanta.

"You aren't planning on stopping already?" Tim asks incredulously.

Tim doesn't trust Matt. And that's a bit of an understatement.

"They'll have road blocks all over the place. We'll need to lay low here for a while. Maybe a couple days. Maybe even a couple weeks," Matt says, his voice tired and flat.

Matt navigates the potholes, speed bumps, and broken-down cars that make an obstacle course of the narrow road onto the campus, his shoulders hunched and tense for each bump Thomas's sore body is forced to endure.

"How are we safe here?" Tim demands.

"It's big," Matt says with undisguised disgust and irritation. "There's a lot of places to hide and it will be more comfortable for the girls than hiding in the woods."

If our options are this place or the woods, I pick here.

Tim exhales a strangled sigh of frustration. We are all at Matt's mercy. Matt knows the world outside of our little town better than we do. We have no option but to trust him.

Matt pulls the decrepit wagon into a parking space adjacent to an auditorium-sized building. With no headlights to illumine the night, it's hard to see where we are or if we're safe. I squint out the windows at the huge brick building. On the roof, a cross stretches up into the night. Moonlight highlights the cross' delicate silhouette. Was this a church? The thought brings a smidgen of peace to my nervous, tense body. Did people worship my Savior here? Perhaps He lingers still in this place set aside for Him.

When Matt turns the key off, the engine sputters and sputters and sputters then finally coughs and quits. I know there weren't many cars left for Matt to choose from, but I wonder if this one has enough life left in it to get us to Atlanta. And what will we do if it doesn't? Thomas still needs a wheelchair and Rosa is so small, I'm guessing she's just three or four. The kids can't handle a hike to Atlanta in the wintery February weather.

Parked in the weak moonlight, we sit silently in the car, unsure of what to do, waiting for direction from our zombie tour guide. Thomas and Harmony have put their tears on hold in the tense stillness. I stay perched against the front seat feeling responsible for our predicament and, therefore, desperate to help.

Matt lays his head back on his seat and sighs. Then, looking past me - tilting his face towards Tim - he asks, "Can you help me?"

Matt's questioning tone is full of meaning, almost pleading. Vulnerable. A glimpse behind the mask of his tirelessly cocky self-confidence. Matt's green eyes stare past me at Tim, begging Tim to work with him and not against him. He's asking for a truce. Tim's lips are pressed in a hard line and his bushy eyebrows are furrowed. His brown eyes glare back at Matt behind the glint of his thick glasses. He looks as angry as he did the other night when he found out I had been out alone with Matt.

Tim has always been overly upbeat, so much so that his persistent nerdy cheerfulness drove me crazy. Only recently have I seen this angry, darker side of him. Close contact with me and my chaos seems to bring out the worst in people. I think Tim would rather die than cooperate under Matt's leadership.

Tim nods with a terse bob of his chin and says, "Whatever you think is best. We need to keep Ivy safe."

There's the nausea again. What about everyone else? We need to keep Harmony safe. We need to keep Rosa from ever being hurt by one of them again. We need to keep Thomas safe.

I cringe knowing Harmony heard Tim's obvious agenda. Everything is all about Ivy lately. Who am I? A short, slightly too curvy, curly haired, virgin? A Living one? Those things don't define me to the rest of the world. To them I'm the one Pravda would like to see drained of blood and turned into an easy to take pill for the cure.

"Can we just all keep each other safe?" I ask.

Neither of them answer me.

"What do you need me to do?" Tim asks in a begrudging whisper, as though saying it any louder would've taken more submission to Matt's leadership than he could muster.

An unwilling partnership.

Matt looks out his side window for long seconds that feel like minutes before answering, "We need to cover the car with dirt and tree branches so it blends in with the other cars here. Put stuff behind and around the tires like the wind blew it there. Then we'll scout a safe place to move Tom and the girls to. We don't have to unload the car tonight."

"Okay," is all Tim says.

Tim and Matt push the car's front doors open and the rusted hinges cry eerie, oil-deprived shrieks. In the venomous dark, the ghostly noise fills me with terror. We all freeze breathless, listening for any sign that we've drawn attention to ourselves. An ominous quiet is our only answer. There's no way to know if anyone is out there in the dark watching us. Hunting us.

"I want to come too," I whisper urgently at them.

They both push their squealing doors shut without answering or acknowledging me. I guess they want me to stay here.

Thomas whimpers again, alone in the front seat. His breathing is heavy and punctuated. His meds probably wore off hours ago. I dig through the bag at my feet for the bottles of medicine I hastily packed before leaving Jose and Ellen's. I find the Tylenol and dump the contents into my hand. Only 9 little capsules left. Only a few days worth of partial relief. I don't have any water for him to take the pill with.

I lean over the seat with one of the precious pills and ask in a whisper, "Can you swallow it without water?"

He nods and lets out another pained whimper. I put the pill to his lips and he opens his mouth to take it. His face feels too hot against my hand.

We sit in nervous silence while the guys throw dirt and leaves over the car. Their shadowy forms wisp back and forth outside the windows while they work their camouflage magic. A bright light flashes in my peripheral vision. Harmony and I gasp and duck low in our seats. She pulls Rosa down to the floor with her and I whisper for Thomas to lay down on the front seat. I risk sitting up and searching the back of the car for two blankets. I toss one over Thomas who is laying on the front seat whimpering.

Ducking down next to Harmony and Rosa, I pull the other blanket over us and we squish together uncomfortably on the floor of the back seat. Where are Matt and Tim? They must be hiding nearby. They won't risk opening the noisy doors now. How long will we have to hide like this? The light is suddenly bright through the blanket - someone is looking into the car! Are we hidden enough? Did Matt and Tim do a good enough job in the short time they had? The light moves away and I whisper for everyone to stay hidden.

My left foot is falling asleep and my right arm is pressed painfully against something sharp sticking out near the floor. There is no room for me to move and I try to focus my thoughts on something other than the pain. I feel under the seat in front of me and my hand finds the cool metal barrel of one of Matt's guns. The cold danger chills my fingertips and gives me butterflies. I find myself, once again, considering if I could use it.

I held a gun last night in the tunnel. I know how heavy it will be if I pick it up - so much heavier than I expected it to be. I don't know how to use it. I don't believe in using it. But I desperately want to protect my friends. I remember that one of the guns is still tucked in Matt's pants. I hope he won't use it. Enough people have died tonight because of me. I don't want anyone else to pay the price for my freedom, even my enemies. But Matt won't see it that way.

We wait in the dark for forever. My foot and arm have gone from uncomfortable to so crazy painful that just staying still has become a maddening test of willpower. I have no idea how long we've been crouched here when I hear the back hatch pop open. The hatch door whines as it resists being lifted and I stop breathing as the car sinks with the body weight of someone climbing in.

"Ivy?"

Tears of relief flood my eyes when I hear Tim whisper my name.

"You can get up. The coast is clear. Whoever it was moved on to the other side of these buildings."

I groan in pain as I pull myself back up onto the seat, excruciating pins and needles stabbing at my numb foot and hand.

"Where's Matt?" I ask rubbing my neck and turning to see Tim crouched close to my seat. He fills what little space was left next to our supplies in the back. He smells like smoke and sweat. I meet his eyes and they are full of the frustration I knew I would find.

"He's looking for somewhere safe to spend the night. He'll be back." Tim spits his disgust for Matt with every word.

I'm sure Tim wishes Matt would prove his negative, judgmental expectations to be true and desert us sooner rather than later; but it's short-sighted of him. I'm certain we can't survive out here without Matt. We can't even buy food without him. I can just picture the commotion it would cause if four Living people walked into a Blood Center to give blood for credits. My picture is probably plastered all over the walls of every compound and B.C. in Georgia. Thanks to Chuck Fox.

Harmony and Rosa have stretched and reseated themselves. Harmony continues to give us all the silent treatment. As much as I hate her grieving silence, I'm afraid of what she'll say when she does finally start talking. I lean up front to check on Thomas and, lifting his blanket, I find him sleeping. How he is able to sleep with all this stress is beyond me. Tim sits sullenly behind me, sighing in frustration as the minutes pass and stretch into an hour - maybe more. We don't speak.

I stare out of the windows and search the night. My eyes blur in and out as I watch for hints of movement and my mind races around endless tracks of what-ifs. The apprehension of what or who is out there, just beyond my sight in the dark shadows, grows. The nerve wracking shadows morph and collect, growing into blurry enemies in the dark. Growing into raw fear and then panic. I stare into the moving ink of night, my fingers curled where the door meets the window. I pull in sharp breaths and the cloud of steam on the glass blurs my view. I feel myself beginning to hyperventilate and I fumble for the door handle, ready to flee. A quick knock at the back window makes me shriek in terror.

Tim lays a hand against my neck and shoulder and whispers in my ear, “It’s okay.”

Matt is looking in the back window. It’s just Matt. I take a trembling breath as Matt opens the whiny back hatch and motions for us to follow him. Grabbing my little bag, I help Rosa and Harmony climb over the back seat. Harmony accepts my help but never meets my eyes. Rosa stands close to me in the chilly night and wraps an arm around my leg. My heart is racing. I stare at the swarming shadows that move all around us as the wind blows. Just trees. Just branches. Calm down.

Matt and Tim climb in and wake Thomas. Together they lift him over the front seat, over the back seat and into the hatch. I have my backpack over my arm and Thomas’ wheelchair unfolded and ready. Tim and Harmony have nothing of their own to carry so they help with the blankets and Thomas’ bundle of belongings.

I was prepared to go when the time came to leave. I had been out of the fence with Matt, had seen the armed mobs forming whose sole purpose was our destruction. I knew our safe time in Toccoa had come to an end. The bag of mine and Rosa’s necessities was ready when the alarms went off. I had even packed a few sentimental items, the most important memories I could fit in my small pack. Tim and Harmony have nothing to remind them of their loved ones. Not a single belonging between them. Not even a toothbrush or change of underwear.

Because of me.

Chapter Three

Let's Make A Deal

We follow behind Matt, who is pushing Thomas, our footsteps like nervous whispers in the dark. The wheelchair makes a gentle whirring and only creaks when Matt tips it backwards to mount a curb. As we emerge from the shadow of the tall brick dormitory, the moon abandons us - hiding its dim light completely behind smoke-induced clouds. We strike out into the darkness, weaving around smaller buildings and parking lots full of abandoned vehicles. My eyes adjust to the thick black night and my stumbling feet find their way.

I have become accustomed to the dull heartache that hasn't left since Aunty died. It's like learning to live with an amputated body part or a chronic illness. The lonely ache has weakened my body but given strength to my fears. I keep expecting zombies to spring from behind the abandoned cars we pass or to reach out from behind dark broken windows. I hear my heart beating in my ears as I hurry to stay as close to Matt and Tim as possible.

Rosa is between Harmony and I, holding our hands. I'm tugging the two of them along like a chain behind me. Matt brings us down a hill that I recognize - we are close to the entrance of the waterfall. I strain to hear the sound of rushing water, but the wind is blowing and my heart's pounding has only gotten louder with exertion. If the falls are near, I can't tell. The wind and my heart are deafening.

As we approach another tall dormitory at the bottom of the hill, a beam of light cuts the road just to the right of me. I whip around for the source and see the light's origin at the top of the hill behind us. Matt ducks behind an SUV with broken windows. I search the darkness, frantic for place to hide Harmony, Rosa, and myself. The light has stopped in the woods on the far right side of the road and I know any moment it will sweep back to where we stand. A shout at the source of the light tells me that the searcher isn't alone. He's alerting others. We've failed already. We got one mile away. A pathetic attempt of an escape.

Tim lifts Rosa into his arms and grabs for my hand. He tugs us down into a damp ditch next to the car that Matt and Thomas disappeared behind. The dead leaves smell like oil and my pants are instantly wet through at the knees. Crawling forward, Tim deposits Rosa under the car. I thank God again that she is mute. Any normal child would be screaming by now. Tim pushes me from behind, shoving me under the car, and Harmony comes unceremoniously behind me. The car has high clearance but we are running out of space. Tim presses himself in with us, his body almost completely covering mine.

Harmony looks over at me with wide terrified eyes. She is panting and crying the way she did two nights ago when Matt shot her. Being my friend is a terminal disease these days. As the light arcs back to envelop the car, I see tears pouring down her cheeks. Tim reaches across me and puts a finger to her parted lips.

Tim cups Harmony's chin with a tender touch and breathes, "Shhh" in a gentle murmur, his breath close to my ear.

Harmony clamps her lips between her teeth and breathes staccato, snot filled snorkels of air through her runny nose. Her face is white like a mouthless mask frozen in fright. Tim's weight is even heavier on me with his hand still petting Harmony and I feel the air being crushed out of my lungs. Instead of fear, I find myself - irritated. At Harmony.

My spirit tells me that it's not fair of me, but the nudge to my conscience only fuels my irritation. She needs to keep it together. She'll get us all killed if she can't muster a little bravery. I look away from Tim's tender caresses on her tear stained cheeks. Like a seedling breaking through the soil, a thin tendril of disgust surprises me as it blooms in my heart. I close my eyes and force Harmony's face from my mind. A rock is digging into my stomach and I fight a desperate foolish desire to scream.

Tim twists above me and the pressure on my lungs is relieved. I open blurry eyes and stare out towards the legs that are walking down the hill towards us behind the ever brightening light. The light only stays for a moment, oozing under the car and glistening on the pavement, before moving suddenly off to the right.

"Whoa," I hear someone say in an easy, unthreatening tone. It's Matt. I can't see him but I picture him putting his gloved hands up as though surrendering. The light has swiveled and stopped on his legs just ten feet from our hiding place.

Tim's body is tense against mine and his breath in my ear stills. We lay frozen and helpless.

“Are you with Pravda?” asks an older man with a demanding wheezy voice, the holder of the flashlight.

“No. I’m just looking for some extra credits,” Matt answers and I hope for the hundredth time that we can trust him.

“This is our territory. If that carrier is hiding here, those credits are ours.”

I swallow hard and feel my heart pound harder. He called me a carrier? What’s a carrier? I’ve never heard anyone use that term before. Carrier of the cure? Carrier of what?

“You interested in a little help?” Matt offers the man who knows more about what Pravda wants from me than I do. Tim’s hand clamps tight around my arm.

“We don’t need it,” the man barks with a phlegmy voice like a cigarette smoker.

“You got a big group here?” Matt asks.

No answer. My stomach pitches fits.

“How ‘bout if I find her, I’ll split it with you 60/40?” Matt offers pleasantly.

He wouldn’t!

“This is our territory. You find her, you bring her to me. Maybe we’ll work something out.”

“That’s not a lot of incentive,” Matt says with good humor.

I hear a “clack.” That clipped, ominous ratchet that lets you know a bullet is loaded and the owner means business. I don’t know which of them is holding the deciding steel.

“I could kill you now?” the chain-smoker offers Matt.

Matt isn’t in charge right now and a group of who knows how many murderers are searching for me. And I’m lying on the ground ten feet away. Screwed as usual.

“I know her.” Matt’s admission sends an icy shiver through my shoulders and I shake under Tim’s warm arms. “I know what she looks like and she might trust me. If I find her, it’ll be easier to bring her in alive. You only get the credits if she’s alive.”

After a long minute of quiet and wondering what each face is telling the other, the other man says, “Fifteen percent. That’s the most I can give you. We have families to feed here.”

“Twenty-five,” Matt counters and I’m feeling more annoyed than angry.

Tim grunts quietly in my ear and I couldn’t agree more.

“Twenty and you walk away from here with no holes in yah.”

“That sounds like a pretty good deal,” Matt says and I could swear there was a little bit of fear in his voice. “Where do I find you when I have her?”

“You try to take that carrier off our territory, we’ll find you,” the man wheezes venomously.

The light wanders back up the hill and away from us, but we stay still. I don’t hear Matt anywhere around the car and the sudden lack of light has made the dark darker. I can’t make out what is beyond our small rectangle of limbs and shadow. Tim’s breathing regulates in my ear and I realize my free hand - the one not pinned between me and spiky cement - is holding tight to Tim’s big hand. Our fingers are intertwined and I don’t remember weaving them together. I glance sideways at Harmony and see her face is hidden in Rosa’s Mickey Mouse hat as she whispers to her. Are we safe?

Will I ever be safe?

Will anyone close to me ever be safe?

Matt didn’t give us away and I should feel relief. I knew he wouldn’t. He cares for me. I feign a small stretch and unlock my fingers from Tim’s. I feel bad. He is so good. I keep seeing his hand cupping Harmony’s face and irritated, confusing feelings come with the memory. I don’t want to be with him. It would solve everything if he fell in love with Harmony instead. But I don’t want that at all. Am I being selfish? Harmony needs someone. Maybe Tim would be perfect for her.

Matt’s voice startles me and I jump in Tim’s arms, “Are you ladies done napping? Mind if we keep going?”

Matt leads us down cracked sidewalks and uneven cement stairways. Tim is always ready to help with the wheelchair without a word being spoken. We move slower now. Every sound amplified in the dark. My heart is the loudest sound of all. On a little walkway next to another tall brick building, Matt stops in front of a low window. He slides the glass open and drops noiselessly into the black hole. Tim lifts Thomas and hands him in to his brother then turns to fold the wheelchair and hands it in as well.

Harmony and I glance over our shoulders as the wind rustles the leaves in the shadows around us. Matt and Tim work together to get us all inside as though they can read each other's thoughts. A fluid motion of silent teamwork that belies their true feelings about having to work together.

Once we are all together again inside, Matt slides the window closed and pulls a thin curtain across it's rod to cover the glass. Then he and Tim lift and push a large metal cabinet over in front of the window. No one else will be coming in that way. Without a word, Matt pushes Thomas's wheel chair out into the hall and we shuffle behind.

The rubber wheels whir against the linoleum, a hospital kind of noise. The nerve-wracking silence of the old building is punctuated by our echoing footsteps. How well could Matt have searched in the short time he had? This is crazy! We can't stay here! What if that group finds us? Who knows how many there are of them and how well watched these dark halls are? My exhausted nerves are set on edge and I long for somewhere safe to curl up and sleep this nightmare away.

Matt's flashlight as our guide, we traverse several hallways with a directness that conveys Matt's familiarity with this place. Finally, we emerge together into a large common room that must be in the very center of the old building because it has no windows. Matt and Tim walk around the large room and check each door. They lock and barricade every possible way in before circling back to us.

"Okay. Everybody pick a couch and get some rest," Matt says in full voice.

It sounds so loud in the echoey darkness that I cringe, wishing he would whisper.

Pulling my small flashlight out of my bag, I grab Harmony's unwilling hand and whisper for Rosa to follow us. Dragging Harmony along, I sweep my light over several moldy, questionable couches before finally coming across one that seems less likely to be full of bugs and/or mice.

"You sleep here," I whisper to Harmony.

Her empty eyes stare back into mine, her face a wilted flower. I take the softest blanket from the pile we brought and cover the old couch with it while she stands and watches. I lay Rosa down at one end; and, holding Harmony's shoulders, I gently shove her down on the other end. She turns away from me without a word, curling up towards the back of the couch. I tuck another blanket around them and turn to search for my own spot to spend the night.

None of the other couches look safe. I find a fluffy chair with almost no holes and minimal mystery stains. It'll have to do. Despite my discomfort, horrendous guilt, and worried thoughts of how many spiders live in this dark room, I am asleep almost instantly.

Chapter Four

When You're Sliding Into First

I count the time by two kinds of dark. I feel like we're in a cave. It is dark when I'm awake and the cave smothers me with boredom and too much time to think. We have flashlights and a few lanterns, but we use them sparingly. When I'm sleeping, nightmares chase me through Toccoa's burning streets. Masked faces grab at me and wrestle my friends away. We've been in the cave for five sessions of second guessing and hating myself and six heart-racing runs through zombie filled nightmares. So, it's been five days and six nights. God has hidden us away in this cave, so we wait. Matt is the only one who leaves.

Thomas is sick. His fever is off the charts. I don't lay my hand against his skin anymore. I feel the heat radiating off of him when I sit near him. Harmony sits by him a lot. She and I still haven't spoken; so, I only take my turn at Thomas' side when Harmony is sleeping. Thomas sleeps almost constantly these last couple days - shivering and moaning under a heavy pile of covers.

Tim changes Thomas's bandages every other day because we have so few supplies. He says they really should be changed at least twice a day. The infection smells through the scant bandages and I'm nervous that we are losing him. The day after we arrived here, Tim made Matt hold the flashlight for him and he checked under Thomas' clothes for the offending wound. The grim way they both walked off in different directions spoke volumes.

It's not just Harmony and I who are on the outs. No one is speaking to each other. Tim is angry and worried. Harmony obviously hates me and I have less and less hope that we'll ever be okay. Thomas is lost in a fever induced haze. Matt can act tough, but I know he's terrified about losing his Tom. The cold, emotionless facade that he wore when we first met is back in place. He's such a zombie.

The cave is huge. It holds six different couches that we've turned into beds. It took some rearranging and cushion swapping, but we eventually all settled into our own little comfortable places. There are several tables and chairs scattered around the room, one of which I turned into a fort for Rosa with an old sheet I found. She has spent her time crawling around the room collecting scattered playing cards, dominoes and checkers and making little games with them. She's like a little wild animal, darting around all day. She brushes past my legs and scares me to death and then scampers away to her fort.

Matt raided the dorm rooms above and around us and came back with a pitiful offering of institutional food. We've been eating cold canned corn and mushy canned beets with Gov. Bars from the car for "dessert". You can imagine what a diet of canned vegetables and fiber does to a person's system. We found a little bathroom behind one of the doors around the perimeter of the room. I'm glad we at least have that convenience. Though, I count it a blessing that we don't have more light when I'm in there.

We've searched the room for anything useful, turning over cushions and emptying cabinets. Our search yielded textbooks, mismatched socks, a few plastic plates, one red plastic cup, a real fork, and a bottle of chocolate syrup. When Tim found the chocolate syrup, he let out an excited "whoop!" and we all hurried to see what treasure he had found. We passed the bottle around in the dim lantern light, taking turns squirting the chocolaty goo in our mouths. It was the best thing I've ever tasted. I looked up and saw my friends smiling. And I smiled back with joy and relief.

They met my eyes and then each other's. One by one their smiles faded back to the expressionless ghosts I've become accustomed to. There is still more liquid chocolate in the bottle. It has been sitting on a table in the center of the room for four days. Like a test of stubborn willpower or something. None of us wants to be happy. Not even the small happiness that sweet syrup would bring. We are sad on purpose.

It wouldn't be this way if Thomas wasn't so sick. If he were well, his sunny disposition would spill over onto all of us and we'd be coping better. His decline has made the cave even darker and harder to bear. He is dying.

Just because we aren't speaking to each other doesn't mean we've been completely quiet. We have been speaking to God. We've prayed out loud over Tom several times a day, Tim and Harmony and I. Matt stands across the room and stares at us with a cold intensity. I think he's mad at me that it isn't working.

He wants me to do another miracle like I did for Harmony. It's not for lack of sincerity. I'm begging God with all of my heart, but He is silent to our pleas and Thomas is only getting worse. After all that Matt has gone through to get his little brother back, if we lose Thomas now - I doubt Matt will stick around to help the rest of us. Thomas is the link keeping us all together. And the link is fading.

*****

I jump awake, a scream in my throat. It takes a few seconds to remember where I am. The cave. I'm embarrassed that my friends heard me scream, then lonely when no one cares. Thomas moans and the painful sound echoes around the room. I feel like I'm losing my mind in this incessantly dark, moan-filled cavern. Sitting up, I see that Harmony is sitting with Thomas. Tim is pacing near the door, waiting for Matt to return.

A light blinks like Morse Code. Rosa is scampering around the room with my flashlight playing imaginary games. Thomas' moans don't seem to affect her like they do the rest of us. Maybe she's just too little to understand. Alone and more desperately lonely than usual, I reach for the little devotional I brought from the Inn. I don't know what the date is, so I decide to open it at random and hope that The Lord will have something good for me. By dim lantern light I read:

> July 9
>
> STOP WORRYING LONG ENOUGH to hear My voice. I speak softly to you, in the depths of your being. Your mind shuttles back and forth, hither and yon, weaving webs of anxious confusion. As My thoughts rise up within you, they become entangled in those sticky webs of worry. Thus, My voice is muffled, and you hear only "white noise."
>
> Ask My Spirit to quiet your mind so that you can think My thoughts. This ability is an awesome benefit of being My child, patterned after My own image. Do not be deafened by the noise of the world or that of your own thinking. Instead, be transformed by the renewing of your mind. Sit quietly in My Presence, letting my thoughts reprogram your thinking.

The verses at the bottom are:

Deuteronomy 30:20 "and that you may love the Lord your God, listen to his voice, and hold fast to him. For the Lord is your life, and he will give you many years in the land he swore to give to your fathers, Abraham, Isaac and Jacob."

Genesis 1:27 "So God created mankind in his own image, in the image of God he created them; male and female he created them."

Romans 12:2 "Do not conform to the pattern of this world, but be transformed by the renewing of your mind. Then you will be able to test and approve what God's will is - his good, pleasing and perfect will."

I've been reading my Bible every day here in the cave. It was only a few weeks ago that The Lord brought me back to His side after I had strayed in self-pity and laziness. Every day, I think of that night in my bedroom at the Inn. I remember how cold and afraid and alone I felt before I crumpled to my face and wet the carpet with repentant tears. I promised Him - no matter what - that I would put Him first and stay safely under His loving wing from now on. But those feelings, that rush of closeness with the God who created me and died for me didn't stay as strong as I would like.

Because life is stupid hard.

It's hard to know He's proud of you when you aren't proud of yourself. It's hard to feel peace when you live in a cave with people who hate you because you caused the death of their loved ones. It's hard to stay excited when it seems as though you've gotten yourself into more trouble than you know how to get out of. I've been reading my Bible every day. But today, for the first time in too many days, God speaks to me. Loudly, in spider web analogies that I can relate to.

I've been so worried and so anxious about whether or not I had messed everything up, I didn't see how all this mess could possibly be His will. Everything happened so fast and I did my best to make the right choices as they flew by me. He created me. And He made me a girl. A hormonal, emotional, guy-loving girl. Genesis says so. He promises that if I sit quiet and listen, refusing to let the spiders of doubt weave their webs of anxiety and fear, that His thoughts will become clear. So, here I am God. I'm listening.

Chapter Five

Old Person Smell

I'm sitting at the kitchen table eating granola with Aunty when I'm shaken awake. Her sharp blue eyes fade away from my view, dissolving into shadow. I sit up in the dark – disoriented - and realize with cold regret that Aunty is gone. A wound reopens in my chest and the raw ache that comes with it is excruciating.

I'm in the cave.

Tim is sitting close to me and as my thoughts line up with the here and now, I'm suddenly afraid that something is wrong. Tim hasn't spoken much to me since we've arrived. I know he's waiting for me to respond to his strange proposal. That's really what it was. A "Pick me. I love you" proposal. There's no time for date nights and hand holding in our world. Barely any time left for life. Tim wants me to marry him and spend the last of our days together. But his face close to mine in the dark tells me that isn't why he woke me.

"What is it? Is it Thomas?" I ask with rising dread.

"Shhh." Tim puts a finger to my lips, his face just inches from mine. My stomach flip-flops in his unexpected closeness and I instinctively think of how bad my breath must be. Tim reaches up and takes off his thick glasses. I used to want to barf at the sight of him. But, last week, when he sat at Aunty's bedside with me, I found myself appreciating his friendship. Throughout the process of losing and grieving Aunty, he became my biggest support. He grew on me. It would be a lie if I said I've forgotten how handsome and muscular he looked when I walked in on him in just a towel.

He whispers, close to my face, looking into my eyes, "I have to go. Will you take over my watch?"

"Go where?"

"Don't worry, I'll be back. I promise."

"Where is Matt? Is he going with you?" I whisper.

"No."

"Will you be gone long? I don't want you to leave -" and I really don't.

Tim gives me a sad smile. He knows how I feel about Matt; and we both know it's foolish of me. He starts to stand up and I reach for his hand. He looks down at me and I know how horrible I must look. So many days since I've had a shower.

He surprises me by bending and planting a quick kiss on my forehead. Then he's gone. I sit on the side of my couch bed and see Harmony watching me with her haunting stare from across the room. Her dead gaze fills me with guilt - and the creeps. I stand quickly to lock the door and take over Tim's watch.

*****

Tim has been gone for more than a day now. I'm really worried about him. Matt was furious when he got back and found Tim gone. He doesn't trust Tim - though I don't know why. What could Tim gain from betraying us? Tim is the outlaw, not Matt. I don't understand why Tim left or where he would've gone. Maybe he walked back to Toccoa in hopes of finding his brother Andrew or to search for more survivors. Matt will totally freak if Tim tries to add any more of the Living to our entourage.

Using precious batteries to light Aunty's Bible, I search the old pages for something. I don't know what really. Am I hoping to find a verse where God says, "Thou shalt stay in the cave until it is safe; and I will heal Thomas; and Matt will find life; and Tim will come back; and Harmony won't hate you; and keep up the good work with Rosa?" Because as much as I look there isn't anything that sounds at all like that.

If I put my nose close to the old pages and flip them quickly, they smell like Aunty's perfume. I fan the old pages against my cheek and listen to the soft flipping noise. On my third flip through, a small piece of paper falls out onto my shirt. It is folded and it must have been in here a long time, the crease is so tight and the paper so thin. It had almost become one with the pages it hid between.

Opening it gently in the light, I'm disappointed. There isn't any of Aunty's handwriting on it. It isn't anything special. Just an old devotional from a ladies conference, written years ago. Before He came back. Before Aunty even really knew Him - back when she was just going through the motions. I wonder why she kept it all this time. I would give anything to have her here. To ask her about it and hear what it meant to her. There is so much I would ask her about if only I could have her back.

Training my flashlight on the old words that she must have cared enough about to keep all this time I read:

Trade Anxiety For Peace

August 26th, 2013 G. Rodgers

"Do not be anxious about anything, but in everything, by prayer and petition, with thanksgiving, present your requests to God… And the peace of God, which transcends all understanding, will guard your hearts and your minds in Christ Jesus." Philippians 4: 6 & 7

God calls us to guard our hearts and minds carefully. (Proverbs 4:23) We need to choose wisely and bring our thoughts and concerns to Him for His help. And then God does the amazing and gives us a peace in our hearts that is beyond understanding! This peace itself guards our hearts and minds from dangerous stress and hasty, unwise choices. Thanksgiving is key.

Everyday there is much to be thankful for. There is also much to keep one feeling anxious and worried. Yet God calls you to live in thanksgiving and in peace. Worry only gives way to fear and fear will displace your faith causing anxiety to grow. God tells us to let faith take the upper hand and cover over the fear that tries to slip in and rob you of peace. Let the truth of His word change your anxious heart and mind and let worry be your call to prayer.

Dear God,

Fill my heart and mind with the recollection of all I have to say "thank you" for. Thank you that as I take responsibility for guarding my heart and bringing my fears to You, You also guard my heart and mind with Your amazing peace. What a wonderful exchange! Today I turn my worried thoughts over to you and ask You to preside over the details of my life. I pray this in

Jesus' name, Amen.

The canned little prayer at the end of the devotional is too generic. I bow my head and dig in for a long chat with Jesus. Aunty used to tell me to count my blessings. I search my heart for things to be thankful for and hope that He'll come through on his end of the bargain.

Chapter Six

I'm A Super Hero

Thomas hasn't been coherent for two days. I sit by his couch and pet him and sing hymns softly for most of my waking hours. Harmony sits by him less and less. I don't know if she's giving up on him or if she knows I need to be the one to sit. Rosa sits near me and today my happiest moment was hearing her softy hum along. Just hearing her make some noise is a joyous breakthrough, a small relief in this dark nightmare.

This is my second deathbed vigil in two weeks. I keep begging God to heal Thomas and I worry more by the hour that He is saying "no." Matt is gone more than he is here. I don't know what he's doing out there and I don't ask. I know he's in agony over Thomas.

Thomas wouldn't be like this if Matt hadn't insisted on taking him away from us. Matt never speaks about the attack. I know he is overwhelmed with guilt. By the time Matt carried Thomas back to us, there was little we could do for him, and our medical supplies were scant. Tim and his dad, Dr. Markowitz, worked tirelessly over Thomas' little broken body with my Aunty's help. I believe Aunty gave her last strength to helping save Thomas. She went downhill so fast after that day and died just a few days later.

Thomas was healing fast before the fences fell. I think he would've continued to heal and would've been fine if we hadn't moved him through the tunnel to escape. All the moving and jostling most certainly ripped sensitive internal injuries and caused this infection. Our lack of access to a doctor and some simple penicillin will be the death of him.

It doesn't seem fair. If Thomas dies, Matt will hate God all the more. I'm in love with a zombie who hates my Dearest Love. We'll never be right together unless Matt finds faith and the healing that I'm dying for him to accept. But Matt seems more hard and bitter by the day.

As I sit here by Thomas and dwell on all of the wrongness, the bleak depths of our situation, I surrender to the nagging surety that I made a selfish choice. I should've turned myself in to Pravda. Maybe they would've left our community in peace. Thomas would be sitting happily in his bedroom at Jose and Ellen's being cared for by Dr. Markowitz and continuing to get better. Tim would still have his dad. Harmony would still have her mom. Someone would've adopted little Rosa and she'd be safe and happy.

My mental state deteriorated, my bravery sapped, I dissolve into wracking sobs at Thomas' bedside. I can't hold back the torrent of tears anymore. I've been holding it all in. My grief for Aunty and all the people we lost. My unbearable guilt for Harmony and Tim and Thomas' losses. My fear of the future and what Pravda will do when they inevitably find me. I can't take it anymore. I want to die.

"It's not your fault, Ivy." Harmony speaks to me for the first time in so many days and her lies only make me sob harder. "You didn't choose this. This isn't your will. It's His. Our families are gone," she says softly and resolutely. "He took them home. They are all safe now," she reaches out a hand to pet my shoulder, but I angrily jerk myself away from her touch.

Now she'll speak to me? What? She had to wait until I wanted to die, had to see me rightfully punished before she'd give her friendship again?

No thanks!

Ivy, what is wrong with you? Where is the compassion that said you would understand if she never forgave you? Why are you angry at her?

Humility beats pride by a slim margin in my internal debate and I sob, "I'm sorry," to my best friend.

"I know. I'm sorry too. Please?" she pleads, holding out her hand to me, asking me to take it and be okay.

I weakly lift my hand to her and she clasps it with more strength than I expect. She's stronger than me. She might look frail but she has Sampson-like strength in her spirit. She scoots over closer to me and we hold each other tightly and cry together. Rosa sits behind us and pats our backs, one hand on me and one hand on Harmony.

Matt walks into the room from wherever he's been and, seeing us crying at Thomas' bedside, assumes the worst. He curses a loud string of profanity and throws several heavy objects at the shadowy walls and then runs back out of the room.

Harmony and I share a wide-eyed moment of panic. I have to catch him! Thomas is still alive. What if Matt leaves us here! And if Tim doesn't come back we'd be alone! I don't know how to drive the car, I can't find us food,

Harmony and I can't do this alone!

"Matt!" I yell out, stumbling to my feet and running through the door after him.

The hallway is dimly lit by the sunlight that creeps out from under a long row of closed doors on either side of me. The hallway floor looks like a runway as I sprint down it, my shoes slapping the silence. I hear another door slam at the far end. I rush towards the sound hoping I'm fast enough to catch him.

When I push through the heavy door at the end of the hall, I am paralyzed by the brilliant sunlight. It is midday and I haven't seen the sun in over a week. My eyes burn in the light, already watery from my tears, and I can't see to take a step. I shade my eyes with my hand and blink furiously, trying to adjust to the glare so I can resume my search. When I finally feel capable of sight, I look out at the huge blurry campus in dejection. It's so big. Matt knows it so well. There are overgrown bushes everywhere. He could be anywhere. I'll never find him. I don't even know which direction he went.

"Is he gone?" Matt asks quietly from behind me.

I spin to see him sitting on the ground against the wall behind me.

"Oh thank God! No, he's not gone. He's the same. I wasn't crying about him. Well he's part of it, but -" How do I explain my horrible guilt to him?

"I see. I thought -"

"Yeah, I'm sorry. I can see how it looked. I was just having a girl moment."

Though it's only been seven or eight days of the lamp lit darkness, I feel like I haven't looked at him in weeks. His brown, wavy hair is getting long, hanging down to the hallow in his thin cheeks. He reaches up and tucks a soft strand behind his zombie ears. He defies religion and science somehow, the disease present but mysteriously halted. His ears look no worse than when I first met him.

A little of the disease shows on the top of each ear in red and white patches. His face looks dry and his neck looks splotchy. He's wearing his usual - long sleeved black T-shirt, black jeans, black shoes. His skin has some tan to it, like he's been out in the sun a lot. His beautiful leaf green eyes look striking as usual, and the dark circles of exhaustion beneath them somehow add to his intense handsomeness. As I appraise him, I realize how terrible

I must look. Twisting my straggly hair into a messy bun, I sit down next to him.

It's still chilly out, even in the bright afternoon light. I left my coat inside, so I wrap my arms around my legs and try to soak in the sunlight. It's definitely warmer than it was when we arrived here a week ago. Matt drops his chin to his chest, sighs, and then reaches over to put an arm around my chilled shoulders. Now that the panic of catching him is over, it feels so good to be out of that room and just sitting still next to him.

It's been ages since we've had a moment together. His arm around me, his closeness, does what it always does to me. Excitement and life break through the stone wall of depression in my heart and pour shivery anticipation over my chilly skin. I feel the blush on my cheeks and I'm embarrassed at how flustered I always get whenever he's near.

He stares at me while I look around, my eyes now comfortable in the bright sunlight. Little signs of spring are showing. The daffodil leaves, always the first sign that winter is losing its hold on the world, are already a few inches tall. They poke resiliently through the long dead decomposing leaves of last autumn. Another week and the daffodils will be blooming.

The air is cool but still. In the absence of the wind, I hear the gurgle of water over rocks. A beautiful brook curls around in messy ringlets until it disappears into the forest. I know the stream's source is the majestic waterfall that Matt took me to see - was it two weeks ago? Three? I've lost track of time. It feels like it's been months, but I know that can't be right.

Matt continues to stare at me with a burning question in his eyes - those eyes that change with the light and captivate me with a glance. Sometimes they are dark and magical. Today, in the sunlight, they match the bright green daffodil shoots on the hill. His too intense gaze is starting to make me feel a different kind of awkward. The attracted awkward I felt at first is fading into just plain nervous.

I've run out of things to look at. It's obvious I'm avoiding his face, but I'm uncomfortable under his piercing stare. He wants something from me. Something I'm sure I can't give. I should slip back into the cave and escape the question I feel his eyes asking. Besides, Harmony will be worrying. I should go tell her we're okay. I sigh. I really don't want to go back in there.

"Why do you keep looking at me like that?" I finally confront.

"Like what?" he says still squinting at me.

"Like - I don't know what it's like but it's freaking me out. So stop it."

"I'm just very interested in you, Ivy."

I squirm and look down at my fidgeting hands. What does that mean? Interested? Interested like he wishes he could marry me or like he wants to sell me to the highest bidder? After too many seconds of silence, I glance up from my nervous knuckle cracking.

He gives me his patented half-smile and shrugs, "I guess I find you fascinating."

"I'm not fascinating. I'm just Ivy."

"The same Ivy that the whole world is after? That normal, boring Ivy?" he says sarcastically.

"Yeah. That one." We are quiet for a moment and then I blurt, "But I don't know why! There isn't anything special about me or my blood. They are wrong."

"Ivy. I watched you bring the dead back to life!"

"I DID NOT bring the dead back to life!" I insist.

"Ivy, I was there. I shot her! She was gone. She was, without a doubt, dead."

"I didn't say she wasn't dead."

He looks at me like I'm being stupid.

"I said *I* didn't bring her back. I don't have the power to raise the dead, Matt. He does. God brought her back to life. I can't believe you still don't get it. You saw a miracle and you still don't see God?"

We're fighting about Him again.

"Ivy, it's cute that you don't see yourself for what you really are, but I do."

"And *what* am I Matt?" I don't like being called a what.

"Ivy, Pravda is right. You probably are the cure to this whole thing."

"What are you saying? You promised me you hated Pravda! Now you're agreeing with them?"

Panic erupts in my empty stomach. Is he considering turning me in?

"I'm not going to let them have you," he says with gentle firmness, "but they're right. You are evolved somehow. The next step in evolution. You have power to give life to someone! They found it in your blood and they want what you have!"

"Oh my gosh, Matt. I don't have crazy super powers. I'm not the missing link! God does stuff like that all the time. He's the Giver of Life. Haven't you ever read a Bible? God used His people to heal the sick all the time. I'm not the first follower of God to see Him bring someone back to life. This isn't new! And the sad thing is I think He did it for you. He showed Himself to you in one of the biggest ways He ever does and you think I'm Lois Lane."

"Lois Lane didn't have super powers, Ivy. Superman did."

"Whatever!"

We sit silently again. Me stewing over his stupidity, and him still staring at me. I take a deep breath of the fresh air, intent on enjoying it before saying goodbye to it again for who knows how long. I know the cave will smell horrible now that I've had a break from it and a taste of fresh air. It's full of Thomas' sickness and empty rotting food cans and mildewed couches. Ugh. It will be hard to adjust to it now that I've been out for awhile. I look around, wondering again where Tim could've gone and if he's okay.

Matt must've realized what I was wondering because he breaks the silence with his flat pessimistic voice, "He isn't going to make it."

I'm irritated and wishing I hadn't come looking for this impossible, frustrating, handsome guy I hate and love. I won't let him talk me into giving up. "Tim will come back. He promised."

Matt laughs, but there's no humor in the sound. "You trust him with your life don't you? But I didn't mean him. I mean Tom. Tom isn't going to make it."

Oh. That might be true but I don't want to believe it either.

"Don't say that!" I argue with Matt and my own logic. "You don't know that. God can still heal him."

"When he goes, will you do what you did for Harmony? Bring him back?"

"Thomas is going to make it," I say, my voice full of a confidence that I don't feel.

"Promise me," he says grabbing my chin roughly, demanding. "Promise me you'll bring him back."

He holds my face so that I'm looking into his angry, heartbreaking eyes. I feel none of the attraction I normally feel when locked in his gaze. These eyes are the eyes of a lost child. These eyes are terrified and dangerous. I want to tell him what he wants to hear, but it would be a lie. He thinks I have some magic power, that I can Lazarus his brother back from death. How I wish I really could.

"I can't." I say sadly. "I can't make that promise."

He doesn't let go of my chin and the sting of his pinch brings tears to my eyes.

"Don't touch her." Tim says angrily from my peripheral vision.

I jump at the sound of Tim's voice. I would be thrilled that Tim is back but for the uncomfortable situation he's found me in. Unfazed, Matt leans close to me, close enough for a kiss, but I have no desire to close the distance. I lean back, my chin still pinched between his calloused fingers. I know his roughness is from fear and grief over Thomas, but it will be awhile before I forget this moment.

I remember Aunty's warning to me the night we talked in the kitchen. The night Matt brought Thomas back to Toccoa near death. I can hear her words as though she were sitting right next to me, whispering in my ear, "I insist that you not go looking for that boy. He isn't for you... I don't want you to even consider the thought. He was very angry and violent...."

"Ivy?" Tim says with concern and growing impatience.

I look away from Matt's intense stare, my chin still locked in his grip, and look up diagonally at Tim. My face crinkles into a cringe when I see his heavy brown glasses have slid down his sweaty nose. He wants to be my knight in shining armor, but he emblazons nerdyness like a crest on his shield. Even his clothes betray him. His shirt is partly tucked in with a tail hanging out in the back and his pants are too short. Mismatched socks show above his black velcro tennis shoes. I forgot how unattractive he was while we were in the dark. I look back at Matt who is still holding tight to my chin.

The anger in Matt's eyes fizzles out and leaves him looking hollow and lifeless. He lets go of my chin and stands up slowly, stretching like a cat, as though the tension of the moment doesn't exist to him.

"Where have you been?" he asks Tim coolly.

"I brought some strong penicillin for Tom." Tim has been calling Thomas "Tom" lately, like Matt does. "I remembered my dad telling me about a hospital near here. I'm sorry it took me so long," he says softly just to me.

"Yeah, we missed you." Matt says sarcastically.

Tim ignores Matt and reaches for my hand as he walks by, pulling me with him back into the building.

"Are you alright?" he asks angrily.

"Yeah."

"Why were you out there with him?" he asks, his voice no longer soft but accusing. He spoke gently when Matt was listening. But, when Matt's not here to battle for me, Tim wants me to know how frustrated he is with my fickleness.

I'm too tired to defend myself. Too tired to explain why I went running out after Matt. I'm sick of being stuck between the two of them. I follow behind him in the thick shadows of the hallway and notice a brown backpack over his shoulder. It looks full and heavy with supplies. Thank God.

"We need to try to get something into Tom's stomach. This medicine is strong and it will help almost immediately but it will make him sick if there's nothing in him."

"I could mash up the last of the beets. They're pretty soft. We could prop him up and try to make him drink it," I suggest. It sounds terrible but there isn't anything else to eat.

"Do it." Tim says.

As he pushes the door to our cave open, I notice the stethoscope hanging around his neck. Just like his dad. Dr. Markowitz always had his stethoscope around his neck, even at U.R. meetings. Tim must have taken it from the hospital he scavenged. I remember that I robbed Tim of his father. My eyes tingle with apologetic tears as I follow my friend back into the reeking darkness.

Chapter Seven

It's All Fun And Games Until Someone Loses An Eye

Thomas' cherubic voice echoes through the inky room as he plays with Rosa. She laughs - another new sound she's been making - and I smile to myself in the dark. Tim's hospital run was a Godsend. Thomas is almost completely recovered with just three days of the strong penicillin in him. Though, Tim says he'll need to continue to take the pills for another seven days.

Tim also got bandages on his run; but, today, for the first time, Thomas's arm didn't need to be rewrapped. Tim's medical training under his dad's tutelage is extraordinarily ideal. He knew just what Thomas needed and where to find it. We would've lost Thomas without Tim's knowledge and bravery. I wonder if Matt even appreciates it. Does he realize just how miraculous it is that God put Tim in our group of survivors?

Thomas is still adjusting to his mutilated hand. He lost all four fingers and his thumb is mangled. He has a lot of nerve damage that keeps his stump of a hand mostly numb. It may never heal better than this. He won't ever be able to do much with it. I watched Matt closely the first day the bandages came off. He looked sick with guilt at the sight of it.

Thomas started wearing the zombie glove with biotechnology almost right away. I know he doesn't like the glove and I'm almost certain that he wears it to spare Matt the sight of his ruined hand. The glove makes life a lot easier for him, filling in for the lost fingers and making simple tasks like eating a little easier.

I thought Thomas' recovery would cheer Matt up, but he is more aloof every day. He's gone most of the time, leaving Tim in charge of our safety here in the cave. I'm beginning to wonder if there is any threat out there. It's up to Matt when we move on towards Atlanta. We're all resigned to trusting his judgment on the matter, but I'm starting to get desperate to get out of this place and on towards rescuing Dad and Aunty Betty. Thoughts of what Pravda is doing to them have filtered into my nightmares.

Matt doesn't tell us anything. He brings us food occasionally, who knows where from, and whispers quietly with Thomas once or twice a day. Other than that, we don't see him.

It nags at me.

Where does he go? Is he walking back to Toccoa every day? It's only a little more than a mile away. There is food, drink and "entertainment" there for him and his kind. I suppose he'd rather spend his days with hedonistic, pleasure seeking fellow zombies than be stuck in the dark with our band of boring, God-fearing cave dwellers.

With the fear of Thomas' death lifted from my shoulders, a new burden has taken its place - jealousy. I'm sick with thoughts of who Matt is spending his time with and how. I fluctuate back and forth between wishing I had the courage to ask him and despondency about it being none of my business. We haven't had a private conversation since the day Tim came back with the meds.

Tim doesn't talk much either. I have lots of questions for him, too. Why was he in the garage instead of at the U.R. the night Pravda attacked? Did he see the attack? Did he see what happened to his dad? And what happened while he was out looking for the meds for Thomas? If the hospital is so close by, why did it take so long?

I need answers. These questions are pestering me like mosquitoes on a humid summer day. Thoughts of Tim and what he's feeling are heavy artillery in my head, warring against my thoughts about Matt. The two of them wage a relentless battle in my mind, regardless of the fact that either boy is actually speaking much to me.

*****

With Thomas better and Harmony speaking to me, the cave is friendlier. Harmony and I watch closely as Tim teaches Thomas how to fold a paper football. The four of us are sitting at a table with the lantern between us. Tearing pages from an old textbook, Tim hands paper to Harmony and I so we can make our own.

Thomas has been practicing using the biotech glove, but the precise folds are a challenge. Tim helps Thomas make the tiny folds that are too hard for him. Tim is patient and he wears an easy smile. I find myself watching him and then looking away when he meets my eyes. Harmony folds the thin glossy paper faster than I can, as though she's familiar with this distraction.

Tim folds faster still. A small pile of paper triangles grows beneath the lantern.

"Hold it like this," Tim models, a paper football standing on its points between his thumb and middle finger. "Then, flick."

Tim's football hurtles towards me and hits me solid in the chest.

"Hey!" I smile and try to make my football balance for a return fire.

An all out war ensues. Three-sided projectiles fly across the table and each of us duck and run for our own cover. Thomas can't walk well yet, but I hear him drop down beneath the table we were sitting at, giggling.

Huddled against a couch balustrade, I wait for a football to come at me so I can send it flying back. Harmony surprises me, popping up behind me and flicking three footballs in a row. I dodge and crawl through the dark to escape her hawk-eye precision. Tim shouts out a point system and we battle to make the most kills.

We run and duck and dodge and flick for so long that my legs burn with exertion and my dry mouth begs for water. Thomas isn't very mobile, but he has mastered the art of flicking and his couch cushion barricade has him well protected. The little stinker is winning. I wish Matt was here to play with us. I know he would smile to see Thomas being a kid.

I stand slowly, looking for a target, and footballs fly at me from three different directions. I shriek and dive into Rosa's fort. My breath is loud in my ears and my cheeks hurt from smiling. I'm not alone for long. Tim dives in next to me and we fill the small space with whispered plans to upset Thomas' lead. I'm about to plunge from the tent and make a run towards Thomas when Tim catches me by the hand. I turn to see what he wants to add to our scheme.

His glasses are off and his face is close to mine in the gray darkness. I stare back at him and feel a flock of birds take flight in the pit of my stomach. Still holding my hand, Tim reaches out and weaves his other hand into my tangled hair, holding the back of my neck tenderly, firmly.

I consider what it would be like to kiss him. I consider the love I feel in his hands and the urgency in his breath. I'm euphoric from our game and I want to keep feeling happy. I want the moment to last. Tim leans closer to me and I know I'm going to let him. I've decided. The door to the cave swings open and Matt's voice fills the room.

"I'm back. Where is everybody?"

"Here!" Thomas chirps.

Tim's lips close the distance and brush against mine as I pull away and scramble out of the fort. The sheet falls between us as I crab-walk away from Tim, my guilty heart hoping Matt won't see. I will Tim to stay where he is as I crawl through the dark towards the bathroom. I shut myself in the dark water closet without a lantern or a flashlight. I sit on the toilet lid, my heart still beating too fast, and wait for my stomach to stop churning.

Chapter Eight

Blood Is Thicker Than Water

The life-sucking darkness is threatening my sanity more than normal today. My flashlight is out of batteries again and I can't get more until Matt gets back. He keeps a stash of them in the car. Most of the supplies have stayed in the old Station Wagon. Just in case we leave here in a hurry, we don't want to lose all the gear.

I know spring is budding outside and I have the worst case of Spring Fever in history. It has rained a lot lately. We hear the thunder and sometimes Matt comes "home" all wet. I just know the waterfall will be glorious right now, its flowing tendrils swollen from the storms. I have to see it one more time.

Matt's been gone for almost a day now. Tim paces near the door a lot and I know he's hurt. It was obvious that Matt was the reason our kiss didn't happen. I was there with him in the moment and then I wasn't. I considered him and then I ran so Matt wouldn't see. I feel bad. I want things to be okay between us. I want to be friends. Maybe now is the perfect time to convince him that we need a little fresh air. I slink through the darkness without stubbing a toe, all the obstacles memorized now.

"Tim?" I say my voice just above a whisper but it seems to echo throughout the room.

He sighs, irritated, and makes a small grunt to acknowledge me, no pause in his pointless back and forth striving. We haven't spoken directly since the fort.

"I'm worried about Matt, maybe something happened to him?"

It might be stupid to lead with my concern for Matt, but I've got a plan. I've decided to go with this tactic, bear with me.

"Maybe we should go see what's going on out there?"

"No."

"But what if he was caught? Do you think he'd be able to keep all this a secret? Don't you think we should just see what's going on out there? I don't know, scan the perimeter or something?"

No answer. Hopefully I've cast some doubt. Is it enough to get me my walk though?

"You and I could just slip out and peek around a bit. First sign of trouble we can be back in here and packed up in minutes. Besides," I pause enticingly, "I have something I want to show you."

Another sigh is my only answer.

I sidle up to him when his pacing brings him closer to me. He starts to pace away from me again, but I grab his hand and hold it tight. "Please? Just a short walk?"

"I'm sure he's fine Ivy," Tim says, his voice heavy with dejection.

I can tell he's assuming I'm just worried about Matt. Okay, so it wasn't my best plan.

"I just want to see the sun for a bit. I know you won't let me go alone, so come with me. Please?" I whisper to him, not really wanting Harmony to hear and not sure where she is in the room right now. "I have something beautiful to show you."

I wait, holding his hand, hopeful.

"Make it quick." He says tersely.

Yes!

I pull him towards the door but he drops my hand. When I turn back, afraid that he isn't coming, I bump into him - following close behind but not willing to hold hands. Fine. I'm just happy we're getting out! I hope it's daytime. If it's dark out, Tim will probably nix the whole walk.

In the hallway outside of our cave, slim cracks of sunlight ooze out from under all the doors lining our path towards freedom. I can tell it's going to be beautiful outside. I hurry down the hall towards the exit, longing to feel the sun on my skin. To smell fresh air and see the sky. Tim steps ahead of me at the end of the hall, pushing the door to outside open slowly, just a crack. Peering through the slit for what feels like longer than necessary, he finally pushes the rest of the way through.

The sunlight hits my face like a welcome bath of warmth and energy. I feel like a solar panel, recharging my drained cells in the golden light. Tears of joy spring to my squinting eyes. I hold my arms out and stand still, reveling in just being alive and free right this moment. It's almost warm out!

Winter is behind us and Spring's beauty is on the horizon. *Lord, let it be spring in my life, please?* My eyes lifted up to the puffy white clouds, I thank God for the chance to see the world again.

"What do you need to show me?" Tim asks, his troll-like demeanor unaffected by this beautiful day.

I offer my hand again and, sighing, he takes it and lets me lead him away from our haven. I don't hesitate. Fond memories of my date with Matt are still vivid in my mind. I know the way. The rusted iron gates that guard the path to the falls are just around the bend from where we've been staying. Without letting go of Tim's hand - mostly so he won't back out - we squeeze through the narrow opening.

The picturesque trail is etched between budding trees on one side and tall bushes that hide the babbling creek on the other. It's so much more beautiful in the Spring. When I was here last, this magical place awed me. Now, covered in a canopy as vivid green as Matt's eyes, it takes my breath away. Overgrown Azalea shrubs lining the path are covered in burgundy buds and the daffodils are showing their lemon-colored petals on the hillside. The soft sound of water grows louder as we walk and I smile in anticipation of what we are about to see. I glance back at Tim and he looks more puzzled than expectant. He'll love it when he sees it, I know he will.

I skip towards the last bend in the trail, my soul readying a song for the sight of the huge waterfall, pregnant with the recent rain. Its cottony white cascades plunging downward and yet looking like wisps of cloud - weightless. I love this place. It might be my favorite place on earth. But, as we turn the corner, I stop in shock. My eyes scan the small cove in utter disbelief. Tim stumbles into me from behind. Just as I remembered it, the waterfall soars high above the budding tree branches at the end of the little canyon. But the water is blood red. Bloody water gushes over the orange and gray cliffs.

"What happened?" I ask Tim. "Why is it red?"

Did some terrible slaughter happen above the falls, filling the water with the liquid life of fallen people?

"It's another judgment," Tim says in my ear, staring up at the gory sight. "The disease was the first. Now, God has turned the water to blood."

"Real blood?" I ask astounded and repulsed.

I remember them telling us that this would come. I remember studying it at the U.R. But seeing it, it's terrible. God shouldn't have done it. It feels evil - and so unlike Him. I guess it felt that way with the disease at first. It took time to see that the disease was God's mercy, His revelation of how broken we were and how much we need Him. I can't imagine how any good can come of this new curse. God's punishments are huge and unrelenting. They are terrifying. I am so used to the God who is my friend and the Lover of my soul; I forget He is so scary sometimes.

"I don't think it's real blood, but I'd have to test it to be sure. I think it's just contaminated somehow. Some bacteria or something. This is going to make life a lot harder," Tim says with sad foreboding.

"What will we drink?"

I didn't need another insurmountable challenge in my life. I already have a full tank of troubles.

"It must have already happened to the oceans. I think freshwater was the third judgment. I don't know. But He won't leave us to die of thirst. We should still be able to get water," Tim pauses and then adds, "I hope."

We stare at the bloody torrents falling with our hands interlocked. I feel small and alone as I stare at God's justice.

"I read that this is punishment for the murder of so many saints. The wicked of the last days are blood thirsty and God has given them blood to drink," Tim says in a small voice.

A chill runs up my spine.

Is Tim right? Is this a curse of revenge? The disease brought people to God. The sickness turned many hearts to Christ - including mine - our sinfulness too obvious to ignore anymore. Could this new bane have some mercy in it? Couldn't it be God calling the world to drink His cup, His blood shed for them? I know God is justice and holiness, but He is equally love and grace, too. I like the latter traits a little bit more.

Just ahead are the boulders where Matt and I laid and talked while watching the sky fill with the neon colors of sunset. I drop Tim's hand and walk over to the smooth, gray elephant-sized rocks, picking my footing up to the top. As I stand there, just above the tumultuous dark red pool, high off of the ground and so near the blood stained water, I feel overwhelmed with dread and a little scared of the God I belong to.

Chapter Nine

Aunty Was Cheating

It takes a few minutes for Tim to join me atop the boulders. He's picks his way up but doesn't sit with me. I am perched on the edge, my legs dangling over the side. I wanted to show him something, wanted to share this place with him. It feels like everything I try to do to make things right with Tim ends up disastrous. The misty vapor of the falls moistens my skin. I rub my arms and face dry and scoot back towards Tim to avoid the contaminated red spray.

He doesn't speak.

My irritation overflows and the words finally burst from my mouth, "Aren't you at least glad that we know about this now? It was supposed to be beautiful, but we needed to know this was happening, right?"

"I'm just wondering why you brought me here to begin with, Ivy."

What kind of question is that?

"I just wanted to share something with you! Just relax for a minute and actually enjoy life for a second."

"It's a beautiful place," he says quietly.

"Why are you so unhappy with me? I miss - I really like it when we're friends," I mumble. "I thought we bonded after -".

"Ivy, you're so - dumb sometimes."

"Excuse me?"

"How did you know this place was here?" He asks angrily, his words coming out in a rush.

I flush red, ready to yell, but then I realize why he's so mad and I regret bringing him. I get it now. I never thought about how Tim would feel about the fact that I've been here before, foolishly far from safety. And, even worse, with Matt - alone.

Stupid, Ivy. Stupid.

"I um. I -"

I sigh, I've got nothing. There's no good way out of this. Of course he's upset. This place is just another one of my screw-ups. But, if I hadn't gone out that night, I wouldn't have known the attack was coming. I tried to warn everyone - a lot of good it did. They all died anyway. And now, again, I feel that this trip was important. I feel like God wanted us to see this new problem. But it's pretty convenient of me to be constantly assuming God is behind my foolish interests. I worry that I'm more off base than I realize. What if none of this is what our terrifying God intended for my life?

"You were here with him," he says, not hiding the hurt in his husky voice. "Is he who you want Ivy? Why did you ask me to come with you to Atlanta? To torture me? If you want him, tell me now. I need to know. I don't want to do this anymore."

I pick self-consciously at my shoe. How do I answer that?

"I'm sorry," I try.

"Oh, how nice of you," he says bitterly.

"I can't figure it out. I don't have a good answer," I say meekly, my focus on the small rock stuck in the tread of my shoe.

"I need you to figure it out, Ivy. You know how I feel. I love you. I've loved you for years. You are the first girl I noticed and you've had me ever since. When we lost -" he pauses, "When you lost your Aunt, I thought maybe you could love me back."

"I used to hate you," I say and then cringe. Why do I always say the worst thing possible?

"I know," he says nonchalantly, surprising me.

"Why did you keep - uh - caring," I can't say the word loving, "when I was so obviously not interested?"

"Your Aunt was part of it. Whenever I wanted to give up, she'd wink at me and whisper, 'Keep trying.'"

Don't I know it? Aunty made no secret of her matchmaking agenda.

Tim's face flushes with embarrassment, "She found that little set of cookie cutters and gave it to me to give to you the week you were attacked. She reminded me a lot of my mom and she was always so great to me. When she and my dad had dinner together she'd always spend some time with me, just asking me about my studies or what I hoped to do someday."

I sit in stunned silence. What is he talking about? This is confusing, heart-breaking, incomprehensible news to me. Aunty had dinner with them?

Without me?

Often?

What's up with that? She had, like, a secret life or something? Why didn't she feel like she could tell me? I guess she knew how much I despised Tim. Did she think I'd hate the thought of her caring for Tim's dad? I probably would have. I didn't want to share our life with anyone else. It was her and me and that was great. I feel like I'm finding out that she cheated on me and she's gone now and I can't be mad at her. I can only be hurt and confused and feel somehow guilty about it.

I'm glad my messy hair is hanging down, hiding my hurt. I don't want Tim to see what I'm sure is written all over my face. I feel like an idiot that he knew things about her that I didn't. Selfish Ivy strikes again. Ivy can't be trusted to be accepting and giving so just keep her in the dark so you don't have to deal with her.

Choked up but trying to hide it, I ask robotically, "Did your dad love my Aunt?"

"Yes."

I nod. This new truth hurting my heart more than it should. Did I keep her from having a happy, fulfilled life? Did caring for me require such self-sacrifice that she died a lonely spinster instead of in the arms of the man who loved her?

"I promised her I would take care of you. And I want to keep that promise, Ivy. I just don't know how to if you decide to go with him."

"I thought we agreed Atlanta was the right place to go," I whisper through the lump of emotion in my throat. "I thought you understood."

He scoots next to me and leans closer to my hidden face, trying to see me.

His shoulder touches mine as he says quietly, "I don't mean Atlanta. I mean, I don't know how to take care of you if you are going to choose him. I wish I could be that selfless, but I don't think I can."

"I haven't made a choice. I'm only sixteen."

"You'll be seventeen next month," he reminds me. He knows my birthday is in April. He knows everything about me. So much more than Matt knows.

"The world is ending soon - probably. I - I didn't know I had to make some iron clad commitment," I say still avoiding his eyes.

He sighs again. So much sighing lately. I feel like I'm constantly disappointing him.

"You don't have to marry me, Ivy." Another sigh, "I just don't know how to feel about you anymore. I'm tired of fighting for someone who isn't interested."

My eyes fly up to meet his.

"I am interested," I defend and it surprises both of us.

I've admitted it now. I have feelings for him. Not exclusively for him, but it's true my feelings have morphed from disgust to decency to thankful friendship and finally into some interest that I can't quite explain.

"But you love him." Not a question, just a statement.

"Yes." I say quietly, ashamed for some reason.

Tim is like my conscience. I know I shouldn't love Matt. I know he's dangerous and that Aunty was probably right. He's probably not God's will for me. But I can't help it. The attraction thrives despite his antisocial, temper-filled, nonexistent presence in my life.

"Well, keep me posted," Tim says almost lightly. "I'm just a couch and two end-tables away."

I smile and drop my eyes back to my shoes. He's persistent and occasionally adorable.

"We'd better get back. We didn't even tell Harmony we were leaving."

"Okay," I agree reluctantly, standing up and brushing dust from my backside.

"Thanks for bringing me here, for wanting to share this with me. Even like this." He gestures towards the bloody torrents, "It's beautiful. Scary but beautiful." he says, catching my chin gently and looking into my eyes.

I hadn't realized that he wasn't wearing his glasses. When did he take them off? He does look better without them. His huge brown eyes stare into my same color eyes and tell me that it's me that he thinks is beautiful, not just the waterfall. His touch on my chin is so different than Matt's harsh pinch from a few days ago. They couldn't be more different. I blush and move past him to find the path down.

Climbing down and making our way back towards the cave, I'm different. I don't notice the trees or the bird's songs. Sad and introspective, I can't stop thinking about Aunty's secrets, Tim's devotion, the curse and the blood. And, above all, I brood on my inability to escape my own curse of self-centeredness that seems to hurt all who know me.

As the gentle roar of water recedes behind us, a new sound prickles at my sub-conscience. Is that a bird? Maybe a hawk? But then the cry becomes suddenly more human. A little child?

Rosa!

Chapter Ten

Dodge This, Spider Man

Tim recognizes the emergency simultaneously. We share a terrified glance and then bolt towards the cave. Slipping single file through the tight space in the iron gate, I shove at Tim to move him through faster. We've been found! Someone has Rosa! I can't think of anything but those two panicked realities.

How can we fight them?

How many of them will there be?

Is it over already?

Sprinting around the bend, Rosa's frightened squealing has me terrified. What is happening! Turning the corner past overgrown bushes, my nightmares materialize before me. A group of the infected stands in a tight circle on the sidewalk outside of our hideout. Rosa is crying from inside their huddle.

"No!" I scream, running towards them. I don't have a plan or any guess at how we'll handle them I'm just desperate to get Rosa away from them at all costs.

I see three things. First, all the masked faces have turned to focus on me. Second, Tim is backing slowly away from me, leaving me like a coward. Desperation pounds in my ears. Then, I see Rosa's small form lying still, too still, on the ground behind them. A sob tears from my throat. If she is dead, I'm going to kill them. Every last one of them.

Red anger displaces my terror and I feel my fists clenching in hatred. I charge at the masked men, a scream ripping out of my throat. I hear a gunshot and it shocks me to a halt. There must be more of them coming and they're armed. This is a suicide fight, but I don't care about anything anymore. I just want to feel their skin beneath my nails a few times before they kill me. I run towards them lost in rage and anguish over Rosa. I feel capable of murder.

Another shot echoes closer and louder in my ears. One of the zombies collapses slowly, blood spraying towards me through a hole in the front of his plastic Spiderman mask. The other four masks dart towards me, closing the short distance quickly. They must not be suffering from the nerve damage or infected feet that many of their kind are dying from. They are lightning fast and the fastest one meets me in the middle of the road and grabs for my arms. I scream a guttural war cry and swing at the black ski mask in front of me.

My weak, unskilled punch does no damage and the thin man laughs at me. His blue spandex-suited arms wrap around me like a vise grip and the smell of his body odor and skin rot makes me retch. His tight body suit feels obscene. I feel too much of him against me. His ribs poke into my back and his slick suited legs feel naked next to mine. I struggle and scream and thrash in a desperate attempt to free myself from my enemy and his nauseating scent.

Another gun shot. Then, a third. I haven't been hit yet and the man holding me is spinning me towards the shooter. He holds me like a shield as another zombie approaches cautiously. The shooter wears a nondescript ski mask. He's holding a gun up, pointing it straight at me. He isn't wearing a body suit like the others. Just a long sleeved t-shirt. I know that zombie!

"Matt!" I scream.

"Stay back!" The blue man rasps, pulling me closer, ducking his head behind mine to hide from the gun - his voice is right in my ear.

Somehow his breath is as bad as the rest of his stink. He jerks me hard and then releases me, crumpling behind my feet and knocking me down. Tim stands over me panting, a dead tree branch hanging from his hands like a club. The blue-suited zombie lays next to me unconscious, maybe dead.

I sob and scrape myself across the pavement to get away from the gross man. His touch and his smell haunt me, following me as I crawl away. I shiver in disgust. I feel violated. I climb to my feet, stumble, find my footing again and hurry over to where Rosa lays in a little ball on the hard ground.

My eyes are full of tears and Rosa's tiny frame is a lifeless blur. But, as I reach her, I feel her trembling violently and I wail my relief. Picking her up in my arms she tries to fight me. When she realizes it's me, she wraps herself around my neck so tightly I feel choked. I don't try to loosen her grasp. I just hug her back and cry with her while I gasp for breath.

So thankful she's still alive.

So thankful.

Thank you, God. Thank you. Another gun shot behind me shocks my body. I jerk to see Matt standing over the blue suited man, gun still pointed at his now unrecognizable head. More death. More murder.

Harmony bursts out from behind the door to our building, crying and running towards us. Tim helps me to my feet, Rosa still strapped to me like a monkey clinging to her mother. Tim pushes me towards the door and Harmony follows us.

Harmony's panicked questions assail me like wolves at my heels. "What just happened? Was it Pravda? What should we do now? We have to run! Where were you?" Harmony sobs as we hurry down the dark hall to our cave.

Guilt hits now. Gut-wrenching guilt. I had to see the falls. I talked Tim into leaving them unprotected. What if Rosa had died? I can't answer Harmony. I can't tell her that I was out getting some fresh air, leaving them in terrible danger.

"We were looking around for Matt," Tim lies for me, but it only makes the guilt more unbearable. "Where were you?" he demands angrily at Matt who comes in the door behind us.

"We have to leave now," Matt says in the bored, calm voice he uses when the whole world is falling apart and he's the last tough guy standing.

"Now?" Tim's disgust is unveiled as usual.

"One of them got away. I could try to track him and kill him, but if I don't catch him," Matt sighs the way Tim always does, "he'll bring more. He'll bring Pravda. We have to move fast," Matt says as he hurries over to Thomas, searching for Thomas' shoes in the dim light. "Try to find everything. We leave in five minutes. Don't leave anything behind."

I hurry to gather my few belongings into my backpack as Thomas bombards Matt with questions. I hand Rosa to Harmony who is sniffling and looking like a frightened deer who can't decide which way to bolt. She doesn't have anything to pack. After I gather our blankets, I grab one of the lanterns and begin to sweep the room for evidence. I find nothing but Gov. Bar wrappers and garbage. I check the bathroom and cringe at what the lantern light reveals.

I've always had my flashlight in here, never the lantern. Several large spiders reign in the upper corners of the little room. Gauzy webs like Halloween decorations droop from the dirty ceiling. I knew I wouldn't like this room in the light. I've been peeing in here just underneath their malicious nests. I shake with the heebie-jeebies as I walk backwards out of the door. I can't wait to get out of here.

Thomas is in the wheelchair and Matt is pushing him towards the door. Tim's arms are full of gear - lanterns, more blankets, flashlights. On his back is the brown backpack he brought back from his medicine run. I look behind as we head out the door. The only testament to our time here is the lonely bottle of chocolate syrup still sitting on the table in the middle of the room.

As a group, we leave the cave.

As a group, we leave safety.

As a group, still together, still alive, we move forward.

Matt whispers while we walk down the hallway towards the exit, "I've been staying close to them since that first night. They live in one of the other dorms. They weren't Pravda, but they've been searching the woods and the other buildings for Ivy. They wanted her for the reward."

Matt peers out through a crack in the door to see if the coast is clear. Standing behind him, I can see through the crack as well. Blood runs down the gray cement hill just beyond the door. Like the bloody waterfall pouring over the stone cliffs. The legs of the blue-suited man stick out across the road. The blue-suited, raspy-voiced man is the one who called me a carrier the first night that we came here. I am no closer to knowing what he meant. But he was right, I am a carrier.

A carrier of The Cure. A carrier of The Light. I do have their precious cure. If only they would put their guns down and listen. Even though they tried to kill us, I feel sorry for them. Their disease was hard in life, but so much more terrible now in death. There is no cure for where they are now.

"I've been hanging out with them to keep an eye on them and keep them away from our side of the campus. They weren't bad guys. They have some girls with them. And kids." Matt says with what sounds like regret. "This wouldn't have happened if you had stayed inside like we agreed!"

So that's where he's been going. And apparently he liked them? Enjoyed "hanging out" with them? And then he shot them. Just killed them all like it was nothing. I remember them standing malevolently around Rosa. They were horrible people. The memory of the blue-suited man's breath in my hair sends a shiver through me.

"Where are we going to go?" Tim asks through gritted teeth. "And how long has the water been red? Why didn't you tell us?" Tim yells and it echoes down the hallway, back to the cave.

"Atlanta." Matt answers him with that flat voice, still staring through the crack. "And it's been red for three days. I didn't see why you needed to know."

Tim makes a guttural noise of anger and disgust.

"Is it safe now?" I ask. "Safe to go to Atlanta?"

"It's never going to be safe," Matt says darkly. "Might as well get moving."

Chapter Eleven

The Girl Behind The Mask

I've never heard so much cursing. The foul, rage-filled expletives coming from the driver's seat are worse than any derogatory cat-calling I've ever heard from the other side of the fence. And in this scary moment I find myself - embarrassed. Embarrassed that I like him. Embarrassed that I've stood up for him and hailed him a "good guy." Tim is hearing this and is definitely judging me for having any feelings for this potty-mouthed zombie. Harmony's face is an equal amount of terrified and horrified. Another long string of swearing erupts as Matt tries for the tenth time to start the coughing Station wagon.

"What's wrong with it?" Tim shouts for at least the third time.

"How would I know?" Matt roars back in frustration.

Thomas is sitting quietly between them, less fazed by his brother's anger than the rest of us. I would guess he's seen this side of Matt more than a few times. Holding tightly to Rosa in the backseat - still guilt-stricken that we almost lost her - I can't stop pivoting back and forth. Searching both sides of the parking lot for the onslaught I'm sure is coming. It's only been twenty minutes since we blew our cover here and Matt sent several zombies to eternal damnation. One of them got away. What that could mean to our survival has me jerking my head left and right like windshield wipers in a downpour.

"We should pray," Harmony says, uncharacteristically speaking up when she would normally cower in silence during the tension.

Taking her suggestion to heart, Tim speaks to God out loud. "Father, we need you. Please make this car start. Please get us out of here safely. We desperately need your help, God."

Matt stares at the torn green fabric ceiling in frustration, looking up at nothing. My heart wishes that he was praying with us. That his upturned gaze was one of reverence instead of unveiled antagonism. At Tim's "Amen," Matt turns to meet Tim's eyes with an unreadable cold expression. Blankly holding Tim's gaze, Matt turns the key in the ignition with a hint of challenge in his sharp green eyes. As if to say, "it still isn't going to work, and you are a huge idiot."

The engine coughs once and catches, hiccupping, but holding on to its grumpy growl. A smile spreads across Tim's triumphant face. Harmony and I exchange proud grins. Proud of our God who always comes through for us.

"Yes!" Thomas says in his sweet, high-pitched prepubescent voice, thrusting a happy fist towards heaven.

Matt and Tim continue to stare at each other. I have goose bumps on my arms. Matt's face is slightly less dead. His eyes a little wider, though I can tell he's trying to keep his expression the same. Can he still doubt? Does he chant "Coincidence!" behind that unreadable facade?

A bullet explodes loudly against the back of the car and I feel the vibration in my legs. Harmony and I scream and duck low in the seat, both of us hovering over Rosa. Matt throws the car into gear and launches us backwards out of the parking space towards whoever just shot at us.

I want to look, want to see how bad it is and how many of them there are. When I raise my head a few inches for a quick glance, the back window on Harmony's side explodes in a shower of glass. We scream again and feel the G-force as Matt puts the pedal down and we shoot forward.

Tearing away through the obstacle course we wove slowly through on the way in, the Station Wagon bravely jolts over speed bumps that should be taken at much slower speeds. Unbuckled in the back, Harmony, Rosa and I lift off at each bump and come crashing back down. My spine and neck ache at the rough jarring and my stomach feels like it's full of nails. One more shot sounds behind us but doesn't find its mark and then we are barreling around a bend away from the danger.

*****

I don't recognize this road. Matt seems to know his way and he says that this is the safest route to Atlanta, but the way he drives - leaning forward in his seat, his shoulder's curled with tension - I know he doesn't feel as confident as he acts. The wind is blowing wildly through the shattered back window, whipping my already impossibly messy hair into an even tighter rat's nest. I need a shower. I miss my home. I brood silently, lost in memories of Aunty and the Inn. Gone now. Never going back.

Little Rosa is sleeping, her head on my lap and her little legs draped across Harmony's lap. She cried herself to sleep, hungry and scared from the day's terrors. I tried to get her to eat a Gov. Bar but she refused, crying all the more until her overwhelmed tears finally trailed off and exhaustion claimed her.

What kind of life is this for such a sweet, broken little girl? Beneath her clothes are the horrible marks of abuse that the missionary Jack rescued her from. When she speaks, if she speaks, it is only in Spanish. I heard the lilting chords of her tiny voice the day the fences fell. Thomas' adopted dad Jose told her for me that I would always care for her. I could tell by the look on his face when I asked him to translate that he didn't think I should be offering such promises.

Jose was right. I'm a total failure. She was almost killed today. We all could've been killed. Part of me, a large part of me, wishes we had been. I'm too tired to keep doing this. I want to go home. I want to be with Aunty and Jesus and not have any more failure, guilt and terror. I want to be done.

"Ivy!" Tim rasps in a sharp whisper, waking me from my accidental nap.

We're slowing down. Are we there? Peeling my face off of the window, I sit up and look out ahead - blinking sleepy eyes in the afternoon sun. When I see the reason for Tim's fearful whisper my stomach clenches in a sick ball.

Bandits!

The road is lined on either side with dense woods and guard rails that protectively block deep ravines. Straight ahead is an ambush. Several large vehicles block the road, facing towards us. There are at least twenty masked zombies arrayed on roofs and hoods and perched behind open car doors armed to the teeth. Frantic, I look behind us. Can't we just turn around? A short distance behind us I see a bridge that we must have just crossed - blocked now as well. Two more cars have pulled out of hiding to block the way back. We're stuck.

"Matt!" I whine.

"Just be calm," he whispers with intensity. "They probably don't know anything about you. We'll give them our gear and that will be it. They're going to make us get out. They are going to search us. There are masks on the floor for you and gloves. Put them on quickly!"

Nodding, I see that Thomas and Tim have already found their masks.

They bend down out of my sight and come up covered in neon orange ski masks. On the floor, tucked under the back of the front seat, I find the kind of masks that I always saw on the zombie ladies - sparkly, sequined, feathery masks. There is a mask for me and one for Harmony. I don't remember seeing these the night we hid on the floor of the car. Matt must've put them here for us during our time in the cave. I'm beyond thankful that he has done so much to care for us. Even having a mask ready for Tim. I'm sure that was for my sake.

Harmony looks at me through her sequined eye holes and we reach out to grasp each other's hand. Her hand shakes in mine.

"What about Rosa?" she asks with a quiet quiver in her voice.

"She's too young. No disease. She doesn't need one," Tim says, muffled behind the thick fabric of his mask.

As Matt slows to a crawl, Harmony produces two pairs of gloves from the floor on her side. I can't believe my eyes. Harmony has the pink mittens from my date with Matt. The ones he gave his own blood to buy for me. Harmony is pulling them on her hands, leaving me the ugly brown pair. I want to argue, *those are mine!* But the Station Wagon's brakes are whining to a stop at the gun waving command of a silver spandex-suited zombie. I pull the scratchy brown gloves on and start a desperate barrage of prayers. *Please Heaven hear us and rescue us. Please don't let any of my friends get hurt. Please! I give up. They can have me. Just get everyone else out of here alive, please Father?*

"Won't they make us take our masks off?" I ask the obvious.

Matt just shakes his head in the negative and says with uncharacteristic foreboding, "You're going to have to be tough. This could get bad. They'll let us go in the end. Just be tough."

The silver-suited man waves his machine gun with a muscular arm to indicate that he wants us to get out. Matt takes a deep breath and opens the squeaky front door. The rest of us sit frozen. Shivers rip up my arms and my tense muscles quiver with dread.

Chapter Twelve

Stupid Is As Stupid Does

Matt stands next to the car with his hands in the air.

The silver-suited man strides with militant purposefulness towards our car and shouts, "Everyone out!"

We still sit. I can't get control of my shivering muscles as I stare out the window at the thirty or so odd guns trained on us. Chills shake me like hypothermia, but I feel sweat beading on my face. Most of the men wear masks, though a few faces are real flesh. The faces without masks look almost healthy. More like Matt. More who defy the odds with skin that looks almost untouched by the disease.

The silver-suited man walks a few steps closer, his face hidden behind a white plastic nondescript face mask. The telltale symbol for man, a circle with an arrow pointing up to the right, gleams on his metallic suit. He's one of Pravda's hired muscle. That's what they wear. It's the moment I've been dreading. Today is the day. All the death. All the running. All for nothing.

The silver man whips his gun into a more serious position and enunciates with malicious staccato, "Everyone - out!"

Tim's door squeals its rusted song as he pushes it open slowly. He sits for a second longer and then slowly pulls himself out, hands raised like Matt's. He steps two steps back to stand protectively in front of my door and the silver man swivels abruptly, training the gun directly at him.

For the second time in my life and, coincidentally, the second time this month, I am suddenly, super-naturally filled with a blanketing peace where only a heartbeat ago there was panic. I open my door with a surety that no one here can hurt me unless God allows them to and that whatever He allows is what is best for me.

"It's going to be okay," I whisper to Harmony. "Get out now."

She obediently opens her door and climbs out on shaky legs. I gather Rosa in my arms and climb out of the backseat. Rosa buries her face in my wind tossed hair and whimpers in my ear. I hug her tight and silently plead with God to keep her safe.

"Everyone!" The silver man insists again, indicating Thomas.

"He isn't well. He can't walk." Matt says haughtily, spitting at the silver man's feet.

My peace falters for a moment wishing Matt could be civil for once. The silver man curses and, taking a step forward, he rams his gun with brutal force into Matt's stomach. Matt doubles over and drops to one knee gasping. He draws a few ragged breaths before cursing at the silver man with an effort I find confusing. It's like he's trying to pick a fight.

"Get him out now or die."

Tim reaches into the front and gathers Thomas in his arms. Thomas was on the thick side a few weeks ago, filled out from his adopted mother Ellen's wonderful cooking. The last couple weeks of sickness and lean provisions have thinned him out considerably. Tim is strong. He lifts Thomas easily out of the car and stands cradling him beside me. I'm sure we look like a couple. A zombie couple with two kids.

A few men separate themselves from the wall of guns and approach us with confidence. We don't convey any threat, our arms full of children. The first man takes Thomas from Tim's arms and dumps him unceremoniously on the ground, drawing a sharp cry from delicate Thomas. Tim, Harmony and I, all step towards our friend - his painful cry pulling us to defy wisdom. The sound of many guns clacking into readiness all around us stops us from running to Thomas' aid.

But it doesn't stop Matt.

He is on his feet and quickly around the car, his arm drawn back in inevitable wrath for the man who just dropped his brother. Tim lunges forward and grabs Matt before the punch is thrown, fighting him to stop, clawing at Matt's flailing arms. Matt unleashes his incredible powers of profanity, shouting obscenities that would make the nastiest zombie pause. Tim continues to fight to hold him as the silver man walks over to him and pistol whips him again, this time lower than his already bruised gut.

Matt doubles over in pain and retches on the ground. Tim's confining arms become supportive, holding Matt up in a caring embrace. Tim whispers to Matt and I watch helplessly as Matt slumps to the ground at Tim's feet. The Pravdanian puts his gun to Matt's head and gives a silent nodded command to his goons.

They hurry over to us, guns drawn and in mere seconds we are all on our knees, our hands behind our heads. I feel the cold point of a gun on my skull and I imagine the others share my fate. Rosa is crying softly and all I can do is desperately beg God to hold her still. To keep her safe and not give them any reason to hurt her. Toccoa is happening all over again. Is this another chance to make the right choice? If I tell them who I am would they let these people who I love so much go?

Tim is next to me in our kneeling line and I hear him whisper quietly, "Don't do anything stupid, Ivy."

He knows me so well. He knows what I'm thinking. If I love him at all, I should ignore him and do it. Pull my mask off and tell them, *I'm who you want!*

They pull all of our stuff out of the car. Matt's stash of guns brings a lot of excitement, but then they find our stash of bottled water. The happy cheers and shouts over our water sounds like crows in a corn field. Scavengers and thieves. But thieves with an obvious chain of command. The silver-suited man barks commands and his henchmen jump to comply. Why is Pravda working with bandits?

The urge to tell them who I am is growing, becoming unbearable in me. My throat is tight with fear and I feel the words climbing out of my gut. I open my mouth, so close to ready. Little short breaths come fast from my panting turmoil. I feel the admission forming on my tongue.

"No!" Tim whispers again. This time the man behind him bumps him roughly in the head, shoving him slightly forward.

I can't let this happen to them. Not when I might be able to save them. But what if I'm wrong? What if they are shot on site for helping me? Matt said if we're tough we might somehow make it through this. How can they not take my mask off though? I would think that would be Pravda's first order of business - before searching the car.

What should I do, God?

The man behind me lifts me up to my feet and starts to drag me toward the larger group by the vehicles. I want to fight him, but I'm terrified of being shot and even more scared of losing my mask. Harmony is crying and fighting behind me. They have her too. Will they search us because we are girls and they know they are looking for a girl? Why not take our masks off back at the car?

Matt and Tim are shouting behind us and I hear the sounds of them being beaten and restrained. These sounds flood me with new terror and the words that were in my mouth a moment ago are flooded away with bile. I have to pinch my lips closed to keep from being sick. It takes great mental effort to hold my bladder.

I'm being led to my death. There's no way we will get out of here alive. The crying gets so loud I wish Harmony would stop - but then I realize it's me! I'm screaming and sobbing and I can't control it! I feel my spirit retreating far inside to hide from this horrible place where it all will end.

I'm shoved down to the cold, hard ground and my mask gets pushed slightly off center. Rocks jab at my back and someone kicks up the dirt near my face. I smell the old leaves around my head and feel sticks and dirt in my hair. My mask is still covering my face but it is pushed so askew that I can't see straight through the eye holes.

My left eye is close enough to the right eye hole to make out feet standing around me. Through the peripheral cracks I see clothing dropping to the ground around the dirty shoes that seem to surround me. Suddenly I understand why Matt was so sure that they wouldn't take our masks off. They don't want to see our diseased faces. That would damper their desires and they plan to have me. Me and Harmony.

Dear God! I am fear and I am fury. The murderous rage from hours ago fills me again - righteous anger. If they hurt Harmony - If they put one mark on little Rosa or even touch her - *Dear God please! Rescue us! Kill these awful zombies! Strike them with lightening! Do something! We are your precious ones! How can you let this happen!*

Several hands reach out to grab me and I feel my clothes being roughly torn away. I try to shut down. Try to hide and find a place in my head to cower and scream silently. I struggle to resist, but weakly.

Then someone calls out a harsh command to stop.

And the men around me curse and dissipate, like a foul odor displaced by a gentle wind.

I feel myself sobbing again. I wrap my arms around my head in exhausted fear mixed with some relief. I don't know why they've gone and

I'm too afraid to hope that they won't be back.

New hands are touching me and I jerk and scream, trying to fight them away.

"It's okay, Ivy. It's okay." Tim's gentle whisper is a confusing, wonderful, life-giving relief. I sob as he pulls me onto his lap and fixes my shirt gently, covering my exposed stomach. I cling to him and cry while shivers shake my body.

"I'll be right back," he says, scooting away.

I grab at him like a desperate child, wailing. I need him! He can't leave me here!

"I have to check on Harmony," he says with his soft voice full of compassion and anger all at once.

I don't want him to go, but I remember how terrified I was for her. I let him pry my fingers from his shirt and sit me gently back down on the cold ground. I'm so damaged and hurt that I can't feel my spirit wherever it went to hide. I feel cold and numb and angry. I have no prayers and no relief, just shivering emptiness. I want to rip my mask off and curl into a ball, but some tiny whispering wisdom helps me to fix it back over my eyes, keeping it on. The horrible mask helps to hide the shame anyways. I don't want anyone to see my face ever again.

I'm sitting on the back seat of the Station Wagon, numb to the world. The door is open. The spring breeze blowing through the holes in my mask keeps drying my tears but to no avail, more come to replace them. I can't stop crying. Rosa is next to me on Harmony's lap. The three of us sit so close together that we barely take up one of the back seats. I feel Harmony shivering, but she makes no sound behind her mask. We don't speak. I don't know what's happening. I keep trying to care; but hurt is holding me captive in a dark place deep inside.

The zombie's cars still block the way and, though no one is holding a gun to our heads, we are still trapped here. A camouflaged army tent suddenly shimmers into view. It has been there, hidden in plain view, blending into the woods. I see a zombie emerge from the tent carrying a smaller masked zombie. The man in the orange ski mask carries the little man in his arms over to our car and, at the front door on the passenger side, he stands looking at me. With an empty stare, I look back at him from behind my mask.

"Ivy?" The masked man asks with Tim's voice.

My disorientation clears a little and I remember that Tim and Thomas have masks on. It's Tim. He's holding Thomas. I continue to stare.

"Ivy?" Tim asks again with more impatience.

I look at them. Study them in their zombie masks and gloves. Ski masks have never had good connotations. People used to look like bank robbers or criminals in them, despite their actual design for nothing more than warmth. I wish they still meant thief. Now they mean so much worse. These masks triumphantly claim the title "Rapist." They proudly acknowledge "Baby Killer." "Human Flesh Eater." "Zombie."

Harmony deposits Rosa into my lap and climbs over us to get out of the car. She opens the front door for Tim and helps him situate Thomas into the front seat. I watch them, detached, while Rosa wraps her little arms around my neck and lays her head against my chest.

Tim whispers something to Harmony and she nods.

I don't care.

Who are they talking about?

I don't care.

What are they talking about?

I don't care.

What else can go horrifyingly wrong in my life today?

I don't care.

Harmony climbs back over me as I sit woodenly, staring at the back of the front seat. She unwraps Rosa's arms and pulls her back onto her lap, scooting to the far side of the seat away from me.

Tim squats in front of me, outside of the open door. Glancing all around us, he gently lifts my mask up to reveal my tear-stained face. I don't want him to look at me. I feel so ashamed. My shame glows red and more tears streak down salty trails that burn on my chapped cheeks. I lower my eyes to my hands, twisted in white-knuckled balls in my lap. Tim reaches up and gently pulls leaves from my hair. I wince as he tries to unravel a stick that is caught in the rat's nest of my ugly curls. He leans closer and works the stick free.

Tim speaks quietly, "The Lord is gracious and righteous; our God is full of compassion."

I look up from my hands and meet his eyes. I don't want to hear this right now. I feel - abandoned. Let down by God. Tim's brown eyes are full of love and watery with concern. I can't bear the emotion in them. I look back down at my hands.

Tim runs a finger across my cheek to dry a new tear. He speaks again:

> "The Lord protects the simple-hearted; when I was in great need, He saved me. Be at rest once more, O my soul, for The Lord has been good to you. For you, O Lord, have delivered my soul from death, my eyes from tears, my feet from stumbling, that I may walk before The Lord in the land of the living. I believed; therefore I said, 'I am greatly afflicted.' And in my dismay I said, 'All men are liars.' How can I repay The Lord for all his goodness to me? I will lift up the cup of salvation and call on the name of The Lord. I will fulfill my vows to The Lord in the presence of all his people. Precious in the sight of The Lord is the death of His saints. O Lord, truly I am your servant; I am your servant, the son of your maidservant, you have freed me from my chains."

"Psalm 116:5-16," he finishes softly, quoting the book and verse of what must have been a comfort to him once. So much so that he memorized it.

God's word is powerful. It goes out like a boomerang to touch people and then returns back to God. The Bible says that God's word has never gone out to touch someone and returned without doing its job. It is power and healing. It works on me again, like it has so many times before. The precious words weave through my wounds like a surgeon's needle and thread. Painfully poking and stabbing at flesh, but then drawing together and curing. Tim's faith-filled speech lays the balm on my infection. It isn't all better, but the Doctor has tended to it and therefore it must eventually heal.

Tim is quiet, leaning close and searching my face for some sign of response. So many feelings are warring inside of me. Longing to be held, but afraid of being touched. Wanting to reach for Tim, but hating him and everyone else. Tim's hand gently cups my chin and he dips his head down to look into my eyes. I squeeze them shut in defiance. Suddenly, he is scooting me over and wrapping his arms around me. Part of me wants to push him away, but mostly I'm so relieved. I let him hold me as I bury my face into his shirt and feel a little safer. A little loved. A little better.

Chapter Thirteen

Dealer's Choice

Our car has been reloaded. The cars blocking the road have pulled to the side. A zombie in a clown mask put air in our front right tire. Bozo also taped a thick cardboard covering over the shattered back window. The car is running, ready to go. Tim is in the front seat with Thomas and Matt is standing outside speaking with another zombie. The silver-suited man stands just behind the two of them in a proud yet subservient stance.

The man speaking to Matt is barefaced and clean shaven. He has dark hair, slicked back neatly, and he is dressed in camouflage like an army man. He looks almost healthy, though his skin has the same yellowish tint that Matt's has. He wears the special zombie gloves that Matt almost never takes off. I wonder if his hands actually need them. Matt only wears the gloves to hide how healthy he is.

The two of them shake gloved hands and the dark haired bandit captain says something that makes his silver-suited lieutenant salute Matt with respect and humility.

I'm in the twilight zone.

Matt strides over to the car and hops in, pulling the now squeak-less door shut. The clown man oiled the doors, too. How weird is that?

"Anyone need the bathroom before we go?" Matt asks lightheartedly.

Yeah, right. Like any of us would delay leaving this place as fast as possible. If I had to pee, I'd rather pee my pants than get back out of this car.

"Okay. Here we go," Matt says, accelerating slowly past the group of masked zombies who stare vacantly at us as we drive away, their hedonistic hungers still unsatisfied.

I hate them so much.

"They took your guns?" Tim asks Matt, pulling his ski mask off now that the zombies are behind us.

"Yeah, and all of the water. I think they missed a few of the guns I had hidden. They hadn't finished searching the car when Gerry showed up and realized who they were beating the crap out of. Your stuff is still back there," he says to Tim.

"So, you're a dealer?" Tim asks, helping Thomas take his mask off.

"I guess the jig is up," Matt says with a sarcastic smile.

"Makes a lot of sense, now." Tim says enigmatically.

"What's a dealer?" Harmony asks.

I glance over at her and see that her mask is off too. I'm leaving mine on. Maybe forever.

When Matt doesn't explain, Tim says, "He's a blood dealer. He steals clean blood from Pravda after it's been processed and he sells it to people for less than they would pay at a blood center."

"What's a blood center?" Harmony asks.

I know a little bit about it from one of the missionaries, but I still get the chills hearing Matt it explain it to her.

"Pravda has found ways to clean some of the LS out of the blood. They haven't found a way to get rid of it entirely," he glances back at me in the rearview mirror and his implication doesn't escape me.

He still thinks I'm the cure.

"You can take that mask off now, Ivy," Matt says and then continues explaining to Harmony, "So people go to blood centers and pay credits for blood transfusions. Pravda takes out the diseased blood and replaces it with much healthier blood and it slows the disease's progress in most people."

So that's his secret. That's why Matt and some of the bandits that we saw today look so much healthier than the zombies we saw through the fence in Toccoa. He's giving himself treated blood to slow the disease. I can't believe it works. I can't believe people have found a way to lessen God's judgment, to circumvent the spiritual disease that God has poured out on mankind.

Matt continues, his voice laden with disgust, "Only the very wealthy can afford treatments and Pravda is making billions. It's not fair. If a person is poor, they don't deserve to live in Pravda's eyes. So I get clean blood to those who really need it at a much lower cost," he finishes with obvious pride in his voice.

This is why I like him. There's more to him than just a selfish zombie. He obviously cares for the down-and-outers. But he isn't giving it away for free is he? He's still profiting from something he is stealing. I called him zombie Robin Hood once and he laughed. I wasn't that far from the mark.

"So why did they let us go?" I ask, speaking for the first time since the attack. The plastic of my mask rubs against my lips and echoes my muffled voice back to my own ears.

"I've sold to them on more than one occasion. I promised to bring them a big shipment as soon as I get going again. On the house."

"Get going again?" I ask.

"I've been gone for awhile. My team probably thinks I'm dead. I don't know if they've kept things going while I was gone. There's a lot to get straight when we get back to my place."

"Your place?" Harmony asks in a mousy squeak.

I haven't given much thought to where we'll stay when we get to Atlanta. I guess it makes sense to stay at Matt's house. I've been so focused on getting my dad and Aunty Betty out of Pravda, but who knows how long that will take? We'll need a base camp, a place to plan and prepare. Matt knows the way in and out. He knows it firsthand. It must have been his blood dealing that landed him in a cell next to my dad. I wonder where he lives? I hope it isn't another cave. I can't take that again.

"Jessie will be so excited to see us," Thomas chirps up from the front seat.

"I hope so." Matt says with a sigh.

I had forgotten about the mystery that is Jessie. Jealousy flares hot in me and I wish we had somewhere else to go. Does she live at his house? Is she his girlfriend? I don't want the answers to those questions. I wonder if we'll have to wear the masks the whole time we're there. I guess so. We are fugitives now. There is nowhere safe left for us.

Tim and Matt start into a conversation about how Pravda transports the blood and where Matt gets his contacts and the process of stealing blood from an armored delivery truck. I stare through the eye holes of my new identity at the hills and trees around us. Their new green leaves don't refresh me. The wind whipping against the cardboard window panel behind Harmony has a hypnotic, dulling effect. I zone out in my own private pity party while they all chatter as though nothing horrible has happened.

*****

We are close to Atlanta now. It's strange to see this civilization of the uncivilized. Everywhere I look, everything we drive past, is drowning in evil. Gigantic billboards offer drugs cheap and babies cheaper. Sometimes the advertisements have pictures. I feel so sick that despite my hunger, I consider never eating again.

I remember all that Ben Morvose, the missionary, told Aunty and I the night he ate pasta at our table. He told us about stem cells and girls who get pregnant just to sell their undeveloped babies for the rich man's table. About unspeakable "entertainment" that I wish I wasn't seeing live advertisements for at every corner. How did we get so bad? How did humanity degrade to this Sodom and Gomorra depravity on a worldwide scale?

"We need gas," Matt confesses quietly. "We won't make it to the house without a stop."

"Is that going to be a big deal?" Tim asks just above a whisper.

It's weird that the two of them are talking now. I thought I'd like it if we could all get along and I'm surprised that it only makes me uncomfortable.

"It shouldn't be. I have to find a B.C. first, I don't have enough credits."

"How long will it take?" I only hear Tim's question because I'm leaning forward to listen. The two of them are trying to keep Harmony and I calm and uninvolved. I refuse to be either.

"I'll need you to drive afterwards," Matt mumbles to Tim. "Do you know how?"

"Yeah."

"Gas is expensive."

So Matt will have to give so much blood he won't be able to drive. Our tour guide and zombie expert will be out of commission.

"It's warmer out now. Can't we just walk the rest of the way?" I ask, leaning over the front seat, involved and far from calm.

"It would take at least another day if we walk. That's twenty-four hours of opportunities to run into the wrong people and carting the kids through dangerous places. If I get gas, we'll be home in a few hours. This is the best way."

Tim sighs, "We've trusted him this far Ivy, let's let him finish the job."

Tim just sided with Matt. Tim just told *me* to trust Matt. I guess we'd better hurry up and get this trip over with before the rest of the world turns upside down.

"Gas is usually cheaper here in Buford. The rich don't come out this way. A lot of interesting characters live around here, so we just keep our heads down and blend in. Do as I say and we'll be fine." Matt says with confidence.

Interesting characters? The worst of the damned sounds like unwise company to keep. Harmony, Tim and Thomas put their masks back on as we reach the busier streets. I'm getting used to mine, but it's starting to chafe against my cheek bones.

"It's actually pretty great that we're driving this tin can. No one else will want this car either. We're much less likely to be hit by car thieves," Matt says to Tim as though making normal, pleasant conversation.

I laugh out loud, a weird crackly sound I've never made before. Harmony and Tim turn at the sound and then share a look. They think I'm losing it. I think I am too. The nerves, the fear, the ridiculousness of the situation we're in is doing things to me. I don't feel good.

Matt has a lot of contacts here in the hellacious town of Buford. Big surprise there. We're hoping to find some guy named Herb who rents rooms by the hour. Matt wants us to stay hidden while he's out giving blood, getting gas, and doing whatever else it is that he needs to do in this godforsaken place.

At a busy street corner, Matt has a nauseating conversation through his window with some half-naked masked women. With their skanky help, we finally locate Herb. Herb is downright icky. He's a large man with greasy black hair that curls at his shoulders. He wears a black half-mask, just around his eyes. He looks like Zorro's out of shape uncle.

Herb owns several of the good-time flaunting she-zombies and he offers us a group discount several times. Apparently he owes Matt a favor. Matt turns him down brashly, but I seethe at the thought that Matt probably accepted this form of payment in the past.

Herb's face turns the shade of a fresh tomato below his black mask. "I insist. I don't like to owe anyone," Herb says darkly with an accent that produces a spray of saliva.

"I understand. I'd be willing to cancel the whole thing for a few hours in one of your nicer rooms and some fresh water," Matt says with easygoing camaraderie.

"Water is expensive," Herb counters.

"Well, you owe me quite a lot," Matt says. "A room doesn't cost you and we aren't taking any credit-makers from their post."

Herb's tomato paste complexion lightens to a calmer shade of sunset pink. He smiles to show only a few broken teeth left in his mouth - the reason for the extra spittle. It's a good deal for him.

"How much water do you need?" Herb asks.

"A gallon would cancel our debt."

"Oh, you gonna be busy? Eh?" Herb keeps jerking his head in a nod towards the back seat at Harmony and I. He sticks his tongue out of the side of his smile and says, "Eh? Eh?" at Matt like he knows why Matt wants the room.

Quiet up to this point, Tim cracks his knuckles and coughs an irritated warning. Somehow nerdy Tim manages to look intimidating for a moment. It's the mask. You can't see his thick glasses. The masks make anyone look tough. Herb casts a nervous glance at Tim and then gets the conversation back on course.

"This will square our debt, yes? I owe you nothing now?" Herb asks leaving spit drops on the partially rolled down window.

Matt nods and shakes Herb's gloved hand.

Chapter Fourteen

Seedy Isn't The Half of It

We park the car outside of Herb's "establishment." The place looks condemned. The long brick building was a business park when it was built. Doctors, dentists and lawyers had respectable offices here. They offered respectable services. That is a time forgotten.

A quarter of the left side of the building is nothing but a burnt skeleton of blackened stone block. The fire that claimed it must have been years ago because kudzu vines have woven lengthy patterns of green latticework over the black cement. The windows are cracked and boarded up.

Dying trees and bushes decorate the garbage strewn lawn. I try to imagine it as it once was. I try to envision the once beautiful landscaping and the trim work freshly painted. It's like trying to picture an innocent little girl in place of the disease ridden, tassel clad hookers that Herb owns.

Next door to Herb's love shack are more of the gruesome signs of the baby market written in Spanish. As we spill out of the car, all of us nervously scanning the area for any sign of danger, Rosa starts bawling. She claws at my shirt, overcome with fear, and tries to pull me back into the car with her. I've never seen her like this. She's making too much noise and I'm worried it's going to draw the wrong kind of attention.

Tim picks her up, pulling her arms from my legs and tears spring to my eyes. I know he's trying to help, but I want to hold her. Something is wrong and I don't know what or how to fix it. He wraps her in his arms and coos soothing words into her ear. She buries her head in his shoulder, shivering. Her cries sound more like a word now. I hear it forming through the sobs. She repeats it over and over into Tim's shoulder.

"Carnicero, carnicero, carnicero." The word gets clearer as she mumbles it between sobs and hiccups.

I glance back at the shop that borders Herb's and see the sign, "Carnicería."

"What does that mean?" I ask Matt.

"Butcher Shop," he says, his voice cold and empty.

"Tim, what if this is where she's from?"

I hurry closer to them and press myself to Rosa, shielding her from view. Tim and I glance around nervous, unsure of what to do.

"Let's get her inside," Tim says with emotion thickening his voice. He loves her like I do. She sort of belongs to both of us now.

Herb's nicest room is the dirtiest room I've ever been in. And that's including the bathroom in the cave. The carpet is brown; but, when we move a large chair to make room for Thomas' wheelchair, I see the carpet's original beige color beneath. The room has a few pieces of cheap broken furniture, a matched set because they are all wrapped in the same color of Duct Tape. A king sized bed fills the center of the small room and faces an old television.

Thomas smiles and asks, "Can we watch cartoons?" when Matt wheels him into the room.

"Don't turn that on." Matt says to Tim, his stern expression and lifted eyebrows conveying an easy to read message.

So, no. No cartoons.

Harmony sits on the edge of the bed and Matt calls over to her, "I wouldn't sit on that if I were you."

She jumps to her feet and brushes at her backside.

"I'll bring in some of our blankets. We can lay them over the bed," Matt says, disappearing back out through the wooden door.

Tim closes the door behind Matt and I see that it has two different dead bolts and two separate chain locks that draw across. The sight doesn't engender confidence. I hope Matt's errands don't take long. I miss the Inn.

It's true, you know - you never know what you have until it's gone. I hated my life in Toccoa. I hated all the cleaning and dusting and toilet scrubbing. I hated being bossed around by Aunty and feeling trapped inside our fence. I wanted out. I wanted freedom.

I was such a fool.

I *was* a princess. The way the rest of the town looked at me, like a spoiled girl - they were right. I had it all. I had family that loved me and cared for me. I had good food, safety and friendship. I had a place I belonged - like nowhere else in the world will ever be for me again. If I could go back, I'd appreciate the heck out of it.

*****

Matt has been gone for too long. He said he would only be an hour, but it's been more like two or three. Harmony, Thomas, and Rosa are stretched out asleep on the blankets that Matt spread over the dirty bedspread before he left. Tim is pacing by the door. I'm standing by the heavy window curtains, watching for Matt - worrying.

If he doesn't come back -

No. Stop. He will. He always does. He has to.

A zombie in a black ski mask catches my attention. Watching him causes a smirk of disgust to grow on my face. He's bobbling slowly, drunkenly, down the sidewalk. His head sways in erratic dips. The overgrown shrubs that line the path towards Herb's exquisite resort make a stage of sorts for the drunken puppet head as it wobbles comically along. My smile fades as I think about who is holding that puppet's strings. He doesn't belong to God, and there is only one other option for master.

At the edge of the hedge, where the sidewalk meets the driveway, the zombie's full body stumbles into Herb's parking lot. The puppet stands still for a moment and then collapses. My mind registers his dark jeans, his black long sleeved T-shirt.

"Matt!" I yell through the crack in the curtains. The glass is thick and I know he can't hear me. He lays unmoving on the driveway. Tim is across the room and by my side in a moment, looking out the window through the blinds above my head.

"Where?" he asks, not seeing Matt's still form on the road near the bushes.

"He fell! There! By the bushes!" I say through tears.

Is he hurt? I'm worried and simultaneously concerned that he may be drunk - in which case I will be mortified. If he blew our gas credits on booze.

I turn to push past Tim and hurry to the door, unlatching the deadbolts and fumbling with the chains. Tim is quickly behind me again, his hands on my shoulders. He moves me away and pulls the mask I'm still wearing off of my face. The air feels cool on my damp skin and I feel too exposed. I want my mask back.

Putting his cool hands on either side of my face, Tim tilts my head up to look at him. I shut my eyes and try to pull away from him. His hands leave my face and clamp onto my arms in restraint. I'm impatient with him, holding me back. Always trying to keep me from Matt. I have to get out there! When he doesn't speak, I open my eyes and find his face too close. Tim's brown eyes look enormous, magnified behind his glasses. He holds me so close to his face that I see the individual whiskers that have started to pepper his cheeks and chin.

Silent for another moment, he finally speaks when I struggle against his grasp, "I'll get him. You stay here and lock the door behind me. I'll be right back."

Tim wipes a tear from my cheeks with his thumbs. Then, he pulls his mask on and slips out of the door. I lock the four locks with fumbling fingers and run back across to the window. Harmony is staring out the window and I slide in next to her. Outside, Matt lays motionless. I bite my lip as warm tears fall. Harmony and I watch Tim as he jogs across the parking lot to where Matt lays.

Tim kneels next to Matt and checks for a pulse. He holds his finger to Matt's neck and glances around nervously. I press my hands against the window as Tim proves his strength and lifts Matt's dead weight up into his arms. Like a war hero on the battle field, he carries his comrade back to our place in the trenches. I run back across the room to meet them at the door.

Both of them safely inside and the four locks reengaged, Tim arranges Matt's unconscious limbs on the bed as Harmony helps Thomas into his wheel chair. Pulling off his own mask, Tim adjusts his stethoscope in his ears and pulls Matt's shirt up. Putting the metal cylinder on Matt's chest, Tim holds up a hand for silence while he listens.

I clamp my hand over my mouth, terrified that Matt is dying or dead. Harmony presses tight to my arms on either side in a strange embrace that is also a restraint. I can't lose Matt! I need him! Tim pulls Matt's mask off and I inhale a strangled cry through my fingers. He's as white as a ghost.

Beside me, Thomas asks in a small, frightened voice, "Is he dead?"

Tim sighs and straightens, "His heartbeat is faint but regular. Judging by his color I'd say he just gave too much blood. I don't see any wounds or signs of a fight. I think he's just very weak. Basically, he's an idiot."

I can't hold myself back any more and I lunge onto the bed by Matt's side.

"He'll be okay?" I ask Tim, daring to hope.

Tim gives me that look that makes me feel wretched. Hurt and condemnation fly like banners on his sweaty, stubbled face. I look away. Kneeling next to Matt on the bed I hold his arm and hand and pray for him to get better. I pray for him to find Jesus. I pray for him because I love him.

"I'm going out," Tim says to Harmony behind me.

She locks the door behind him. I don't look at them. I am focused on Matt as he sleeps. I pull his shirt back down to cover his white chest. His stomach is hairy. I brush his shaggy dark hair away from his eyes and settle myself next to him.

I've never seen him sick or vulnerable. He's always so strong and together. Nothing is ever a big deal to him. He did this for me. I've saddled him with this group of the Living to care for. He has done everything I could've hoped for and then some. He kept us safe in the cave, brought us food, saved us from the bandits. He gave too much blood because he's trying to get us safely to his house as soon as possible. His acts of service and selflessness won my respect long after I had already given him my heart.

The boundaries that exist when he is awake have been removed by my concern. Knowing Tim isn't watching me makes being close to Matt even easier. I touch him. I run my fingers gently down the side of his face and neck. With only Harmony and Thomas as witnesses, I bend close to his ear and study the disease that bubbles and cracks the skin on the very top.

There are scars on his right ear that I hadn't noticed before. A hole has healed in the lobe, and I try to picture him with an earring. Higher up it looks like something tore through his ear and it healed in a jagged line. When I stare at him, this close in the light, I can see that his skin looks different than mine. It's dryer all over. The white paleness of his bloodless face gives away splotchy patches near his lips and nose. Hints of new places the LS will feast on and thrive.

I'm starting to feel - familiar with it. With him just the way he is. I should be repulsed or at the very least worried. But, because I love him, I'm not bothered by his flaws. The disease is part of him as I've always known him. I stroke his messy hair and comb through it with my fingers. He looks sweet and young in his sleep, his eyelids imprisoning the green irises that make him look so intense. His long lashes flutter slightly and I see his eyes moving back and forth behind his lids. He's dreaming.

Harmony has settled into the chair by the door with my Aunty's Bible. She has made herself at home with my few belongings and I'm glad. Thomas is in his wheelchair playing with a small paper origami animal that Tim made for him. Thomas' lips move quickly and silently. I know he isn't talking to himself. He's praying for his big brother. Rosa has managed to stay asleep through all the commotion, curled into a little ball on the top corner of the bed. I don't know where Tim went, but I'm not worried. He's smart. He can take care of himself.

No one needs me right now. I embrace the opportunity and lay down on the bed. Another glance at Harmony - she's not watching me - I lay gently in the crook of Matt's arm. He smells spicy like deodorant and I bury my nose in his side and try to memorize the scent.

"Hey," Matt whispers breathless and weak.

Surprised and embarrassed, and I sit up quickly.

He chuckles quietly and says, "Jumpy."

I smile down at him, my face red.

"I pass out for a few minutes and you're all over me. I knew you wanted me," he whispers.

I scoot off the bed, incapable of staying so close to him when he's awake. What felt tender and innocent isn't anymore.

"Are you okay?" I ask in a timid whisper.

"Never better," the characteristic reply makes me smile and eases my worry, though his eyes are closed again.

"Do you need anything? Some water?" I ask.

He doesn't answer me. His breathing is deep and slow. He's out again. I lay my head down on my folded arms and watch him rest.

Chapter Fifteen
No Habla Espanol

Pounding. A grumpy question I can't understand. Someone is rapping on the door with urgency. I jump up, not sure when I fell asleep and see myself in the mirror beside the bed. My cheeks are crisscrossed with red sleep lines from my sleeve. My hair hasn't been washed in weeks. The top of my head looks flat and greasy but the rest of my hair is a halo of frizz. But, worse than all of that, are the empty eyes that look back at me like they belong to someone else. Some thin, hallow, sleep deprived, depressed stranger.

Who is she? I don't like her. I want me back. Am I gone forever? The door rattles again with the force of an angry fist.

Breaking eye contact with the nether version of myself, in the reflection behind me I see Harmony staring at the door. She glances over her shoulder and meets my eyes in the mirror. Neither of us speak. Neither of us offer a smile of encouragement nor suggest a course of action. We stare stoically into each other's empty eyes. I look away first, my eyes drawn down to Matt where he lays still asleep on the bed.

The lamplight from the bedside table spills over his pale face coloring him a sick jaundiced yellow. Thomas sits near him on the other side of the expansive king-sized bed, fingering the black glove Matt gave him with his good hand. Tom's mutilated hand is tucked beneath him. He rarely lets us see it. The lamplight glistens on the shiny fabric of the zombie glove and I notice the shadows. I notice the night. It's dark outside. I check the curtained windows and I see only night behind them. We've been here longer than we had planned. Matt blinks slowly but doesn't seem coherent. How long will it take him to get his strength back?

The angry pounding intensifies and is accompanied by a stream of Spanish that I don't have to speak to understand. The woman the fist belongs to wants us to open the door and let her know what's going on *or else.* What should I do? I draw a shuddered breath as my cloudy mind continues to wake up and deal with the moment. I realize Tim is still gone. Where is he? Why would he stay gone so long? We need him!

Matt mumbles behind me, "Tell her we're leaving. Say, 'Nos vamos.'"

"Nos Vamos?" I repeat softly, trying the foreign words and feeling stupid.

Matt nods.

I take a deep breath and cross the small room to stand at the door.

"Nos Vamos!" I say uncertainly, too loudly.

An angry question flies back at me through the door. How do they speak so fast? How could anyone understand that? I look over my shoulder at Matt. He looks like he's asleep again and my stomach clenches with panic. His lips move though his eyes stay shut. He whispers something that I can't hear and Harmony moves closer to him, bending to listen.

Harmony calls in a shaky voice, "Estaremos fuera -" then looks back down at Matt as he mumbles to her again. She calls out the rest of the repeated message, "en cinco minutos!"

"What did you say?" I whisper to her aggravated.

"I don't know!" She whispers back intensely.

The Spanish woman outside sends another rant through the wooden door, her voice trailing off as she moves away down the hall.

"What just happened?" Harmony asks me.

I shrug frustrated. Where the heck is Tim? What are we supposed to do?

"We have to go now," Matt says with enough strength for me to hear him this time. "You told her we'd be out in five minutes. My deal with Herb was for three hours. How long have we been here?"

I look to Harmony for the answer. I don't know how long I slept.

"Five hours, maybe more," she answers apologetically as though it's her fault.

"Can you move yet?" I ask Matt.

Five minutes ticks down towards only four. And how can we leave without Tim?

My heart drops again, "Where is Rosa?"

Harmony nods towards the window and for a brief second I misunderstand - for a terrified instant I think she's somehow gone - then I see her tiny feet beneath the curtain and my heart floods with relief. She's hiding.

I am so exhausted. Constant tension and constant fear are my constant reality. Rosa is probably starving. I am. Where will our next meal come from? Where will we sleep tonight? Will we make it to Matt's? Will it be any better there? Despair pierces my limbs like needles and injects them with heaviness. My shoulders slump with the weight of impossible responsibilities. I can't do this anymore.

I reach for my mask where it lays on the bed beside Matt. As I pull it over my eyes, I decide to pull on a different personality. A persona that matches my empty eyes. Someone tougher. Someone jaded. Someone used to hardship - in fact, she likes it. She says, "Bring it on."

"I'll take Matt to the car first," I say to Harmony who is fixing her mask into place. "Then I'll come back for Thomas and you can carry Rosa."

Harmony nods and helps me pull Matt up into a sitting position. She has gotten used to him. A couple of weeks ago she cringed in his presence, shrieked at his touch. Matt accidentally killing her had a lot to do with that. Now we all need each other so badly. Instead of familiarity breeding contempt, contempt has somehow grown into familiarity.

I lift Matt's heavy arm over my shoulders and with a "one, two, three", Harmony and I labor to lift him to his feet. He is so weak that as soon as we have him standing he swoons and crumples to the floor despite our efforts to hold him up. Harmony's expression is unreadable behind her plastic mask but I assume her face wears the same frustrated, helpless expression mine does. Matt moans from his slumped position on the filthy carpet. Maybe the smell of filth roused him.

"Come on Matt," Thomas whines in frightened encouragement. "Get up!"

"Let's try again?" I ask Harmony.

"What about the wheelchair?" she suggests.

Duh!

I nod and cross the room for the chair, pulling it close to the bed. Harmony bends and pulls Matt's arm over her shoulder and I hurry to help. The two of us strain with all of our strength and manage to pull Matt up between us, the burden of his dead weight across our shoulders. My knees wobble as we lunge to the right and deposit him unceremoniously into the squeaky seat. We'll wheel him outside and hopefully the two of us can get him into the car. Then what? I guess we'll wait there, in the car, for Tim. With no one to protect us. In front of the Spanish butcher shop with starved, terrified Rosa and a little boy who can't walk.

"God, please help us!" I whisper through my gritted teeth.

Harmony and I use up two precious minutes loading and maneuvering Matt through the room and out into the now empty hall. I pull the door shut behind us and pray that the kids will be safe for the few minutes we're gone. Matt is unconscious, his head lolling against his chest, as we push him towards the front door. We roll hesitantly towards the barely lit parking lot.

Outside, the car sits alone on the gloomy, potholed lot. Harmony walks so close behind me that she steps on the back of my shoe.

"Sorry," she whispers.

I grunt in response, never breaking stride. The night is full of sounds. The beat of nearby night clubs, a scream somewhere down the street, a keening siren in the distance. The wind carries the smell of the butcher shop next door and my stomach turns. I search the shadows for - Help? Danger? Someone to shoot me and put me out of my misery?

I crouch as I hurry, bouncing Matt over uneven pavement, the last few yards to the car. Maybe I can get it to start. What if I have to get us out of here? How hard could it be to drive a car? Where is Tim? I jump when I see someone in the front seat. A masked man sits up and stares out of the window at me and then lunges towards the door, throwing it open. I stumble backwards into Harmony and she shrieks in my ear.

"What happened?" Tim asks, his voice surprising me from behind the mask.

"Where have you been?" I yell at him, equal parts fury and relief.

"I - there wasn't enough room on the bed for me and I was tired," he spits at me coldly.

I'm too tired to care. Too exhausted to muster offense.

"We're in trouble. Again," I say tiredly. "The kids are still inside and we have less than a minute to get out of here before more problems come."

"More problems are already here," Tim says in a whisper, jerking his head for me to look behind me.

A heavyset man in a blood soaked apron is staring at us from the door of the butcher shop on the other side of the parking lot. I can tell he is looking me over. Worry digs its claws into my spine as the man adjusts his weight and takes a step in our direction. He's walking towards us.

Crap.

Crap, crap, crap.

As he closes the distance between his shop and our car, the lights throw shadows over his face and his features morph back and forth between demon and man. He is only a few feet away when the light above us consumes the shadows and displays his true form. Half of his face is gone. He wears no mask to cover the decay. He is gruesome. One side rot and one side face, one side hell and one side earth. My stomach climbs into my throat as the butcher smiles a jack-o-lantern grin at me, his oozing left side glistening under the street lamp.

"Whas goin' on here?" The demon man asks with a strong Spanish accent. "Do you nee' some help?"

Tim stands up from the car and positions himself in front of me, "No, thank you. We're fine."

"Your frin doesn't luke fine," The fat man says with another mutilated smile.

I think it must hurt terribly to smile in his condition and then I remember that LS deadens the nerves. He probably doesn't feel any pain at all.

"He's just tired. Over did it. You know." Tim says in a friendly tone. "He gave too much blood because we're short on credits. He'll be fine. We're heading home so he can rest."

Tim sounds too upbeat and the infected man squints a fleshy right eye at him. The man's other eyelid hangs dead and unresponsive, part of the lifeless tissue on his left side. Tim opens the back door of the old Station Wagon and turns his back to the butcher to lift Matt into the car.

We can't know for sure if this horrible man is the one who hurt Rosa, but just being near him makes me feel cold. His expansive belly protrudes like a beach ball beneath his blood swirled apron which is tied tightly beneath his paunch. Very few people are overweight these days. Food is scarce and you have to work hard for it.

I feel bile in my throat as thoughts of his trade, his diet, bring tears to my eyes. He eats babies. He kills children. He's a cannibal. A murderer. I glance up and meet his eyes and I see darkness in them. Tim yanks on my arm so hard that he almost pulls it from its socket and I break eye contact with the smiling man. So much blood on his apron. Is it animal or human?

Tim motions for me to help him lift Matt. The infected man pushes me out of the way with bloody hands and clamps them around Matt's legs. The fat man expels an exaggerated groan as he lifts Matt's bottom half. Straightening, the butcher jerks his thick neck to the side - cracking it - and then begins to whistle as he helps Tim fit Matt's limp form into the back seat. The butcher's whistle sounds like a siren, like a haunting signal for demonic backup.

The fat butcher straightens and cracks his back, leaving Tim to finish situating Matt into the car. The bare musculature on the left side of his face shimmers as though it wears a coat of varnish and I can't help but stare at his inhuman countenance. Behind me a high pitched scream fills the night. I spin to see Rosa at the door of Herb's hotel, her mouth open wide in a bloodcurdling scream of raw terror. She has seen the face of the devil and I know beyond a shadow of a doubt that this devil is the one who hurt her.

Rosa's Mickey Mouse hat rides low over her forehead and her messy hair is draped around her face. I pray fervently that the butcher won't recognize her in the parking lot's scant light. Harmony runs to Rosa and wraps her in her arms, lifting her back into the shadows of Herb's dark hallways. The butcher stares into the inky doorway with a puzzled, too interested look on his face. Tim and I lock eyes and I know we both hide panic behind our zombie disguises.

Tim clears his throat and successfully draws the fat man's dark eyes away from their search.

"Thank you for your help," Tim says, extending a hand to shake the butcher's thick bloodstained one.

The butcher looks down at Tim's hand in confusion. I realize Tim's mistake before he does. Too cordial. Too mannerly. Too Living.

"Where deed you say you're goin?" the butcher asks Tim with ice in his thick voice. "Is that your geerl?" he questions with a clipped nod toward the hotel.

"I didn't say. And our group is none of your business." Tim lowers his hand ungratified. "Get in the car," he says tersely to me as he pushes the wheelchair towards the darkened doorway that Harmony and Rosa disappeared into.

Seconds later, Harmony emerges with Rosa's face buried in her neck and Rosa's little arms and legs wrapped around her tightly. Harmony keeps her eyes on the ground, avoiding the fat man's keen stare and ducks quickly into the back seat. Tim comes barreling out of the building behind them.

Tim is pushing Thomas at a jog. A petite masked woman - her gray hair pulled up in a bun - is hot on their heels. She is shooing them out with a long rant of angry Spanish words and a shot gun trained on their backs. Herb's hospitality has run out and I realize my stuff is still in there. My bag is all I have left in the world!

As Tim reaches the car with Thomas, I start back towards the hotel. I can't leave Aunty's Bible in there.

The little gray haired Hispanic granny stands between me and the door back in to the hotel. She spreads her legs and cocks the gun on her shoulder, aiming it at me. The painted eyes on her mask are cheerful but her mouth wears a snarl beneath the colorful plastic countenance.

"I said get in the car now!" Tim yells at me like I'm a naughty child.

"Dat ees my geerl!" the butcher yells into the windows of the Station Wagon, slamming meaty fists against the glass.

He tries for the door handle of the backseat door and finds it locked.

"I wheel pay you for her!" he pleads with Tim who is loading Thomas on the other side. "You need credits! I wheel give you 50 credits for her!"

"Ivy!" Tim barks, his voice strangled by panic.

Tim loads Thomas and shoves the wheelchair away from the car. No time to fold it and load it. As Tim slams the door, the butcher grabs at his shirt. Tim slaps the man's bloody hand away and screams my name, "Ivy!" I hear the front door slam shut as Tim disappears into the car. The car starts its labored cough, the engine unwilling to wake up and get moving.

"Geeve her back to me or I will keel you!" the butcher screams at me.

He turns abruptly and sprints towards his shop. He isn't giving up so he must be going for a weapon - or more help - or both.

I stand between the car, the shotgun wielding old woman, and the door the butcher disappeared into. I can't believe I'm losing Aunty's Bible. My conscience makes my decision because my heart and my head are still desperate to retrieve my most precious things. I turn back to the car and run around to the other side where Tim has opened the front door for me. Tim shoots me a deadly glare as I climb in. He turns the key in the ignition again and again the car argues lazily. If it won't start we are all dead.

"Father!" Tim shouts a desperate prayer and pumps the gas pedal with his foot.

The car is still hemming and hawing, undecided as to whether or not it will oblige. I smell gasoline and I know the engine is flooding. I lean past Harmony to watch the door of the butcher's shop. A scream erupts from my throat when the fat man appears in his doorway with a long gun. He starts towards us and flips the gun up to aim - firing off a cannon shot that hits our car and reverberates in my teeth.

In the "boom" of the gunshot, I don't hear the engine catch. I'm thrown against the seat as the car lunges forward and shoots towards the road. Another shot of the butcher's gun hits the old car and wounds it. The tire. The car limps onto the road and takes us shakily away from the demon butcher. One more shot rings out after us, but doesn't find its mark.

Chapter Sixteen
Jagged Paper Heart

Tim maneuvers the wounded car down semi-lit, obstacle-filled streets. Harmony and Rosa cling to each other in the back seat. Thomas sits close to Matt, who moans and blinks as though waking. Tim and I sit far apart, alone, in the front seat, unspeaking. The Station Wagon's ruined tire thumps sickly, forcing Tim to drive slower than any of us feel comfortable with. My conflicted heart is pounding against my panting lungs. "Go back," my heart begs. I can't leave Aunty's Bible behind. I've lost everything else. I need that leather bound souvenir more than food. More than water.

Matt drifts in and out of coherency, helping us find a gas station, teaching us how to scan his plastic card with its electronic credits. Our tank back up to half-full, our next priority is finding a tire. The full service gas station that Matt directed us to had lots of "services" available, but none of them the kind we needed. The faded sign above the old Chevron station gave me the impression that vehicle maintenance and car washes could be found here. Instead we found several helpful attendants selling drugs, sex, and discounted blood. Not a one of them able to change a tire.

It's late now, I'm not sure of the time. The streets are alive with loud music and neon advertisements. Packs of girls in short skirts and see-through tops cross in front of our car and disappear into night clubs. I struggle with hatred as they laugh and bump into our windows. I don't want Matt to look at them. I know Tim won't look, and if he did they would only make him sad. But how many nights has Matt spent with girls like these? I can't ever - won't ever - be part of this world. Matt's world.

Our car limps another block or two before Harmony spots a rusted pick-up truck behind an overflowing dumpster. The truck is in the late stages of automobile decay but one of its tires is still good. Tim sets to work pulling the tire off while I stand guard over him and hold the flashlight.

Tim's fingers work quickly with tools I've never seen before. He knows what he's doing. I'm thankful and relieved for at least the three hundredth time that Tim is with us. Aunty's education of proper grammar and how to stain-treat satin has turned out to be grossly inadequate training. The Station Wagon is idling behind us and Harmony is in the front seat. Tim gave her a thirty second crash course on how to drive.

We are only a mile or two from Herb's hospitable love shack. Only a mile or two from the butcher. I swivel nervously - checking and double checking each intersection, every corner, and every zombie - expecting the bloody aproned man to materialize at any moment.

"Stand still, would ya?" Tim says through gritted teeth as he pries at the corroded orange lug nuts of the tire we need. "You're drawing too much attention."

I take a deep breath and look around without moving my head. He's right. Several small pockets of zombies are staring at us. Below a flickering street lamp directly across the street, a midget in a Darth Vader mask is pointing at the Station Wagon. The short, Imperial Commander from the dark side tilts his formidable black mask towards me and I feel his eyes on me. I stare back through the eyeholes of my sequined mask. Little Darth is one legged. His beige body suit dangles in an empty knot where his right leg should be. He leans against a metal crutch that is too tall for him. He is wearing a cape. Though the streets are cacophonous with people and the heavy beats of the dance club's music, I imagine Vader's electronic breathing from the movie.

It's not my flashlight or the Station Wagon that is drawing their eyes. It's not even my nervous behavior. They are staring because we don't fit in. My mask says zombie but my clothes say otherwise. I'm dressed neatly and conservatively. My sweater buttoned all the way up, my jeans baggy from two weeks of not enough food. My tried and true ugly tennis shoes round off my anything but sexy outfit. If I had the pink high heels I got in Commerce and a mini skirt I'd be *less* interesting out here.

Darth says something to a werewolf sitting near him and the werewolf looks me up and down and laughs.

"Hurry!" I mutter to Tim.

"I'm trying!" he says back, lifting the tire away from the old truck. "Ugh!" Tim exclaims in disgust.

Directly behind the tire, only a few inches from Tim's face, is the carcass of a long dead dog. Tim rolls away and gets up with the heavy tire in his arms.

Across the street, the werewolf stands up from his plastic chair. A rubber-faced President Clinton dressed in filthy cutoff jean shorts emerges from the darkened door of the tattoo parlor next to Darth Vader and the wolf. They stand staring at us. We're going to have to put this tire on somewhere else.

*****

I'm sure God's angels have been working overtime for us today. By no small miracle our car limped to a safer spot and Tim changed the tire like a pro. We are back on the highway heading for Matt's house. Tim is driving. Matt is awake now, giving directions and laughing with Tim and Harmony in the front seat. I'm in the backseat with a kid asleep on each shoulder.

Things are changing.

Harmony giggles at all of Matt's jokes. Tim and Matt share pleasant conversation about long gone sports teams and their favorite cars. I can't figure myself out. I don't know why it irritates me so much that they are enjoying each other. Somewhere down deep I recognize jealousy. I blame exhaustion.

Brooding quietly, pretending to sleep, I stare up at the night sky. The clouds frame the moon in eerie beauty, a wispy gown wrapped around the thin crescent. The stars are bright and clear and they make the night less scary. I can see over the trees and fields that streak by under the translucent star light.

When the heavens are lit up at night, I think of my sister, Hazel. She had those glow-in-the-dark sticker stars on her ceiling when we were kids. Mom and Dad never took them down after she ran away. I used to sneak into her room for years after she left and I'd sit in the dark and stare at the constellations she had designed. I would wonder where she was and if she was okay. The stars always bring her to my mind. I hope someone told her about the True Light. I hope she's alright somewhere.

The stars light the road before us, and Atlanta starts to grow around us. More and more cars share the road with us. Semi-trucks with Pravda's logo shake the Station Wagon with their gusts of wind as they fly past us. Armored trucks delivering blood line the exit ramps. I start to notice the road signs on the highway.

Twenty miles to Pravda.

Fifteen miles to Pravda.

Ten miles to Pravda.

Exit 89 Pravda.

"Tim?" I lean forward and both kids slump behind me still asleep.

"I know," he says quietly.

Tim slows the old wagon and the breaks squeal as he pulls over onto the side of the highway. A semi-truck with Pravda's emblem flies by us on the left and our car rattles and shakes in the wind the truck produces.

"Why are we so close to Pravda?" Tim asks Matt.

Matt doesn't wear his mask like the rest of us but his pale face is unreadable.

"You're going to have to trust me," he says to Tim.

"Where are we going?" Tim asks with more frustration seeping through.

"My house. We're almost there."

"Is your house on Exit 89?" Tim says with his head down, his thumb and index finger pinching the bridge of his nose through his orange knit mask.

"Yes."

"We aren't getting off at that exit." Tim says angrily.

"My house is safe," Matt insists, his voice calm and level. "Yes, it is close to Pravda, but it's as safe as anywhere else. They don't look in their own backyard! It's pretty brilliant," he says, proud of his brazenness.

"You said you would keep her safe. This is ridiculous. I'm not taking her to their front door!" Tim shouts.

Instead of cringing about Tim's obvious agenda for my safety above all others, I feel relief. It's stupid, but - with all of them enjoying each other so much - I felt alone. As much as I want to rescue my family, it seems terribly foolish to be this close to Pravda. I don't want to be close to that evil place until I'm ready to storm the gates and get my dad and Aunty Betty out. And even then I hope to do that as quietly as possible.

"My house is secure. That's where we're going. I'm strong enough to drive, so you can move over and trust me or get out and leave," Matt says with a gun in his hand that appeared out of nowhere.

Tim's shakes his head in disgust and exhales a small sigh of disappointment. His shoulders slump as he looks out the window to his left.

"I don't want to be this close to them." I say to Matt pleadingly.

"I can't help you get your family out without my team. My team is at my house. Do you want my help or not?"

He doesn't talk to me the way Tim does. Tim bosses. Tim demands. Matt - coerces. He seems to care for me at times and then at others - I fiddle nervously with my fingers against the front seat. Tim is completely silent.

Matt says, "Ivy?"

When I meet his vivid green eyes the spark ignites. His nonchalant "take it or leave it" speech always works on me. I'm desperate to see his house. I need to know about Jessie. I'm not ready or willing to leave him or the mysterious life he dangles like a carrot out of my reach. I have to go there. I have to know.

"Tim," I say hesitantly, with my own coercive plea.

"I know," he says sadly. He opens the front door without another word and walks behind the car.

Matt slides across Harmony and settles himself into the driver's seat. Tim is taking his good old time getting back in the car. Matt puts the car into gear. Tim hasn't made it around to the passenger side yet. Matt starts coasting slowly down the side of the road, checking his mirrors to merge back onto the highway.

"Wait!" I shout, waking Thomas and Rosa.

"Wait for what, Ivy? He isn't coming. And I need to get home."

The car accelerates and bumps back onto the road.

"Stop!" I yell, whirling backwards in my seat.

Tim is walking away from us down the highway. Tears flood my eyes as Matt gasses the car up to highway speed and Tim grows smaller in the window behind me. He doesn't look back as we hurtle away from him.

"Go back!" I sob over my shoulder at Matt. "Tim!" I cry his name with regret.

Why did he leave me? I need him!

But I know why he left. Time after time I chose Matt over him. Time after time my heart shouted its choice. He loves me. I know that. It's the only reason he stayed as long as he did. I sink into my seat under a wave of guilt and grief. What if I never see him again? What if something happens to him and he's all alone out there. Harmony stares over the back of the front seat at me through her sequined mask and I see tears slipping out beneath it.

My heart feels thin like paper being torn inside my chest. In a perfect world we'd all be happy together. Tim would be content with his smaller place in my heart and Matt would be happy with the larger portion. In a perfect world no one would choose or get hurt. But if my life has taught me one thing, just one thing, it's that this world is as far from perfect as it gets.

Chapter Seventeen
On Wings Like Eagles

My chest hurts from trying to hold in the heaving sobs of regret. I am dumbfounded. Shocked that Tim is suddenly gone, without a word of goodbye. Gone because of my rejection. Gone because I let him down. He's in danger, out there alone because of me. Harmony stares straight ahead in the front seat and I know she must be blaming me. It was an impossible task to put on my shoulders, and I search the past for where I must have gone wrong. This feels so painfully wrong that I know it must be. Some foolishness of mine, some sin, some lack of decency or honesty on my part has caused this painful rip in our little family.

Matt drives. He seems unmoved and unconcerned by my guilt and loss. I feel anger growing in my bitter tears. Anger towards Matt. Anger that he left Tim behind, when Tim has been nothing but helpful and kind. Without Tim, Thomas would be dead! Doesn't Matt feel any debt of gratitude for that? Is his pride so huge and ugly that he couldn't care a little for another human being that has helped him every step of the way? Is he really so selfish and self-centered to be glad that Tim is out of the way? Was Tim nothing more than a burden and a challenge that is finally out of Matt's path? What kind of man have I trusted myself with? What if Tim was right and Matt really can't be trusted? I long to undo what I've done.

But - What about my dad? What about my family? They are what's really important. Not crushes and feelings and untrustworthy boys. Tim couldn't help me get to my dad, and my dad needs me! That is why I came to Atlanta. When I get my dad and Aunty Betty out of Pravda, maybe it will all feel worth it. I just have to swallow this grief and move on with my mission. Finding my family and then finding a safe place for Rosa and Harmony. If I'm only concerned with my loved ones and their safety, why does my heart shout accusations of selfishness at me?

Matt stops the car in front of a massive iron gate. Pulling up to a security box, Matt swipes a card and then punches in a series of numbers by the light of the street lamps above. The iron gates swing open before us and we drive through into an unexpected sight. The name "Paradise" welcomes us in golden block letters set into a marble wall. Nothing could have prepared me for this.

My tears stop falling as I gaze at this strange place. Paradise it is. As Matt drives slowly down perfectly paved roads lit overhead by antique looking street lamps, exquisite mansions appear on either side of us, the smallest one bigger than the Inn. Deep red brick, pristine white stone, sandy beige stucco, each one more immense and more immaculately kept than the one before. The yards are spotless and fresh green grass grows in manicured lines. Gardens of tulips in rainbow colors line gazebos and swimming pools that are lit up with twinkle lights and Tiki torches. It's like I've gone back in time. The world used to look like this.

Fresh.

Cared for.

I'm so engrossed by the homes and their artistic landscaping that I don't notice the cars until the second or third street of mansions. Each house is unique, each yard, each garden, but the driveways hold a common denominator that makes me sink low in my seat like a child. I peer over the rim of the door so only my eyes are visible in the window.

Pravda.

Pravda.

Pravda.

Every car says Pravda. Company vehicles for company employees. Matt lives in Pravda's private community. Tim would be sick. I ache at the thought of him. This is the most dangerous place in the world for me. Following Matt was the dumbest thing I've ever done.

We twist and turn slowly through the immense community cruising past castles with tiny turrets and Manors with five garages. When I can't believe that this many wealthy people still exist and I can't fathom how I'd ever find my way out, Matt pulls the station wagon into a wide driveway that winds up green slopes to end at a magnificent gray stone Manor. White marble columns hold up a wrap around balcony on the second floor. The entry way is massive. The double doors are made of dark wood that looks hundreds of years old and fortified with iron filigree like a castle's gate. The shrubs lining the front walk are sculpted into different animal shapes and lit with colorful lights.

"Stay here," Matt says.

Without another word, he is out of the car and walking around the side of the expansive home and out of our sight.

"Ivy, we've got to get out of here," Harmony says looking back at me over the front seat.

"Don't worry, you'll be safe here. You'll see," Thomas says with pleasant confidence.

I look between them both and say nothing. Harmony is probably right. If we left now and started walking could we ever find Tim? How long would Harmony and Rosa and I last out there on our own? The butcher, the werewolf, Darth Vader and a million more like them are out there. We have nowhere to go. No money. But God would take care of us, I think. Or is this His plan? Am I supposed to be here with Matt in this house? I've been trying so hard to hear Him. To put Him first and listen for His still small voice. I thought I was on the right path until Tim left. I don't know anything now. It's a little too late to second guess things.

Matt is back at the car only a minute or two later. He gathers his brother in his arms and leaves again without an explanation. Harmony and I sit quietly. I'm sure that we are in terrible trouble and I feel like a worm for getting her into this mess. I have no idea how to undo what I've done.

*****

Harmony huddles close to me beneath the front porch lights as the giant sized wooden doors swing open before us. A thin young man with dark circles under his eyes stares at us as we follow Matt into the warm glow of the foyer. The mansion draws my eyes away from the black-clothed stranger who looks bored at our arrival. I take in the opulent rooms around me in total awe.

Massive crystal chandeliers hang above us and also in the rooms to my left and right. Straight ahead, an airy staircase carpeted in luxurious red carpet spirals up to the second floor and more sparkly chandeliers. The wooden floors around us shine waxy in the light with rugs that look invitingly soft. The room to my right has a beautiful white Baby Grand piano sitting inside a marble circle in the center of the room. Windows climb towards twenty foot ceilings and end in leaded glass points. Velvet curtains drop from great heights to puddle dramatically on the floor.

The room to our left is an enormous library. Wooden shelves hold thousands of volumes. I remember the night I found Matt in the kitchen at the Inn with a book. I was surprised to find him reading and embarrassed when I realized he might be smarter than me. Now I see why. Leather couches and recliners sit around the room on carved wooden feet. Silk lamps at each side table match the silk drapes on the windows. A carved wooden eagle with a wingspan of at least five feet is frozen in flight above a rose marble fireplace. A fire burns with well fed flames in the hearth. This place - it feels like a castle. Like the castle in Beauty and the Beast after the curse is broken. It's magical. And I smell food. Something delicious is cooking somewhere.

"Well, come on," Matt says. "Let's get the introductions over with."

I realize I'm about to meet Jessie. Jessie who lives here with Matt. I was so proud of our Inn. I felt sure that it must've impressed Matt. And it was nothing but a shabby old house compared to where he lives. I'm sure I will feel equally shabby next to Jessie. If only I could've at least showered and brushed my hair before having to meet his girlfriend.

We follow Matt down a long hallway papered in elegant blue and gold wallpaper with golden sconces that light our path. Ahead I see a brightly lit room and I hear people and music. My stomach growls loudly and I realize the amazing smell is bacon. The kitchen invites us in with its towering ivory wood cabinets and state of the art appliances. A woman with pixie length silver hair has her back to us as she opens an oven twice as big as ours at the Inn. After pulling several pans of sizzling bacon out of the oven, she turns to face us with a smile on her face and pot holders on her hands.

"Well hello! Come on in and sit down. We're just about to eat lunch. Can you eat a BLT? Are you allowed pork?" she asks kindly.

"Ivy, this is Jessie. Jessie this is Ivy and that's little Rosa and this is Harmony," he points us out to Jessie who is old like Aunty.

A goofy smile of relief takes over my face. I blush embarrassed behind my mask as Jessie walks over to me to shake my hand. She doesn't take off the pot holders so the handshake is awkward. Harmony gets an unexpected hug from Jessie and looks at me with wide eyes over Jessie's shoulder. Matt smirks at me from where he is leaning against the large kitchen island. I think he knows how much I've dreaded who Jessie was to him. The jerk could've told me and put me out of my misery.

"You're skin and bones," Jessie says reprovingly to Harmony. "You can take those masks off now."

I hesitate, but Matt nods a go ahead so I lift my mask away and Harmony does the same. No one seems to care that we are Living. Matt must have told them when he brought in healthy, Living Thomas. I bet that was a shock for them. I'll never forget Matt's face when he saw Thomas Healed. Thomas was close to death before the missionary told him about Jesus. I wonder where Harvey met Thomas. Surely not here in this community of Pravdanians?

Jessie pulls Harmony over to a huge oak table and calls, "Come and eat!"

From the adjacent room where the music is playing, the guy with the dark circles obeys Jessie's call. Behind him slouches a girl about his age. She also wears her hair in a pixie cut, but hers is blond. She isn't feminine, but she is still beautiful. She wears dark eyeshadow that makes her look pale. Her bra shows through her black lace top and there are holes in both knees of her jeans. Aunty would be horrified.

Lagging behind the depressed looking couple, a large man lumbers into the room carrying Thomas and laughing with him. The portly man has a reddish complexion that stands out against his white shirt. As he steps into the well-lit kitchen, I see that the disease has taken both of his ears and is covering his nose and lip as well. He has the black spot on his forehead just like Thomas. He glances at Harmony and I, but doesn't look friendly like Jessie.

"Well? Can you?" Jessie asks me with impatience.

"I - I'm sorry?" I stammer confused.

"Eat pork?" she asks with a touch of annoyance, rolling her eyes.

"Yes ma'am," I reply with growing insecurity.

Jessie jerks her head towards a place at the table for me to sit down and I hurry to comply. She seems to like Harmony more than me already, and I feel less and less hungry. I pull a seat up close to mine for Rosa and unwrap her arms from my neck as I put her down.

"I thought you people didn't eat pork," Jessie says with fake pleasantness as she sets everything for fresh BLT sandwiches on the table. Her hostility bleeds through and I look down at my plate instead of meeting her eyes.

They are green like Matt's - green and cold. Is she related to him?

"That's Jews, Jess," says the man with no ears. I guess he can hear just fine without them.

"Jim, this is Ivy, Harmony and Rosa. Girls, this is Jim," Matt says indicating the red faced man who sits and stares at us after gently setting Thomas into a seat at the big table. "That's Nora and Wes," Matt says, introducing the other two.

"It's nice to meet you," Harmony says quietly.

Rosa and I stare at our plates without speaking.

Everyone starts eating before Jessie sits down. They all wear the black gloves, even Jessie who had them on under her oven mitts. It's strange to be sitting at a table with all of these black gloves. I feel awkward and I look to Harmony.

Neither of us has taken a bite yet. We pray before we eat. Always. We acknowledge God's provision and thank Him for it. Harmony drops her eyes to her lap and I realize she's praying in her head. I follow suit, praying a silent prayer quickly and hoping it isn't noticeable. When I look up, Nora and Wes are staring at me. I blush red and hate myself for it. Matt winks at me. It helps, but just barely.

The bread is soft. The kind you used to get at a grocery store. The tomatoes are juicy and ripe and I wonder where they get them. Tomatoes won't be in season for months. The iceberg lettuce is so crisp it crunches as much as the bacon. I wipe real Mayo from the corner of my mouth with a white cloth napkin. A cold can of Coke sits at my plate but I'm afraid to open it. It's so valuable. So rare. It seems like a crime to waste it. Matt reaches across the table and opens my Coke with a refreshing pop and sets it back down by my plate. I look up embarrassed at his help and notice everyone pretending they weren't watching.

Harmony and I take turns politely disguising yawns during "lunch." It's close to two a.m. now, which is prime time for zombies and bed time for decent people. We've been on the run all day, and the intense stress of the day has taken everything I have. And I can't stop worrying about Tim. Every time I think of him my BLT feels like a brick in my stomach. How will he eat? How will he survive? I ruined his life.

Matt captures my attention when he mumbles a question to Jessie, "How's the water here?"

"Fine," she replies confidently.

"Rationing?" Matt asks quietly again.

"Of course not. We have as much as we want. They wouldn't dare."

Jessie makes it sound like Pravda is beneath her. Her presidential home at the back of this opulent community makes me wonder just what she does for them and how on earth Matt thinks she won't turn us in.

Harmony offers to help with the dishes and everyone looks at her like she just passed gas at the table.

Jessie presses her lips together to hide a smirk and says, "That's the maid's job, dear."

"I'll take them up and get them settled in the guest rooms," Matt says to Jessie but there's a hint of subservience in his voice.

Like he's asking not telling. Matt lives here, but it's obvious that this is Jessie's house.

"Not the purple room," is her only response.

Chapter Eighteen

A Naivety Worth Keeping

Matt offers the first room to Harmony. We walk in together and find a bed so beautiful it looks like a queen's. The whole wall is quilted in white satin with tufted buttons to make an enormous headboard behind the king sized bed. White fur pillows fill the bed above a white ruffled bedspread. A zebra skin rug lays across the floor in front of a massive white limestone fireplace.

The room is extravagantly luxurious and yet so pure. White wooden blinds hang from the picture windows framed by zebra print curtains. A white tufted chaise lounge sits beneath a delicate crystal chandelier with white iron leaf embellishments and crystals that drip almost to the floor. Matt shows Harmony her private bathroom, complete with a white claw-footed bathtub. A closet next to the bathroom is stocked with clothes and Matt tells Harmony to help herself to anything she wants.

I follow Matt back out of the room with Rosa in my arms. As I turn to pull the door shut behind me, Harmony stands alone and dirty in the middle of the white room. She looks small and lonely. The firelight from the fireplace throws shadows across her gaunt cheeks. She's probably never seen anything this beautiful, but I can tell she'd rather be anywhere but here.

"Goodnight," I whisper apologetically.

"Ivy - don't - Just be careful okay?"

When we first met and became friends, what drew me to Harmony was her innocence. She was so unburdened, dancing obliviously through life. These days her face wears worry like a zombie wears a mask. I nod and pull the golden door knob closed.

Matt leads me down the hall away from my friend with eloquent words and intriguing descriptions. In an even tone, like a tour guide, he tells me facts about the house - the square footage and where the marble in the piano room came from. I slump behind him, carrying Rosa, trying to listen. My tired thoughts distract me with hopes that my room will have access to a bathtub, too. I'd kill for a good soak.

Still upstairs, but at the opposite end of the house from Harmony, Matt opens the door to my room and motions for me to walk in first. I gape in the doorway. An elaborate canopy of golden lace hangs from a four poster bed carved to look like delicate tree branches. Thick golden carpets lay on dark wood floors that look like the floors at the Inn. The whole room has a gilded antique feel.

A smile tugs at my tired cheeks. He chose this room for me so I would feel more at home. It's the kind of room that would've taken Aunty's breath away. She would've loved the delicate golden picture frames and the tapestry style curtains. She would've admired the intricate Moroccan tiles that cover the expansive fireplace. A golden fan spread across the front of the fireplace glimmers in the fire light. I do a double-take when I realize that we had the exact same one at the Inn! I set Rosa on the bed and walk over to the fireplace to run my fingers across the golden finial at the top of the screen.

Next to the fireplace, between two marble pillars, French doors open into a bathroom even bigger than Harmony's. The tub is big enough for four people. Why would anyone even need a tub this big? The sink basin is a large golden bowl with a spigot that looks like a disk. I stare nervously at it, not sure I'll be able to figure out how to work it. I've never seen anything like this place.

A mirrored cabinet next to the sink has oatmeal soaps and body washes and bath oils. No clear peach sparkle deodorant, but I think I'll manage. An enormous walk-in closet next to the bathtub is full of clothes and shoes. Men's, women's and even children's shoes and dresses and hats hang neatly as though just pressed. Why does Jessie have a closet with all different sizes of clothes and shoes? Whose stuff is this? A beautiful silk bathrobe hangs sideways atop the clothes as though it has been laid out for me. I wonder if I'll find a nice comfy pair of yoga pants to sleep in.

Rosa is playing with the pearl tiebacks that hang from the curtained bedposts. Matt has made himself comfortable on the velveteen sofa at the foot of the bed. He's staying? I'm so tired. I am suddenly aware that this is my bedroom and there is a boy in here. Aunty wouldn't like that. But she's gone. These are my decisions now.

I take a deep breath and sit down on the burgundy velveteen cushion next to Matt. The sofa is soft and my tired limbs sink into it. Matt stares at the fire crackling behind the golden screen. Nervous at being so close to him, I move away and hope it just looks like I'm trying to get comfortable. Matt chuckles next to me and I glance shyly at him. He locks his green, appraising eyes on me and I wonder how he can possibly see anything desirable. I didn't see a toothbrush in that cabinet. I hope there is one. I wish I had my toothbrush. I wish I had Aunty's Bible. I wish I could get Aunty out of my head.

Matt reaches over and caresses my hands. I hadn't realized I was wringing them until he touched me. His touch is like lightening on my skin. My breath catches and I glance behind us to see if Rosa is watching. She isn't. Matt closes the distance between us on the couch and pulls me into his arms. I look up at him and I see the gold of the fire flickering in his eyes.

Matt tilts his head closer to mine and I know he's going to kiss me. I feel shivery with anticipation and terrified at the same time. My limbs are responding without me telling them to. I press myself closer and close my eyes. Matt's breath is warm on my face and no one is watching. I want to be near him. I want his adoration. I want to not make a fool of myself.

At this inopportune moment I think of Herb's hookers. Matt has probably been with lots of experienced girls. I have no idea what I'm doing. And I know there's a line I shouldn't cross. Is a kiss okay? Some kissing? Can we just sit close like this and breathe each other's air until I hyperventilate and pass out?

Then, the moment for decisions is past because his lips are on mine. Turning my thoughts into heat. His lips are soft and hard simultaneously. His nose bumps against mine and I giggle nervously while our mouths are still touching.

"You're adorable, you know that right?" he says, still so close to my lips that his lips brush mine while he speaks.

I smile and blush and open my eyes to see his beautiful eyes just inches away. Oh, those eyes. The fire's glow has each distinctive fleck of green sparkling. Like a glittering green star. They are dazzling. He nuzzles my cheek with his nose and breathes in my ear. His breath is intoxicating. I shiver and he puts his gloved hand against the skin of my back.

I freeze.

He moves his satiny fingers along my spine and without knowing why I shove him hard away from me.

He looks stunned and says, "What's wrong?"

"I can't," I stammer.

"Of course you can, I'll help you."

"No!" I say pushing myself as far back as the couch will allow.

"Ivy," he whines.

"I can't do anything," I hold my hands up in front of me like a force field.

I want to apologize but I can't find the words. My spirit is back in charge again and my body shamefully in check. I can't believe that just happened. It was so fast. I just didn't realize.

I'm holy. Holy means set apart for special use. Not for ordinary things. I'm not supposed to let the world in. But if anyone could tempt me - If anyone could make me consider it - it would be Matt.

"Is this a religion thing?" he asks with thinly veiled disgust.

"It's not religion, Matt. It's not rules. I - I love Him. I want to be what He wants me to be."

"Who? Tim? You love Tim?"

"No! God, I love God."

But now I'm thinking of Tim. Super.

"You love God," he says laying his head back on the couch and laughing as though I just told him a joke.

"I belong to Him."

"You're a nun, now?" he says flatly.

"No, it's just - He's my best friend. I -"

I know I sound stupid. These aren't the eloquent words I had hoped to use to win him over. And this isn't the way it was supposed to come up in conversation.

"Yeah, well, you can let your best friend know he's a real jerk, okay? And I hate him," he practically spits the words at me. "Will you let him know that for me the next time he shows up? Let him know who saved you from an angry mob and rescued you from bandits and offered you a safe place to stay and a new life?"

I sit quiet and ashamed and confused and hurt and sick. Matt covers his face with his hands in irritated frustration. I don't know what to do. What if he tries again? Standing up, I realize someone is watching us at the door. A girl, about my age. She wasn't at the dinner table. She glares at me and then disappears down the hall.

"Who was that?" I ask with a dark premonition in my heart.

"The maid," Matt says, still angry. "Later," he says coolly, walking to the door.

He stalks out of the door without looking at me and I let the tears fall. I give into the self-pity and the overwhelming emotions of kissing him and wanting him and then losing him. He said he hates God.

He told me once that he didn't believe in God. Despite his acknowledgment of God's existence, somehow hating Him feels like we're losing ground. Aunty was right. He's not right for me. She wanted me to be with Tim and now Tim is gone forever. The only person who knew Aunty like I did is gone.

I stumble to the door to pull it closed and see the girl again. She's knocking on a door down the hall. She looks at me with venomous eyes. Someone opens the door she was knocking on. I can't tell who is inside, but a black gloved hand reaches out to pull her into the room in an intimate way. Like she was just pulled into a kiss. The door shuts behind them. What if it was Matt. What if he -

Rosa pulls on my hand. She must have seen us fight. She looks up at me with worry on her innocent face. I wipe my tears and pull her close. Taking one more look down the empty hallway, I shut the door to our room and lock it.

Chapter Nineteen
My Sunday Best

After bathing Rosa and tucking her in, I took a long, bubbly, candle-lit bath. The aromatic soak - did I mention the back massaging jets - felt like it healed the life-sucking damage done by the last few weeks on the run. Laying my head back on a soft bath pillow, I drifted to sleep. I woke up in the cold bath sometime in the night. I wrapped myself in the soft silk robe and stumbled, shivering, into bed next to Rosa. The heavy covers engulfed us like a cocoon and we cuddled and slept dreamless sleep long after the sun peeked through the heavy tapestry curtains.

Blinking my eyes beneath a golden canopy, I gradually remember where I am. Rosa is sitting on my stomach, her chubby hands patting my cheeks to wake me. I smile up at her, so thankful for this little cherub who loves me and makes me feel important and needed. Her dark curls have dried in soft waves around her face. Last night I found a soft pink nightgown in the wardrobe that fit Rosa with a little room to spare.

The wardrobe seems to only offer fine things. I found no jeans or sweatpants for us, but today, Rosa will have several fancy dresses to pick between. That should be fun. This place is so different from the life we're used to. We could take another bath, play dress-up, and explore the many drawers and cabinets of our room's fine furniture. We could light another fire and relax on the fluffy golden rug in our p.j.s. I don't think anyone in the house is expecting anything from us. Maybe one day of downtime would be okay. Then, tomorrow, Matt and I can start planning how we'll get my family out of Pravda.

Matt. Will he act different with me? Though I am used to his fluctuating zombie moods, the heat of last night's kiss is still burning and I wonder how he'll treat me today. What about the rest of them? Matt's team or family - or whatever they are - were polite for Matt's sake. If Matt is mad at me, will they be mean? I saw how much the maid hated me in the cold glare she gave me. Whose room did she go in last night? I want to know and I don't.

Rosa points at her belly and I realize I'm starving too. Matt said we should make ourselves at home. Am I welcome to help myself in the kitchen or should I ask someone first?

"Eat," I agree with her and pinch her little nose.

She bounces up and down on the bed excited that I understood and agreed.

I pull my aching body out of bed, stretch, and head for the wardrobe. I rifle through the fancy dresses for something that looks close to my size and not too formal. I used to feel chubby. A month or so ago, I was ashamed of my curvy shape. The last few weeks of running and scavenging have changed me physically. I'm leaner. My size 7/8 pants are way too big. I'm probably a 5 now. I didn't enjoy our time in the cave, but I'm not bummed about the pounds I left behind.

Holding up a silver dress that looks like it will fit and wouldn't make Aunty clear her throat, I ask Rosa, "How 'bout this one?"

She smiles and points at her belly again. She doesn't care what I wear as long as it gets us to breakfast faster.

I dress quickly. The fancy underwear and bra from the wardrobe make me feel too grown up. I'll wash mine and hang them to dry later. The silver dress has short sleeves so I search the closet for a sweater. Nothing. I wrap a fancy white shawl around my shoulders and hope that Matt was right about us being allowed to help ourselves to anything we want. I glance in the mirror before leaving the bathroom. I look so different from me. My thin physique, my long hair that hangs wavy and soft from the special shampoo, this dress - It's some other girl in the mirror, not dorky Ivy Mae Lusato. I feel like I'm being given a chance to decide which girl I want to be. The girl before me is what I always wanted.

I leave Rosa in her nightgown. She's gotten no better at table manners and the pretty dresses in the wardrobe wouldn't last ten minutes. We tiptoe down the hall to Harmony's room, hand in hand. At Harmony's door, I knock gently.

No one answers.

I knock again a little louder and wait a little longer.

Fear creeping around the edges of my concern, I push the door open. The room looks like it hasn't been slept in.

"Harmony!" I call out concerned, checking the bathroom.

The bathroom is spotless and she isn't there.

I grab Rosa's hand and hurry from the room. I carry Rosa down the twisting staircase. Trying to remember the way to the kitchen, I pull Rosa behind me as I speed through the blue and gold hallway.

Nora is sitting at the big kitchen table with her bare feet up on the table. A mug of coffee with a swirl of whipped cream sits next to her manicured toes. She looks up from her book and smirks at me as I enter the kitchen. Her mocking smile takes away all the confidence I felt in front of the mirror upstairs. She's dressed simply again, black leggings and a gray T-shirt. Her makeup is dramatic and impeccable. Thick black eyelashes flutter beneath rosy eye shadow and thick black eyeliner. Her lips are deep red and I notice red lipstick marks on her coffee mug. She looks like a model.

I've been worried for weeks about Matt having a girlfriend here. Jessie might be old, but my worries weren't ridiculous. How could Matt not want this beautiful girl? I don't hold a candle to her.

"On your way to church, freak?"

My insecurity strikes me dumb and I stand staring at her with no reply.

"Help yourself to some coffee and breakfast before you jump on the Jesus bus, okay?"

Nora stands up, closing her book and picking up her coffee in her black-gloved hand. She stalks out of the kitchen without looking back at me.

I need to find Harmony. Nora's smug demeanor hasn't made me feel any more comfortable in this strange house. The coffee is calling to me and I see homemade sticky buns on a plate on the counter. And bananas! I haven't had a banana in years!

Harmony first. Then, food.

I tiptoe lightly across the kitchen and peek in the adjoining rooms. A grand dining room is dark and devoid of people. The next room is where everyone came from last night when Jessie called them for dinner. I take a step through the door and find a theater. A large movie screen is playing a movie with barely dressed women and I'm horrified. Jim sits in the front row in front of the massive screen with head phones over his non-existent ears. I back quickly out of the room, pulling Rosa with me. Where could Harmony be?

Back in the kitchen, I glance out of the glass patio doors and see verdant landscaping and gardens behind the house. Harmony's mom loved to garden. She helped her mom with it all the time. An epiphany tells me I'll find her there. I grab two bananas and peel them for Rosa and me. She claps as I hand her one and takes a huge bite of the soft white fruit.

I motion for her to follow me as I step outside reveling in the taste of a fruit I thought I'd never taste again. I hear laughter close by. I follow a stepping stone path lined with lilies and tulips. Bird baths and bird feeders sit near vine covered arbors over wooden benches for afternoon naps. The trees around the yard are all in full spring bloom. When the wind blows at my white shawl, the trees give up some of their petals and the scent of cherry blossoms fills my nose. I hear the laugh again and I walk through a pair of shrubs sculpted into the shape of prancing stallions.

Beyond the leafy green horses, a rose garden spreads out before me. Jessie and Harmony are laughing as they work amidst the beautiful blooms. Both of them are kneeling as I approach, relieved to find my friend in such a happy place. They look up at me with surprised faces and my smile quickly fades into confusion. Harmony is wearing jeans and a comfy cotton shirt. Her hair tied up with a bandana. Jessie's garden pants show their age and a colorful shirt peeks out from behind her muddy gardening apron.

"Well, where are you off to?" Jessie asks with her fake polite smile.

"I -"

"You look very beautiful, Ivy," Harmony says kindly.

"I thought -"

"We usually have a less formal breakfast," Jessie says looking back down at her rose bushes.

"My closet only had dresses," I say humiliated.

Why does Jessie like Harmony so much? I keep making a fool of myself in front of this woman. It's really important to me that Matt's people like me. I don't know what I'm doing wrong.

"Most closets do," Jessie says still looking down, but I can tell she's mocking me. "Usually find pants and shirts in drawers. But maybe your kind does it the other way around."

I look at Harmony and she looks down and blushes with embarrassment for me.

"I found these in my dresser drawers," she explains as though she needs to apologize. "Do you want to see if the things in my drawers fit you?" she offers.

"No. I didn't check my drawers. I'm sure I'll find something," I say backing away. "I'll see you later," I mumble as I turn and reach for Rosa's hand.

"Oh, leave her here with us," Harmony calls. "She needs to play outside."

I'm so embarrassed and irritated that I don't argue. I nudge Rosa towards Harmony and hurry back through the stupid horse shaped bushes to get out of Jessie's sight. I hate it here.

Chapter Twenty

Hypocrites Live In White Washed Tombs

I stop only to pour myself some coffee, hell bent on getting to my room as fast as possible to change out of this dumb dress. I couldn't find the whipped cream, but real milk and sugar are just as heavenly a treat. I hold my hot caramel colored coffee out in front of me, careful not to spill on Jessie's fancy white rugs.

Please don't let me run into Matt. Please don't let me run into Matt. Please!

"Morning, Ivy" Matt calls as I'm halfway up the stairs.

Dang it!

I turn around with a smile and force my voice to sound pleasant, "Morning."

Maybe if I act confident he won't notice.

"My, my," Matt whistles, impressed. "All you need is those sexy shoes you had on when we met and you'll be the perfect party girl," he says with a chuckle.

I flare my nostrils and try to keep my smile. Will he ever forget those ridiculous shoes? I don't feel like laughing at myself right now.

"Yes," I lie, "I just felt like looking my best today."

"Well, I was going to take you for a walk to show you something. I think maybe you'd better change into something less frilly."

My fake smile feels more like a snarl as I nod and say, "Oh, I guess I could change. I'll be right back."

Taking long fast strides to my door, my coffee sloshes over and drips on the hallway carpet. I barrel into my room and push the door shut behind me. I lean against the door in humiliation, my partially spilt coffee clutched against my chest. When I take a deep breath and open my eyes, I find the maid staring at me from the bathroom door.

Shut. Up.

Why is this the worst day ever? Can I seriously not embarrass myself in front of absolutely everyone? I didn't get a chance to "dazzle" Wes with my silly girly get-up. Maybe I should go find him first before I change. Perhaps I could add some dangly gold jewelry and an up-do for my hair first?

I think even God is laughing at me and I don't appreciate it.

"Why are you in here?" I ask too demandingly to the girl holding my dirty underwear.

"Just cleaning up your mess," she pauses and adds, "Ma'am" with fake respect.

She is my height but Harmony's build, thin and willowy. Her brown hair is cut as short as Jessie and Nora's. A thick tube-shaped plastic earring hangs from her right ear. She doesn't wear one in her left ear and I wonder if the tube is for fashion or something else entirely. The black spot stands out on her forehead. Bitterness shades her large brown eyes and her cheeks are blushed with hate. Why wear makeup when shades of disgust compliment your features so dramatically? If she didn't make me so nervous, I'd pity her. Her face could be pretty if she had an emotional makeover.

She wears a formal white shirt, pressed perfectly, with tiny black buttons down the front. Her thin legs are bruised beneath a short, black skirt. Her shoes are too large and too thick for her, like something a monster would wear. She holds her head high and limps across the room towards me. She must have the disease really bad.

"What are you looking at?" she accuses.

I lift apologetic eyes to her face, she saw me staring at her feet.

"I was going to make your bed, but if you are laying back down," she says as though accusing me of being pampered and lazy, "I can come back later."

"No, you can make it."

"Oh, thank you!" she says with exaggerated sarcasm.

"I can make it! You can do whatever you need to do," I stammer.

I feel her disgust for me - the way the zombie ladies on the other side of the fence in Toccoa despised me. Aunty said it was jealousy, but I never thought she was right. The malevolency in the maid's eyes isn't jealousy, it's pure loathing.

I hesitate before asking, "Can I please keep my underwear?"

"I was just going to wash them," she barks.

"I can wash them myself. Thank you." I reply as gently as possible.

She glares at me and drops my underwear on the floor.

"What's your name?" I ask as I cross to the dresser drawers and start pulling them open in search of normal clothes.

"None of your damn business," she returns bitterly.

I feel heat on my cheeks from her rude, hostile remark. I bite my lip and pray for her. *Lord, help me love this terrible person.*

*****

I meet Matt back downstairs. I feel loads more comfortable in my new soft gray leggings and a pretty purple shirt that hangs asymmetrically on one side. A simple pair of gray canvas shoes that fit perfectly was in one of the drawers, new with tags still on them. Finding new shoes was definitely the best moment of my day so far. Well - it's between the shoes and the banana.

Matt leads me down the hall to the kitchen and back out through the French doors. Rosa is eating another banana outside and the remnants of sticky bun are all over her face and her nightgown. She is swinging on a white porch swing with Nora and Wes and they are smiling at her. Harmony sits at an umbrella canopied table with a cup of coffee - complete with whipped cream. They all seem happy. I feel Wes and Nora's eyes on me as I walk away down the stepping stone path with Matt. I feel certain that if I look back they wouldn't be smiling anymore.

The sun is sinking lower in the sky and I've only been up for a little over an hour. My body is falling into zombie schedule. I don't see how that could hurt anything. Might as well be up when the rest of the house is. Matt seems happy. He reaches for my hand and I'm thrilled to let him hold it. He isn't mad at me for last night. He still likes me. I push away the questions about last night. I'm sure it wasn't Matt's room that the maid went in. She's a foul person and I pity whoever she shares her bed with.

We walk the meticulously manicured gardens and pass by some of the workers who maintain this masterpiece. Men in gray uniforms are up on ladders pruning the uniquely shaped bushes. As their heads turn to stare at us, I see that they wear the same tube shaped earring in their right ear that the maid wears.

"Why do they have that earring?" I ask innocently, making conversation.

"They belong to Pravda."

The name makes me go cold. I glance backwards at the men who continue to watch us as we walk hand in hand.

"What do you mean 'belong'?"

"Belong. Serve. They are the property of Pravda," he says with no indication that he finds people owning other people wrong.

"That's terrible," I blurt. "Why?"

"Most of them owed debts they couldn't pay. Drugs, blood treatments, who knows how they got themselves under Pravda's thumb. Some of them were sold to Pravda by other people who owed debts. Some of them are just criminals out on a 'work-release program' of sorts."

"And Pravda marked them with those ear things?"

"It's a leash. If they disobey, or run, they die."

I have no words. I can't imagine such technology. I can't believe how diseased the world really is. It's constantly gob smacking me. I'll never adjust to the wrongness. My thoughts darken. Matt is holding my hand and we're walking through a garden as beautiful as Eden. And I have new shoes. But those things don't please me.

I suddenly remember the scars on Matt's ear.

"Did you have one of those in your ear? Is that how you got those scars?"

Matt looks quizzically at me. He was asleep the night I studied his scared ear. Maybe he wears his hair so shaggy to hide the scars.

"Yes. You know I spent some time in their prison. That's how I met your dad."

"Does my dad have one of those?" I ask alarmed.

Matt nods. My dad is out there somewhere with a device in his ear that says he belongs to Pravda. A device that can kill him. My heart hammers its outrage.

"How am I - I mean how are we safe here with them?" I ask, nodding at Pravda's servants who follow us with their dull eyes. "Shouldn't I be wearing my mask and staying inside?"

I look back and the men are still watching me. The butterflies that reside within my stomach take up their nervous fluttering.

"They have no way of knowing you aren't one of us. Everyone around here gets weekly, if not daily, blood treatments. Besides, Jessie is highly respected at Pravda. Making Jessie look bad would be the last thing any of these cattle want to do."

Cattle. His flippant disregard for their value puts yet another wedge between us. The gulf is growing wider. I wish it could go back to just him and I having tea, late at night in the kitchen at the Inn. It was simpler. We walk in silence, still holding hands but not connected. Not really.

"Ivy, I'm sorry - about last night."

"I'm sorry, too."

"I know God is important to you. He's screwed me over too many times for me to forget, but I know He's the reason you and Tom are well."

I stop walking and look at him with moist eyes. Is this the breakthrough I've been waiting for? Why now?

"You believe?" I ask with joy flooding over me.

He faces me with an apology on his handsome face. "Believe? Sure. Want anything to do with? No," he says softly, knowing he's let me down.

"Why?" I beg. "How can you believe and not want? Why wouldn't you want to be Healed?"

"Hah. He can take His healing and shove it," he says, pulling his eyebrows together and frowning. "I can't take something from someone who gives to those who don't earn it."

My joy dwindles. He gets it. He knows how it works. Grace is a gift, it isn't earned. Grace is the binding agent between us and God. I thought if I could just help him see, help him understand. But he does understand. And he still wants nothing to do with it.

"No one deserves anything from God, Matt. He's better and bigger than all of us. The Bible says, 'All have sinned and fall short of the glory of God.' That's the disease. It's all the falling short. We're awful at heart, all of us."

"Some people are worse than others."

As we walk, hand in hand, I try to think how to answer that. It definitely seems that way. If I compare Aunty to the Spanish Butcher there's a clear winner in the "more evil" debate. But that's not the point.

"It's not so much about who is worse than me. It's simpler than that. It's just between me and Him. I'm not perfect and I know it. Are you perfect?"

He snorts, "I'm a lot better than most. I take care of my family and I care about the people that everyone else steps over. I never claimed to be anything special and I know my place."

"What about those people Matt?" I nod over my shoulder. "Those cattle? Those people are slaves and prisoners, but you don't seem too worried about their rights."

"They got what they deserved, Ivy. That's exactly my point. I only help people who deserve better than what they got."

"Like the bandits on the road? They deserved your help? They're good guys who just need a hand up?"

I'm starting to get loud and I try to calm myself down. At least he's talking. I don't want to push him away again.

Matt drops my hand and stalks a few feet away, and then abruptly turns to face me. His lips are pressed together and his hands are on his hips. Classic signs of frustration and defensive behavior. Taking a deep breath, I smile and I walk over to him. I reach out and put my hands on his hands, hugging his hips.

Looking up into his flashing eyes I ask, "Why fight Him? If you believe, if you see how good He's been to me and to Tom, why hate Him?"

He stands rigid, not softening despite our closeness.

"Because - I can't stand the hypocrites," he says, finally meeting my eyes.

His eyes aren't angry like his posture. I'm surprised to see hurt and pain in them. The anger has drained from them like dirty water down the drain.

Shaking his head slightly he says, "My dad was one of you."

Does he mean his dad was a Christian? I remember Matt telling me that his dad left them when Thomas was little. Matt had to step up and take care of his family and his mom. A father who would abandon his family? Matt must be wrong. His dad wasn't one of the Living.

"It was before 'The Rapture'," he says making air quotes with his fingers, his voice thick with disdain. "My old man was a preacher!" Matt intones loudly over my shoulder at an invisible audience. "He left my mom for his secretary. Then that a-hole went and started another church." His eyes wander back to mine and they are wet with emotion, "And, you know what Ivy? Your people loved him. They went to his new church and no one put that S.O.B. in his place for leaving his wife and two kids."

He turns away from me to brush at his eyes. I stand mute and shocked by his openness and his sad past.

"And the best part?" he asks, turning to look at me with wide, incredulous eyes. "The best part is, he disappeared with the rest of them! He was on the good list! I'll tell you right now, Ivy. If he's on that list, I'll NEVER sign my name there."

My heart aches at the hurt on Matt's face. I understand now. I wrap my arms around Matt and hold him and he holds me back. There's nothing else to say. I can't fix this damage. I know Jesus can, though. I think now, more than ever, that Matt is meant for Life. God has had a hand on him since he was young. I fell in love with a preacher's kid. Peace springs up in my heart. For some reason, I'm positive that "He who began a good work in Matt will see it to completion."

Chapter Twenty-One

What Can Come Betwixt Us?

Matt and I struggle to reach the top of a grassy hill, far from the mansion and the eyes that were watching. He led me through to the other side of the gardens and then through a small patch of woods. After crossing a meadow of dandelions, this hill rose before us and now we are almost to the top. Matt reaches the summit before I do. I'm using my hands and feet to climb the last few steep feet. Matt reaches for my hand and pulls me up to where he stands. I stand panting and sweating with my back bent and my hands on my knees. When the darkness of overexertion recedes from the edges of my vision, I turn to where Matt is standing, looking down the other side of the mountain.

Down at Atlanta.

Down at a massive silver building.

Down at Pravda.

There it is. Within my sight. My destination. My enemy. My family. I want to run and hide. I want to bound down the hill and up to the front doors, calling for my daddy. My head hurts from the pressure of the climb and the urges that pull me in two different directions. I sink to a squat, making myself smaller, hoping that no alarms begin to sound announcing that Ivy Lusato has been spotted.

Matt sits down next to where I am squatting and pushes me off balance playfully. I sprawl out on the ground, scraping my hand against a stick and not at all enjoying his good natured bullying. I collect myself as coolly as possible and reseat myself.

"Why do all our dates involve hiking?" I ask with feigned irritation. "It's like you don't know me at all. I prefer dinner and a movie."

"Well my dear, I brought you dinner," he says pulling a Twix candy bar out of his back pocket.

"Oh my gosh! Matt! Where did you get this?" I grab at the chocolate bar and greedily tear back the copper-colored foil paper. I haven't had a candy bar in years. Harmony's mom's homemade chocolate was always a welcome treat, but it never tasted like real chocolate used to.

He chuckles and I look up from the chocolate to see him enjoying my delight. He likes to make me happy. He loves me, too. I know he does. The way his eyes grab for mine and the peaceful look he wears when I'm happy. I smile at him, and swallow a mouthful of caramel and chocolate.

He reaches out and slides his fingers through my hair, holding the back of my neck. I tense at his touch, but I'd be lying if I said I haven't been hoping, wanting. Then, his lips are on mine again and I want them more than I want the chocolate. More than I want oxygen. I breathe heavy against his mouth and kiss him back. My fingers tingle like they're asleep and I literally can't feel the rest of my body. I feel weightless and lost in his gentle kisses.

He pulls away from my persistent lips and looks back down towards Pravda. I pant alone in the one foot of space that I shared with him a moment ago. I let it happen again, and he stopped for me. Tears of frustration, want, and appreciation gather in the corners of my eyes. I feel exhausted by all the things Matt makes me feel. There are too many all in one heartbeat. Too much to process and understand.

He reaches over and holds my hand, cradling it between both of his.

"Eat your dinner," he says with smile.

I hold out the other half of the pair of Twix and we eat while we stare down at Pravda. The sun has reached the horizon and the sky is a watercolor painting of tropical oranges and pinks. Someday maybe he and I will sit like this by the ocean. Someday when this is all over and it's just the two of us. Maybe we'll be married and we'll call it our honeymoon and I'll let him kiss me as much as he wants.

*****

Turning our backs on Pravda, Matt holds my hand as we trek back. I struggle to follow his ramblings, my thoughts wavering back and forth between not falling down the hill and how amazing it feels to be so close to him. Matt gabs about contacts on the inside and when he last saw my dad. He's worried about how hard it will be to get Aunty Betty out since she is older and we don't know how fast she can move. If she's anything like her sister, we shouldn't have any problems.

Hiking home, the shadows wage war against the waning light. We make it back to the gardens as the darkness claims victor over the day. The stars are out again tonight and it's chilly now that the sun is gone. Matt wraps an arm around me as we follow the stepping stone path back towards the warm glow coming from the kitchen patio doors.

We linger in the shadows. Matt holds me close, his arm around my waist. I'm not ready yet to cross into the light that spills off of the back porch and shades the green grass into silver blades. We walk slower and slower towards the boundary line between privacy and surveillance. I find myself dreading going back inside.

"You okay?" Matt asks as my footsteps slow with anxious hesitancy.

"Mmm," I answer.

Jessie doesn't seem to like me. I've won no points with Nora. Wes and Jim are creepy. The maid may or may not try to kill me in my sleep tonight. I'm in no hurry to face the zombies who are sharing their home with me.

I do want to see my Rosa. Harmony is always great with her, so I know she's been well cared for while we were gone. I love Rosa's smile and her cute chubby hands and the way she hugs me while we sleep. I feel like I need her as much or more than she needs me. Lost in my thoughts, I look up as Matt pulls me to a stop by a little bench. The seat is lit by moonlight beneath an arbor of silver leafed vines.

"I'll be leaving in a few hours."

"Leaving?" I ask with growing nervousness, "For where? For how long?"

"A few days."

"Days!"

"You're safe here. Please, don't worry."

Matt pinches my cheek gently when my face says I'm having a hard time obeying his request.

"Wes and Jim and Nora will be coming with me. We have some business to take care of."

"What about my family? I don't want to be here without you."

Pulling me down on the bench with him, Matt whispers, "I have to go. I'd rather stay here and take moonlit walks with you, but I have business to take care of. You'll have Tom and Harmony. And Jessie is an incredible woman. She just takes some time warming up."

"Yeah, she's about as welcoming as frostbite," I pout.

"Jessie is a very old friend. I trust her with my life. She knows how important you are to me," his voice is husky as he holds me closer.

I'm scared to be here without him, but comforted to hear that I'm important to him. I'll try to be strong. I'll trust him. He's been faithful to his word since we met. I can handle a few days.

"You'll be safe?" I ask.

He smiles at me in silver light, his face close to mine, "I promise."

Chapter Twenty-Two

If God Is For Me, What Zombie Can Stand Against Me?

As Matt and his team are leaving, he pulls me aside. He looks uncomfortable and I assume it's just his aversion to showing emotion during goodbyes.

"We're getting rid of the car, it's too junky to go unnoticed here," he says.

I have no fond feelings for the old Station Wagon. Does he think I want to keep it or something? He stares at me with frustration on his face and I look back in confusion.

"I don't care about the car, Matt."

"Yeah. Well, I don't know if - it's that -" he humphs a deep breath of irritation, "I figured you'd want this."

He lifts his arm to hand me a backpack. Tim's backpack! My hand flies to my mouth and my eyes condensate with guilty tears. Tim didn't take his pack! Not only is he out there alone because of me, but he's out there with nothing. This is the backpack he brought back after being gone for days looking for Thomas' meds. Maybe it's full of medicine and nothing else. But what if it has something dear to Tim in it? I'll kill myself if he's alone in the world with nothing and I have no way to apologize or return this to him.

"You should open it with Harmony," Matt says cryptically before slipping out the backdoor behind Jim, Wes and Nora.

I watch him go from the kitchen window. He follows Nora around the house and out of my sight. Matt will be with Nora on this secret mission that I'm not allowed to be a part of or even know about. He trusts her with his life and she knows more about his life than I do. I furiously force the jealous thoughts to leave me alone.

Harmony sits at the foot of my golden bed. Rosa is splashing and swimming in the mini swimming pool in our bathroom. I hold the backpack in between us and take a deep breath as I unzip the zipper. I already know I won't find anything as boring or simple as medicine. Matt told me to have Harmony with me. He looked already and he knows what's in here. I look with dread into the shadows of the brown pack.

The first thing that catches my eye ruins me. I reach for it, but I can't really see it for the tears that are falling now. It's the silver picture frame of Aunty Coe and Aunty Betty when they were young. The picture that sat on Aunty's bedside table. The glass is cloudy. Ash from the fire that claimed the Inn clings to the delicate grooves in the frame. Tim went back to Toccoa. He went back to the Inn. I stroke the fancy silver scrolls that frame the faded picture of two smiling young women.

Aunty Coe looks so young and so alive. The snapshot is small and old, but her blue eyes are still noticeable. Aunty Betty looks something like me. I'd never noticed it before. This picture, a piece of my life and my history, is so dear to me, so valuable. And I can't thank Tim for it.

"Ivy," Harmony says with tears streaming down her face.

I look up to see her holding a photo of her mother and father and a necklace that must have belonged to her mom. Tim went to her house too. He's the most thoughtful man I've ever known. His trip for Thomas' meds took days. Days because he was risking his life to care for our hearts. And then I trampled on his.

We dig into the bag and find a set of physician's tools. Are they from the hospital Tim found or did they belong to his dad? We both cry out with joy when we pull out a Bible from the bottom of the bag. Opening the cover, the dedication page says it was given to Tim's mom, Leila, when she accepted Jesus' gift of salvation at age ten. Leila's delicate penmanship shows the birthdays of Tim, Andrew and their sister, Eva - who died with Leila in a car accident. Each child's spiritual birthday is written on the inside cover as well. This is precious and I shouldn't have it.

Harmony and I lean into each other and cry over the emotional bag of precious gifts. We cry for our lost loved ones, we cry for Tim, we cry because there's no going back.

"Read some," Harmony says after we've sat sniffling and quiet for too long.

I feel like a horrible traitor opening Tim's mother's Bible. I'm sure he didn't mean to leave it. I wonder if he meant to leave at all. Maybe he was sure I'd stop Matt from driving away. Maybe he expected me to jump out after him and beg him to get back into the car. He would never have walked away from his mother's Bible. Or from me. He trusted me to not leave without him, and I just let Matt drive away. I did nothing. I push the Bible over to Harmony. I can't read it.

Harmony looks sadly at me and then opens the book and begins flipping the thin pages. She flips towards the back and leans close as she searches for the verse she's looking for. Depression pulls my shoulders down and tells my heart to beat slow, painful beats. I'm tired of feeling. Always feeling. Always sad or hurt or scared or guilty or worried or exhausted or lonely or grieving. I ache inside and I'm so tired of aching.

Harmony clears her throat and reads quietly:

> **Romans 8:18-39** "Yet what we suffer now is nothing compared to the glory he will reveal to us later. For all creation is waiting eagerly for that future day when God will reveal who his children really are. Against its will, all creation was subjected to God's curse. But with eager hope, the creation looks forward to the day when it will join God's children in glorious freedom from death and decay. And we know that God causes everything to work together for the good of those who love God and are called according to his purpose for them. For God knew his people in advance, and he chose them to become like his Son, so that his Son would be the firstborn among many brothers and sisters. And having chosen them, he called them to come to him. And having called them, he gave them right standing with himself. And having given them right standing, he gave them his glory. What shall we say about such wonderful things as these? If God is for us, who can ever be against us? Since he did not spare even his own Son but gave him up for us all, won't he also give us everything else? Who dares accuse us whom God has chosen for his own? No one -for God himself has given us right standing with himself. Who then will condemn us? No one - for Christ Jesus died for us and was raised to life for us, and he is sitting in the place of honor at God's right hand, pleading for us. Can anything ever separate us from Christ's love? Does it mean he no longer loves us if we have trouble or calamity,

> or are persecuted, or hungry, or destitute, or in danger, or threatened with death? (As the Scriptures say, "For your sake we are killed every day; we are being slaughtered like sheep.") No, despite all these things, overwhelming victory is ours through Christ, who loved us. And I am convinced that nothing can ever separate us from God's love. Neither death nor life, neither angels nor demons, neither our fears for today nor our worries about tomorrow - not even the powers of hell can separate us from God's love. No power in the sky above or in the earth below - indeed, nothing in all creation will ever be able to separate us from the love of God that is revealed in Christ Jesus our Lord."

The promises of a God who calls me His child work over me. He reminds me that He has a plan that is working for my good. He promises me that nothing bad I go through here can begin to compare with how wonderful it's going to be there when I'm with Him. He promises that nothing - not even my gargantuan failures - can make Him love me less or take back His promises. I can cling to these words like a life ring in the middle of a stormy black ocean.

Harmony closes the Bible and offers it to me. I shake my head no. I feel less like dying, but I still don't want to keep Tim's dearest possession.

"You keep it in your room," I whisper.

Harmony nods her understanding and hugs me before leaving me alone with my thoughts, Aunty's picture, and the sound of Rosa's carefree splashing. Alone on my bed I find that my tears were nowhere near close to running out.

Chapter Twenty-Three

Drink From The Well That Will Never Run Dry

Time passes slowly here in the big house without Matt. Harmony and I spend time studying Tim's mom's Bible every day, but there are so many more hours to fill. Harmony spends time outside in the garden whenever the weather is nice. She and Jessie talk and enjoy each other, but it always gets awkward when I try to join in. I quit trying, but it still bothers me.

On the rare occasion that I cross paths with the maid, she treats me with cold ambivalence. I find myself intentionally avoiding her. I have yet to figure out where she sleeps or what her name is. She is like a ghost in the house. She moves through the spacious rooms with her heavy clod-like shoes, grumbling and groaning as she works. Her presence in a room brings tension and haunting coldness.

Thomas is a cheerful playmate. Jessie's mansion has a basement level completely dedicated to entertainment. There are comfortable couches positioned for optimum viewing before large screened televisions. Ping-Pong tables and pool tables and, unbelievably, a small indoor swimming pool keep us busy long after we tire of movie marathons.

One corner of the basement has a room that Thomas calls the "panic room." If anyone dangerous comes in the house, we can escape by hiding in the hidden room with the electronically locking door. Thomas says it's stocked with food and blankets and everything you could need to survive for weeks. Why would the inhabitants of Paradise need such a room? They are Pravda's spoiled children. They have no fear of their over-indulgent parents.

Thomas and I read books to Rosa and play games with her. We watch all nine Star Wars movies in one day. We eat tacos for dinner with real shredded cheese and fresh sour cream. And, though I've never been anywhere so full of pleasure and entertaining distraction, my mind is always elsewhere. I have unlimited food, new clothes, no responsibilities, games and distraction to last for years, but I feel more trapped than I did in the cave.

Worrying about Tim keeps me from enjoying my food or my sleep. Missing Matt steals any contentment or comfort that Paradise has to offer me. Knowing my dad and Aunty Betty are rotting in Pravda's prison while

I snack on fresh baked chocolate chip cookies is killing me. Aunty would be so disappointed in the choices I've made and where I've ended up. I know.

It's been three days since Matt left. I'm lying on the little sofa in front of the fireplace in my room. Rosa is playing with a pile of fancy jewelry on the floor. Rings that I suspect hold real diamonds decorate her chubby fingers. She holds a large ruby necklace up to the fire's light and red prisms sparkle around her. She laughs and grabs for another necklace. The fire makes me think of Matt. I stare into the flames and picture his face, his eyes. I remember how he kissed me here and I long for him to get back. For the one hundredth time today, I worry about what I'll do if he doesn't come back.

The sound of music slowly registers in my love-sick brain. It is pure and beautiful. Carrying Rosa, bedecked in her jewels, I follow the complex notes down the hall and down the twisting staircase. At the doorway to the piano room, I find the source of the emotion-filled melody. Jessie sits with her back to us, her fingers crawling over the ivory and black keys. The chandelier above the white Baby Grand piano filters golden light down over Jessie's short gray hair. Her sandaled feet press the bronze foot pedals with expert timing, giving crescendo to her overlapping notes and chords.

Harmony sits near the piano on a white pin cushioned love seat. Her smiling face invites me to join her on the love seat for the private concert. I'm afraid if Jessie sees me she'll stop playing. Leaning against the wall, I slide to a seat on the floor by the door. Rosa looks up at me with mesmerized eyes, enraptured by the beautiful music. She lays her head back on my chest as Jessie's trained hands pull a story from the keys.

I imagine men waging a fierce battle against a brutal enemy. The eerie chords promise that the battle was won, but that many lives were lost. The survivors make their way home to loved ones waiting for them and their fallen comrades. Lovers are reunited and triumphant peaceful notes tell the song of their embrace. Jessie ends the tragic melody with quiet chords of finality. Rosa runs over to Harmony and the two of them clap their hands and beg for more.

"Alright, one more," Jessie says, enjoying their delight. "Matt never likes it when I play. I only play when he isn't home," she says smiling.

"Why?" The question slips out of my mouth before wisdom can restrain it.

I didn't want her to know I was here listening.

Jessie turns to see me sitting on the floor, but doesn't look surprised or put off by my presence.

She looks sad as she answers me, "It makes him think of his father and the past."

"Why?" I ask again.

"Those were hard times. We try not to remember them," she says as though she was there.

Matt said she was a very old friend. Maybe she knew his father. Then, quite suddenly, I know how she knew him.

"Did you play the piano in Matt's father's church?" I ask, sure of the answer already.

Jessie studies me with a scowl.

"He told you about his father," she says - a statement of disbelief, not a question. "Yes. I played the organ in his parent's church." Her lined face settles into a frown and she turns back around to face the piano keys.

"Please," I ask timidly, "please play an old hymn for us. It's been so long since we've heard one."

Jessie sits with a straight back at the piano, her fingers poised on the keys. She shakes her head, then sighs and begins to play again. The familiar notes of Amazing Grace roll majestically from her gentle hands. I close my eyes and lay my head back against the wall. The sound of the precious hymn washes over me and fills me with contentment. Jessie plays on. She transitions seamlessly into the minor melody of The Old Rugged Cross. Aunty loved this one. Rosa has laid her head on Harmony's lap and Harmony is stroking her dark brown curls. Harmony and I smile at each other across the room and reminisce with wet eyes as the piano fills the dark house with The Light.

*****

It's early morning and the sun is rising on the fifth day since Matt left. I'm in my room getting ready for bed, my body having completely switched over to zombie schedule. I grab for Rosa as a blaring alarm begins to sound. It is coming from outside and it sounds just like the alarm that went off the day the fences came down in Toccoa. I know something bad is happening and instinct warns me that the alarm sounds for me. Pravda has found me again. I look around the room for a hiding place, frantic to find somewhere safe for Rosa and me.

The Panic Room! I have to find Harmony and Thomas and get them safely into the little room. What about Jessie and the maid? What if they close the door before I can get us down there? I know the maid will do anything to keep me from the safety of the little hidden room. Which would be worse? Trapping myself in there with her hatred for who knows how long, or letting Pravda take me? For Rosa's sake, I'll endure being trapped with the girl who despises me.

An ear-piercing announcement echoes even louder than the still blaring siren:

"Attention Paradise! Pravda requests your attendance! Attention Paradise! Pravda requests your attendance!"

Harmony bursts into my room looking as terrified as I feel. We stare wide eyed at each other while Rosa cries and holds her hands to her ears. Then, as suddenly as it started, the alarm cuts off. Rosa is still crying loudly in the wake of the alarm and I pull her tight to my chest to shush her.

"What's happening?" Harmony whispers.

I wish I knew.

We tiptoe down the stairs, hoping to get to the basement without being seen or stopped. If the alarm did sound for me, will Jessie hide us or turn us in? Will Pravda take Harmony and Rosa too or will they let them stay here? If we make it to the hidden room, can it be opened from the outside? If Pravda is here for me, and Jessie tells them where I am, we'll die of starvation in the small room before they give up trying to take me. I know what I have to do. I have to put Harmony and Rosa in the panic room without me. Harmony and Rosa will be safe after Pravda has me. If Tim was here, he'd yell at me. He'd make me hide.

I miss him.

At the bottom of the stairs, the front door hangs open. Harmony and I peek out of the open door with dread. From our vantage point on the hill, Jessie's house looks out at the other mansions of Paradise. Peering out, I see the inhabitants of Paradise standing in their front yards. Jessie stands with her legs spread and her hands on her hips near the bottom of her hill, not far from the street. I can't see her face, but her posture says she's annoyed by the interruption.

Thomas stands next to Jessie and the maid kneels just behind them. The other homes I can see are the same. A single person, a couple, a family. And then, just behind them, servants down on their knees. I'm distracted from my fear by the curious spectacle before me. All of the neighbors I can see have large groups of servants. There are anywhere from five to fifteen people in black skirts or pants and white shirts - kneeling, yet at attention - behind their unaffected masters. Jessie, in the largest house on the hill, has only her maid kneeling behind her. I wonder why?

The families with children draw my focus. The kids are relaxed. Some boys Thomas' age wave at Thomas from where they are sitting on their well-kept lawns. They seem completely uninterested in the long row of white Pravda vans that are playing follow the leader in the open turnabout at the end of the road.

Pravda employees in silver suits are waving the vehicles to a stop in an orchestrated pattern on the street. There is one van per home. One white Pravda van stops directly in front of each driveway. But the wealthy members of this community seem unfazed. They chat on their lawns and wave to their neighbors as little ones Rosa's age run and play in the morning sun. Whatever is happening, it's normal. My heart slows down a little.

As the white van in line for Jessie's house pulls to a stop in front of her long driveway, the van's side door slides open. I'm too far away to see what is inside, but I can tell from here that the chatter in the other yards has stopped. Are they afraid of what they see inside or do they merely pay attention now because it's time to participate in this strange parade?

A disembodied voice barks via megaphone: "Serving Humanity, Curing the World!"

Harmony and I reach nervously for each other as the crowd below returns the man's chant in unison, "Serving Humanity, Curing the World."

Three driveways down from Jessie's, a silver-suited Pravdanian in a white mask emerges from the parked white van. He moves forward confidently into a yard where a smiling couple with a young son stand watching. The little boy is perched on his father's shoulders. Walking past the family, the silver-suited man grabs hold of a black man who kneels next to ten other servants. Dragging the servant to his feet, the Pravdanian punches and kicks at the dark skinned man as he pulls him back towards the van. A woman kneeling in the line screams and lunges to her feet as the other servants grab at her to keep her from following the Pravdanian and his prey.

The hysterical woman breaks free from the hands that hold her and rushes towards the van. In an instant, the woman and the other nine servants respond to something I cannot hear, see, or understand. The black man screams, paralyzed by pain, as the Pravda employee drags him past the white van and into the street. The eight who still kneel keel over and writhe on the fresh green grass. The woman arches her back and crawls slowly as though in horrible pain. Unwilling to give up, she creeps towards the van as she fights against some terrible force.

As my heart pounds harder, horrified by what I'm witnessing, the woman drops to the ground. She is still. The other servants on the lawn simultaneously cease their twitching. They lay like white and black stones on the lawn; some of them slumped over into a colorful bed of tulips. The black man in the street wails in grief and drops to his knees, covering his face with his hands. The way his body moves - grief stricken and devastated but not twitchy or stiff - I can tell that the physical pain has stopped. His emotional pain is just as hard to witness.

The unseen man with the megaphone announces, "This slave was caught stealing and selling Pravda's water. Theft of Pravda's resources will not be tolerated."

The black man arches his back and throws his arms out, enduring some torture I can't imagine before falling backwards, dead, on the pavement.

The disembodied voice continues pleasantly, "Pravda's water is for you, her beloved family. She will not allow her family to be disrespected and taken advantage of. You will always be loved and protected in Paradise. Do not fear. Please enjoy all that Pravda offers you. You are precious to the future. The Director wishes you all longevity and peace."

As the disembodied voice proclaims longevity and peace for the people of Paradise, they respond by raising their right fist to the sky. The van doors slide closed and, once again following the leader, they drive down the street and out of sight.

The family whose lawn is polluted with dead servants looks embarrassed. They wave apologetically to their neighbors and then walk quickly towards their front door. The little boy on his dad's shoulders calls out through his tears for the dead people on the ground and holds out his hands for them as his father ducks into their red brick mansion.

Chapter Twenty-Four

Did You Know You Could Die From PMS?

Harmony and I are sitting quiet and horrified at the bottom of the winding staircase when Jessie and Thomas come in the front door. I lift my eyes to meet her old green eyes and I'm surprised to see sadness lurking in them. The people of Paradise seemed so unaffected by the brutal murder that took place right before their eyes. Thomas looks frightened and there are wet tracks on his cheeks. From where Harmony and I spied on Pravda's community meeting, I couldn't see Thomas' face during the murder. It hurt me when I saw him raise his fist towards heaven as though he belonged with these people who hate our God.

"Jess, that man. Those people," Harmony says distraught.

"I know, hun." Jessie replies, holding Thomas close and petting his back.

My anger and sadness for what just happened has to skootch over just a little and make room for the irritation of Harmony and Jessie's close relationship and nickname status.

"Jeremiah stole water?" Thomas asks Jessie.

I didn't realize that Thomas knew the man. I should have. Matt and Thomas have lived here for years. These neighbors are his friends and their children have been his playmates. He just witnessed the torture and murder of people he knew by name. Pravda may treat them like disposables, but children know the truth. Children haven't been ruined by the world yet. They know that a person is a person. That every life has value. The cries of the little boy on his father's shoulder are pressed into my memory. His little hands reaching for the dead people who cared for him. Another brutality that I'll try to forget.

"Humph," the maid grunts angrily, closing the door behind her as she comes in. "Jeremiah didn't steal anything!"

"Trish!" Jessie barks."

"It isn't right!" the maid - named Trish - yells back disrespectfully.

"Leave." Jessie says coldly.

Jessie reaches into her shirt and pulls out a plastic pendant that hangs from a thick silver chain around her neck.

Trish looks murderously angry as she clomps away.

"Jeremiah wouldn't steal. He's like me," Thomas says to Jessie. "Like us," he says to Harmony and I.

"One of the Living?" I ask him.

He nods and sniffs, "A lot of them are like us."

I thought there weren't any Living ones in Atlanta. But they are still here. Being tortured and killed because they are criminals - criminals for their faith. The only thing unique about me is that I'm here in Paradise by invitation. I hate Pravda. I hate this fake paradise. I seethe.

"It doesn't matter now. He did. He didn't. It's over. If it wasn't him, it was someone else in Paradise and they chose Jeremiah for the demonstration on our street," Jessie says with growing impatience.

"Demonstration?" I ask incredulous.

"Someone took Pravda's water and sold it. So they let the servants know that that was unacceptable. There are a lot of streets in Paradise. They gave the same show to each street. Only one servant was guilty, the others were collateral.

"Collateral!"

"It's late. I'm going to bed," Jessie says in her defensive, clipped tone.

"How did they die?" Harmony asks.

"This," Jessie says, pointing to the pendant that dangles against her blue floral shirt.

"It sends a signal to the earring?" I ask.

Jessie glances at me - it's almost a glare - and then nods that I'm correct.

Harmony asks, "How did it kill everyone on that lawn and not the others?"

Jessie sighs looking at Thomas and then decides to answer Harmony's question, "Each van had a transmitter. It works on a certain frequency and a certain radius. My transmitter is only for Trish. I can discipline her or terminate her with this button."

"Are you -" I blurt in fury and Harmony squeezes my arm with a sharp pinch to quiet me.

“Most of them are criminals! We need these for protection,” Jessie retorts, self-righteous and defensive. “Each home controls their own slaves.”

“Trish? Is she a dangerous criminal?” I push, still furious that Pravda has given the people of Paradise carte-blanch to kill their slaves with the touch of a button.

And not just kill. They can torture them with terrible pain. Jessie just threatened Trish with her button. What about the people of this community who aren’t decent like Jessie? Do they get drunk and torture their slaves? Do they press the button on grumpy bad days because someone looks sideways at them? Do innocent people die because the lady of the house has a bad case of PMS? This is insane!

“This isn’t your home and you have no place here,” Jessie says staring with cold, angry eyes just at me. “When Matt gets back you will leave.”

“Matt is a blood dealer!” I shout at her. “He is stealing blood off of armored trucks! If Pravda kills for water, what will they do to him if he’s caught?”

Jessie has already turned her back to me. She stalks down the hallway to the kitchen without another word.

I turn my furious eyes to Harmony. Whose side is she on now? It had better be mine.

“Ivy,” she starts apologetically, but I can tell she wants me to calm down.

“Just don’t,” I spit my words.

Picking up Rosa, I march up the stairs to our room and shove the door shut behind me with my foot. The door closes a little louder than I meant for it to. I lock it. I can’t wait to give Jessie exactly what she wants. When Matt gets back, we’ll go get my dad and then I’m never coming back here again. I’ll put Atlanta behind me and head for the coast. Maybe the Gulf of Mexico.

I fall asleep holding tight to Rosa and picturing a little house - maybe a hut - on a sandy beach. The sky is turquoise blue and so is the water. The place in my imagination calms me. Washes away the anger. The sand feels soft beneath my feet...

Chapter Twenty-Five

Ladies And Gentlemen,
The Moment You've All Been Waiting For

I feel his arms around me. My breathing is heavy and the covers are too warm. A hand, Matt's hand, runs gently up and down my side. He is close to me, curled against me. I am groggy and tired. Is he really here? Am I dreaming? He lays a soft kiss against my ear and pulls my hair off of my sweaty neck. The cool air feels good. I roll towards him.

"It's you?"

"It better be me," he says with humor, "were you expecting someone else in your bed?"

In my bed.

I come up fully awake. Rosa is sleeping right next to me!

"How did you get in here?" I whisper, scooting against Rosa's back and pushing Matt away with my knee. I know I locked the door last night. Or this morning.

The bright afternoon sun filters through the curtains. I haven't been sleeping for long. It won't be evening for hours. I should be exhausted, but Matt being home - in my bed - has me wide awake. Matt's long brown hair is damp and fresh like he just took a shower and he smells so good it makes me weak.

"I thought you'd be missing me," he says, "but I guess I'll just go."

"No!"

I know he's playing with me, but I don't have the wherewithal to fight back right now.

"Don't go. What time is it? I'm glad you're home safe," I whisper.

He smiles at me, that adorable crooked smile, and reaches out to hold my hand. I feel nervous because he's in my bed and I know he shouldn't be, but I feel a lot of other feelings too.

"I missed you," he says genuinely, a trace of sadness on his handsome face.

I'm disarmed. I snuggle close to him and let him wrap his muscular arms around me.

"Where did you go?"

He doesn't answer me, instead he nuzzles my hair with his nose and breathes a contented sigh.

"Was it dangerous?"

Still no answer, but he squeezes me close and I sense that it was dangerous, wherever it was that he went.

"I prayed for you."

"Thank you," he whispers.

We lay quiet for awhile. I'm nestled against his chest and I listen to his heart beat. I pray silently for that heart, that God will keep it beating. Keep him with me. Change that heart. Make him Living.

"How are you holding up?" he asks.

I tell him about Jessie. About how she said I have to leave. I tell him about Jeremiah. And how terrible it was to watch Jeremiah and the others die. About how worried I am that he'll get caught stealing blood again and what Pravda would do to him. I don't have very many people left. If he was gone, I'd be so alone. I start to cry.

He pulls my face up to his and wipes my tears and kisses my lips, "I'm not going anywhere. I'll always be with you, okay? I love you."

I cry harder, burying my face in his neck. He loves me. I should be smiling and saying it back, but I can't seem to pull myself together. He loves me and I'm so desperate for him, but something feels broken. It's one of those times when once the tears start, there's no stopping them. I built a dam to hold back the worry, the guilt, the want, and the desperation for Matt's love. Now, when he is giving me what I've yearned for, the dam is breaking. I should be happy, but my ugly tears just keep coming. I'm ruining this moment.

"Baby, why are you so sad?" he breathes in my ear.

I smile and hiccup - he called me baby! - and then snot comes out of my nose and I'm so embarrassed. I release a laugh that sounds more like a sob and I brush my nose clean with the bed sheets. He grins and I smile up at him. My breath is still shuddering from my heavy sobs and I feel like a basket case.

"You love me?" I ask when I can finally speak without my words getting caught in my chest.

"I do," he says running his hands under my shirt against my stomach, against my skin.

I close my eyes. His hand is on my skin. I love it. I love him. I'm confused and longing. Longing to not ruin this moment and to stay still and let him touch me.

"I love you," he whispers again, stroking my side, giving me goose bumps.

I grab his hand and pull it out of my shirt and away from my skin. I feel sick. I'm going to ruin this moment and I feel sick.

"Please Matt. I can't."

"Why?" he asks sadly.

Genuinely sad. Not mad at me like before. Not manipulative like he can be. Genuine and real and honestly wanting to hold me and touch me because he loves me and really not understanding why we can't.

"I almost lost my Healing once. It was -" I look up into his faceted green eyes and swallow, "It was terrible. I don't want to lose Him again. I need Him. He is the only reason I'm okay. He's the only thing keeping me sane. He is so good to me and so in love with me and I don't want to hurt Him. I want you,"

"Then let me," Matt interrupts.

"But I won't risk losing Him. Hurting Him. I can't."

"Then how can we be together, Ivy? What is the point? Me wanting you and you wanting me back? Does He want to torture us? Why give us these feelings if we aren't allowed to have them?"

"We are allowed, in the right way."

"You want me to marry you?" he asks with too much humor in his tone and a snort.

I switch from intimacy to insecurity and embarrassment in 1.2 seconds. I roll away from him, towards Rosa's sleeping form, hating this moment. Disgusted. Upset. Frustrated. Ashamed.

"Okay," He says behind me. "Okay, I'll marry you," he grabs me around my waist and pulls me back close to him until we fit together like nestled spoons.

"I can't marry you," I whisper.

I expect him to get mad. I just told him I can't be physical with him because we aren't married, and then to my great shock he offers to marry me. I know I can't and it's not fair. It's not fair, God. I don't want this. Life hurts too much already. My heart can't take anymore stinging lashes from love's whip.

"I'll change for you. I'll be like you and Tom."

I turn to look into his beautiful eyes and find them teary. His cool, calm, collected, zombie green eyes are full to the brim with emotion.

"You can't do it for me. It has to be for you. It won't work unless it's for you."

"I - I don't think I can. I really would do anything for you, Ivy. Anything," he promises fiercely. "But loving Him? I promised myself - I swore I never would."

"That's like promising to starve yourself or hate yourself. It doesn't make sense! Take back that stupid promise and be Alive, Matt. I know your dad hurt you. I'm so sorry," I say with all the apology that I genuinely feel. "But God is so sorry, too. He never wanted that. He hurt *with* you. He kept you alive so you could know He loves you. So you could find Him! He *sent* you to me and Aunty. Out of all the places Thomas could've gone, do you think it was coincidence? He has been loving you and following you and keeping you safe your whole life because He loves you. Can't you feel it? Can't you feel Him?"

Matt blinks and two tears slide out. He closes his eyes to trap the tears that betray him and the feelings he always pretends aren't there. I'm so humbled that he's letting me see the real him. So in love with him and amazed that he loves me back. He is quiet for a while. Holding me. I realize that I'm holding my breath. Could the moment I've been praying for, hoping for, finally be here? Is it now? I breathe in and wait.

"How do I do it?" he asks like a little boy, vulnerable.

I feel a sudden rush of nerves. I have to do this right! What if I don't explain it well? What if I mess it up? It's the most important moment of my life. God, please help me.

"Well," I start hesitantly, wishing I was more prepared, hoping I'll remember the verses, "The Bible says we have to admit that we are sinners and that we can't fix our broken relationship with God on our own."

"No argument there," he whispers lightheartedly, his eyes still closed.

I smile.

"You asked me why your dad got to go to heaven when he had done such an awful thing, and I've been thinking about that. We all sin all the time, you know? Like, what if I was super good and I only made one mistake a day? Just one bad attitude or one moment of self-centeredness, or one mean word slipped out. Just one a day. Every year, that would add up to 365 sins. Now that I'm sixteen, I've sinned like 5,000 times at least.

"So what if Pravda caught me for stealing water 5,000 times. They'd never let me off. It wouldn't matter if I was a good person. There isn't enough good I could do to get out of that much theft. They would punish me. The Bible says God is good and He is just. He is a just judge. He can't let that much sin go unpunished. But what could He do about it? We're human. We're all going to sin. And way more than once a day. Every human being would have to die to pay for their sin. But God made us because He wanted us to be with Him! He didn't want us to die.

"So God made an incredible way to get us out of our punishment. He came to earth and died for us Himself. He paid our ransom. We were being held captive by this sin we couldn't do anything about, and He paid this huge ransom that we totally didn't deserve. He died in our place. His blood was perfect because He lived on this earth for thirty-three years and never sinned. His blood was spotless. No disease in it. His blood IS the cure. The Bible says Jesus is the Lamb of God who took away the sins of the whole world. That's why we're cured, Matt. Thomas and I and Harmony, we've been covered by His blood. It washed the disease away."

I grope for Matt's hand and hold it tightly in mine. His eyes are closed, but I can tell he is listening. He opens his eyes when I pause and stares into mine. I keep going, hoping he's really understanding.

"You said the other day that you believe it's really God who Healed me and Thomas. But believing it is true isn't enough. The Bible says that even the demons believe that Jesus is God, and they shudder! But obviously the demons aren't children of God. Remember that day you took me to the falls?"

He nods that he remembers and continues to stare at me. I blush and look away from his intense gaze.

I stare at his lips and continue, "I asked you if you believed that George Washington was real, and you said yes. You can believe that Jesus is God's Son and that He lived on earth and died on the cross and still not KNOW Him. You don't KNOW George Washington. He was real, you believe in him, but he has nothing to do with your life today. God wants you to believe in Him first and trust in Him second. He wants you to acknowledge that you're a sinner, and that you can't get to Heaven on your own; that you want to follow Him and be like Him and make Him the boss in your life instead of you."

I see the argument building in his eyes before he even voices it, "I'm not good at that, Ivy. You are simple and sweet and innocent. But I've seen too much. I have to be in charge of myself. It's the only way I've kept Thomas and I alive this long."

"Did you keep Thomas alive? Was he doing well under your care?" My words are harsh, but I say them with love and gentleness. "You said Thomas was close to death when he left to follow Harvey to Toccoa. Were you enough to keep Thomas alive or did he need more than what you could give? He would've died under your care. God gave him what he really needed when you couldn't."

Matt doesn't answer me and I hope that I haven't pushed him away.

"We can't do this life on our own. We weren't meant to. He made us with a missing piece. We need Him. I know you can feel it. I know you feel that thing in your heart that says there is something more and you're missing it."

I see his Adam's apple bob as he swallows and he nods. Accepting my words. Validating them. Agreeing. Understanding.

I sit up in my bed and look around the room, "Do you see that chair over there?"

He rolls away from me and follows my gaze to the pretty sofa we sat on together, "Yes."

"Do you believe that chair would hold your weight if you sat on it?"

"Obviously," he says, sounding slightly irritated at my childish question.

"Is it holding you now?"

"No."

"It takes more than belief, Matt. You have to get up and go sit in the chair for it to really hold your weight. You have to ask God to forgive you *and* let Him take charge of your life - admit that your way won't work. Then, He'll heal you like He did for me and for Thomas. Then, you'll be His. And it's amazing. It's so amazing Matt. Will you?"

He is quiet, looking across the room at the sofa. I sit next to him quiet, barely breathing. And I pray. I pray because a war is happening in my bed. God has been chasing Matt his whole life, but Satan has triumphantly held him captive all this time. Satan does not want to lose his trophy. This pastor's son who hates his sinful father's God.

The battle in Matt's mind can't be fought by me. It's up to him to hear the right voices. I picture an angel and a devil perched on each shoulder. Each of them whispering in his ear that the other one is wrong. Who will he believe? The one he has followed his whole life, or hope? Hope that humility is worth it. Hope that God is who He says He is. Hope that the longing inside will finally be satisfied.

"How?" Matt croaks in a voice heavy with emotion and labored by the fight he is fighting.

"Pray with me."

He nods.

"Lord Jesus," I start and wait for him to repeat.

I nudge him and he says quietly, "Lord Jesus."

And then Matt starts to sob. Painful, heartbreaking sobs of defeat. The defeat of years of stubbornness and the defeat of his own anger. He is giving in, and it has broken him. I cry with him. I wrap my goose-pimpled arms around him and sob. I want to help him finish the prayer but his raw heartbreak is so intense that I can't stop crying for him and with him. It is the death of him, but it is Life. I am so full of joy that I can't stop shaking.

Chapter Twenty-Six

One Step Forward, Two Steps Back— And That Last Step Is A Doozy

Matt lies quietly next to me. His eyes are closed, there's a small smile on his lips and his face is glowing like the afternoon sun. I am nestled in the crook of his arm, grinning so hard my cheeks ache. I'm not worried that we didn't finish the prayer. I would've had him repeat after me that he was sorry for sinning, that he knew Jesus died for him and paid for him and that he was thankfully accepting that undeserved sacrifice. I would've led him to say that he wanted to follow God's plan for his life and that he was relinquishing his own command. But none of that was necessary. Matt's heart did what my humble words could not do. He gave his zombie heart to God and God changed him from the inside out.

Matt's skin is radiant. His face that used to be pale and dry looks as pink and healthy as a new born baby. His ears are soft and pink too. The disease is completely gone. I won't miss it. I thought I loved him just the way he was, but this reborn child of God next to me is incredible. He was handsome before - now he is stunning.

We are the same now, he and I. We are both Living. I have wanted this moment for so long and the longing and wanting and pain can't compare to the elation I feel now. Just like the verses Harmony read to me. You think that the pain is too terrible and that you'll always remember it. But, then, the good that comes later is so phenomenally better and the pain is forgotten. Or, if not forgotten, totally worth it. God is so amazing!

"Your skin is healed. Your ears. It's all new and perfect," I whisper, staring up at him.

Matt turns his head towards me and opens his eyes. I inhale a small gasp. His emerald eyes sparkle with a new clarity. Deep green pools that are full of love and wisdom and dazzling with excitement. I stare into them, lost.

Suddenly, Matt jumps up, ripping his arm out from under me and flopping me unceremoniously back on the bed. He tears his shoes off and then his socks. I'm freaked out by his sudden stripping. Does he think I'll sleep with him now because he's Living? I'm trying to get the words out, trying to form the question about what he could possibly be doing when I realize he's upset. He is unrolling layers of gauzy bandages from around his feet and toes.

"Did I do it wrong?" he asks bewildered.

"What's the matter?" I ask just as bewildered.

"He didn't fix them," he says.

I look closely at his feet and see that they are curled and disfigured. I never knew how bad the disease was on them. His shoes are the special zombie shoes that compensate for missing toes and make walking normally possible. He looks so disappointed and, though his feet look awful, I'm frantic to downplay it. I don't want him to already be frustrated with our God.

"Thomas was completely healed. Did I not do it all the way?" he asks me, truly worried that he has done something wrong. "Pray it with me, Ivy. The whole prayer. I have to say it all!"

"You *are* Healed, Matt. There's no halfway. It's all or nothing. God doesn't always give the same Healing."

"Thomas' feet were much worse than mine. Now - Well, I've seen them! They were completely restored! Why wouldn't He fix mine?"

I search for words. Words that will encourage. I avoid looking at his tragic feet and stare instead at the sheet that I've balled up between my hands.

"Sometimes we keep our scars. Sometimes they make us a better person. He wants us to lean on Him and He says His strength is made perfect in our weaknesses."

I believe the words I'm saying with all my heart, but they sound trite when I look up at his disappointed face. "I don't know why He didn't make them whole, but He always does the right thing for us."

I hate those words sometimes. I claimed them when Aunty was dying. I claimed them when Toccoa was burning. I claim them every day that I'm stuck here on this God-forsaken planet, being hunted, running for my life. I know they can be small comfort at times. It takes faith to believe in Him during our greatest disappointments.

"I don't understand," he says, staring at his feet.

This skin on his feet is healthy. There aren't any open wounds. But several toes are missing and the few that are left are bent and deformed. He'll have to wear the special shoes until Jesus comes back.

I look up from Matt's feet as Jessie bursts into my room followed close by Trish the maid.

"See!" Trish yells, pointing at Matt.

Jessie's face is full of fury and disgust. She looks back and forth between me on the bed and Matt on the floor. He looks up at her with an apology on his face.

"You?" Jessie asks Matt, incredulous.

"Jess," Matt pleads, "We knew. We knew what was true."

"Not in my house!" she yells.

She isn't mad at him for trying to sleep with me - like I first thought - she's angry because he gave his heart to God.

"I want you out," Jessie says freezing the room with her icy anger.

"Not him! Just her!" Trish whines.

"Get out!" Jessie whirls around and slaps Trish. "This is none of your business!"

Rosa starts crying behind me.

Trish falls to her knees and lifts tear-filled pleading eyes to Matt, "Matt?"

I know that look.

Trish loves Matt.

Envy and anger stab ruthlessly, ripping jagged holes in my heart. It *was* Matt pulling her into his room the night we got here. He was sleeping with her. I'm going to be sick. I grab for Rosa and lunge from the bed. Tears fall as I reach the bathroom and slam the door shut behind me.

I hear screaming. It's Trish screaming. Screaming in terrible pain. Jessie is pushing the button.

"I want all of you out of my house!" Jessie screams before leaving my room.

I slump down on the floor against the bathroom door. Betrayed.

"I'm sorry, Trish," Matt says from the other side of the door. "I shouldn't have used you. I'm sorry."

Trish screams, no longer in physical pain, but angry and heart-broken, "Go to Hell!"

Then everything is quiet. She is gone. Jessie is gone. Matt, who loves Jesus, is out there on the floor in his ruined bare feet. And I hate him.

*****

"Ivy?"

Matt has been begging me to come out. Pleading with me to forgive him. Promising me that she meant nothing to him. Every time he makes that promise, I hate him more. He was sleeping with her and she meant nothing to him. What kind of horrible person does that? He said he loved me. How could he love me and sleep with her?

I know it was before. Before he gave God his heart. But that doesn't loosen the knife in my chest. I'm not God. I can't forgive the way God can. I can't forgive him for this. I'm a virgin. I've never slept with anyone! I've been so tempted by Matt. So close to giving him what he didn't deserve. I am a delusional moron. Aunty was so right. She was always right.

What am I going to do now? I don't want anything to do with him. I can't stand to see those eyes and know that she was looking up at them from his bed. Ugghh... The thought of her in his bed makes me nauseated. I crawl forward to the toilet, sure I'm going to barf. Rosa whimpers and follows me. I hate when my life makes hers scary. I promised myself she'd be safe and happy with me, and I've failed at that too.

I can't go get my dad without Matt's help, and I can't stand to look at Matt or speak to him ever again. Jessie wants me out of her house, and I doubt she'll give me long to comply. She may even call Pravda on me now. I am so screwed.

Chapter Twenty-Seven

God Help Me

Rosa is crying quietly and shaking me. My eyes blink open to see the bottom of the toilet. I must have fallen asleep on the floor. Why am I here?

It hits me like a punch in the gut.

Matt slept with the maid. That horrible girl who hated me and now I know why. Pain and hatred pucker my face as I pull myself off of the floor. I hear noise in my room, just beyond the bathroom door. Rosa is whimpering and trying to get me to understand something. Muffled thumps register in my depressed mind. Someone is out there.

"I know," my voice sounds flat and dead and I hate the sound of myself. "We have to go."

I stand up and open the wardrobe. I want to be fully dressed and ready to walk out of the door when I leave this bathroom. I'll take whatever clothes I can find in here, I don't care if it's a freaking prom dress. I have to get out of this house.

The door to the bathroom flies open - breaking the lock - and bounces off of the wall. I turn to yell at Matt. Breaking my door down won't get him any closer to me. I'll close my eyes and tell him every terrible thing I think about him and then we'll leave.

But it isn't Matt.

A cluster of bodies dressed in silver Pravda bodysuits advances slowly into my bathroom. Their faces are hidden behind horrible white plastic masks. The round dark eyeholes make the Pravdanians look hollow, as though their thin suits are wrapped around a vacuum of formless evil. Their physiques are fit and strong, more than enough muscle to drag me away to whatever end Pravda has for me. I scream and stumble backwards.

There's no way out!

Nowhere to hide!

The tangle of white ghostly limbs moves towards me like a pale octopus. An arm towards the front lifts a gun and trains it on me. I push Rosa behind me. I wish I could tell her how sorry I am for failing her. I wish she had never had the misfortune of meeting me. The cluster of zombies shoots me in the shoulder, and I scream at the sharp pain. My scream echoes in my ears in the small room.

And it keeps echoing. It doesn't stop echoing. It rings in my ears until blackness consumes me.

Where?

beep

beeping

weird smells

HELP!

Someone!

beeping. steady. beeps.

so

heavy

Help!

Hands touching me!

pain.

d a r k n e s s

"......effective Doctor. Do you want to move her?"

beep.

beep.

beep.

Soooo

heavy.

soooo....

sick.

".....2ccs. Put her back under."

No!

Help me!

God?!

d a r k n e s s

I'm exhausted. I've been running for so long.

I've been searching.

I can't find her. I have to keep looking. I know she needs me. She's here and she needs me! I hear them coming behind me. Why can't I elude them? They scream in my ears, almost reaching me. Almost, but never quite. My legs are exhausted, a weariness I've never known. My whole being is diminishing like melting ice. I am less and less. Where is she? I keep trying to call her but I don't know who - I know that I know, but I can't remember. Where would she be? Why is she so hard to find? They breathe down my neck. They smell like death.

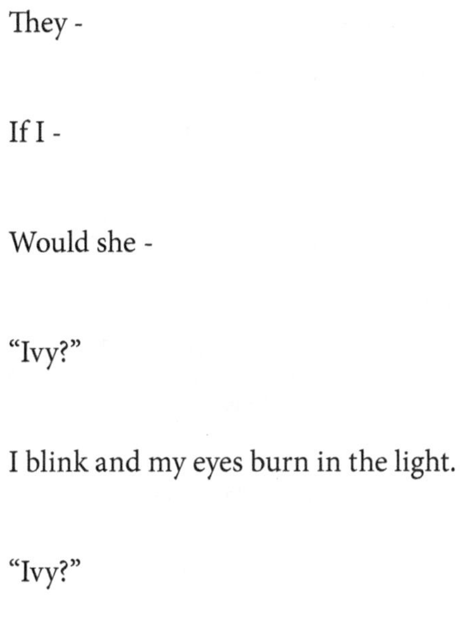

They -

If I -

Would she -

"Ivy?"

I blink and my eyes burn in the light.

"Ivy?"

Something pulls my eyelids apart and the burning comes back. A light is shining into my eye.

I'll hit it.

My arm won't move.

"Ivy?"

"hgmr wilmdber," I respond groggy.

"Wake up, dear," says a blurry feminine voice I don't recognize.

My eyes focus slowly. I don't know where I am and I feel so heavy. I feel like I am made of rock.

I am a boulder.

A blob.

I don't have arms or legs.

I can't feel my face. I don't know if I have feet.

Thick. Everything is thick. The air is thick. My nose is thick. I can't get enough air through my thick nostrils. I hear a beeping noise. It is accelerating. I have no idea what it means, though I suspect I should.

The woman I don't know calls out for someone.

I feel the darkness coming again and I don't want it to. I'm afraid of the dark. The hands live there. The hands that grab at me and chase me. Please don't send me back there!

The hands grab me and yank me under.

d a r k n e s s

"Ivy?"

"Ivy?"

I've been awake for some time. Staring at a small crack in the ceiling above me.

The crack is a river on a map.

The crack is a rift in time.

The crack is an arrow pointing to something important. It's a clue to where I am. Why I can't move.

My eyes blink and I'm relieved. It is the first muscle I have moved. The first small step towards finding me.

"Ivy?" the voice calls out again and I realize that word has meaning.

What is Ivy? Ivy is something. It's a word I've heard. It means something to me.

"I know you are confused, but you are just fine. You are alright. Do you understand?" the blurry voice says words to me.

"mlphh" I move my tongue.

I have a tongue and I moved it!

"Can you squeeze my hand?"

I realize with profound impact that there is another crack, not far from the first. I don't know if it is above it or below it. To the left or to the right. I know it's there. Near. And it must mean something. I study it with all of my might.

*****

I sleep. But it isn't the darkness. It is restful. It is light and breezy. I feel content.

"Ivy?"

Aunty is calling me. I must have overslept! I have to get up and help her feed the guests!

My eyes snap open to the white room.

"Ivy?" the voice asks, but it isn't Aunty.

I start to cry.

Someone presses a button and my bed hums to life, lifting my head and my body. Making me sit up. My stomach turns inside of me. I feel burning in my throat. I am choking on something in my mouth. It is hot and it comes out of my mouth. I don't know where it goes after that.

Where is Aunty?

She's dead isn't she? I'm alone. She left me. Where am I?

Pravda!

I remember things in a dizzying whirl.

Gleaming silver suits. Plastic faces. A werewolf. A garden.

Rosa? I've lost her!

Matt!

Where is he? He loves me!

No! The maid, I can't remember her name, but I remember what she did. What he did. It hurts. It hurts worse than the hands. Send me back to the dark where the hands are. I don't want to live.

Someone is wailing. It sounds like the woman who wailed for the slave they killed in the street. But it can't be her. They killed her too.

The wailing is terrifying.

The wailing is me.

Who is me?

Ivy.

I am Ivy.

I am Ivy and Pravda has me and I am alone.

Chapter Twenty-Eight
This Is All A Big Misunderstanding

The woman looks at me and I look back at her. I am expressionless and so is she. She waits for me to speak and I wait for her to speak. I am up in bed, but only up because the bed has been raised to the sitting position. I threw up again. The woman was waiting for me to be sick. She had a little silver pan to catch the acid that burned its way out of me.

Beep. Beep. Beep.

I don't know why I feel so sick. I know I was sick last night when they came for me. How many hours have I slept here? Maybe I have the flu. Maybe it's a side effect of what they used to drug me. The octopus shot me with a tranquilizer. The drugs are taking forever to wear off. I feel like a limp noodle. With intense effort and concentration, I wiggle my fingers. Breathing is irritating. The air feels too cold and sharp in my nose. My mouth feels swollen and fluffy, like it grew feathers while I slept.

Beep. Beep. Beep.

I am worried, but not for myself. What happened to Harmony and Rosa? Did Pravda take them too? Would the woman tell me the truth if I ask?

Beep. Beep. Beep.

The beeping noise that never stops its obsessive cadence has become part of my thoughts. I feel the beat in my head. I feel it in my chest. The beeping is the sound of my heart. They have me hooked up to a machine that is monitoring my heart beat. The machine beeps at me while I think. My heart is loud and irritating.

I have to know where Rosa and Harmony are. I have to know what happened to them. I decide to end the staring competition and be the first to speak.

"Where is Rosa?" I ask, but it sounds like "merr wwosaa".

What is wrong with me?

Why can't I speak?

The woman doesn't acknowledge my attempt. She continues to stare into my eyes, but I can tell she isn't looking at me. She is looking through me. Her thoughts are elsewhere. I thought she was staring me down, trying to intimidate me. But the older woman is merely bored. She looks down at her lap.

"You have been in a drug induced coma for three months, Ivy," the woman reads, looking down at a chart as though she is reading me the latest newspaper headline.

She is dressed in white clothes. A white shirt and pants. And a white lab coat. She wears a silver pin with Pravda's emblem near the pocket of her cotton coat. She has silver hair like Aunty. My eyes pool with moisture. I blink and a tear escapes.

"Do you understand me, Ivy?" she asks. "You have been asleep for three months," she stares at my face as she speaks.

I watch her lips make the words. I have been asleep, she says. For months. I blink at her. Why would she lie to me? Is she trying to trick me? Trying to freak me out? That must be it. Does she think I'm stupid? I feel a small smile form in the corners of my mouth. They'll have to try harder than that if they want to manipulate me.

"You are smiling, that's very good," she talks to me like I am a little child, her voice coddling and too cheerful. "Most people take weeks to regain muscular functions. You have moved your fingers and smiled since I sat down. You are going to be just fine."

My lips flat line. My brain works hard to understand, and it makes my head hurt. I feel my brow furrow. I feel it because it takes great effort to move my brows a millimeter. Could she be telling me the truth? Have I been here, in this place, for a long time?

Why?

For what purpose?

Why haven't they killed me? I thought they wanted my blood. Is that why I'm so weak? Maybe they've only left me with enough to survive. They drained me almost dry but not quite. So I'll make more blood? Will it go on like this forever? Them draining me down to almost nothing? Me rebuilding? Them draining? Me rebuilding?

"We woke you because it is best for the fetus to have an active host."

What is she talking about?

"If you can't handle being awake, we will put you back under for the duration of your pregnancy."

What?

"If you become a danger to yourself or Pravda's fetus, your pregnancy can be completed in the coma. Do you understand?"

I feel my brows furrow again. I try to look down at my body. I can't possibly understand because it can't possibly be what she said. She has the wrong chart. There has been a mistake. That must be it. I look back up at her expressionless, pinched face and I feel bad for her. I feel sorry because I can't tell her she's wrong. If I could talk, we'd clear this all up. I hope her mistake doesn't get her in trouble. I'm not mad at her. I'll tell her when I can talk. She'll come to apologize, "sorry, wrong chart" and I'll tell her "no problemo."

I wish I could ask her about Harmony and Rosa. Should I though? Maybe they didn't know Harmony was in the house. Maybe Jessie hid her. Jessie liked Harmony. And I'm okay with that now. I bet Jessie hid Harmony and she's just fine. If I asked about them, it would send Pravda looking for them. I won't ask. They wouldn't even want Rosa. She's an innocent. Not even Living yet. She's just another child in a terrible, cruel world. She doesn't have special blood. She's probably safe with Harmony. I'll picture them together and safe.

"Ivy? I need you to show me that you understand and that you will comply. I can't leave this room until we have an agreement," the woman says, glancing across the room at the large gray panel that fills the center of the wall near my bed.

I follow her eyes to the gray panel. The empty gray square on the wall makes me nervous, but I don't know why. I look back at the woman in white and see that she has a name tag on her white v-necked shirt. Patrice. Her name is Patrice. I've never known anyone with that name. It's pretty. I wonder if I'm saying it right in my head. *Paatrease.* Patrice wears white gloves. Like the zombie who shot me. I remember his white-gloved hand holding up the strange gun. Patrice has scaly red patches all over her neck and chest that are thinly veiled with makeup. Her face is tinted orange from the thick layer of makeup and the outline of her lips is a penciled red line.

"Ivy? Lift your finger."

I lift my finger.

"Good. Now lift your finger if you know your name. Is your name Ivy?"

I lift my finger.

"Good. Now lift your finger if you understand that you are three months pregnant."

I stare up at Patrice's puckered orange face as I contemplate. She still thinks I'm pregnant. I will lift my finger so she'll go away. I lift my finger.

"Good. Now lift your finger if you promise to be a good girl and listen to your nurses and eat your food and take good care of your baby."

She called it a baby that time. Ha. Fetus, baby. Lift my finger. I'll be good. She'll be back soon to correct her mistake.

Chapter Twenty-Nine

It's Not You, It's Me

I am waking again. The crack on the ceiling is still there. I know now that it doesn't hold any answers, but it is straight above me and therefore I stare at it. I am blinking my eyes and breathing and it doesn't hurt.

Beep. Beep. Beep.

On the fourth beep, I remember that I am in Pravda. The realization attacks me and clubs me mercilessly. I am robbed of the momentary peace I feel each time I wake up - those few precious moments before I remember where I am. Before I begin the tormented wondering of what will become of me. Each time I wake, I have only a few breaths of freedom before the depression is thrown over me like a heavy black blanket that blots out the light.

My chest hurts. Not my chest, my breasts. My breasts hurt. Every time I wake up it is only to do battle. I am fighting the terror and paranoia of what happened to me over the last three months. I'm on a catheter. When Aunty was dying, Tim's dad explained to me how a catheter works.

Someone looked at me *down there* and I'm humiliated. I've never been looked at. I feel violated. I'm worried that other things could've been done to me while I slept. My body doesn't feel like my own anymore. I wish I could leave it. I feel like the only part left that is me is hidden inside my brain. I don't want to be connected to the rest of me anymore.

I don't want to live. I've lost everything and everyone. All the running and hiding we did was for nothing. No more friends. No more family.

Family.

It is always my first thought after the depression pushes down heavy on my heart. My dad is here somewhere. My dad and Aunty Betty are in this same building somewhere, but I have given up on them already. The first time I realized that we were in Pravda together I thought, "Maybe I will get well and I can escape and find them." I thought, "Maybe this was God's plan all along." I don't indulge that fantasy anymore.

God?

He is my second thought in the train of thoughts that haunt me, that chase me down the long dark tunnel of my defeated spirit. God wasn't in the dark with me. The hands chased me through nightmares and God didn't intervene. Where is He? He gave me Matt and then ripped him away. I am super mad at God. I know I shouldn't be, but it can't be helped. I could lie to myself and say He has been great to me. But, trapped in my own head, I have only myself for company. I feel like I should at least be honest with me.

Was it all in my head? His plan. His will. Did I jump from the narrow path long ago when I followed Matt out of Toccoa? Maybe God gave up on me and left me to my love lust and boy-crazed bad choices to punish me. Yes. I am definitely being punished.

The softness of someone's skin against my own is comforting. It occurs to me that someone is holding my hand, petting my thumb. I pull my eyes from the crack on the ceiling and they make the long journey down to my hand. A plump woman is holding my hand in hers and patting the top of my hand like a mother would. I don't think she is my mother. No, she isn't. I remember what my mom looked like, thin and freckled with pretty teeth and straight brown hair. She had bangs, my mom. The woman patting my hand doesn't have bangs.

"Hello," she says kindly.

Her eyes shift from me to the gray panel and then back to my eyes.

Her hello and her gentle eyes make me cry. I cry for a long time until I sleep again.

Chapter Thirty

Count Your Blessings, Name Them One By One

The nurse who takes care of me is very nice. She doesn't wear zombie gloves. She is old like Aunty, but heavier. Her hair is cut short like Jessie and the tramp maid. The nurse's name is Gladys. I don't think I know how to say her name right. But I don't know how to say anything right.

Pravda has done something terrible to me, and I'm not me now. I can barely move. I am sick when I am awake. My neck moves now, though slowly. I can look down at my body where it lays in lumps under the thin white blanket that always covers me. I am worried. My body doesn't look like me. It looks thin. And when I turn my head, I can't feel my hair on the back of my neck. Nothing in the room is reflective and I think that is on purpose.

The room is all I have now. I've studied my surroundings for clues - and out of sheer boredom. There is the gray panel. I think Pravda is watching me from behind the panel. I've seen movies where the police had windows that only worked one way. I think that's why Gladys and Patrice glance so often at the panel. I don't want to be watched, but I'm not doing anything interesting. I feel bad for the people who have to watch me. They must be as bored as I am.

The rest of the room is white and silver. The walls are white. The floor is white. The ceiling is white. The rest of the stuff in the room - that makes it a hospital room - is silver. Silver instruments and silver cabinets that roll. Silver bars alongside of my bed to keep me from falling out. Silver carts full of silver tools that make me nervous when my eyes fall there.

Long, rectangular florescent lights hang from the ceiling instead of being part of it. Above the foot of my bed, two bulbous silver lights that are never lit hang from the ceiling. They point towards my feet.

I have an IV. It is near the head of my bed. The tubes dangle down out of sight and then climb back up to disappear into my arm. I don't know what the clear liquid is, but I believe it is feeding me.

I've been here for three months. She told me that. I've been here for three months. That's why I'm thin. That's why I'm weak. I was in a coma in this room for three months. I am seventeen now. I missed my birthday while I fought the darkness and the hands, locked away inside my own body. In Pravda. Alone.

I've lost everyone. I don't have anyone. I'm alone until I die. Until Pravda kills me.

Movement in the corner of my eye compels me look up. A man is standing in the doorway to my room. He is dressed in blue scrubs like a doctor but he wears the white plastic mask. I don't know how long he has been there, staring. He wears a stethoscope around his neck and it reminds me of Tim. Tim who loved me and took care of me. Tim who I hurt. Tim who is probably dead. The man in the doorway takes a step into my room. What does he want with me? Where is Gladys?

Beep. Beep. Beep.

I hear my heart rate getting faster.

I am afraid.

I wish I wasn't. I want to be courageous. I want to face Pravda and their devilish intentions with stoic bravery and a fierce grip on my faith - but it just isn't there.

I feel my breathing get harder and faster.

The man takes another step into the room and lifts his gloved hand towards me.

Beep. Beep. Beep.

I am gasping now, trapped in my own feeble body. Incapable of crying out. Incapable of running or fighting. I'll lie here and scream in my head alone while he does whatever he came to do. Maybe it's time to take my blood again. What if he drains so much that I go back into the coma again? I can't go back in there again!

I gasp again and I feel my lungs rebelling.

A panic attack. I've had one before.

The beeping on the machine next to my bed gets more and more insistent.

The man stands close to my bed now and stares at me. He turns to study my IV bag and then, with one last look at me through the empty plastic eyeholes of his mask, he hurries from my room. I can't calm down. I don't know why he came in, but it doesn't matter now. I can't breathe!

Gladys charges into my room, her stocky legs swishing the fabric of her pink scrubs. She kneels at my side and bends close to me, petting my forehead.

"Shhh," Gladys murmurs, her breath sweet like peppermint.

Tears slip out of my eyes as I continue to gasp. I can't get control!

Gladys runs her fingers through my hair and I realize that my hair is gone. She is running her fingers through hair shorter than her own. With herculean effort, I lift my hand up to touch my hair. My arm shakes with the exertion. My skinny fingers tremble like an old woman as they reach my head. My hair is so short, less than half an inch.

My gasps are desperate, like someone coming up out of the water after almost drowning. But each gasp brings another. The air won't come in!

Panic clamps down even harder and stabs my tortured lungs. A horrible wheeze-like scream is erupting from my chest. I can't get any oxygen! Gladys is cooing to me, telling me to focus, to breathe. I can't breathe, Gladys! I can't! My trembling hands touch my too thin face. I grasp at my head and face like a blind person trying to "see" with my hands. My fingers brush against something hard. Something is in my ear!

I have a tube in my ear!

A tube like Trish the maid! Somewhere there is a button that can torture me and kill me! My eyes start to go dark. I don't have any air left and I'm dying. And I'm glad.

Let me die, Gladys. Put a pillow over my face and let me go home. I just want to go home. Aunty is there. She's waiting for me. I promised her I'd meet her there.

Gladys croons softly at me, a comforting noise. A noise like she cares about me. I don't know why, but I believe her. I believe that she cares. I look up at her with dimming sight. My eyes are wide, so wide they are trying to find breath for me.

"He cares," she whispers in my ear.

Not the ear that says I'm a slave, the other ear.

"He cares."

She means God. She says He still cares for me. Somehow the next gasp brings air. And then another gasp brings a little more. My eyes find the ability to focus again and I stare at Gladys as she shows me how to breathe. She breathes in and I breathe a weak, shaky breath in. She breathes out and I try to push the air out of my contracting lungs. Each breath feels like it takes too much thought. There is no rhythm to it.

As Gladys sits and pets my hand, I breathe. I breathe and I stare at the rod in her ear. Gladys is a slave. A slave who knows how to be a nurse. Pravda has given me a nurse who knows Jesus. Jesus has given me a nurse who knows Him. We are slaves. But we are loved. Jesus loves me. I know He does. I know He does and it makes me cry. I love Him too. No matter what. No matter where I am or what they do to me. I love Him.

*****

No one has taken blood from me since waking from the coma. I thought I was here because of my blood. I only see Gladys and she is only nice. She checks my heart machine and washes my face and rubs the needles out of my feet. She helps me sip water. She holds the pan when the water comes back up. She is trying to get me better. Why?

They are watching her through the gray panel. They know she is helping me, but they let her keep caring. Why am I here? Will they take more blood after she has rehabilitated me? Did they do something to my brain? Is that why I can't talk? Is that why my hair is short? I need to know!

I lay and stare at the gray panel. I squint my eyes at it. For no reason at all, I stick my too dry tongue out at whoever is watching. Then I feel stupid. Then I don't care.

*****

Gladys says I have to try to walk today. She says the sooner I try, the sooner I'll feel better. I can barely lift my arms. I think Gladys is overly optimistic. I've kept down salted crackers today. And when I drink water it usually stays where it's supposed to. I want to walk and I also don't. When I start walking, I'll be more independent. I'll be able to use the bathroom on my own. They'll take the catheter out. Someone will have to look at me *down there* to take the catheter out. So - I don't really want to walk. I still would rather die.

I've been contemplating killing myself. I've been thinking about God and how He would feel about it. I promised Aunty I'd meet her in Heaven. She wouldn't want me to kill myself. But, I can't see the point in going on. I'm a prisoner in my body and a prisoner in my bed. I know it is unrealistic to hope for escape. Pravda went to great lengths to get me. I don't know why or what they've done to me, but I know they'd have killed me by now if they were done with me. It's safe to assume that I am never leaving.

Gladys comes into my room and changes my IV bag. She leans over me and plumps my pillow. She winks at me and squeezes my hand. She left something in my hand. Gladys bustles back out of the room and I look down at my hand. I turn it over and see a red and white mint in my palm. An unwrapped piece of candy. I look at it and it makes me remember. I remember Aunty. I remember being twelve years old and Aunty telling me about Jesus.

Aunty gave me a candy cane. She said the white stood for Jesus who is sinless and perfect and the red stood for His blood shed for me. She said if you turn it one way it was a "J" for Jesus and if you turn it the other way it's a shepherd's staff. The Lord is my shepherd, I shall not want. I lift the peppermint candy to my mouth and cherish the sweetness and the refreshing mint.

I remember the 23 Psalm. The Lord is my Shepherd, I shall not want. He makes me lie down in green pastures - or a white Pravda bed. He leads me beside still waters. He restores my soul by giving me a Living nurse who cares for me.

Yea though I walk through the valley of the shadow of death -Yea though I wait alone for Pravda to kill me - I will fear no evil. I am not afraid! What can they do to me except my dear Savior lets them! And if He lets them, it is for my good.

Thy rod and Thy staff, they comfort me. The shepherd's staff was a comfort to the sheep. It rescued them when they got tangled in the briars. It fought off the wolves who came to hurt the sheep. The Shepherd cares for me.

Thou preparest a table for me in the presence of mine enemies. I am definitely surrounded by enemies. I've never been more "in the presence of my enemies." But I sit at Christ's table. He will provide for me. I belong to Him, not to Pravda.

Thou anointeth my head with oil. My shaved, short-haired head.

My cup runneth over.

Does it? Am I just lying to myself again? How does my cup runneth over right now? On bad days, Aunty would tell me to count my blessings. If I didn't count them, she would count them for me. What would she count for me today? My eyes get moist as I think of her. Her brilliant blue eyes, her glamorous silver hair, her caring hands. I picture her standing here by my bed, counting:

1. You know Jesus, Ivy. That's more than most of the world can say. You have riches untold! An inheritance in Heaven. God calls you His legitimate child. You stand to inherit every amazing thing God owns.

2. You are loved, Ivy. I love you and your parents love you. Tim and Matt and Harmony and Rosa and Thomas, they all love you, Ivy. Your life has been full of love.

3. You are still alive. God has more for you to do. Maybe you will meet more Pravdanians. Maybe you will get to share Jesus with them. Maybe you will have the wonderful privilege to add more jewels to your Savior's crown before you come to be with me. Maybe one less person will suffer horrible separation from God because you are still here.

Yes Aunty, I have blessings to count. I will choose to think about them instead of the darkness. When the cloud of depression threatens its acid rain, I'll put up my umbrella and count until the Sun chases the clouds away. Thank you, Father. Thank you for this day. Thank you for Gladys. I love You. Surely goodness and mercy shall follow me all the days of my life, and I will dwell in the house of The Lord forever.

Chapter Thirty-One
If I Make My Bed In Hell

Three doctors stand at the foot of my bed. Gladys is standing by my head, hovering and petting me maternally. Her nervousness is making me nervous. The doctors don't usually come in my room. These doctors don't wear masks. There are two men and the woman, Patrice, who first spoke to me when I woke up. I wonder if either of the men could be the man who came in last week and gave me the panic attack. I'm trying to focus on my breathing. I don't want another attack. I have to stay calm. Gladys' frazzled patting isn't helping.

I haven't seen Patrice since that first day, and I was worried that she had been fired - or worse - for her mistake. She thought I was someone else, and she told me I was pregnant. That was crazy. I can only imagine how awful it would be to be pregnant. I'll never know. I came in here a virgin and, sadly, I will die in here a virgin. I'll never know love or marriage. Don't think that way. Count your blessings, Ivy.

The two men and Patrice have been mumbling quietly to each other. Their conversation comes to an end and they pivot to face me. I feel my stomach turn and I lift my hand to signal Gladys. She puts the little vomit pan beneath my face and I take deep breaths, trying not to fill the pan for the third time today. The nausea is the worst thing about my slow recovery.

One of the men reaches for a switch and the two lights at the foot of my bed beam white light at my legs. Gladys takes the empty pan away from me and presses the button that lowers my bed. She lays me down flat for the first time in days and I begin to panic. I hear my heart rate accelerate faster and faster on the tattle-tale machine. I can't even pretend that I'm not terrified. They can hear my fear in loud, staccato beeps. Gladys puts a mask over my mouth and the oxygen rushes in. I try to look past the clearish hump covering my mouth and nose to see what they are doing. Is it time to take my blood now?

Patrice pulls my bed covers off of my feet and legs. My heart rate beeps faster and louder in my ears, they are going to look at me *down there*! That's what the lights are for! I try to move away. I try to push the covers back down over myself with frantic hands. I cross my legs and lock them as tears pour from my eyes. I've never been so humiliated and full of shame. I fight with adrenaline fueled strength to escape the hands that are clamped around my ankles. But I am not strong enough.

Gladys grabs a hold of my hands and lies across my chest, pinning me down. I am filled with malignant fury at her betrayal. Her bulky form blocks my view of the doctors and leaves me with only the feel of their white plastic gloves on my legs.

I scream into the oxygen mask and hear myself yelling, "Stop!"

It is the first word I have spoken since waking. In the terror, I have found my voice again. It is no comfort to me in the darkest moment of my life.

*****

The two men are gone now, but Gladys and Patrice are still in my room. I'm turned away from them, my legs unstrapped and re-covered with my blanket. I still have the oxygen mask over my mouth and nose. My chest is heavy with the shame of being looked at. I'm crying quietly into my pillow when I hear Patrice greet another unwelcome doctor into my room.

"Set it up right there," Patrice says.

I curl into a ball. My armpits feel sweaty with the dread of what they have planned for me next. My catheter is gone now and it really hurt when they took it out. Without it, maybe I could escape. I ask God to give me the strength to make a run for it. He has done that in the past; given His people extraordinary strength to defeat their enemies. Would He do that for me now? I can't stay here. I have to try to get out. I know I can stand, but can I run? Please, God? Please! Help me!

I slowly lift the oxygen mask away from my face and ease it up over my forehead. At least I don't have to worry about it getting caught in my hair. The elastic of the mask slides through the short stubble and slips easily over my shaved head. Nothing else is holding me down. The IV came out yesterday because I've been eating solid food for days now. I begin to inch my legs towards the edge of the bed, praying that no one is looking at me.

I'm almost there.

I'll slide off and move as fast as I can to the door. If God will just keep them looking the other way, I might have a chance. I think of the rod in my ear. What if they push the button? If I get far enough away from the signal will the button still work?

Sliding my legs over the side of my bed, my bare feet hit the cold linoleum floor. My eyes come up level with the gray panel. I forgot about being watched. I also forgot about the heart monitor. I pull the wires from my chest and run. An unending tone blares from the heart monitor as I stumble through the doorway into a white hallway.

I'm alive and aware. Aware of the cool tile beneath my bare feet. Aware of the tremble in my atrophied muscles. Aware of the shortness of my gown. Aware that I am being chased.

At the end of the white hallway, I come to a T. To the left is more of the white hallway, to the right a pair of double doors. I plunge through the swinging doors to my right and my momentum carries me into a metal railing. The metal railing keeps me from falling a hundred feet to my death. I am standing high up on a grated metal walkway in a noisy, auditorium sized room. Looking over the railing, the massive room buzzes with activity.

Pravda workers, below me and unaware of me, move between computer monitors and strange machines. Large red pipes run all around the room. The pipes are shiny and they draw my gaze, zigzagging around and over the machines, sometimes running straight through them. The hum of a pump is loud in my ears. In the lull of each pumping noise, I hear a sloshing sound - like the slosh of the ocean when it breaks on the shore. In the center of the room below, the starting point - or ending, I'm not sure - of the red pipes is a gigantic glass cylinder of churning red liquid.

It is blood.

The pipes aren't red.

The pipes are filled with blood. Gallons and gallons of blood is circulating around the room.

"It's something isn't it?"

I start at the voice behind me and feel the vertigo of how high up I am. I turn towards the familiar voice. I feel weak like a spaghetti noodle as I lean against the metal railing behind me.

"They sent me to bring you back. They could walk through this door any minute."

I stare in disbelief at a face I know.

A face that has haunted my dreams for weeks.

A face that is covered in sores that don't make sense.

Tim's face. Tim is dressed in blue scrub pants and a white doctor's coat. His father's stethoscope hangs from his neck. I remember the man who stood staring at me in my room last week. I was so terrified of the man in the blue scrubs and white mask. He had a stethoscope around his neck, too. It was Tim. But it can't be! I'm imagining he's here because I'm crazy and this place is crazy.

Tim's brown hair is cut short and it looks wet and spiky. His brown eyes stare intently at me, but I can't take my eyes from his skin. He has advanced patches of the disease on his cheeks and down his neck. His top lip is all bubbled and cracked. It looks like the diseased skin is hanging off of him, like it might fall off at any moment and leave only gory holes in his flesh. How could this happen? Did he lose his healing?

"How?" I whisper and it sounds mostly like English.

"No time," he replies with a sad shake of his diseased head. "This isn't what it looks like and I'm here for you."

I have a million questions on my slow, thick tongue when Gladys pushes the doors open behind Tim.

"She's waiting," Gladys says to Tim and he nods.

Gladys stands waiting. Watching.

"You aren't going to jump, you must come with me now," Tim orders me in the bossy tone he has used on me so many times before.

He winks at me and Gladys can't see it because she is standing behind him. I stare at him, overwhelmed by what it means that he is here. Overwhelmed by the disease on his face. Can he get his Healing back again? Did he lose his Healing because of me? He is here for me?

He found a way to get to me. Somehow, he will get me out of here. I let go of the railing behind me and take a weak step towards him. The exertion and the vertigo take hold of me and my legs crumple beneath me.

Chapter Thirty-Two

Rock A Bye Satan's Spawn

I blink as the blackness clears. I am being carried. I stare at the white hallway and my stomach sinks as I realize we are almost back to the room. The room where they held me down. The room where they watch me. Gladys bustles down the hall ahead of us. Her short pudgy legs hurrying back to her post.

I look up at Tim. I'm in his arms. He doesn't look down at me. I wonder if he is still mad at me. I let him leave. I remember his backpack and his mom's Bible. The Bible is at Jessie's house. When we get out of here, could we get it back? What if Jessie threw it away? Jessie's mansion - that's where Matt is. When I think of Matt, which I try not to do, a dull ache starts in my chest that often takes hours to dissipate. Tim turns his brown eyes down at me, as though he could read my thoughts. As though he knew I was thinking of Matt.

Like Old Faithful, the shame that I always feel under Tim's gaze gushes forth, covering me in self-loathing. I've hurt Tim so many times. Why does he bother with me? I'm not even pretty anymore. My hair is gone and my ear has the tube in it. I'm wearing an ugly hospital gown and my body looks alien beneath it. My stomach is distended and my legs and arms are too thin. Pravda's coma changed me. I'm not at all worthy of Tim's bravery. Not worthy of a good man's faithfulness.

Tim's strong arms hoist me closer to his chest in an embrace. His muscular arms trigger memories. I remember the Inn. The day Aunty died. Tim in a towel. His big brown eyes close to mine without his glasses. I look up again and realize he doesn't have his glasses on. I want to ask, but I know I can't. I can't act like I know him. The sores on his face look strange this close up. I reach up to touch them but Tim jerks his head away and fumbles as though he might drop me.

As we approach the end of the hallway and the door to my room, we pass a large window that looks into my room. I see Gladys and Patrice waiting inside for me. This is the gray panel. It isn't a room for people to watch me, it is a window in the hallway. There isn't anyone sitting by the window and it gives me hope. I'm not being watched all the time like I feared.

Before turning into my room, Tim whispers, "I'll get you out of here. I promise."

Tears slip down my cheeks in response.

"Back in bed now," Tim says loudly for Gladys and Patrice to hear as he lays me gently in the narrow hospital bed.

"Ivy!" Gladys says, clucking her tongue the way Aunty would when she was ashamed of me. "We'll have to restrain you if you try that again."

I wonder if her lecture is for Patrice's sake. Is she really such a loyal slave that she would keep me from escaping? If she is so loyal, could I have been mistaken about her knowing Jesus? How can she love God and serve Pravda?

"We had a deal, Ivy? Remember?" Patrice says as she walks over to us.

I try to remember what she said to me the day I woke up. Something about putting me back in the coma if I disobey. Patrice flips switches on a new machine that Tim has plugged in near my bed.

The machine is white with a black monitor. It looks like a computer. It has a screen that sits above a panel of colored buttons. A wand with a long cord is attached to the side in a little holder. It looks like something I saw in the dentist's office as a child.

"We're going to look at your baby now, Ivy," Patrice says.

This again? I look at her, incredulous, and then look to Tim. I check to see if anyone is watching before rolling my eyes at Tim and shrugging my shoulders. I try to silently convey to him that Patrice is crazy. Tim returns my "this lady is crazy" face with a subtle head shake and sad, downcast eyes.

Tim thinks I'm pregnant too? Intense frustration churns in my chest and I dig for words. I think about how to form them, how to communicate with these people that I am not who they think.

"I'm – not - pregnant!" I find the words I've been searching for and they come out small and quiet instead of strong and defiant like I wanted. At least they sounded like the words I wanted.

Tim looks down at the machine and presses buttons.

Patrice and Gladys pull the covers down below my stomach and I swat at their hands.

"Please, dear," Gladys says, her eyes pleading and maternal again. I still haven't forgiven her for holding me down and I scowl at her and hold tight to my blankets.

"Ivy, if we are wrong and you aren't pregnant, the machine will show us. Let us look and put this whole thing to rest, alright?"

Patrice makes a good point. Let them look and see that I am not pregnant. I look at Tim and he nods imperceptibly. He's here to rescue me. If he thinks I should let them use their machine, I'll trust him. I desperately hope he can get his Healing back when we get out of here. I hope I can trust him in the state he's in now.

Gladys pulls my thin hospital gown up and I see my stomach for the first time in a long time. Months, I guess. My stomach looks strange. I am even thinner now than I was when I left Matt's house. The thinnest I've ever been in my life. But my stomach looks hard and bloated. My confidence falters.

What if I am - pregnant?

How can that even be possible! What did they do to me while I slept like the dead?

Tim moves close to me and reaches for a bottle that sits in a little cup holder on the machine. He squirts cold, clear gel on my stomach. It's like thick, icy water on my skin. Reaching for the wand that is connected to the machine, Tim puts the wand in the clear puddle on my stomach. His face is fixed on the little screen on the black monitor. The wand makes a scratchy sound as it slides over my belly. It sounds like broken headphones when they're plugged into an iPod. The machine's speakers send out a loud crackle.

I let out the breath I've been holding as I stare at the screen. There isn't anything there. Flashes of gray on an otherwise empty black screen. I knew this was a mistake. I can't believe I even entertained the thought! Tim continues to swirl the jelly on my stomach with the noisy wand. I feel my shoulders relax and I lay back against my pillow. A new sound registers on the machine. The static takes form and becomes a syncopated beating. A fast thumping; like water dripping from the rain gutter outside my window at the Inn. I jerk my head towards the screen and lift myself back up onto my elbows.

It can't be!

"There she is," Tim says quietly.

A creature is writhing on the screen. The tiny gray silhouette moves and turns and then rests against a black background. The gray moving thing has a profile; I see a face with a little nose. Tiny hands move into view with fingers so minuscule they are like strands of thread. The machine says this is in me. Tim says this is in me. I blink with confusion. My hands are gripping the rails of my bed and I don't remember lifting them there. There is a thing in me! How did the thing get there? What did they do to me while I slept!

"You can tell the sex?" Patrice asks with surprise.

"No - I was -"

"That's unprofessional, Hale."

My eyes flash from the black and gray movement on the screen to Tim's face. Patrice called him Hale. He chose his father's name for his new identity.

"There is the head," Tim says drawing lines on the computer screen, taking measurements of the writhing alien inside of me.

As I watch it move, I wonder that I can't feel it. How can it move in me, exist in me without me knowing? Tim expertly maneuvers the wand on my belly showing various views of the unmistakable tiny human growing inside of me. He takes several more measurements as I stare at the delicate creature on the screen. Panic begins to well inside of me as my mind finally accepts the truth. I am pregnant.

"How?" I squeak. "What did you do to me?" I wail at Patrice. "Who did this?"

"You have been chosen to be a carrier, Ivy. This is an honor. You may carry the baby that will cure humanity. We impregnated you when you first arrived here."

She says "arrived" as though I came by choice. As though it was the best thing that could ever happen to me, coming here to this shop of horrors. As though they didn't hunt me down and shoot me with tranquilizers and rip me away from the last people who loved me.

Tim gently wipes my stomach clean and then turns to shut down the machine. I feel frozen. I'm still propped up on my elbows just staring at my sticky, shiny stomach. There is something in me, and I don't want it there!

Her propaganda has gone on like a planned speech, "- 12 weeks old. This fetus is a combination of years of genetic experiments and it carries the genetic code of several others who are immune like yourself. We are very hopeful about this baby. You may be the mother of humanity's savior."

Everything she says is wrong.

Everything.

She says the baby is a combination of genes from others like me that they've hunted and captured. They are playing God in their blood worshiping, mad scientist labs - messing with things that only God can control. And they've made me their satanic Petri dish. I'm the devil's Mary. An immaculate conception, a virgin birth, a baby created to save humanity from their disease. I raise my hand to signal Gladys in the nick of time. My vomit fills the little tin and my stomach heaves with the nausea of what they've done to me.

How could this happen? Did God want this to happen? Am I an abomination to Him now? I feel cold and dirty and, for a brief instant, I envision ripping the thing out of myself. My split second daydream is a gory scene of blood and flesh. I flop back on my thin pillow and stare at the delicate crack on the ceiling. I try to leave my body and my pounding heartbeat behind as I float into that small space in my head that still feels like me.

*****

I lay in my small bed with my arms and legs strapped down. My thoughts wander down lightless gray tunnels in a stupor of deep depression. I don't remember deciding to run again, but I do remember them finding me. I remember hiding under a bed in another room after getting lost in an impossible maze of white hallways. I wanted Tim to find me and take me away from here. Dr. Hale Shepherd. That's what Patrice called him.

But it wasn't Tim that found me. It was another doctor. He cursed at me and called for the men in the silver spandex suits. Two of them with white masked faces carried me back to my room. Back to Gladys and her clucking tongue. Back to Patrice and her lectures of broken contracts. Back to prison. Back to the place where they stole from me and turned my womb into a sick genetic experiment. I'm not me anymore. I'm us now. Me and the thing. Me and the It inside. There is more than just me now, but I feel like so much less. I feel lost. I feel so alone.

They took vials of blood from me after Tim showed me the thing. Blood for tests. I wish I still believed that I was here because of my blood. I wish their intention was to drain me dry and let me go to Heaven. This new reality is much worse. The thing inside me won't cure them. Then what? Will they do it to me again and again in the hopes of finding their savior? Am I to live here as a prisoner forever, making unholy child after unholy child for Pravda's hellish purposes?

Even if Tim could get me out of here, I would still be full of Pravda's dark science experiment. I can't kill it. I know I wouldn't be able to do that. I know Tim wouldn't either. I am going to be a mother. If I stay, Pravda will take the It. Will I be sad? Will I be able to watch them pull the small life from my body and then take it away? Will I care? If I run away before it comes out, I would have to keep it. I could never care for it. I don't want to be a mother.

Chapter Thirty-Three

Would You Rather?

I haven't seen Tim since the sonogram. The first few weeks after my escape attempt, I foolishly watched for him. Hoped he would come for me. Then they moved me. Patrice and a silver-suited faceless guard walked me to my new room. No, my new prison. I don't know if Tim even knows where I am now.

I am pregnant. I am pregnant. I say it to myself over and over, but it never feels real. I know it is true, but it doesn't feel real. This thing they put inside me moves now, like a little butterfly inside of my gut. I feel it flutter when I lay down or sit still. It doesn't make me happy. It doesn't make me love the thing.

I haven't spoken much to God. I don't have much to say. I'm not mad. I'm just not anything. I'm not feeling. I am a void. I have become used to the moment by moment failure that is my life.

The first few days in the new room, I tucked myself into a corner near the door and did nothing. I slept excessively, curled in a ball on the padded floor instead of on the pillow-filled, full-sized bed. It was the only rebellion I could come up with. In those first few days, I sat and stared at the sunshine yellow walls.

I am certain the walls were painted yellow to induce cheerfulness, but that color has the opposite effect on me. When I look at them, I think of the golden yellow walls in the African room at the Inn. The room where Matt stayed when he first came to Toccoa. Yellow is a depressing color. To avoid the walls, I slept some more and found Matt in my dreams as well.

The room has a shower, a treadmill, and a TV bigger than the one at the U.R., but not as big as the one in Jessie's basement. There are books and snacks and a microwave. There aren't any windows in the room, but I think there might have been at one time. The far wall has panels, painted the same vomit yellow, but the panels look out of place. I think there were windows behind them. I guess I should be thankful for a prison with so many amenities, but gratefulness is an attitude I can't muster. It is hard to be appreciative when you wish you were dead.

"They" are always watching me in the new room. Not through a mysterious panel in the wall like the last room, though I'd prefer that. Here, in sunshine yellow hell, they have better technology. A camera mounted above my door follows me around the room with an unnerving electronic hum. The only place I am safe from the camera's glinting eye is in the bathroom. The bathroom is a tiny closet with only a toilet. The room is so small I can do nothing in there but what was intended.

After the first few days of my pointless existence, Patrice came to visit me. In her clinical, white-noise tone - as though speaking to a child - she offered me my old room and my old restraints. I looked despondently at her from my place in the corner. She handed me a list of requirements and reminded me that my pregnancy could be completed in the coma if I didn't "comply." She left as pleasantly as she arrived. Her head high and her shoulders back. She disgusts me.

I wish I had been brave enough to continue in my rebellion. I wish I was made of better stuff. But the coma was a fiend-filled, soul-sucking place that I never want to re-live. I asked myself, "Can you spend the next six months being chased through the dark by the hands that claw and drag you beneath black waves, drowning but never dying?" I answered myself, "No, no I can't."

I began to follow the list.

1. Walk or jog gently on the treadmill for thirty minutes at least once a day.

2. Shower after exercising.

3. Take your vitamins.

4. Eat the three meals delivered to your room each day.

5. Do one hour of Yoga.

That first day on the treadmill, I walked. Patrice's list said that I could jog. She may as well have said I could try flying. My legs found the back and forth motion of walking as foreign as my first time roller-skating. Even on the slowest setting I was only able to walk for ten minutes. I shut down the moving belt and collapsed in a crying heap.

Number one on the list was hard, but number two was appalling. The shower is next to the bed, right out in the open - where the camera is always watching. A sink and a towel rack are on the other side of the shower and a red bathrobe hangs from a hook next to the shower door. The shower glass is thick and opaque. To test its transparency, I hung the red bathrobe in the shower and then crossed the room to stand near the camera. The camera followed me to the door with its whirring noise.

From across the room, the bathrobe hanging inside of the white glass shower was an amorphous blur of red and nothing more. Whoever watches will see my skin, but no definition. But that's still too much! The thought of the coma is only slightly more terrifying than the thought of being watched while I shower. I racked my brain for a solution.

Searching the room's drawers and cabinets for the first time, I found extra bed sheets. Draping my extra sheet over the shower wall, I attached it at the top with five pieces of chewed gum. I took my first hot shower in total privacy - and reveled in the small victory I had won against my captors.

Next on the list, take my supplements. The vitamins are a meal in themselves. I take a prenatal vitamin, a vitamin D supplement, a vitamin B supplement, and a vitamin A supplement, Folic Acid, Iron, Calcium and Zinc. Those are each separate pills. I spend several minutes each day swallowing them. The irritating thing is that the back of the prenatal vitamin label says it has ALL the other vitamins in it for 100% of my daily need. So why am I taking them all again? And let me tell you what the side effect of all that Iron is. A lot of fruitless time in the tiny bathroom closet. And a lot of snacking on dried prunes.

Patrice's list requires me to eat three meals a day. The meals are delivered through a flap in my door. Just like prison. Three times a day the flap goes up and a tray slides through. Meal time makes me miss Jessie's kitchen with bacon and Coke and whipped cream; which in turn makes me think of Matt - which in turn makes it hard to eat because of the lump in my throat. But, I force the food down so I won't have to face any more visits from Patrice.

The meals are bland, salt less and uber healthy. Weird varieties of rice, thin slivers of chicken breast or turkey and copious amounts of fresh vegetables. For desert, I get fruit. The only bright side? I haven't had a Gov. Bar in months.

Yoga is the last thing on my list. I spent the first couple of days wondering what in the world a Yoga was. I stood at the camera and asked, "How can I Yoga if I don't know what it is?" No reply came. I don't think they can talk to me through the camera, but you'd think they could at least slip me a note through the door or something. Answerless and Yoga-less, I worried that Patrice would come haul me back to the other room for "breach of contract". But she didn't come. Maybe I was already doing Yoga without knowing it?

Pravda has supplied me with material comforts to assuage my loneliness. The double bed is wonderfully soft and overflowing with pillows. There is a cozy rocking chair in front of the huge TV and a DVD player with hundreds of movies to choose from. The microwave oven is great for heating a cup of water, and there is an unending supply of "pregnancy safe" herbal teas.

Above the microwave is a shelf of snacks - mostly dried fruits and vegetables, canned nuts, and rice cakes. Above my bed, there is another shelf with books for me to read, half of them about my changing pregnant body and the other half steamy romance novels. For the record, I haven't read a page of either.

There are strange things in my room, too. A giant sized purple bouncy ball sits in a corner near the TV. I outgrew bouncy balls about ten years ago. Does Pravda expect me to play with it? Another oddity is the floor itself. The entire room is carpeted in blue vinyl padding like the walls of my elementary school gymnasium. It is squishy, like walking on thick sponges, and it makes a whooshing-suctiony sound with each step.

It took me a few days to notice the lack of anything reflective in my room. There are no mirrors and no metal surfaces. The microwave has a coat of white paint over the door, dulling the reflectiveness of the plastic. The TV screen is flat and absorbs the light instead of reflecting it. Even the faucet of the sink is a dull metal instead of shiny. I have no way of looking at myself.

Pravda has provided me with three changes of clothes. All three are identical flesh-colored body suits. I hated the peach spandex suit when I first put it on. The constraining spandex made me feel like a zombie. And it makes my belly look huge. As the days went by, I grew used to it and comfortable in it. The suits that always looked like one piece are actually two. A thin seam around my ribs conceals a magnetic zipper. I can lower the bottoms of the suit without taking off the top. This is convenient as I now require a hundred pee breaks a day. Another distasteful side effect of being pregnant with Satan's spawn.

Following the list is getting easier. I did twelve minutes on the treadmill the second day. The third day I did fifteen. I have found a surprising sense of accomplishment in watching my progress on the electronic screen. I have begun to enjoy the exertion. I like to picture Toccoa as I walk. I'm passing the UR, there's the old school, there's Harmony's apartment. I hope she's doing okay. I walk to Thomas' house and back each day on my imaginary trek. It doesn't make me sad to remember. I am beginning to build up endurance and I'm sweating by the time I'm done.

*****

Today is my sixth day following the list. After a twenty minute walk on the treadmill and a hot shower in total privacy, I decide to watch a movie. Squatting before the neatly organized movie racks, I look through the hundreds of DVD's. I haven't watched anything yet. I've been trying to hold on to my rebellion by rejecting Pravda's comforts.

But today, for the first time, I'm tired of being sad. I look through the movie titles for something funny, something to make me feel happy again. In the bottom drawer of movies, I make a discovery. The Yoga DVDs: "Yoga for Pregnant Women", "Prenatal Yoga", "Yoga for the First Trimester", "Yoga for the Second Trimester", "Yoga for the Third Trimester", "Yoga Poses to Prepare for Labor and Delivery", "Yoga Poses to Turn a Breach Baby", "Postpartum Yoga", "Yoga to Lose Weight After Pregnancy".

I glance at the camera, irritated. They could've helped me find these days ago. Whenever something goes wrong in the room, I find myself blaming the camera. The watchers are my only option for interaction. When I get mad, it is at them. Interested to finally learn about the Yoga, I put the first DVD in.

"Trinity Divinity" scrolls across the screen in delicate lettering set to calming music. My spirit perks up interested. Maybe Yoga has something to do with God? Maybe Pravda is indulging my faith? Trinity means three. The three persons of God: God the Father, God the Son, and God the Holy Spirit. And Divinity means God. I squint in confusion and skepticism as a woman appears on the screen. She is wearing a spandex suit, but not a silver one like the Pravdanians wear. Hers is black with purple stripes on the legs and it is sleeveless. She is sitting on a blue mat in the middle of an empty room and she greets me with a smile as the music fades.

"Hello. Welcome to Yoga for Pregnant Women. I'm Trinity. I am going to help you ready your body for the changes ahead."

I settle myself onto the floor in front of the television and follow Trinity's instructions. She leads me through strange poses that make me feel self-conscious because I know I am being watched. The poses aren't hard, though they are awkward. I bend my body in half over my protruding belly - reaching for my toes - feeling a burn in the back of my unstretched leg muscles. I find out what the purple bouncy ball is for as Trinity shows me how to support myself on it as we exercise. Trinity folds herself like a pretzel and I attempt to copy her, following her soothing voice through position changes and still moments of deep breathing.

Chapter Thirty-Four

A Room With A View

I am finishing a satisfying lunch of fresh peas and cold turkey when someone enters my room for the first time in over a week. I look up from my rocking chair surprised as Gladys wheels a small cart into my room.

"Gladys!" I chirp, happy to see her - happy to see another person!

Gladys smiles but her smile is forced and doesn't make it to her eyes. Her eyes look sad and nervous. I scowl when I notice the deep purple bruise around her left eye.

"I'll only be a few minutes," she mumbles apologetically. "Just here to change your sheets and do a quick clean up."

I watch in confused silence as Gladys bustles around my small room, changing my sheets, hanging new towels, wiping down the sink and shower. I know we are being watched and I know something is wrong. I don't want to endanger her more by asking her what happened. I mentally run through other things I could ask. Questions I'm dying to know the answers to.

"Gladys?" I ask as she readies a vacuum cleaner. "Did anyone else come in with me?"

Gladys glances nervously over her shoulder at the camera and then back at me. She tips her head in a small nod and then turns on the noisy vacuum cleaner.

Her nod isn't enough information. It could mean that they have Harmony, too. Or even Rosa. Or Gladys might only mean that there are other girls trapped here like me. I try to think of a way to ask her a more specific question without Pravda understanding. I'm dying to know if Harmony is here with me or out there with Matt. That question has been twisting my stomach into knots for weeks.

Gladys vacuums backwards to the door and then hurries to push her cart from my room. She doesn't look at me on her way out or say goodbye. Her absence leaves my room feeling emptier and lonelier than ever. I lie down on my bed and let rivers of depressed abandonment leak from my eyes.

*****

I must have fallen asleep crying because a strange new sound disturbs my dream. I fight to hold onto the imaginary world my dream created—Matt and I are walking outside in the sunlight, hand in hand. I struggle to stay asleep, but the struggle wipes my dream away like Aunty's scrub brush on a stained shirt. Matt's translucence is rinsed away. I open my eyes and remember what he did and where I am. Just like that, the ache in the pit of my stomach returns. Even sleeping brings me pain.

The strange, mechanical noise is grating near my head. It sounds sort of like the movement of the camera, but louder, as it buzzes in my ear. My yellow walls grow brighter with natural light. I sit up astonished as the panels on the wall behind me finish moving to reveal a large window near my bed. I blink in the buttery sunlight and stand up on my bed to look out at a yard full of people.

My room must be partially below ground because my window, though it is at least five feet off the floor, shows a view only a few inches above the green grass outside. I press my hands against the thick warm glass and stare jealously across the neatly trimmed lawn at its inhabitants. It is summer time out in the world. My April birthday went uncelebrated in the nightmare world of my coma. I'm seventeen and pregnant and missing out on the flowers and heat of my seventeenth Georgia summer.

The sun beams high above in an aqua-marine sky full of billowy clouds. A large green courtyard is surrounded on all sides by Pravda's silver paneled walls. The vibrant green lawn is crisscrossed with a perfect grid of lawnmower lines. There are flowerbeds in each corner of the yard and a three-tiered round fountain smack dab in the middle. The fountain sprays diamond faceted streams into the sunlight. Silver-suited masked guards stand stationed in the two corners I can see from my low vantage point.

Young women clothed in peach spandex are scattered across the lawn, enjoying various activities in the fresh air. I long to be out there with them enjoying the beautiful summer day. Some of them are synchronized in graceful Yoga, mimicking an instructor who wears a silver Pravda suit. Others walk leisurely laps around the courtyard in small groups of two or three. A few of the girls are laying on reclining lawn chairs reading books or napping in the sunshine.

The peach-suited young women before me share one common trait. They are all pregnant. I spy openmouthed at Pravda's colony of Carriers. They all look young, around my age. I'm surprised to see how many of them look infected. I thought the carriers would be Living, like me. Some of them look healthier than others, but from what I can see, most of them are showing signs of the disease. All of them have short hair and they all have the tube in their ear. The only difference I can find between us is they are outside and together and I am shut away in this solitary confinement.

I search the faces for Harmony, but she isn't part of this group. I thought I'd feel relieved, instead jealousy surprises me. Harmony is free out there somewhere with Matt. They are both Living now. They have lost me. They have only each other for consoling friendship. They are a church now, two believers together in His name. My lunch of turkey and peas turns like a corkscrew in my stomach.

With bi-polar elation, I recognize one of the girls on the lawn. Her name is Chloe. She was part of our group in Toccoa, but we were never close. She's a few years older than me and she didn't hang out with us much. She was always with her mom. They must have taken Chloe the night they attacked Toccoa. It's been awhile since I felt the stab of guilt for those who died in Toccoa. Chloe probably lost her mom because of me. If I was out there with them, what would she say to me? Maybe she hates me. Maybe that's why Pravda keeps me inside.

Chloe's belly is only a small pooch, she isn't very far along in her pregnancy. She looks less pregnant than me. How can that be if she's been here much longer? Chloe's curvy figure looks provocative in her peach spandex suit. Pregnancy has augmented her already voluptuous chest. Chloe was always pretty. Her curly blondish-brown hair has been shaved, but she wears the pixie cut well. Her skin is red and the disease has cast a shadow over her tan complexion. She walks past my window with another carrier, her lips moving in a conversation I can't hear.

None of the girls notice me down near the ground, built into the cage they seem to be enjoying. I wave furiously and pound on my window but no one turns in my direction. I scowl angrily at the camera on my wall and then turn my gaze back to the yard. Why are they letting me look outside? Is this supposed to cheer me up? Is this some sort of incentive?

Some of the girls are much farther along in their pregnancy than others. I study them and notice with concern that the girls who are farthest along in their pregnancies are equally advanced in the disease. The girls who barely show in their tummies also show the least amount of disease on their faces and hands. The girls with the most protruding bellies are wearing Pravda's special gloves.

I don't think it could be a coincidence. The longer I stay here with this thing in me, the sicker I will get. I've already noticed that my skin is dryer. I can't see my face, but I know it doesn't look healthy anymore. I can feel it in my pores. The disease is taking me again. The buzzing noise makes me jump in surprise and I step back on my mattress as the panels close over my windows, shutting me back into my lonely prison. I turn and stare at the camera. What was the point of that? Five minutes of staring out at a freedom that hasn't been offered to me.

I usually do my Yoga after lunch, but I can't come up with a reason to follow the list today. I lay on my bed, curled in as tight a ball as my belly will allow, and think about Chloe and the other girls. They have something I long for, but at what price? How did they lose their healing? Is it this place? This building? Is that why Tim is sick, too? But that can't be it. Gladys is still Alive. She has her Healing. That means it isn't the tube in my ear. Besides, Tim doesn't have the tube and he lost his Healing.

Is it the baby? Can Pravda's science take away my Healing? I search my heart and mind for Bible verses that have grown dim in my memory. Will God judge me for the thing they put inside of me? The disease is His judgement. And His Love. We're supposed to see it and remember our sin and our need for Him. Rev. Depold said it should drive us like a bullwhip into His healing embrace. At the first sign of a spot, we should run with abandon to the river of His shed blood and plunge head first into the fountain that flows from Immanuel's veins.

I hum the old hymn.

"There is a fountain filled with blood, drawn from Immanuel's veins.

And sinners plunged beneath that flood, lose all their guilty stains."

I sing the old hymn out loud to the camera, my voice cracking pitifully. I don't care how I sound, I only hope they can hear my decision. In that moment of turning to Him, I find a new mission. I feel rejuvenation flow through me. I won't let Satan take my Healing from me. I won't! I belong to Jesus and His Word says NOTHING can pluck me from His hand. Not even this baby.

As His Spirit comforts me, I feel full of new purpose. Someone is watching me. Someone is being paid or forced to watch what I do. I'm going to give them a show. I'm going to sing to my Savior and get on my knees to my Savior. I'm going to stay fresh and untouched by the disease no matter how far along I get in this pregnancy. I'm going to show them what a life of faith can do. No more glaring at the camera. I'm going to pray diligently for whoever it is that is watching and I'm going to show them Jesus.

Chapter Thirty-Five

Is That A Trick Question?

A month of routine has gotten me nothing but a bigger belly and a clear conscience to match my clear complexion. I follow the list: walk, shower, vitamins, food, and yoga. I'm very careful with which yoga DVDs I put in. Some of them are great exercise and nothing more. Those are the ones I do. Some of the other DVDs I've put in - and then taken back out - have been more sinister.

Trinity Divinity tells me I am part of the Divine. And she doesn't mean as an adopted child of God. She tells me to breathe in the universe and feel it filling me with its power. She says I am part of a cosmic force. She is right, but it's not the way she means. She says I'm a goddess.

She lies.

I suspect her lies have played a part in stealing the other Carriers' Healing.

I kneel before the camera several times a day and pray out loud to God. I ask him for the souls of the people who are watching. I ask for His blessing on the baby inside of me. It isn't the baby's fault it's been created by evil. Every day they open the panels and show me the people outside. I watch them for the short time I'm allowed and I learn about them. It's like watching a TV show with no sound. I've given them names based on their looks and personality.

Chloe has an obvious best friend, it's the only girl she ever talks to. I call that girl "Beachball" because her belly is ginormous. She's the most pregnant girl out there as far as I can tell, and each day I'm surprised to see her out there still walking slow laps around the courtyard with Chloe.

Another girl I named "Twizzler." She has short, bright red fuzz on her mostly shaved head and she is always doing Yoga. The other girls switch things up, sometimes walking, sometimes reading, sometimes Yoga-ing. But Twizzler only does Yoga. I've never seen the front of her. Just her back as she bends her thin pregnant body into strengthening positions to match the Pravdanian Yoga instructor.

One of the girls reminds me of Thomas' adopted mom, Ellen, so that's what I call her. She is Asian and petite. She has a kind face. She looks less pregnant than I do and she doesn't look sick like the others. If I were allowed outside, I would want Ellen to be my friend.

There are twenty-three girls in all. Some days there are less than that outside, but never more than twenty-three. I know all of their faces now, but I don't understand why they are allowed outside and I am not. I've been following my list, I've been doing everything Patrice asked of me. I don't know what else to do to prove my compliance.

Each day when the panels close, I fight my hardest fight of the day. I am jealous of the other girls' freedom. I consider looking more like them. I consider ending my prayer times before the camera and my intentionally too loud hymn sings. I covet that time in the sunshine. I can't stand the thought of never going outside again. My solitary confinement is starting to crack me. I fight the fight with the only weapon I have - His Word.

I search my heart and memory for the scripture I memorized in Toccoa. Aunty would be ashamed at how little I retained in our Bible memorization sessions. Pravda hasn't given me paper to write on, but I did find a pen in one of my drawers. I ripped the back cover off of several of the books on the shelf above my bed and wrote down the Bible verses I could remember. So far I have:

> **Ephesians 2:8-9** "For by grace you have been saved through faith and that not of yourselves. It is a gift of God, not of works, lest any man should boast.
>
> **Romans** (I can't remember the verse number) "All have sinned and fallen short of the glory of God."
>
> **Romans (3:23? 6:23?)** "The wages of sin is death, but the gift of God is eternal life through Jesus Christ our Lord."
>
> **I Corinthians 13** "Love is patient, Love is kind, Love does not envy. Love is not boastful or proud, Love is not rude or self seeking. Love is not easily angered, it keeps no record of wrong. It doesn't delight in evil but rejoices with the truth. Love always protects, always believes, always hopes always perseveres. Love never fails."

Genesis 1:1 "In the beginning, God created the heavens and the earth."

Isaiah (?) "All we like sheep have gone astray, we have each turned to our own way, there is none righteous no not one... And The Lord has placed on Him the sins of us all." (I'm pretty sure I don't have this one all right, but it's close)

John 1:1-? "In the beginning was the Word. And the Word was with God and the Word was God. And the Word became flesh and made His dwelling among us. He came to that which was His own and His own did not receive Him. But to all who did receive Him, He gave them the right to be called children of God. And we have beheld his Glory, the Glory of the only begotten, full of grace and truth."

John 3:16 "For God so loved the world that He gave His only Begotten Son that whosoever believeth in Him would not die but have everlasting life."

Psalm 23 "The Lord is my shepherd, I shall not want. He makes me lie down in green pastures, He leads me beside still waters, He restores my soul. He leads me down paths of righteousness for His name's sake. Yea, though I walk through the valley of the shadow of death I will fear no evil for thou art with me. Thy rod and thy staff, they comfort me. Thou preparest a table for me in the presence of my enemies, thou annoinest my head with oil, my cup runneth over. Surely goodness and mercy shall follow me all the days of my life and I will dwell in the house of The Lord forever. Amen."

Jeremiah 29:11 "For I know the plans I have for you, declares The Lord. Plans to prosper you and not to harm you. Plans to give you a hope and future."

Psalm 37:4 "If you find your delight in The Lord, He will give you the desires of your heart."

That last one was always one of my favorite verses. It's my favorite because it's like a trick. Not that God is trying to trick me, it's just that the verse is like a trick question. At first you read it and you think, "Sign me up! I'll do whatever it takes to have God give me all my heart's desires." You're like, "Aw yeah, I'm gonna get what I want from God." But then, you see that you have to follow the instructions first. You have to find your delight in God alone FIRST.

So, you go after Him. You read his Word and you study who He is and what He's like and you fall in love with Him. Because He's amazing. And then, bang! You realize now that you love Him so much, your heart's desires have changed. Now you only want what He wants for you. Before, you wanted to be rich or to marry Mr. Hotty or to have lots of great stuff. But now, you want more of Him. You want other people to know Him. You want His will for your life. Find your delight in Him and He'll *change* the desires of your heart is what it should say. But when you figure it all out you just love Him more for it.

It is my heart's desire to get out of this place. It is my heart's desire to stand in the sunshine. But if it isn't what He wants for me then I will lay it on the altar and believe in His great goodness anyway. He wants me to be alone for a reason and He promises that it is for my good. I am hanging on to that promise like a tightrope-walker dangling off the wire by one toe.

I have bits and pieces of other verses written down. I think about them during the day and try to remember them better. I sing *Jesus Loves Me* and *The Old Rugged Cross* and *Amazing Grace* at the top of my lungs to my captive audience. I can't be sure that they can hear me through the camera, but I sing anyways. And, in between all of that, I make a gazillion trips to the bathroom. Yay pregnancy. I'm also fairly certain I have hemorrhoids. Not cool.

*****

A wailing noise wakes me sometime in the night. It niggles at my sub conscience and pulls me from a restless sleep. I fumble for the light beside my bed as another muffled shriek sends goose bumps up my arms. The painful cry echoes from across my room. I'm baffled and yet unaffected. I'm in Pravda. Who knows what experiments are taking place, what servants are being tortured. I hope it isn't Gladys screaming. I have to pee, as usual, so I shuffle across my padded floor to the little closet I practically live in these days.

In the tiny bathroom, another scream echoes louder and clearer through the vent on the wall. Muffled voices bounce through the ventilation and I bend to listen. One of the voices sounds like Tim! His involvement piques my curiosity and ploughs up doubts that I had barely buried. Why is he part of whatever is making the girl scream in anguish? I've been worried that something happened to him. I'm relieved that he's alright, but new worries about his loyalties flood my mind.

The girl wails and weeps and Tim's voice gets more urgent. I can't make out what he's saying. Other voices shout and echo through the duct work and the tension of what is happening rooms away has me transfixed. The girl grunts and groans and I realize I'm hearing one of the carriers giving birth. I cradle my stomach and pray for the girl who is in painful labor somewhere close by. I think of the different carriers I've seen outside. Beachball is the most obviously far along. I wonder if it's her. Chloe will be worried about her friend.

I lean against the wall, perched on the toilet for hours as the girl cries and labors to birth a new candidate for savior. I hear Tim's soothing voice as he encourages and cares for her and it soothes me. He is still Tim. The best man I've ever known. The girl doesn't know how blessed she is to be receiving his gentle care. I miss him and the girl's cries make me hurt with loneliness.

I hear the voices grow in fervor - all of them talking at once - the baby is coming. A throaty bleat echoes through the pipes, a newborn baby's first cry. I smile and tears spring to my eyes in the joy of the precious moment I've overheard. I stand up and stretch my cramped legs and turn the light off, ready to climb back into bed. Another scream fills my little bathroom and my blood goes cold. I flip the light back on and drop to my knees, pressing my ear to the vent.

The girl is sobbing and begging. She's asking for her baby. The baby is crying. My hands are shaking and my ear hurts as I press it hard against the metal vent. The baby's cries are incessant and I'm desperate to know what is happening, to hear the baby comforted by its mother. The cries cease suddenly and a long silence hangs with unanswered questions. Did they give the baby to its mother? Does it nurse contentedly at her breast?

A heartbreaking wail hurtles down the pipes and fills my bathroom like the cries of the damned. My brow is wet with cold sweat. My back is aching from hunching against the vent, but I can't straighten. I know the baby is dead. The broken girl's raw anguish tells me what happened in the room not far from mine. Whatever Pravda was looking for in this newborn, they didn't find it. Pravda killed her baby. And, somehow, Tim was part of that.

Chapter Thirty-Six

Make Up Your Mind

I dreamed of Matt last night. We were holding each other under the golden canopy by the firelight. We talked and kissed and touched. He told me he loved me over and over again. And I believed him. And I loved him too. It's hard to face the day with the memory of his lips on mine still lingering.

Harder still, last night's haunting cries are still echoing in my head. Questions that sleep didn't erase are pricking at my wounded mind. What is Tim doing here? Is he truly lost? Part of Pravda? Will I have to watch this baby inside me die? Will Tim hold my hand when they execute my child? I know the baby won't meet Pravda's impossible requirements because Pravda is looking for Jesus - and they won't find Him in my womb. He has already come and gone from this earth. Pravda refuses to look up and see Him where He is now.

After my morning thirty minute walk, I'm waiting for the shower to get warm. I'm wrapped in my red bathrobe when the door to my room opens. Gladys cleaned my room yesterday, so I wasn't expecting her back for another week. But it isn't her.

Tim steps into my room, pushing the baby picture machine in ahead of him. No one else is with him and we stand and stare at each other in silence. He ever so slightly leans his head towards the camera to remind me they are watching. I allow the disappointment to show on my face. We can't talk. We can't act like we know each other. I fight the part of my brain that is urging me to run to him and feel his arms around me. God help me; I've never been so lonely, so happy, and so confused in the same moment.

"I'm Dr. Hale Shepherd. Do you remember me?" Tim says, lifting a gloved hand to his chest in introduction.

I stare at his hand. He *is* one of them now. He's wearing the gloves and everything. I remember when he carried me back to my room. He said he was here for me. That he would get me out of here. I want so much to trust him.

I don't know how *not* to trust him.

He is Tim and he has always taken care of me. Is this it? Has he come to rescue me like he promised? Maybe last night was a nightmare for him, too. He won't wait another day to take me and my baby out of here. For the sake of the camera, I take a step back from him. I try to look scared. We've been apart, but I know him well. I see the relief in his eyes. He was worried I would ruin it.

He follows my act, "You know what I am here to do, Ivy. We have to look at your baby. You aren't going to make me call for someone to hold you down are you?"

I shake my head "no" with tears in my eyes. The camera may see fear but my tears are joy, relief, and elation to have a friend in my prison cell.

"Please lay down on your bed and we'll get this over with quickly," he says, his voice husky and quiet.

My lonely ears hear love and concern in his tone, though I may be imagining it. The sound of a friendly voice is like music, a melody from the past. The past when I was safe and when I was loved. It has been so long since I felt either. My body is weak with relief at the sight of him. I want to whoop with glee that he found me.

In an effort to keep the joy from showing on my face, I sternly remind myself that there is no way out of here. How can Tim rescue me from Pravda's security or the tube in my ear that has made me a carrier slave? I feel like a schizophrenic as I argue with my negative thoughts - simply knowing that he knows where I am is a comfort to me.

Tim stands waiting for me to comply, so I walk to my bed and lay down. When it's time to run, he'll let me know. I pull the covers up to my widening waist and open my bathrobe to expose my belly. Tim plugs the machine in next to my bed and fiddles with the colorful buttons.

My heart pounds against my ribs as Tim turns to check if I'm ready. He looks me over quickly and pauses for a moment to look in my eyes. I'm wearing only the red bathrobe. I'm glad the heart monitor is gone so Tim can't hear how nervous I am. I am sweaty after my thirty minute walk on the treadmill and self-conscious of how terrible I must look. My hair has been growing. It's now a 3 inch long halo of frizz around my head. I haven't seen my face in months. I haven't put on makeup or plucked my eyebrows or shaved my armpits. I am hideous.

Tim on the other hand looks - really nice. He must have gotten contact lenses because he isn't wearing his glasses. He works at the computer screen without squinting. The spectacle wearing nerd who left Toccoa with me couldn't see farther than a foot away without his thick brown glasses. His hair is short and styled somewhat messy, but it looks carefree and handsome.

This new Tim - in this new life - looks older, professional and confident. He seems taller and more filled out. He carries himself the way his dad did, smarter than most people yet humble and intuitive. The Tim I used to know was from another place and another life. His overly bright optimism, his lack of finesse, his sheltered dorkyness, it's been rubbed away by the steel wool of loss and circumstance. His Tim-ness is mostly gone and I kinda miss it.

Tim's scattered stubble has grown into a light beard during our months apart. The rugged smudge of hair around his square jaw diminishes the scarlet patches of LS on his face and around his lips. Seeing the disease on him hurts my heart. I know it's mostly my fault. He was on his own with no one. He came here to work for the enemy and I can only assume he was looking for me.

Tim never trusted Matt. He knew if I went with Matt, I would wind up here. And he was right. So he came for me and somewhere along the way he must have made compromises. Pravda stole his Healing. I didn't think he was capable of walking away, but he must've gotten lost.

His lips are pursed in concentration as he types something into his machine. Staring at him, soaking him in, I study his lips. The last time I saw him, he was carrying me. I was cradled in his arms and I remember looking up at the left side of his face. That's where the sores were, on his top lip. But today, the LS on his lips is on the far right side and mostly on the bottom lip. That can't be right. I must be remembering it wrong. I was barely coherent that day. The disease doesn't clear up or move around.

I stare intently at him while he fiddles with the wand that is attached to the machine. Tim shoots glances at me as though he's barely paying attention to the screen before him. He scratches at one of the sores on his lower lip and the cracked yellow skin falls off, drifting down to land on the panel next to his hand. I feel my face cringe in disgust. Then, I realize he caught my grossed out reaction and I feel my cheeks blush.

But Tim doesn't look bothered by my stares. I feel like he wants me to notice something, but I don't know what. With his back to the camera, Tim winks sideways at me. I look away ashamed. Ashamed that I was staring. Ashamed of him for being so blasé about losing his Healing. He seems proud of himself! Mostly I'm ashamed of myself for finding him handsomer as a zombie than I did when he was Living and would have done anything for me. Twisted, Ivy.

"This is cold," Tim says in warning as he squirts the clear liquid on my stomach.

My eyes widen and I inhale through my teeth as the cold goo hits my warm skin.

"We might be able to determine the sex of the baby this time," Tim says quietly.

A shiver runs across my neck and down my arms. I'm terrified and the fear takes me by surprise. I have avoided thinking too much about the baby. I don't want to bond with it. I don't want *it* to be there at all. Going from an "it" to a "he" or a "she" forces more reality on me than I want to cope with.

"Are you alright?" Tim asks in response to the embarrassing chill that just shook me like a small seizure.

I bite my lips and close my eyes. I don't trust myself to say anything.

The wand moves around on my stomach, but I keep my eyes closed. I don't want to watch the screen. I don't want to know. Then the fluctuating echo of a tiny heart beat pours from the speakers of Tim's machine. It's so fast and so alive.

"Look, Ivy," Tim entreats in a whisper.

I find Tim's eyes first. One knowing stare between the two of us that this thing they've done to me is wrong and that neither of us are okay with it. Then, I obey and turn my head to the white-gray movement on the screen. It is fully a baby now. Last time I saw it, it looked like a fish with a face. Now, I watch it move its arms and legs, bend its knees and curl its fingers. Tim moves the wand around to change the view and we see the top of its little head and the profile of a perfect face.

"You are almost twenty weeks along," Tim says, entranced by the life form on the screen.

"How many are there?" I ask stupidly.

"Just one, thank goodness!" Tim laughs.

I squinch my eyes, he didn't understand my question. "Not how many babies, how many weeks?"

"Oh. Haven't you read any of your books? There are forty. The average pregnancy is forty weeks. You are just about halfway. And your baby is eight and a half inches long and just under a pound."

Halfway. Halfway to what? Halfway to motherhood? Halfway through my prison sentence? Or halfway until Pravda kills this baby and then starts it all over again? Halfway leaves months of questions and waiting.

"I think it's a girl. A little rose..."

My eyes fly from the screen to Tim's face. Is he trying to tell me something?

"I have a little girl, myself," Tim says pleasantly as though making doctoral conversation. "I adopted her a few months ago. She's precious. Long dark eyelashes and a sweet smile. She loves Mickey Mouse."

Tears leak from the corners of my eyes and I've lost the will to play our acting game. Tim has Rosa and she is safe? Did he find Jessie's house? Did they bring Rosa here when they brought me? I don't know how he did it, but I'll never be able to thank him enough. Knowing she's safe, knowing she's with him, I lay my head back on my pillow and cry.

"I'm sorry," Tim says.

I cover my face with my hands, spiraling into teary oblivion, and worry that Tim will leave before I'm able to stop. He wouldn't have told me this if we were escaping. He wouldn't have needed to. He could tell me later when we're safe. He's sorry because I'm crying and he's sorry because we aren't leaving. I knew it.

"No, I was wrong," Tim interjects as though I'm not weeping. "It's a boy. You see right here? Yup, that's a boy."

I wipe at my blurry wet eyes and look with confusion at where Tim is pointing on the screen. Did he only say it was a girl so he could bring up Rosa? Does he really have her? I feel like I'm losing my mind! This code thing isn't working and now I'm having a boy and I think Rosa is okat but I'm not sure. I'm so frustrated!

Tim is wiping at my stomach with a towel and I grab it away from him to wipe myself off. He looks at me and I can't read what he's thinking.

Obviously this isn't an escape attempt and Tim's presence has brought more questions than answers. I want to get out of here! I can't stand this place one more day! I try so hard to tell him that with my eyes, but he looks away and gathers the cords of his stupid machine.

Maybe he doesn't want to leave now that he has his dream job. How many opportunities are left out there to be a doctor? Like, none! He has Rosa by himself? Or with someone else? Maybe that's what made it possible for him to leave his Healing behind. He's moved on. He has a family and job. That's more than anyone can hope for these days. Heaven knows someone must have taught him how to fix that awful haircut of his! He's safe, he's got some zombie girl, and he's probably rich because he works for Pravda. How can he do this to me?

"Thank you for cooperating," he says and then he wheels his machine away from me and slips out of my door.

Fury takes me. I scream through my teeth and reach for something to throw. I pull books from the shelf above me and wing them at the camera and at the panels that block my window and at the door that Tim left through.

"Let me out!" I scream at the camera. "I don't want to do this!" I wail and fall to my knees on the blue padded floor. "Please?" I beg through eyes blind with tears.

Chapter Thirty-Seven

Let Me Tell You Where You Can Stick That

I quit eating. I quit everything. No treadmill, no shower, no vitamins. I'd go back to my spot in the corner on the floor, but my freaking back hurts too much. So I've been lying in bed for two days. Two days of non-compliance. Two days of "list" strike. Two days of spitting in Patrice's face. Two days of I don't give a care. Want more? I've got more - I've had two days to think of them.

I can't keep playing their game. I tried. I wanted to do this triumphantly. I wanted to "do all things through Christ" yadda yadda. But I'm not perfect. I'm sorry God. I give up.

The lunch tray came through the hole in my door an hour ago. It smells beyond delicious. I didn't eat dinner last night or breakfast this morning. Whoever drops off my meal has collected the previous meal trays untouched. I imagine I'll be seeing Patrice sooner or later. I've been planning speeches for her in between my "depressed pregnant woman with low blood sugar" naps.

I'm going to tell her where she can put her list. I'd rather live in the coma than in this hopeless solitary confinement. Maybe I haven't learned anything. Maybe I'm repeating my immature mistakes. Toccoa felt like a prison and I couldn't wait to be free. Until I was free and I knew how much I had lost. This room would probably sound like heaven to someone who is starving. Someone who lives with abuse. I'm sure I'm a spoiled brat. But I'm wicked depressed. Insane with loneliness. Desperate for a kind word. Companionship. Maybe I could talk them into giving me a puppy.

They show me the other girls enjoying each other and the sunshine and it is acid in my veins. Tim pops up in my life again and the acid burns through to my bones. I don't even know him anymore. He's got LS all over his face and I sure as heck don't know who has his heart. He didn't even look sad when he left. I guess I'll have to see him again for the next session of "check out your growing Satan spawn baby" pictures. I won't react next time.

I won't care what I look like. I won't let my heart pound. I won't share any private moments of intimate eye contact. Tim can do what he wants with his short time left. If Aunty and the Elders had it right, we have less than a year left on earth. Maybe six months. I'll let Pravda put me back under and the time will slip by. Jesus will be back for me soon. Heaven is just around the bend.

I long to be with Aunty again. And my dad will be there, too. Dad and I will reunite on golden streets, even though we've been in this same building for months. Harmony and Rosa will be there. I can't wait to hold onto that sweet little dark-haired angel and never let her go. It's weird to think about seeing Matt in Heaven. He's Alive now. I wonder if we'll remember all the stuff between us. I wonder if we'll have feelings for each other there. I wonder what he's doing now. Who he's with. If it's Harmony.

It's almost time for the panels to open. It's the same time every day. After lunch, after yoga, short nap, panels open, then dinner. Instead of the panels, it's my door that opens. I don't turn to look. I maintain my blank stare at the puke yellow walls. I know it's her. I don't know how, but I am sure. My pout was as good as sending her a hand written invitation. I hear her shoes as they pad across my squishy floor. She sighs as she sits down near the foot of my bed.

She's like the undead version of Aunty. Aunty would come to my room when I was being "hormonal" and she would sit on my bed. Aunty would pet my back and stroke my hair. She came with life giving words and reminders of who I am and Who I belong too. She came to heal. This woman with silver hair like Aunty's and trim legs like Aunty's comes to control. To threaten. To remind me who she is and who she works for. I hate her as much as I loved my Aunty.

"What do you need, Ivy?" Patrice asks.

I furrow my brow and stare at the lint balls on my blanket.

"We had a deal, Ivy, and you are breaking that deal."

There it is. Here comes the coma talk. She better be ready to put her money where her mouth is. I have no desire to continue on with our deal. Pregnancy sucks. My boobs hurt. My ankles are so full of water they slosh when I walk. My bladder has shrunk to the size of a lima bean. Charlie horses wake me in the night and then heart burn keeps me from falling back to sleep. Mine is a miserable existence. The coma sounds like a vacation.

"Ivy, I can't help you if you won't talk to me. How can I make your stay here nicer?"

I turn to see who is in my room, because it can't be Patrice. Patrice isn't Pravda's concierge; she's Pravda's hit man. Nope, it's her. Unless Pravda has found a way to clone her ugly orange face.

I roll back over.

"Ivy, please. You are so special to us."

"Hmph."

"Would you like some chocolate?" she asks in her patronizing, little kid voice.

She disgusts me.

And, yes, I would like some chocolate, but I need a bigger payoff. I can't believe she is sitting here offering me things. I'm furious. But more with myself than with her. This is working? I was such an imbecile to believe her threats. To let her bully me. I bet I'd be outside right now if I had stuck to my guns a little longer in the beginning.

"Why?" I ask, my voice muffled against my pillow.

"Well -" she starts hesitantly, "many pregnant women crave chocolate and I thought it might make you feel better. It isn't part of a healthy diet, but a little indulgence once in a while never hurts."

She is such a moron.

"Why do you open the panels?" I clarify. "Why open them if I can't go outside?"

"Panels?" she has the audacity to play dumb with me.

"THESE PANELS!" I scream, pulling myself up onto my knees and smacking my fists on the panels beside my bed.

I turn a crazed face to Patrice, meeting her startled eyes with my own eyes wide and crazy and my breath coming out in snorts.

"They've opened?" She asks with an oblivious look on her carrot-colored, made up face.

"Yes! They've opened! Every day!" I shout. "Why?"

"I will have to look into that," she says in a small voice that I find even more irritating than her child-speak voice.

She genuinely seems baffled and I begin to doubt myself. I lose some of my steam.

"Why do they get to be outside?" I ask angrily.

"Ivy, we are keeping you separate from them for your own good."

"My own good! My own good? I'm losing my mind in here! I can't take another second of Trinity Divinity and canned peanuts! I need fresh air," I beg. "I need to feel the sunshine!"

"We are curing humanity here. Serving the world," Patrice defends.

I remember that I've heard those words before. It's Pravda's motto. Patrice is so indoctrinated she's become part of the lie.

"The other girls have begun to manifest the disease after prolonged periods of socialization. We are concerned that there is an element of infection we do not yet understand. Your immunity, throughout the entire pregnancy, is of utmost importance to your fetus. Don't you want to heal humanity, Ivy? Can't you put aside your needs for the good of the entire world? We are asking you to be a hero. A savior. I will give you anything you want. Name it."

"I want to go outside. With the others. I won't lose my Healing. I will prove it to you. I'm not immune. I'm Healed! I want a Bible and a devotional book, preferably something by Charles Spurgeon. Give me two weeks of time outside and I will have a spotless complexion and healthier blood than any of the other girls," I blurt pieces of the speech I had planned, my words running together.

"No."

"I won't eat. You'll have to put me back in a coma if you want me to live long enough to carry this baby. I am sick of this!"

"I'll see what I can do about a Bible. I do want you to be comfortable here."

"Are you -" I start to interrupt.

"Ah ah," she holds up a white-gloved finger to silence me. "You don't understand, Ivy, and I don't expect you to. You've been indoctrinated and lied to since childhood. It is precisely your uneducated, fantastical view of life that keeps you from understanding the science of contagion and what we are protecting you from. Do you know you are breathing filtered oxygen here in this marvelous room? We have purified your air. We are giving you the gift of longer life! Even the Director himself isn't afforded that luxury on a twenty-four hour basis."

I stare at her dumbfounded. We might as well be from different countries. Different planets. We speak different languages.

"I'll work on getting you the books you asked for. I don't see how it can hurt. I'll expect you to eat your lunch now. I imagine it's getting quite cold."

I stare morosely after her as she retreats from my room.

Chapter Thirty-Eight

A Labor Of Love

Another day of not eating. Hunger pains are shredding my stomach like a cheese grater. The trays keep arriving at my door, but I don't roll over to look at them. The temptation is too terrible. A chocolate bar came with last night's dinner. It is still sitting there on the little stand built into my door. I wish they would take it when they take the uneaten trays. I drool on my pillow every time I think about what it would taste like.

The baby is kicking me more often. I think my starving, noisy stomach is keeping him awake. I feel him moving all the time now. I don't hate him. I feel things for him that I can't explain. A lot of sadness and worry. I wonder what it would be like to be pregnant and happy. To have made a baby with Matt and be excited about having him. Would the baby look like Matt or like me? What will this baby look like? Will Pravda kill him before I get a chance to hold him?

An hour after they take away the third dinner I have not eaten, the flap on the door goes up again. I don't want to look, but my starved body rolls to see what is there without the consent of my stubborn will.

There are two books sitting next to the untouched chocolate bar. My stomach growls its frustration with me. Sliding off of my bed, too hungry and too weak to walk, I crawl across my blue padded floor to the door. Refusing to look at the candy, I pull the two books quickly off of the little shelf and turn my back to the door. The first book is a Bible. I hold it to my chest and allow a fresh batch of tears to fall quietly. I know He's been with me all along, but He feels even nearer now.

The second book is a devotional book I recognize. It isn't by Spurgeon, but I already know I will love it. "My Utmost for His Highest" by Oswald Chambers. Aunty owned this book and read it often. God couldn't have sent me a sweeter gift. Still sitting on the floor near the door, I cross my legs Indian style and open the devotional.

A paper football hides inside the front cover.

Tim.

I remember that day in the cave that we ran around flicking footballs at each other. Tim tried to kiss me underneath Rosa's fort. How might things have turned out if I had let him? I would have gone with him instead of Matt. Maybe Pravda wouldn't have found me. But then, Matt wouldn't have found Healing. I unfold the note with a desperate hunger for information. The baby inside me gives a little kick to remind me he is there. I read:

> Can't say much. Don't throw this away. Tear it up in little pieces and let it down the sink drain. I'm proud of you. I see you singing and praying and trying so hard to be brave. Our friend is here, too. She is like you, but not doing well. We can't leave without her. I am working on it. Pray. The butcher's daughter is happy and healthy. Safe. We miss you. You are winning, don't give up. You've almost beaten them. Also, you still have family here. Another has joined them. Not as good at breaking in as he was at breaking out.

I read it over and over. I do my best to show no reaction. My nose runs and my eyes brim. My chest feels like it will explode with the feelings I have locked inside. I read the letter enough times to memorize it. Its contents are better than sunlight and better than chocolate. Tim has Rosa! She is safe! Harmony is here! Matt is here! Tim is going to get us out of here! Tim must still care for me, I haven't lost him to Pravda. I'm relieved, ecstatic, desperate, and ten more emotions I don't have names for - and all of it trapped internally.

As I wash the tiny pieces of Tim's shredded football down my sink, a tear slides unchecked down my cheek. Matt is here. I ache that he is somewhere so close by, but I can't get to him. He must have tried to rescue me. With renewed vitality, I pace around my room. My soul is a tornado of emotions and the pent up energy keeps me walking circles for an hour. Matt came for me. He loves me and I love him. What he did ripped a hole in my heart, but time has been mending the gash. I miss him so much it feels like a tangible thing, radiating off of my body.

Will Tim be able to get Matt out? Tim's letter implies that Matt is in the part of Pravda where they are keeping my dad and Aunty Betty. Matt said he met my dad in jail. What if Tim can't get in there? What if Tim doesn't help them? What if he only rescues me and Harmony? He doesn't know Matt is Alive. I have to tell him somehow. The letter says I have to destroy it and leaves me no way of communicating back.

I feel horrible for the jealous feelings I've been having towards Harmony. All this time she's been here. She's pregnant and alone like me. But Tim says she isn't doing well. Is she sick? Is she falling apart from the mental strain of captivity and pregnancy? Is it her baby that is not okay? I can't believe she's here. I can't believe she's pregnant too. I can't believe how relieved I am that she is not with Matt! I am a horrible friend. I should be crushed that she ended up trapped here, too.

Why don't I see her outside with the rest? Maybe they are keeping her in confinement, too. Which would mean she is holding tight to Jesus and she hasn't lost her Healing. I hope she is okay and I hope whatever is wrong with her gets better. I hope she can pull her fragile self together. Tim says we aren't leaving because of her. If she continues to not do well, will we have to stay here and wait for her?

Ivy! What a horrible thought! Of course we will wait for her!

If Tim knew what a horrible person I was, he might consider leaving me here. He said he sees me pray and he sees me sing. Does he watch me through the camera? It is weird and comforting to know that some of the time a friend is watching me instead of an enemy. He said I'm winning. Does he mean by starving myself?

Patrice didn't know that the panels were opening. Could it be Tim opening them for me from where he watches? He wanted me to know there were more girls here. He wanted me to fight for time outside. This is all part of the plan somehow! I can hold out now. Now I know that I am not alone and this fight is worth fighting. The people that I love are here with me.

I flip open the devotional again and ask God to give me what I need. On the page marked Sept. 18th I read:

> **His Temptation and Ours**
>
> "We do not have a High Priest who cannot sympathize with our weaknesses, but was in all points tempted as we are, yet without sin." **Hebrews 4:15**
>
> Until we are born again, the only kind of temptation we

> understand is the kind mentioned in James 1:14, "Each one is tempted when he is drawn away by his own desires and enticed." But through regeneration we are lifted into another realm where there are other temptations to face, namely, the kind of temptations our Lord faced. The temptations of Jesus had no appeal to us as unbelievers because they were not at home in our human nature. Our Lord's temptations and ours are in different realms until we are born again and become His brothers. The temptations of Jesus are not those of a mere man, but the temptations of God as Man. Through regeneration, the Son of God is formed in us (see Galatians 4:19), and in our physical life He has the same setting that He had on earth.

Before reading more, I look up **Galatians 4:19**, crazy thankful that I have a Bible in my hand again.

> **Galatians 4:19** "My little children, for whom I am again in the anguish of childbirth until Christ is formed in you!"

Okay. That's totally weird, right? How is the first verse I read in this Bible about childbirth? Paul is fretting and exerting himself to help the new believers - his little children - become more like Christ so that Paul can be done "laboring" over them and know that they are born again, with Christ living in them. He's a worried dad, helping these new babies in Christ to realize who they are in Christ so that they aren't stillborn. So Satan doesn't steal their new life. God, you are totally amazing.

Back to Oswald:

> Satan does not tempt us just to make us do wrong things - he tempts us to make us lose what God has put into us through regeneration, namely, the possibility of being of value to God. He does not come to us on the premise of tempting us to sin, but on the premise of shifting our point of view,

> and only the Spirit of God can detect this as a temptation of the devil.

Oswald is so right. That's how the other girls lost their Healing. It wasn't because they were partying or lying or sleeping around. It wasn't fist fights and dirty thoughts. It was letting Satan lure them away from staring at Jesus when they needed His light the most. We may be in prison, but Jesus suffered so much worse. Already His Word is encouraging me. Already I know – again - that I can do anything He asks me to do. I know it isn't a coincidence that the first verse he gave me was about childbirth. He knows I'm pregnant. He ordained it. I can have a baby for Him.

Chapter Thirty-Nine

**sings* I Win, Nah Na Nah Na Nah Na*

"Hello, Ivy"

Patrice stands at my door, looking down at me where I lay on the floor. I am dying. I haven't eaten in too long and my body is ingesting itself.

"How about we make another deal?"

I hear her, but I make no move to indicate that her words matter.

"I've come to take you outside."

I turn my head to look at her and my neck is so stiff that I moan in achy agony.

"This is a risk for us and you have to make it mutually beneficial," she says with sugary encouragement, her foot tapping on my padded floor. "Dr. Shepherd says you haven't read any of your pregnancy books. I think you would benefit from reading them. And, of course, I'm going to need to see you eat immediately. Dr. Shepherd has a lunch tray for you. After you are finished, he will escort you to the garden where you can enjoy ten minutes outside. We will monitor your health over the next few weeks. If your immunity continues, we may consider limited fraternizing with the other carriers. How does that sound?"

I nod my sore neck in the affirmative and feel my short hair rub back and forth on the blue mat beneath me. I won. Kind of. If her shoe was food I would eat it off of her foot. I sincerely believe I would have died soon if I had gone any longer without sustenance.

*****

Tim sits by me while I devour a plate of chicken and rice. I'm too hungry to think about anything but getting the food in my stomach. I don't taste it in my mouth, it goes from fork to throat like I'm a vacuum cleaner. Tim chuckles while I shovel. Tim brought a glass of cold milk with my meal. That I savor, laying my head back against the wall and closing my eyes with each sip. I feel uncomfortably full and it is heavenly.

After eating and drinking, some of my strength returns. I leave my room for the first time in weeks. Tim leads me down white hallways to take me to my promised time outside. We don't pass anyone as we walk, but security cameras blink from recessed corners along our route. I imagine the courtyard will be watched as well. I may not get to say anything to Tim. And there is so much to say.

All the doors we pass are closed, so I am curious when I see a set of doors standing open ahead of us. As we walk by, I look into the room I saw when I tried to run away. The halls are empty because everyone is in that room. Fifty white coats, maybe more, scurry around the pump and the pipes red with human blood. It's sad. They are so desperate. Searching and sacrificing for a Cure that already exists. It's a travesty. A waste of life. A waste of the blood He already shed and a waste of their limited time. Soon they'll know. It breaks my heart. Tim guides me past the room and I follow him.

As Tim pushes open the door to outside, I am distracted. The door is made of reflective metal. I see myself for the first time in months. My legs are thin sticks below my always growing belly. The peach bodysuit accentuates my stomach which is now the size of half a soccer ball. Above the belly bump I am thinner and my chest is bigger.

I'm surprised by my face. It stares back at me like an old friend. We smile at each other, my reflection and I. My cheeks are pink and my skin looks healthy. My hair falls in soft curls near the top of my ears. I stare at the tube in my ear. Sometimes I forget it's there. Somehow the tube is a far greater violation to me than the baby they put in me. Pregnancy is hard, but it is life-giving. It is part of being human. The tube is death.

"Ivy?" Tim asks, still holding the door open.

I step out into the garden.

I feel none of the elation or triumph I thought I would. The sun is hot and the humid air smells like gardenia flowers. I've been longing for the refreshing feel of the sun on my face and I'm surprised that all I can feel is tired. I sit down in one of the white wicker chairs on the lawn and the wood is so hot it burns through my spandex suit.

I study the view I've only seen from inside my window. The fountain gurgles nearby, a marble relief of Pravda's emblem shooting streams of clear water in four equidistant arcs. Neatly trimmed bushes bloom by my chair, but they make me think of Jessie's garden. And Matt.

Why do I feel so let down? The yard is pretty. But I thought it would be better somehow. From inside, it seemed like more. The bright blue sky is framed above the four rectangular walls that close me in. I'm finally outside, but it's just a different view of my cage. The silver walls of Pravda's fortress shimmer in the bright sunlight. Reflective windows encompass the entire courtyard. The glass is tinted black and it's impossible to tell if anyone is watching us from the thirty possible vantage points that wreath us.

Tim sits down next to me, staring at me. I look over at him and lift one side of my lips in a small smile. His skin is redder today. My smile fades. I owe him so much and he's a zombie now.

"It's makeup, Ivy."

I look at him in surprise and mouth the words, "We can talk?"

"I think so," he replies in a normal voice.

I give him my best crazy eyes. That's something we should be sure about I think!

"I tried to show you it was makeup."

I remember when he was in my room and he picked skin off of his face. I was supposed to figure that out?

"You mean when you picked crusty skin off of your lip and it flaked all over the table?"

Tim rolls his eyes.

"I couldn't tell! I though you lost your Healing!"

"Really, Ivy? You thought I would walk away?" He snorts and shakes his head in disgust, looking away from me across the lawn.

Suddenly we are Ivy and Tim again. Stupid Ivy, frustrated Tim. Same old, same old. It makes me smile. He looks back at me and sees me smiling and he cracks a grin at me. It's a nice moment. The nicest I've had since that morning with Matt.

"Matt is Healed. He repented," I blurt.

"I know."

"You know?" I ask incredulous.

"He's making a big ruckus downstairs. He's preaching in the tomb."

"The tomb?" The word sends chills up my arms.

"That's what we call the prison."

"We?"

"Pravda."

It's not good that he considers himself a part of Pravda. Maybe he didn't mean it that way, but it still makes me less comfortable with him.

"Preaching?" I ask.

"Like the apostle Peter, tongues of fire and all that jazz."

I can't even imagine it. Matt, the angry zombie blood dealer is teaching and preaching about Jesus in Pravda's tomb. I shake my head and smile at Tim.

"I'm not sure I can get them out, Ivy."

"You have to!" I lean towards him in a desperate plea.

"Easy. They still have cameras. Sit back and calm down."

I look away from him and lean back in the wicker chair.

"All the prisoners have a Sef I and each one is set to a different frequency. It's a logistical nightmare. I have to take down the whole system, and I don't even know how it all works yet."

"S.E.F. Eye?"

"Sound Energy Flux Incapacitator. The thing in your ear."

"Please Tim? Please find a way? I can't leave them here."

"I'm trying." He sits quiet for a minute before asking, "Aren't you going to ask me about Harmony? Or Rosa? Is he all you can think about?"

Guilt douses me like a bucket of cold water being dumped over my head. I hate Tim. I feel like a piece of garbage and I hate him. No one on earth makes me feel as horrible about myself as he does. I should have asked about them. I kick myself for not thinking of them first. But I won't ask him now.

"I'm tired, Dr. Shepherd," I say with proud indignity. "I'm ready to go back to my room."

Chapter Forty

I'm Rubber And You're Glue

I am proud.

I'm proud of Matt. We've been apart for so long that the past seems like a dream. But I know what we had - what we have - is real. He came here for me because he loves me and I think of him all day every day. I can only imagine how terrible Pravda's tomb is; how hard it must be to endure. But my reborn guy is triumphantly preaching about our God in that dark place. Matt's dad was a preacher and it seems his son inherited the calling. What would Aunty think now? I knew Matt was special. That he was meant for Life.

I haven't seen my dad in many years, but I picture him being pleased. They are down there together. Matt will have told him I'm here; that we are all in this together. I think my dad will be proud of the guy I fell in love with. Maybe when we get out of here, my dad will already think of Matt like a son. Does Matt know about the Carriers? Will he be upset that I'm pregnant? When we leave, will he help me? Be a father to my child?

Every day the baby grows. I fight the attachment that is forming. He has the hiccups all the time. I was worried the first time I felt the rhythmic tapping on my spine. I searched the pregnancy books and found the cause. I guess he is practicing swallowing now and hiccups are a normal thing. The books say he can grip with his fingers and open and close his eyes in reaction to light. He kicks like a champ. I feel less and less alone in my room and I talk to him all the time. I call him baby, but there is a name on my mind.

Life has settled into a pattern. It is my new normal. I'm the healthiest I've ever been - mind, body and spirit. I walk on the treadmill, eat a healthy and balanced diet, spend hours in God's word and in prayer with Him. I read my pregnancy books and do my yoga. Tim comes for me after lunch every day and we walk to the garden for my allotted time of fresh air.

Tim has been filling me in little by little on our short ten minute walks. We can't speak in the hallways, so we make the most of our time as he walks the courtyard with me outside. Harmony didn't wake from her coma. Tim says there is no scientific reason for it. Her baby grows while she sleeps in a room much like the one I woke in. Tim says she's having a girl. He is hoping she will wake on her own. Then, we'll need to wait for her to regain her strength and rehabilitate her muscles. I'm terrified that she won't wake. I know I'll never forgive myself if I lose her.

Rosa is with Tim in one of the houses in Paradise. Pravda gave Tim the keys to his own mansion the same day they hired him as an ultrasound technician. He has servants and a nanny for Rosa. All of the servants in his home are Living. Tim says they are a family, eating together, raising Rosa, praying and meeting for church services. Word has leaked out and Living slaves from neighboring Paradise homes sneak away on their breaks to partake in the communion at Tim's mansion table. It sounds dangerous, but lovely. I get a little jealous when he talks about his new family.

It took several days to hear the whole story of how Tim pulled it off. In the time we were apart, he went back to Buford. Back to Herb. He worked for Herb, though he won't say what he did, and found the contacts he needed to build his fake life. He knew I would end up in Pravda and he knew they would impregnate me. I had to fight feelings of anger and resentment when I realized that Tim knew all along what Pravda wanted with me. I wish he had told me so I could have been more prepared.

Through his criminal contacts, Tim became Dr. Hale Shepherd, child genius and youngest graduate of Harvard's last graduating class before the famous school closed. He also fake specialized in ultrasound and sonogram technology. He spent a few weeks studying so he could pull off the lie and then walked through the front doors of Pravda for an interview with Patrice. He said she was thrilled to hire him. I imagine a "thrilled" Patrice would look a lot like a jack o'lantern.

I filled Tim in on where Harmony and I were before we were caught. Right up the road from his new house, apparently. I told him about Matt and Wes and Nora and Jim. When I told him about Jessie, he almost tripped over his own feet. I guess Jessie was married to the Director when Leprasimilis first hit. The carrier program was her idea.

I felt sad for her when Tim told me more about her. Their daughter found Life through Harvey, the same missionary who brought Thomas to Toccoa. Pravda threw Harvey in the tomb and the Director forced his own daughter into the carrier program. Jessie left him. One of the carriers that I've watched right outside of my window is their daughter, Trudy. I feel sorry for Jessie. Her mysteries and her resentment were born out of tragedy.

*****

After a few weeks of walking outside with Tim, Patrice made good on her word. Today, I get to go outside with the others. They ran their tests and found me no less healthy for my time out in the fresh air. I am excited and nervous to meet the other carriers. Well, really I'm only nervous about seeing Chloe. What if she blames me for Toccoa?

I normally walk with Tim right after lunch, but I remember that the other girls get their time in the sun right before dinner. It takes forever for the time to pass. I am standing by my door waiting for Tim when I hear the outer lock disengage. My smile morphs into disappointment as the door slides open. It isn't Tim. It's a silver-suited Pravdanian guard. He holds the door open for me and I take a deep breath before following him out into the hall.

Just outside of my door, another silver-suited man waits next to a chair that has never been there before. Both of the Pravdanians wear the white masks. It is part of the silver-suit outfit I guess. "Henchmen must wear terrifying white plastic mask." Scary guy handbook, page three.

"Please sit down," the guard who opened my door asks in a kind, humane voice.

I take a step back towards my room. I've never heard any of the guards speak. The human voice behind the mask throws me off guard - no pun intended.

"The Director will permit you time outside if you comply."

They are always asking me to comply. And I never like the results of my compliance.

"You will not be given another chance."

Another ultimatum. That's all I get here. So, this is it. My decision. Do I want to go outside bad enough? Could I do another hunger strike?

I sit in the chair.

The second guard stands behind me and I hear something mechanical buzz to life in my ear. I whip my head around reflexively. A razor is poised at the level of my eyes in the man's gloved hand. Panic gives way to realization. They are shaving me again. I remember that the other girls outside always had short hair. Their heads must be shaved on a routine basis. Pravda can't send me outside with my hair growing back in. Everyone around here has to be equal. Things have to be fair. That's how their game works.

I close my eyes and grasp tightly to the arms of my chair. The razor starts at the back of my neck and mows steadily up the middle of my head. It makes another pass and then another. My hair tickles me as it falls around my ears and down past the front of my face. While they shear me like a sheep, I wonder if this is why Tim didn't come. Maybe he hates to see me looking so much like a slave.

When the buzzing stops, one of the guards - I've lost track now of who's who - wraps his black-gloved hand around my arm and leads me down the sterile white hallways. I have the way memorized now and I don't need his help. I loathe the feel of his rubbery finger pads on my thinly suited arm. My skin crawls at his closeness.

The Pravdanian guards always remind me of the man who attacked Aunty and me at the outlets. They wear the same silver suit with Pravda's symbol on the chest. Though the man who attacked Aunty and I didn't wear the creepy white mask that these guards wear. I think I would feel less nervous if my escort today was wearing the Oscar the Grouch mask. At least this henchman doesn't smell like body odor.

He leads me past the busy room with the pipes and I peer inside as we walk by. Today the pipes are only half full with blood. I wonder if Pravda is running low. My chaperone pulls me along beside him, towards the door to outside and towards new worries and fears.

We reach the reflective door and I give my pregnant self an apologetic nose-crinkle. *Sorry, they shaved us again*, I think as we stare at our nearly bald head. She gets me. She's the only one here who really gets me. I give myself a little wave and think, *wish me luck*, as I'm nudged through the doors and into the populated garden.

My escort doesn't follow me outside and the doors click shut behind me. I stand alone before a group of yoga bent mothers-to-be - instantaneously hot and sweaty in the heat wave of a sunny Georgia afternoon. The yoga instructor pauses in Downward Dog and turns her head to stare at me. The girls who mimic her pose do the same. Ten necks pivot, nineteen eyes appraise me - one of the girls has an eyepatch. New name! I'll call her "Pirate."

I see Twizzler's face for the first time. I know her by her short, bright red fuzz. Her freckled face would be cute if it weren't for the ugly hole in her cheek and the pus filled bubbles around her lips. The other yoga-doers are equally diseased, their faces and necks mutilated by Leprasimilis. Pregnant, peach spandex-suited zombies with their butts in the air scowl at me with gory, upside down faces. My stomach flip-flops with anxiety and I realize this might not have been a good idea.

"Ivy?"

Chloe is walking towards me with a smile on her face. Her pretty features are marred by scabby gray skin and her ears are bandaged. The sun shines on her shaved blondish-brown hair. The moment of truth has come. She recognized me. I'm relieved to see a friendly face. I smile back at her. Chloe has her best friend, Beachball, with her. Jeez, how big is that girl gonna get? Is she having twins?

"So they did get you. I thought it was just a rumor!" she drawls like a delicate southern belle, exchanging toothy smiles with Beachball.

Beachball is more tooth than smile. Her lips have begun to rot away, leaving her face in a permanent snarl. I stare back at them without answering, unsure what the right answer would be.

"I'm so glad my momma didn't die for nothing'," Chloe says, a smile still holding on her ashy face.

Her tone is friendly, but in that fake" southern girl" polite way. Her mom is gone and she blames me and her words are a poisoned dart in my heart. My non-confrontational personality starts squeezing my chest and pumping excess sweat to my armpits. I normally handle confrontation with mean girls one of two ways: talk too much or run. There is nowhere to run. Chloe keeps stepping towards me and I keep stepping backwards. I bump into the white brick wall behind me. She closes the last step between us and our pregnant bellies touch, peach suit to peach suit.

"I'm so sorry, Chloe," I whisper through the lump in my throat. "I know it is my fault and not a day goes by that I don't -"

"Don't do that," she interrupts her voice still sugar sweet. "Don't act like you can make it right with an apology. You destroyed our home and killed - everyone - I - loved," she enunciates while tilting her head back and forth in my face. "And then you ran. You are a piece of trash, Ivy Lusato. And I don't want anything to do with you," Chloe finishes in a gracious tone as though she'd just politely stated that she doesn't care for pickles.

Chloe pivots and walks away, her curvy hips swinging with each step. Beachball follows after her, but not before giving me another snarl through her skeletal teeth. I lean against the wall and let Chloe's words bounce around in my head. *Piece of trash* echoes in my red hot ears. Around the yard, the other girls are standing still, staring at me. I came out here for friendship. To be a part of this surreal group that I felt attached to through the window in my room. Now I want to leave. Just as desperately as I wanted this, I want to never come out here again.

I sink to my butt, my spandex suit catching and snagging against the brick wall behind me. The other carriers stop staring and go back to their activities. I wait out the hour in shame, in exile. Once again I question Tim. Why did he want me out here? How is this helping us to escape? I wish he had never opened those stupid panels.

Chapter Forty-One

Glutton For Punishment

The next day when the white faces come, I decline their invitation to escort me outside. I'm never going back out there again, at least not with the other girls. My dreams last night were tortured. The people I love took turns calling me a piece of trash. Chloe's estimation of me has echoed through my thoughts a thousand times since yesterday. I keep having long conversations in my head where I defend myself to her.

I spend my pre-dinner hour with a better friend, Oswald Chambers.

I've started reading the book from the beginning - even though each devotional is dated throughout the year - because I'm hungry for truth and I don't want to miss anything. Sometimes I read and study two a day. It is July outside, maybe August, but I seek devotion in January's pages.

> **January 11th**
>
> "As they led Him away, they laid hold of a certain man, Simon..., and on him they laid the cross that he might bear it after Jesus." Luke 23:26
>
> If we obey God, it is going to cost other people more than it costs us, and that is where the pain begins. If we are in love with our Lord, obedience does not cost us anything - it is a delight. But to those who do not love Him, our obedience does cost a great deal. If we obey God, it will mean that other people's plans are upset. They will ridicule us as if to say, "You call this Christianity?" We could prevent the suffering, but not if we are obedient to God. We must let the cost be paid.
>
> When our obedience begins to cost others, our human pride entrenches itself and we say, "I will never accept anything from anyone." But we must, or disobey God. We have no right to think that the type of relationships we have with others should be any different from those The Lord Himself had.

> A lack of progress in our spiritual life results when we try to bear all the costs ourselves. And actually, we cannot. Because we are so involved in the universal purposes of God, others are immediately affected by our obedience to Him. Will we remain faithful in our obedience to God and be willing to suffer the humiliation of refusing to be independent? He will care for those who have suffered the consequences of our obedience. We must simply obey and leave all the consequences with Him.
>
> Beware of the inclination to dictate to God what consequences you would allow as a condition of your obedience to Him.

When I'm done reading, I sit quiet in thought - long after the dinner tray arrives through my door. I look up at the camera and hope that it is Tim watching. Not because I have anything to say, not because I wish to send a message, simply because I'd like to have a friend with me. My baby kicks and reminds me that he is there. I cradle my belly with one arm and hum a lullaby.

Cold and sore on the floor, I pull myself up to my feet and shake away the aches of sitting too long. My dinner is waiting and I eat the cold chicken breast in morose solitude. I swallow my broccoli and my emotional throat stubbornly clings to each bite. My food goes down to slow and hits my stomach roughly. I don't attempt to enjoy the sugared pears. I put my unfinished tray back on the little shelf of my door and shuffle to my bed.

I turn my lights out earlier than normal, no longer able to bear the day. In bed, I think about what Oswald said. Is he right? Will other people always have to suffer for my obedience? It seems contrary. I thought I was supposed to be a blessing to the people around me. Chloe has suffered because of me. Harmony has suffered because of me. Tim has suffered because of me. The Elders, their families, our whole community suffered because of me.

All this time, I've been sure that I had failed. I was certain that if I had been smarter, or quicker, or more Christ-like, the suffering needn't have been. What if Oswald is right? What if I've been carrying a guilt that didn't belong to me? It seems like the easy thing to do - letting myself off the hook

- but, as I wrestle with my demons tonight, it couldn't be harder.

*****

My breakfast arrives with an extra garnish in the morning. A paper football is marinating in my applesauce. I wipe it off and tuck it away in hopes that the camera didn't see. I lay the tray on my little table and make an unscheduled bathroom break. Sitting on the closed toilet seat, I read:

Go. It is important.

That's it. That's all he wrote. No encouragement. No "keep up the good work." No "I'm coming for you soon." Only typical Tim bossiness about things that are apparently important, but above my clearance level. Tim and his "need to know" basis.

He can suck on an egg.

I tear up the short message and flush it down the toilet. Resolved to disobey my bossy friend, I walk my thirty minutes, take my shower, read about breastfeeding (and worry that I'll never get the chance), eat my lunch and do my yoga. I'm in the Word when the door of my room opens. I grumble under my breath at Tim and at Jesus as I follow the guard out of my room and down the white hallways. I'm such a pushover. I have that "walk of the condemned on the way to a firing squad" feeling in my gut.

At the end of the line, I avoid my own eyes in the reflection of the shiny door to outside and plunge through to face the prison yard. The mid-August Georgia heat weighs heavy again today and the thick gray clouds filling the sky above Pravda have made the air thick with humidity. Going from air conditioning to humid heat wave has my face wet with perspiration within seconds, like a cold glass of sweet tea dripping condensation in the sun. The yoga crew turns to look at me and I force a smile at the peach-clothed bellies who are balancing their backs on various colors of yoga balls. None of them smile as they turn their attention back to their instructor.

I scan the yard for Chloe and spot her on the far side of the lawn. She is staring back at me across the green carpet between us. Chloe and Beachball glare for a few long seconds and then resume their walk around the courtyard. Always walking those two; wearing a path into the perimeter of the lawn. With their backs to me, I feel like I can breathe and look around. The Asian carrier who reminds me of Ellen is sitting on one of the lawn chairs and there is a chair open next to her. I hurry over to it and sink down on the warm white wicker, hoping everyone isn't staring at me.

"Hi," I say apologetically to the girl I've been calling Ellen.

I'm not sure why I feel apologetic. I guess I feel bad for her for having to be seen with me, but I'm too insecure to continue to stand alone out here.

"Hey," she answers with an easy smile and I know I've found a friend.

"I'm Ivy."

"Helen," she says, holding out a delicate golden skinned hand for me to shake.

"You're kidding," I blurt out without thinking.

She looks questioningly at me, wondering why her name brought such a reaction. I blush and shake her hand.

"Why is that weird?" she asks.

"I've been watching you from my window and I call you Ellen in my room because you remind me of someone I knew. Ellen and Helen are practically the same!"

Helen lifts her black eyebrows at me and I replay my last sentence in my head. Yup. I sound like a crazy person.

Helen smiles and lays her head back, closing her almond shaped eyes as though tanning herself despite the lack of sunshine. Her short, black hair is glossy and healthy and there aren't any signs of LS on her feminine face. Above us, thunder echoes in deep vibrato through the ever darkening clouds.

"I couldn't help but notice your altercation with Chloe the other day. What was that all about?" she asks with her eyes still closed.

"Oh. Yeah. Well -"

Aunty always insisted that polite conversation meant eye contact. I can't decide if I should lean over and look at her or if I'm supposed to lay my own head back and close my eyes. Are we fake sunning ourselves? Is she pretending to be napping so the others don't think she's talking to me?

"Chloe has problems with most of the girls out here, so don't feel too bad about it."

"Oh. Thanks. Okay," I lay back in my chair as though relaxing, but my body is anything but relaxed.

"You're still following Him?" Helen asks.

"Him?" I ask, glancing over at her. Her eyes are still closed.

"Jesus."

"Oh! Yes! And you are too?"

"They all were when they first came," she says sadly.

I glance over at her and see that her dark brown eyes are open and she's leaning over the arm of her chair looking at me.

"What happened to them?" I ask.

"It was a lot of things. No Bible. Pravda's cruelty. Anger and pain. It happened slowly and I don't think they noticed. We used to pray together," she says mournfully.

"Do you think it was Trinity Divinity?" I ask with obvious disdain.

Helen's eyes widen, "I thought I was the only one who couldn't stand that purple pretzel."

I smile at her description of the woman and Helen grins back.

"How far along are you?" Helen asks.

"Um, I think I'm twenty-five weeks."

"You're getting there. I'm at fifteen weeks."

"So you haven't been here very long then?" I ask surprised.

The way she talked about the other girls and the "way things were" it seemed like she had been here longer.

"No," she says in a sad whisper, "I've been here for quite a while."

"Did it take them awhile to make you pregnant?" I ask awkwardly.

"No," she says, looking away across the yard - avoiding my eyes.

Oblivious, I press on, "Then, how?"

Helen turns to meet my eyes and I see anguish in her pretty features.

"This is my third pregnancy."

I open my mouth to speak again and then realization floods me. Pravda has done horrible things to this girl. They have put three babies in her and she has had to watch two of them die. My hand flies up to cover my open mouth.

"I'm sorry," I mumble through my fingers.

"It's okay," she answers, her face the picture of grace. "I'll see them soon. My babies are with my Lord and they are safe. I have a boy and a girl waiting in heaven for me."

"I'm so sorry," I say again.

"It is what it is," Helen says bravely and then settles herself back against the chair and closes her eyes again.

"I'm having a boy," I offer.

"That's nice," Helen answers politely.

I haven't had to endure what she has and I'm impressed that she has clung so tightly to her faith. No wonder the other girls lost theirs. The physical and psychological trauma that Pravda has inflicted on them is unfathomable. How long have they been here? How many times has Pravda put them through the torture of childbirth only to murder their children? And then Pravda hits reset and starts them down the road to pain and grief again. It's horrific. If Tim can't get me out of here it will be my lot too. I don't want to be one of these girls.

"So you've met Dr. Shepherd?" Helen asks with humor in her tone.

I look hard at her, not sure what she's asking me.

"He's the doctor who does the sonograms," she explains. "If you know you're having a boy, he's the doctor who told you."

"Yeah, I've met him." I answer slowly.

"All the girls are completely in love with him."

"They are?" I ask genuinely shocked.

Tim? Tim Markowitz? All the girls are in love with him? I feel a smirk on my face.

"Especially Chloe. She has claimed him."

I sit straight up in my chair.

Chloe.

Tim.

How am I just realizing this? She must have recognized him. She knows he isn't Dr. Hale Shepherd, zombie baby picture doctor. She must know he's here under cover. Why hasn't she given him away? But Helen just told me why. Chloe is in love with Tim.

"Are you alright, Ivy?"

"Huh?" I say as Helen lays her slender hand on my arm. "Yeah, I'm fine. Just - just gassy."

"Oh, don't get me started on gas. Isn't pregnancy delightful?" Helen waves her hand in the air like a Pentecostal woman waving hallelujahs at *a come to Jesus* meeting.

A cry across the yard draws our eyes. Beachball is hunched over on the ground and Chloe is calling for help. Two Pravdanian guards lift Beachball and carry her across the yard and through the swinging doors as she groans in pain.

*****

It's very late but I've yet to sleep. Beachball has been moaning and screaming for countless hours. Her labor cries drift through my room like specters, haunting me. Reminding me that my turn is coming.

Chapter Forty-Two

Six Degrees Of Separation

Three days later, Helen and I are reclining in the same two wicker chairs on the lawn. The sky is gray and cloudy again today, another storm is coming. I glance up at the elephant clouds and wonder if the rain will cut our outside time short. Just a few days ago I would've been relieved if the weather had sent me back to the safety of my private room. Now that I have Helen, my hour outside is the best part of my day.

Chloe hasn't come out since Beachball went into labor. There are whispers around the yard that Beachball didn't make it. I don't tell them what I know. I don't want to know what I know. I heard the baby come.

A good strong cry, her baby had. And then Pravda ended that precious cry. Beachball wept. She wailed. I shared in her grief and cried quietly for her. And then I heard Beachball fight. I heard metal trays clattering and glass breaking. Enraged, she screamed at the people who had taken her child. Then, they pressed her button. I know that that's what happened, even though I couldn't see it. Beachball's shrill screams echoed through my room like a banshee's cry. My room went quiet, but her scream echoed in my head and in my nightmares.

Sitting outside with Helen, I wonder if I should tell her what I know. But I hold back, so thankful for friendship and unwilling to be the bearer of bad news. Without Chloe's persistent glare, even a cloudy day outside is refreshing. I do feel bad for Chloe, but it's a relief to have a break from her hatred.

I breathe in the damp fresh air and wiggle my bare toes. A gardenia bush covered in blooms is within my arm's reach. I stretch out my hand and pluck the largest flower from the dark green, waxy shrub. I love the smell of gardenias. We had a bush at the Inn. Aunty arranged them in vases with Magnolia and Rhododendron. I pluck a petal off and then another.

"Did you love someone before you came here?" Helen asks me.

I thought she was resting. Was it so obvious I was playing the old game in my head? Pluck a petal and say *he loves me*. Pluck another, *he loves me not.*

"Yes," I answer her almond eyes.

I don't offer any more and Helen is good at not asking too much.

"Did you love someone?" I ask her.

"Yes. I was married."

"Is your husband -"

"Holding my babies," she answers with smile that would only make sense to the Living.

"What happened?"

"We were with a group of believers here in Atlanta. We thought our building was safe. Pravda sent a mob and they burned our haven to the ground. That's when they took me. Me and Carly and Crissa."

"Carly and Crissa?"

"Carly is Chloe's friend. The one who just had her baby."

Beachball is Carly? Was Carly. Should I tell Helen what I know?

"My husband, Fin, was part of our security team. He was out with our friend Andrew when they hit us. Fin and Andrew got back just as the silver suits were loading Carly and I into a van. He tried to save me." She smiles at the memory and I watch the smile fade before she whispers, "I saw him fall."

Helen stares up at the tumultuous sky and I see a tear slide down her cheek, "I miss him so much."

I lie back in my chair and avert my eyes, let her have her moment. Something is bothering me. But it can't be. It would be crazy. Are there so few of us left that we are all connected? Could her husband's friend be Tim's brother Andrew?

"Andrew Markowitz?" I whisper to myself.

"How do you know that name?" Helen asks.

I look up into her eyes and see mistrust and accusation. I stare back at my new friend and hope that she'll believe me.

"I know him. Knew him. And his father and his brother."

His brother is here, I want to tell her. But I can't. If she said anything to anyone, we could lose what small chance we have to get out of here.

"Is he still alive? I have to tell Crissa! She's Andrew's wife!"

"Which one is she?" I ask sitting up, scanning the yard.

"Crissa doesn't come out very much," Helen says, standing up.

"Is she like us? Or like them?" I ask nodding at the decomposing yoga devotees.

"She's like - she's like Him. She still holds tight to her Healing, even after everything."

The way Helen says *everything*, I know Pravda has done terrible things to Andrew's wife.

"Do I even want to know?" I ask.

Helen shakes her head no, and I'm relieved she doesn't tell me anything more. I don't want to know what they've done to the girl. This place is colder than the silver steel the building is made of. If hell froze over it would look like Pravda. Within these walls lives an evil iciness that chills the warmest hearts. Lord, insulate me, I pray. Keep me warm.

*****

The sun is back out today, but Helen isn't. We've only been friends for a few days and she already means so much to me. I spend my time in the sun worrying and praying. I fight the negative whispers in my head that say maybe she just needed a break from me. Maybe she'd rather stay inside than make conversation with me.

I sit in my wicker chair next to Helen's empty one and try to look like I'm comfortable; like I'm enjoying my time in the sunshine. Yesterday's clouds emptied themselves during the night, but the hot sun already lapped up every bit of moisture. I blink in the unveiled brightness of the late afternoon and wish I had sunglasses. These last few weeks of being outside have given my hands, face and neck a golden tan. The rest of me is still white as a ghost beneath my peach bodysuit.

I wonder again why Tim wanted me out here. I don't think it had anything to do with my vitamin D levels. If I had to guess, I think it's possible that Tim wants me out here because of Chloe. I know him pretty well and I imagine he won't want to abandon one of our people. I'm fairly certain he wants me to somehow make things right with her and help her find her healing. He isn't the only one adding to the list of dependents. The more I get to know Helen, the more I need to get her out of this place. But, the bigger our group, the smaller our chances.

A new girl sits down in Helen's seat and turns towards me. I look at her and then lay my head back the way Helen did and close my eyes. Like I'm cool. Calm. Unthreatened by her nervous smile.

"I'm Crissa. Helen told me you knew my husband?"

My eyes pop open and I turn to look at the mousy girl next to me. She is farther along than me, her belly almost as big as Beachball's was. She is Living, but she isn't very pretty. Her porcelain white face is thin and pinched and her shaved black hair makes her head look too flat. This is Andrew's wife. Tim's sister-in-law is here. Does he know that? We're going to have to try to get her out, too. Which, obviously, is impossible. Tim might as well rent a tour bus.

"Did you know my Andrew?" ghostly Crissa asks me.

"Yes. I know him or knew him, before here," I answer, trying to meet her eyes, but she avoids mine.

"He's alive?"

"He was in January."

"How do you know him? Where is he?"

"His father and brother were part of my community in a little town called Toccoa about two hours from here."

"Yes, he told me about Toccoa. Are they still alive?"

I avoid her question, "He came to Toccoa after he lost - after he lost you I guess. He was in charge of security in our town when our fences fell."

"How do you know he made it?" the tragic girl asks me, looking somewhere past me.

"A few of us got away. Andrew and his brother and I and my friend Harmony."

"And his father?"

I shake my head no.

"Do you know where he is now?"

"No. I'm sorry. But I know where his brother is."

"Where?" she asks me desperately, her hand on my arm.

Even as she leans desperately towards me, she still doesn't look at me. It's almost as if she is blind.

"I - I actually don't know for sure. He was here in Atlanta when they got me."

"Oh."

Andrew's petite wife stares down at her thin, chalky hands. Her peach belly protrudes too far from her thin body. It looks like it would be too heavy for her to carry. If we don't leave soon and take her with us, Pravda will take another life. This young woman has already lost so much. I would do anything to save this baby for her.

"Keep holding on to your faith. You'll be together soon if you don't let go," my trite encouragement feels hallow.

"Yes, thank you. I will pray for you, Ivy."

"Thanks," I mumble as Crissa Markowitz stands up.

Crissa takes a hesitant breath and makes eye contact with me for the first time. Her eyes are the palest blue-gray. With a new strength that takes me by surprise she says, "I'm supposed to tell you that you and your baby boy will see Him together in the sky."

Then, she turns and speed waddles back into the building.

Chapter Forty-Three

Heaping Burning Coals

When I see Helen in her usual seat the next day, I'm surprised by how much relief I feel. I hurry over to my seat next to hers and beam a smile at her. I want to ask her where she was, but I don't want her to hear my loneliness.

"I met Crissa," I announce, holding myself back from saying how weird she was.

"Yes. I know. She told me."

"How did she tell you?"

Helen wasn't outside yesterday and Crissa isn't out here today. When would they see each other?

"We're roommates."

It's another one of those punch-in-the-gut moments.

Roommates.

The other carriers get roommates. I feel like I'm always on the outside. Aunty's secrets, Matt's secrets, Tim's secrets, they've all left scars. Pravda keeps me away from the other carriers, supposedly for my own benefit. I'm sick of being left out.

"She's a little strange, but she's a wonderful person," Helen says.

Of course, they are best friends. Helen doesn't need me; not like I need her. She already has Crissa. I have to look away from Helen because my eyes are watery.

"Did she say anything weird?" Helen asks, sunning herself and oblivious to my struggle. "She has the gift of prophecy and sometimes she says weird things."

"Uh, yeah. She said that my son and I would see Him in the sky."

"I never told her you were having a boy. You can count on what she said, Ivy. You are going to get to keep your baby."

I lay back and close my eyes, thinking. It must mean we're really going to get out of here. This is confirmation from the Lord that I really will be rescued from this place. A word from God. I've had moments with Him where He speaks to me in my devotions, but I've never heard someone else speak for Him.

"We both know your baby won't have whatever Pravda thinks they are looking for. It must mean you are going to get out of here somehow."

I turn to look at my friend, but she is sunning herself with her eyes closed. Unaffected. I wish I could tell her. I wish I could promise to take her with me.

*****

Two weeks after Beachball - I mean Carly - lost her baby, Chloe rejoins us on the lawn. She stands alone near the door. I take a deep breath and pull my heavy self up from my chair.

"Praying," Helen whispers encouragingly.

I walk towards Chloe, but find it hard to make eye contact with her. I glance at her out of the corner of my eye - as though she isn't my reason for walking that way - and she returns an awkward look. I veer towards her at the last second and stop, my feet shuffling nervously back and forth.

"How are you?" I ask her.

Chloe scowls at me and opens her mouth in some retort, but then closes it again without the bark I was expecting.

"Helen said you and Carly were roommates."

Chloe's angry face twists into sorrow and she turns away from me.

A long silence hangs between us and my legs beg me for permission to walk away, to stand anywhere but here. I'm about to give in to them when Chloe answers me.

"They never brought her back," Chloe whispers. "I came out today to see if -" Tears slide down Chloe's dry, jaundiced cheeks. "I thought maybe you had seen her? Maybe they kept her in your part of the building?"

Chloe came out here just to talk to me. I feel like some important victory with eternal consequences has just been won. I wish I could tell her that Carly was fine. If I tell her what I heard, she'll retreat back inside and never speak to me again. I have a captive audience and my heart is broken for her.

"Have you asked around? Maybe someone else saw her?" I ask.

I tell myself it isn't a lie. I didn't see Carly die. She could've gone silent that night because she passed out. I need more time with Chloe. I need to help her.

Chloe and I interview the other carriers. None of them have heard or seen anything. I feel more and more deceptive with each inquisition. Aunty always said the truth is always the right answer. I struggle with an internal wrestling match, the truth about Carly fighting its way free.

Saving the yoga crew for last, I follow a few steps behind Chloe as she boldly approaches the synchronized group of pregnant zombies. They are paired up in a stretch that is only possible with the counterbalance of another person. Chloe stands over them with typical Chloe confidence. Even back in Toccoa she carried herself with poise and strut.

Not waiting for the instructor to pause, Chloe barks, "Have any of you heard anything about Carly?"

The shorthaired, sin-eaten faces look blankly at her and then avert their eyes. Or one eye in Pirate's case.

Twizzler groans in obvious irritation and I peer around Chloe's shoulder with wide, nervous eyes.

"Chloe, you know she's gone. Just deal."

I expect Chloe to retort, but she walks dejectedly away from the clueless yoga doers.

"Chloe, wait!" I waddle after her as she heads for the door to inside.

Chloe pushes through a set of swinging doors that are opposite of the doors that lead back to my room. I plunge through behind her. No guards stop me and Chloe disappears around a corner ahead of me. I question my sanity as I follow after her down a sterile white hallway in a part of Pravda I've never seen.

As I round the corner, Chloe disappears into a room on the right side of the hallway. Hurrying to catch up to her, I pass several open doors to my right and left. They look like my room. Brightly colored walls, beds, TVs, rocking chairs. Chloe's door is mostly closed but not shut tight. I look over my shoulder, still marveling that no guards have stopped me. I knock lightly on the door and push it open.

"Leave me alone," Chloe says over her shoulder as she stares out her window.

Chloe's window looks out at the sunny lawn filled with roly-poly peach bodysuits. Her view shows the back of the wicker chairs. I see Helen still sunning herself next to my empty chair. I wonder if she knows I'm gone.

Chloe's room is much like mine. Her floor is padded with the same blue gym mats. Instead of one bed she has two. Hers on one side of the room and Carly's on the other. One bed is messy and the other neatly made. There's no shower in their room and no treadmill. They must have a communal bathroom they share with the other girls. They don't have a microwave or a snack shelf either.

With a deep breath, I make a decision, "Chloe, I heard Carly have her baby. There weren't any complications and Carly was alive when the baby came."

"What do you mean you 'heard' the baby come?" Chloe spins to face me with a face distorted by fury.

I pause, taken aback, stunned by her anger.

"Are you one of them?" She spits at me.

"One of who?" I stammer.

"The monsters who did this to us! Are you working with them? Spying on us?"

"What? No!"

"Why don't you live over here with us?"

"I - I don't know," I say sadly, fully aware of what I'm missing out on in my solitary confinement. This unguarded hallway where they all live together is more freedom than I've been given. They come and go as they please and make friends and share their time and their lives. Pravda has taken everything else from me; I don't know why I can't at least have this.

"You walked with him for weeks before you came out with us. Why!" she shouts accusingly.

Him? Does she mean Jesus? I'm still walking with Him and she isn't. I look at her confused.

"We both know who he is," Chloe glares with eyes so narrow they look shut.

Tim. She means Tim!

Chloe nods angrily towards the door and I follow her eyes thinking she wants me to leave. I see the camera watching us above the door and realize she was reminding me we are being watched. At least I'm not the only one.

I look back at the window and stare out at the yard. I look at the chairs where Helen has her nose in a book. Chloe must have watched Tim and me every day behind the one way glass of her bedroom window. It must have driven her nuts. Tim and I walked together and smiled and talked, sure that no one could listen in. Surely he must have realized that she was watching? Could he be that stupid? Chloe cares for Tim. Supposedly she's "claimed" him. I feel sorry for her. He loves me, he always has. No wonder she hates me. Not just for Toccoa and her mom's death, but because the guy she loves cares more for me than he ever could for her.

"They think you all lost your healing because of your close quarters. They keep me separate because they think it keeps me healthy. I try to tell them they're wrong -" I defend gently.

Chloe cuts me off, "You've always thought you were better than everyone else, Ivy. You can judge me all you want, but you'll see soon enough. You'll lose your healing too. It's what they put in us! They've damned us! We're just egg cartons to them and these things -" she shouts, pointing at her baby bump, "- are stealing our healing. This is my second time! The first was a girl. But they sucked her out of me because they saw 'imperfections'!"

"Chloe, you don't have to -"

She cuts me off, "Why were you walking with him!"

"I told you. They didn't want me around - everyone else because they thought I would get sick. I walked with him because I was proving to them that time outside wouldn't affect me. And it didn't," I say pointedly.

"You haven't been here very long, Ivy. And, as usual, you've been sheltered. You have no idea what you're talking about. I'm happy for you that you still have your nice skin," she says with disgust. "But it won't last. They'll kill your baby too and you'll finally know what it feels like to suffer like everyone else."

I open my mouth, but her hatred has stolen my voice.

"You stay away from him, Ivy. He loves me. You made your choice and now you have to live with it."

I stare at Chloe in confusion. The things she's saying don't make sense. Or too much sense. Does she actually know what she's talking about? I'm about to ask a very stupid question when Chloe cries out and drops to her knees, her hands pressed against her ears. Behind her, through the one way glass, I see all the girls outside on their knees like Chloe. All of their faces twisted in pain. It's like what happened to the slaves in Paradise. It's their Sef Is. And I alone am unaffected.

I'm not sure why I do it, but I sink to my knees and clamp my hands to my ears. I see now why our floors are padded. Pravda doesn't want injury to their carriers when they press the button that brings them to their knees. Chloe's splotchy face is riddled in anguish as she writhes before me with her eyes squeezed tightly shut. Why don't I feel any pain?

Chapter Forty-Four
Don't Shoot The Messenger

Chloe's screaming is killing me. I'm on my knees, hunched over my belly, holding my ears to block out her sickening cries. We've been like this for several minutes and I don't know what to do. Chloe jerks and spasms, arching her back and reacting to the pain that I don't feel. I cry and pray and lament our existence.

After at least five minutes of sharing the padded floor with Chloe's thrashing legs, two Pravdanian guards lift me to my feet. I try to act like someone in pain. I twist my face and lock my limbs as they carry me away. One last glance out the window shows Helen in the fetal position on her wicker chair outside. Why is this happening?

The guards carry me through the swinging doors to the courtyard and then straight through the swinging doors that lead to my lonely section of Pravda. No roommates and no friends. Just white coats and red pipes and unabridged loneliness. The silver suits deposit me on my own padded floor and leave me alone with a bigger problem. I don't know how long to carry on in this charade. I have to keep faking so they don't know that the tube in my ear didn't work. I won't know when the other girls are relieved.

Laying on the floor with a million questions and nothing but time I ask God for a miracle. Maybe it is Tim watching behind the camera. Maybe he found a way to shut off my device. Maybe Pravda never pressed my button. Maybe they are watching my pathetic attempt at acting with arms crossed over white lab coats and smirks on their faces. Did Chloe see that I fell later than she did? Did I give her even more reason to hate and mistrust me?

With these questions drilling holes in my subconscious, I fall asleep on the blue padded floor.

*****

A hand on my shoulder wakes me. My eyes open to Patrice's orange crow's feet crinkled in concern.

"She's fine," Patrice says over her shoulder with relief.

I blink confused and the memory of what happened to the other girls comes flooding back.

"I want her monitored for the next twenty-four hours. We can't lose this one," Patrice says, standing up and smoothing her white coat.

She looks down at me with a look of confusion and anger before turning and exiting my room; leaving me alone with Tim.

He helps me to my feet and leads me over to my bed where his sonogram machine is already set up. Unzipping my suit just below my chest, he peels the peach spandex down to expose my belly. Pink stretch marks have been creeping slowly up my domed middle. They started out small and innocuous around the perimeter of my stomach. Over the last few weeks they've drawn lightning bolt patterns in their march towards my belly button.

Tim doesn't seem to notice them. I watch him silently as he prepares the machine and squirts the clear gel on my stomach. His eyes don't look for reasons to find mine. His hands don't move slow and careful when they touch me. The process feels clinical and remote. When did this happen? Could Chloe be right? Has Tim moved on?

Hurt and abandon make my chest feel suddenly full and achy. I don't love Tim. I love Matt. But I did feel something for Tim. Something we had was real. Real and necessary to my sanity and survival. I wince with a made-up pain, testing, not wanting my head to be right. When Tim's brown eyes finally meet mine, the hunger that used to be there is gone. I stare up into his zombie makeup face and I know it's true. Tim doesn't love me anymore.

"What happened?" I whisper.

I guess I meant what happened with the Sef Is, but some part of me meant something else entirely.

"You went missing on the lawn. When you aren't where you are supposed to be, Pravda won't hesitate to discipline you. You passed out from the pain after they brought you back here."

My miracle. Pravda thought I passed out from the pain when really I just fell asleep. Thank you, Father.

"I have to make sure your baby wasn't affected."

Does he know I was with Chloe? Does he know I was doing it for him? This may be my only chance to tell him about Andrew's wife. She's so far along and her baby could come any time. We need to leave here as soon as possible.

“Is everyone else okay?” I ask.

“No.”

“What happened?” I prop myself up, worried that it could be Helen or Chloe.

“That’s not your concern,” Tim says pushing me back down on my pillow roughly. Angrily?

Is he mad at me for this?

“Are Helen, Crissa and Chloe ok?” I ask, scowling and insistent. Sick to death of Tim and his guilt trips and overly high expectations.

Tim’s brown eyes slide sideways to look at mine, while his face still faces the computer screen. It isn’t conspiratorial. There’s no softness to the look. He’s genuinely disgusted with me and his sideways glare brings a wave of hopelessness with it. If Tim doesn’t care for me, why would he get me out of here?

“Crissa is a friend of mine,” I say meekly. “She’s the wife of a man named Andrew who was with my group in Toccoa. I deserve to know if she’s okay.”

Tim’s expression turns to steel. I see his chest rise and fall, breathing harder, fighting fury.

“She didn’t come in with you. How would you even know that,” he says flatly for the camera’s sake.

“I just found out. She told me who she was and I put it together.”

“She’s fine,” Tim answers quietly.

I nod and look away from him. It’s too hard to look at him when he’s like this. It’s like looking at a score card of all of my failures. I’ve never been what he wanted me to be. I love Matt and I should be relieved that Tim has accepted that, but all I feel is loss. Tim swirls the wand around on my stomach and we listen quietly to the heart beat of my son. Tim clacks away at the keyboard and I let my thoughts wander in self-pity. My baby kicks at the intrusion and I think about the name that I have picked for him if he comes. When. When he comes.

*****

An hour later, as Tim wheels his computer towards the door, an expectant silence has grown between us. I zip my suit back over my belly and watch Tim as he walks away.

"Chloe is fine," he says with his back to me as he reaches my door. "But Helen didn't make it. Maybe you'll think about that before you go wandering off again."

My door clicks shut.

I stare at it in paralyzing grief.

Chapter Forty-Five

The Forecast Predicts A Scorcher

I haven't been back outside. I can't go out there again. Helen is gone. I try to picture her at home in Heaven, reunited with her husband and her babies. I try to tell myself it's better this way. I didn't know her well and I hadn't known her long, but she was the only one here who liked me. One of the few who still followed Him, the only one who understood me. She knew what we were really fighting against. What we were really fighting for. I feel so alone on this battlefield, alone amidst the corpses of the dead.

When my door opens, Crissa is the last person I expect to see standing outside of my room. She is flanked by two guards and holding a small duffle bag. She takes two steps into my room and the door closes behind her. I'm on the floor doing Trinity Divinity's *Yoga For Your Second Trimester* video. Crissa stands awkwardly, not looking at me but up at the camera. Trinity moves on without me. I turn off the TV, pull my big belly up off of the padded floor and walk over to Crissa.

"Why are you here?"

"I don't know," she answers softly, her pale blue-gray eyes flitting around my room.

*****

Crissa and I have been alone for days. Gladys hasn't come to clean my room. Patrice hasn't come to do whatever it is she does, and Tim hasn't come either. No one comes to escort us outside. Two trays come through at meal times, so I know they know she's here.

I have two theories. The first is that Crissa and I are the last ones left. The last two who show no sign of disease. When Helen died, it left Crissa alone in the other wing with the girls who have lost their healing. I think Pravda could be putting all their eggs in one basket. They want Crissa and I separate. I think they are losing their faith in the other girls, who, ironically, have lost their faith.

Theory number two is that this is Tim's doing. Crissa is his sister-in-law. How could he leave her here? He is planning on taking her when we leave. Somehow he convinced them that she should room on this side with me. If

Chloe shows up at my door they'd better bring another mattress with them. Crissa and I take up all the room in my double bed.

Crissa is strange. She doesn't meet all my hopes and dreams for a roommate - like Helen did - but I am glad for her company. It is nice to have someone to talk to. Someone who knows what's really happening here. We are alike in faith, but that is where our similarities end. She's like no Living one I've ever known. She's - well, she's weird.

We, the Living, all exist in two realities. We live here in this fallen world, but we know we are IN the world not OF the world. We know we belong to Jesus and His kingdom. We know Heaven is our ultimate home. But still, we live here. We bleed, we hunger, we sin, we struggle.

Crissa seems barely aware of this world. It's like she's three fourths of the way through the door to Heaven with only a toe still touching back on earth. Talking to her is like talking to Jesus. If Jesus was whispering and barely making eye contact. Her pale watery eyes stare off into the distance when she speaks and I wonder what they see.

When Crissa saw my Bible, she almost passed out from joy. She has read ravenously for most of the last few days. Sometimes she reads out loud, her voice clogged with emotion. I'm learning from her. She cares so little about herself. Her whole being lives to bring Him honor. She strives to worship Him in every action. I think she brushes her teeth "to the glory of God."

I told her every detail I could remember about Andrew. How long his hair was, what he was wearing, how much he didn't like me. She smiled and closed her eyes as she listened. I was worried that she might like me less when she heard that her husband wasn't my biggest fan. She wrapped her thin white hand around mine and reassured me that Andrew was just very intense. No kidding. I haven't told her about Tim. The camera is always listening.

*****

Andrew Markowitz's wife and I are lying on my bed when an alarm sounds in my room. It's a whining siren that I have heard once before. It's the same alarm that went off when Harmony and I were in Paradise at Jessie's house. It signaled Pravda's announcement and demonstration of corporal punishment. It brings fear to my heart; but, when I look at Crissa, I see calm contentment on her thin face. I guess it's hard to feel fear when you're sitting at Jesus' feet. Her faith might move mountains, but mine is more the normal kind. I wrap my pillow around my ears. The alarm echoes for half an hour, taking me from fear, to concern, to frustration and finally leaving me with only deep annoyance.

Simultaneously, the alarm bleats its last cry and leaves a punctuated silence as the flap on my door draws my attention. It isn't meal time and a paper football sits alone on the little shelf. Crissa blinks contentedly at me and smiles. She's so bizarre. I roll my eyes at her and hurry to the door.

Tim's note reads:

R16.8 Be ready.

I stare at it in confusion.

"Revelation 16:8," Crissa says, looking over my shoulder at the folded note.

I nod, pretending I already knew that.

"The fourth angel poured out his bowl on the sun, and it was allowed to scorch people with fire. They were scorched by the fierce heat, and they cursed the name of God who had power over these plagues. They did not repent and give him glory." As creepy Crissa speaks out loud another judgment from the throne, goose bumps blanket my face and then emanate down my arms and legs.

Tim said be ready. The distraction of whatever the sun has caused is our window. I don't know if he means for Crissa to come with us, but I've already decided we're bringing her. I turn to face her and take a deep breath.

"Crissa, have you ever played Hangman?"

Crissa squints at me and shakes her head no.

"I'll show you how," I invite with a fake smile.

Crissa is not *worldly wise*. Hopefully she'll recognize my strange behavior as a sign. She follows me over to our bed where I pull down one of the romance novels that Pravda stocked my shelf with. Opening the back cover for a blank space, I write:

> Dr. Shepherd is Andrew's brother Tim. We came here together and he is going to get us out of here. His note says we have to be ready to go.

Shielding my note from the camera, I motion for Crissa to lean closer so she can read it. Her eyes stare at the message and my eyes stare at her face. Always surprising me, she doesn't react. She leans away from my note and stretches her skinny arms behind her back.

"I'm awfully tired, Ivy. Let's play another time."

I nod and pad across the room to my sink where I shred both Tim's note and my message on the back cover of the book; and I wash the tiny pieces down the drain.

Chapter Forty-Six

With Friends Like These, Who Needs Enemies?

Crissa and I are on edge. We jump at every noise and we stare at the door all day long. We've even been sleeping with our shoes on. Something is going on out there and the suspense is killing me. We can't see it, but we can feel the change. There's a volume to the silence. A message in the absence of communication.

Yesterday, only one meal came through the door. One tray piled high with random things that would never please Patrice. There were two Gov. Bars, a bag of chips, a mushy apple, and a piece of jerky. I ate a Gov. Bar and gave the rest to Crissa. She argued, but I promised her I wasn't hungry. I'm way better at lying than she is. She's so small and fragile and her due date is only getting closer. I have to keep her strong for when it's time to run.

We are lying on my bed, quiet but not sleeping, when the lights go out. Like, *out* out. I don't have a clock, but I'm pretty good at tracking the time of day. I'm fairly certain it's late morning. No breakfast tray came today and I'm starving. I know Crissa is too because her stomach has been growling next to me all morning.

"Ivy?" Crissa says and reaches for my hand in the pitch black dark.

I feel for the switch of my lamp by the bed and flick it back and forth with no results. My room has never been this dark. Even at night when I turn the lights off, there are little night-lights around the room that light my nightly trips to the bathroom. But the night-lights are out too. Even the tiny red light on the camera is dark. For once, Pravda can't see me. I can't see me either, but it still feels good.

"I think it's time, Crissa. Let's go sit by the door. He must be coming."

"Ivy?"

"Yeah?" I answer in the dark, opening and closing my eyes with the same resulting blackness.

"Let's pray first."

"Okay."

Crissa fumbles against me, searching for my other hand. I reach for her and we lock our fingers together in the dark. A peace comes when our hands are clasped, like a circuit of faith has been completed and the power of peace that passes understanding flows through us.

"Father, thank you. Thank you that Ivy is here with me. Thank You for your perfect plan. We rejoice, Lord, in sharing in Your sufferings. We exalt You Lord, we worship You. No matter what happens today, we trust you. Your mercies are new every morning. May your great name be broadcasted in this dark place today. Bring new life today and healing. May the people who walk in darkness see Your light. Amen"

I echo her Amen and add a silent addendum to her prayer. *God, get us out of here! Keep us safe!* More selfish than her prayer, perhaps, but real and desperate none the less. We crawl across the padded floor and sit with our backs to the door.

"The angels are coming, Ivy. They are going to fly us out of here."

Her breathy prophetic whisper hangs in the darkness. More confirmation from God that we will leave this place today. But will we leave it alive? I've never seen an angel, but I'm pretty sure they only give rides to dead people. I do want to go home to Heaven, but I wouldn't mind kissing Matt first. Maybe having a life with him here. With my baby.

As the minutes stretch by, my stomach growls and fear and worry begin to creep over me. I wiggle my foot nervously and chew the skin around my already too short nails. What is happening out there? What if Tim gets killed or caught before he ever comes for us.

"This is my seventh pregnancy. Seven is God's perfect number you know," Crissa says.

"Seven!" I exclaim. "How long have you been here?"

"About two years."

"Then how could you -"

Crissa interrupts, "I had five miscarriages and one baby that they killed before it was born."

"Why?" I ask incredulous. "Why would they kill it?"

"Dr. Shepherd said something looked irregular."

"I'm so sorry Crissa," I say reaching my arm around her thin frame in the dark and holding her in a tight hug. "Don't be mad at Tim. He was doing what he had to do to get us out of here."

"I'm not mad at him."

"We're going to get out of here and you are going to hold this baby. Do you know what you're having?"

"A girl."

"Have you picked a name?"

"No, I never named any of them. I told Jesus He could name them."

"Well, we're naming this one. What's your favorite girl name?"

"Maybe I'll name her after Andrew's mother. I think he would like that."

"Leila?" I ask. I saw Tim's mother's name on her Bible and I'm surprised I remember it.

"Uh huh. I never met her, but I know she'll like it."

"I thought she died?" I ask confused.

"Oh, she did. But it won't be long before we meet."

As if the dark wasn't creepy enough, Crissa's etherealness fills my peach spandex suit with goose bumps. Her gift of prophecy could stand to have a better bed-side manner.

*****

I've dozed off on Crissa's shoulder and I fumble in confusion as the door shoves me awake. A bright light penetrates the darkness. I shield my eyes and look up from the floor. Tim and Chloe stare down at Crissa and I. Chloe is scowling at me and holding tight to Tim's gloved hand. My eyes adjust to the light and I realize there is someone else with them. Another carrier. As the light washes over her face, I gasp and jump to my feet.

"Helen!"

Tim, Chloe and Helen step around Crissa and into my room, pushing my door closed behind them. I wrap my arms around Helen and hug her fiercely. I feel tears pooling in my eyes and for once they are tears of relief and joy.

"You said -" I accuse Tim.

"No time!" he whispers back. "She passed out like you did, I declared her dead and hid her, we've gotta move!"

"I didn't pass out," I correct him, "my Sef I didn't work!"

"Why didn't you tell me?" Tim whispers furiously.

"Why didn't I tell you?" I sputter. "You were shooting daggers at me and the camera was watching! How was I supposed to tell you?"

Helen and Crissa hug each other as Tim and I stare each other down. I mentally register the extreme difference. Crissa and Helen have been together for years, friends who've been through a lot together and their relationship is solid. This dysfunction Tim and I have seems to only get worse. And we've added scowling Chloe to our unstable concoction.

"We don't have time for this!" Tim barks in a whisper. "I'm supposed to be in the security booth for the next hour. We have one hour until the next shift arrives."

"Forty-five minutes," Chloe says holding up a watch.

"Why would anyone be in the booth if the cameras are dead?" I ask.

"Two people man the booth around the clock - whether the power is on or off makes no difference. My shift is over in forty-five minutes. Don't ask stupid questions. If the power *does* come back on and we aren't out of here when the next two arrive, we are screwed."

"Where's the other guy," I ignore his warning about stupid questions, so tired of his self-important garbage, "the guy who was with you for your shift?"

Tim shoots me a withering glare and I trade my stupid question asking for a more important one, "How do we get out of here if their Sef Is do still work?" I ask, motioning to the other girls.

"With this," Tim says holding up a small device that looks like Auntie's kitchen timer. "It will interfere with the signal, but it has a small radius. It's supposed to be for one person. They'll have to keep close together and hold it in the center of their huddle. It's all I could get."

I nod, but I have more questions. How will it work when we add Harmony? Is Harmony awake? What about when we add my dad and Matt and Aunty Betty? How is Tim going to get such a big group out of here without being stopped?

“Let’s go,” Tim says turning to the door.

If we get out of here, Tim and I are going to have some words. Tim pulls the door open and we all stand petrified. Patrice stands in front of my door, her mouth hanging open in shock. She is flanked by two plastic-faced guards.

“What is this?” Patrice asks, mystified.

“I was bringing these carriers to a room with auxiliary power,” Tim reassumes his role as Dr. Shepherd.

“It’s you?” Patrice questions Tim with obvious hurt on her pumpkin orange face. “You’re the saboteur? I offered you everything.”

“Let’s be professional, Patrice.” Tim says quietly, caught in her gaze.

Patrice’s eyes are twitching with unwanted moisture. Can evil cry? Apparently it can try.

There’s this still moment where the question of “what now?” builds until it explodes into a blur of action. Patrice claps her gloved hands and the muffled clap signals chaos. The guards jump at Tim. One masked face punches Tim in the stomach and the other guard goes for his neck. Tim fights back, his arms swinging, but not hitting either target hard enough to free himself. Watching them pummel him, I’m terrified and certain that our only chance to escape is already spent.

Chapter Forty-Seven

What's Good For The Goose Is Good For The Gander

Chloe darts into the fray and Helen and I shout for her to stay back. One of the guards grabs her, leaving Tim with only one assailant. Chloe struggles and donkey kicks the guard whose arms are wrapped around her. He curses behind his white mask and grabs her short hair, twisting and yanking it to subdue her.

"Careful with her!" Patrice barks, always protective of her carriers.

Chloe delivers a cobra strike punch to the guard's throat, and he stumbles back releasing her. Chloe runs to where Tim and the other guard are locked in a loveless hug. She slips her hand into Tim's lab coat pocket and then plunges a Taser into Tim's attacker's stomach. The guard releases Tim's throat and drops to the ground, spasming.

Tim goes from defensive to offensive. The second guard rallies from Chloe's throat punch and lunges towards Tim. Tim pulls his fist back and delivers a powerful blow to the second guard's face mask. The thin plastic crumples against the silver-suited man's face. Tim kicks the wobbly guard directly in the chest and, in mere seconds, both guards are down. Tim Tazes them both, ensuring their defeat.

I see Patrice reach into her coat and my head screams at me to stop her. I spring for her and rip the button out of her hand, but not before she's able to press it. Chloe, Crissa and Helen drop instantaneously to their knees. Crissa and Helen are still inside my room but Chloe is in the hallway after helping Tim fight. I hear Chloe's knees hit the hard linoleum floor. The three girls scream and moan, clutching at their ears, writhing on the floor.

"Tim!" I throw him the button.

I wrap my arms around Patrice and hold tight to her as she struggles, bent backwards against my pregnant belly. If she gets away, she'll bring more guards and our escape will be over before it started. I put my hand over her mouth and she yells in vain against my hand. Tim presses Patrice's button in a successive pattern and the girl's bodies relax, relieved.

Chloe's cries go from tortured to tearful. Tim rushes to her side, cradling her head, whispering to her. She pulls her knee to her chest and whimpers.

I stare at them with a tightness in my chest. Holding Patrice tightly, I turn away from Tim and Chloe to check on Helen and Crissa.

Helen is leaning over Crissa just like Tim over Chloe. Crissa is holding her eight and a half months pregnant belly and breathing sharp breaths through her teeth. The pain put her delicate body into labor! This is a catastrophe! I turn back to call Tim over to our more pressing problem and I see him plant a loving kiss on Chloe's forehead as he whispers to her.

One of the guards on the floor moans. Tim stands up from Chloe's side and walks over to the guard with the crumpled mask. Tim holds up his Taser and presses a button. I hear the small weapon's electronic charge build, a high pitched noise that sings higher and higher. Tim kneels next to the struggling guard and presses the Taser to silver-suited man's heart.

Tim discharges the shock and the man's limbs flail. Tim presses it over and over until the convulsing man lays still. I watch in disbelief. My limbs are like stone as my head tells me to do something and my eyes just watch Tim murder. Patrice is still in my arms, watching Tim. I cling to her, less restraining and more relying on her to hold me up. Tim crosses to the other guard and I find my voice.

"What are you doing?" I cry at him.

"This is war, Ivy. I have no way of locking them up. The Taser will wear off and they'll send every guard in this god-awful place down on us. I'm trying to save you and the babies. Pravda will kill your baby, Ivy." Tim says, staring at me as he presses his Taser into the second guard.

The second guard goes still after only two rounds of electric shock to his heart. Patrice is surprisingly still. I glance at her orange face and see respect in her eyes. She admires Tim and his ability to kill. Patrice's acceptance of Tim's actions makes me even more certain that he was wrong. Tim is next to me taking Patrice from me. Patrice slides willingly into Tim's arms. Is everyone in this place crazy? How can everyone here be this enamored with Tim Markowitz!

"Help Chloe," Tim directs me and, woodenly, I move to obey.

Tim drags the dead guards into a nearby room and closes them inside. We file back into my room, Chloe limping with an arm over my shoulder. I pull my door closed and Chloe leans against it.

"Ivy, what do you have in here to tie her up?" Tim asks as Patrice leans against him in depressed resignation.

Something about her posture suggests that she's comfortable in his arms. I turn circles looking around at my room in the dim light of Tim's flashlight. I can't think of anything.

"Can we lock her in the bathroom?" I suggest.

"No. There's a camera in there. They'd see her as soon as the next guard took over."

"What!" I shout. "What do you mean there's a camera in there!"

I'm horrified.

I've been changing my clothes in there. Reading Tim's notes in there. Crying and picking my nose in there! The thought that Pravda saw all my most private moments. That Tim could've been the one watching! I feel sick and furious and violated.

"Think, Ivy!" Tim snaps me back. "We need to tie her up and bring her with us."

"What if we used the button?" Chloe asks, leaning against my door frame, standing on only her good leg. "We could take Ivy's Sef I out and reset it. Put it on Pumpkin Face."

Tim looks at me with his lips pressed in a hard line.

"Will that work?" I ask. "Mine's broken."

"I could possibly reset it. It might just be that it wasn't calibrated correctly."

"How do we get it off?" I ask.

"It would hurt," Tim says quietly.

"She'll be fine," Chloe says with obvious disdain from her place at the door.

"Why don't you do it then?" I challenge Chloe fiercely, hiding my cowardice.

"Theirs still work. The Sef I's would kill them before I could rip it half way out," Tim says quietly.

Rip is a horrible word.

Crissa groans and inhales staccato breaths at my feet. We have to get her out of here or Pravda will take another innocent life. I look up at Tim and see concern for me on his face. I stare back into his eyes and we share a moment. Some part of him still cares about me. We've been through so much together. Losing Aunty, escaping Toccoa, the cave, our almost kiss, the waterfall, the bandits, Herb's place and the butcher. We both loved my Aunty. We both lost Toccoa. We both love Rosa. There is a bond between us that nothing can break. Tim has moved on, but we will always have that. I nod at Tim and he understands.

Tim puts Patrice in my small bathroom, and she looks sorrowfully at him as he closes the door. Tim slides my big rocking chair in front of the bathroom door, sealing Patrice inside. She tries the door once, ramming against the rocker. Then, she is quiet.

Tim points to my bed and I sit on the edge. Chloe hobbles across the room and climbs onto my bed next to me. Tim lays me down gently and scoots me over to the edge. Chloe makes an irritated noise in her throat and I revel in the fact that she doesn't have one hundred percent of Tim's devotion. Chloe lays her pregnant body over my chest, pinning me down with her well endowed torso. The claustrophobia of being trapped and out of control makes me suddenly scared.

I struggle against Chloe's arms and say, "Wait!"

"No time, Ivy," Tim sits down on the floor beside me and I feel his fingers wrap around the Sef I. "I'm sorry," he whispers.

Then he yanks.

The plastic ear piece tears through my flesh and cartilage and I scream. Chloe holds me tight with vicious strength until Tim pulls the Sef I free. When she sits up, I open my tear-filled eyes and look up at her. Her smug face stares down at me compassionless. She couldn't care less about my pain. I feel hatred bloom in my chest. She probably enjoyed that. I shove her away from me and sit up. Tim hands me a towel, and I hold it to my bleeding ear.

Chloe holds the flashlight for Tim as he fiddles with the Sef I.

"Thirty-two minutes," Chloe updates with a glance at the watch on her wrist and Tim grunts in return, his concentration on the bloody earpiece.

"Got it." Tim says and he and Chloe cross the room to my bathroom.

Tim pulls the rocking chair out of the way and he and Chloe go into the little room with Patrice and pull the door shut, leaving Helen, Crissa and I in total darkness. Patrice shouts and struggles inside the tiny water closet and I hear what sounds like a slap. Patrice screams and then the bumping noises subside. The three of them exit the bathroom, Tim first then Patrice with Chloe limping behind. As Tim's flashlight brings back sight to the room, I see my earpiece in Patrice's ear.

"How do you know it will work?" I ask.

Chloe holds up the button.

"Chloe, give it to me, please?" Tim asks.

I blink, startled. Tim never asks. He bosses. Why does Chloe get his respect?

"If you press it, you'll all feel it!" I warn her. "Crissa can't take anymore!"

"That's why Tim brought us this," Chloe says holding up the kitchen timer lookalike.

Tim pats at his lab coat pocket in delayed acceptance of the fact that Chloe picked his pocket. Chloe limps backwards, away from Tim and Patrice to stand close to Helen and Crissa.

"Chloe, let me—" Tim holds out his hand to her.

Chloe ignores him and presses the button. Patrice shrieks and falls to her knees, writhing in the pain that she has caused countless others to suffer.

Crissa shouts out for Chloe to stop. Crissa's spirit reminds me who I am. Though some part of me likes seeing Patrice hurt, I try to grab the button from Chloe's hands. Tim pulls the button from us and clicks the successive clicks that end Patrice's empathy session.

Chapter Forty-Eight
A Specter of The Past

After a quick stop at a medical closet to bandage my ear, our group is maneuvering the hallways at a frustratingly slow speed. Crissa can barely walk from the cramping labor pains and Chloe's knee is probably broken. Helen and I are helping Crissa. Tim is carrying Chloe. I've been entrusted with Patrice's button. She walks like a cat behind Tim and Chloe, her hands in the pockets of her white coat.

The hallways are all dark, and our only light is the flashlight in Chloe's hands. Tim leads us past the room with the pipes, and I see flash lights and lanterns scurrying around. Panicked voices call out to each other. Someone in the room is shouting obscenities. We keep moving.

Two more empty hallways lead us to a hall that I recognize. This is where I woke up from the coma. Tim motions for us to go ahead of him through an open door near the end of the hallway. I'm unprepared for what is inside. In the pale, bluish light from the flashlight, Harmony looks like a corpse. She lays motionless in the dark room on the narrow hospital bed. She's hooked up to wires and machines, but with the power out, they are silent. There is no indication that she is alive.

Crissa cries out with another contraction behind me, but I'm fixated on Harmony. I walk slowly over to my best friend. Her auburn head has been shaved and the horrible Sef I is in her delicate, elf-like ear. Her skin is pure white and her cheeks are thin and hallow. She was always skinny, but now she's emaciated. Tears fall from my eyes as I pet her cool forehead. Under the thin sheet that covers her, her stomach protrudes - pregnant with Pravda's science.

Tim approaches her from the other side of the bed with a needle in his hand. His face mirrors my heartbreak. He holds the needle up and, with a sharp breath, he plunges it into Harmony's arm.

"What is it? What did you do?" I ask.

"It's experimental. A drug that will cool her blood and bring on hypothermia."

"What? Why? How will that help?"

"Some coma patients have responded to hypothermia. I had to at least try before we left her."

"We can't leave her!"

"We can't take her like this."

"How long will it take?"

"If she doesn't show signs of response in the next few minutes -"

"We can't leave her!"

"We can't take her, Ivy!"

"I *can't* leave her!"

"Ivy, I can't care for her. I don't have I.V.s and heart monitors. We don't know if she'll ever wake up."

I hold tightly to Harmony's skeletal, limp fingers with dry eyes. I wonder if I am capable of crying for her, if I have any tears left. I can't leave her here. God has plans for her. He brought her back from the dead! It wasn't so she could lie here alone in Pravda's hell.

"Tim," I gasp, "Pray with me!"

Tim lays his hands on Harmony. Helen and Crissa reach out to touch her feet though the sheet. I put my arms around her like I did that night in Toccoa. My arms feel too empty because she feels so small.

"God! Please!" I beg Him like I did that night.

But no peace fills me. No supernatural power flows through me.

"Please?" I whisper, but Harmony lays limp against my chest.

"Twenty minutes," Chloe reports.

"Ivy, we're out of time. We have to go. If we bring Harmony, we can't get Matt or your dad and your Aunt. You'll have to decide.

It's an impossible decision. I can't choose to leave any of them. I cradle Harmony and tears slide down my cheeks and land in the stubble on her shaved head. I knew they would surface eventually.

Tim is at my side, pulling at me gently, "Ivy, we have to go now."

Crissa cries out, taken by a strong contraction.

"Nineteen minutes," Chloe whispers fiercely.

I let Tim make the decision. He pulls me away from Harmony, and I watch her thin form flop back onto the bed like a rag doll. Her skeletal face slides sideways against the thin pillow beneath her, leaving her neck at a sharp angle. I watch her eyes, and internally, I beg them to open. My prayers and urgent wishes have no power. If only those long lashes would flutter open so I could smile at her beautiful gray eyes again. I think of her mother. Sherry was like a mother to me. She would be horrified to see her little girl like this. To see her in this terrible place. I lay my hand on Harmony's pregnant belly, and the baby inside kicks me. I jump at the feeling and look up at Tim.

Tim pulls me away from the bed. He carefully removes her I.V. and the heart monitors on her chest. Is he bringing her with us? What about Matt and my dad? Tim lifts Harmony who is still wrapped in her sheets. It looks like he's holding a ghost. Harmony's white face looks like death, and the gauzy sheet flutters around her as Tim walks her to one side of the room and lays her on the ground.

"What are you doing?" I croak through my tears.

"Crissa needs the bed, and I think I have a plan," Tim answers leaving Harmony laying alone on the cold dark floor in the corner.

I turn away from Harmony, unable to bear the sight. Tim helps Crissa up into Harmony's bed, and she breathes the sharp "hee hee who, hee hee who" breaths of labor. Tim rummages through drawers and turns to hand out the objects of his search. Each of us pull on nursing scrubs, hair nets and surgical masks.

"Let's go! Seventeen minutes!" Chloe barks.

Tim wheels Crissa's bed to the door and whispers something to Patrice. She nods and pulls the door open, leading the way out of the room. Helen helps Chloe out the door behind them, but I can't bring myself to follow.

I stumble back to where Harmony lays alone on the floor in the corner. I gather her one more time in my arms and whisper how much I love her, how sorry I am, into her cold ear. I promise to try to come back. I tell her how sorry I am that I got her into this. I pray for God to protect my friend and bring her safely home. This isn't goodbye. We'll be together again when Jesus comes back for His bride.

"Ivy," Tim calls from the door.

I look sadly up at him, my heart completely slain.

"Ivy, hurry! Matt is waiting for us. He needs you!"

I crawl away from my friend, and I know I'll always hate myself for leaving her here.

*****

We've only gotten halfway down the hallway outside of Harmony's room when the group stops moving. I brush away my tears and move around Helen and Chloe who are stopped in front of me. Tim is toe to toe with the largest Pravdanian guard I've ever seen. Another hulking guard stands protectively next to a silver-suited old man. The old man's fat gut implies his wealth and importance. There are bandages around his ears and oozing wounds on his face and neck. His eyes find mine staring and they smolder back at me, full of smug hatred.

The Director.

I've never seen him. No one told me who he was or what he looked like, but I know without a doubt that this is him. This is Jessie's ex-husband. This is Trudy's father. This vile man put his own daughter in the carrier program. This short, loathsome man *is* Pravda. He opens his mouth to speak, but Crissa interrupts him and addresses the guard in front of Tim.

Crissa's labor pains seemed to have ceased, and her voice booms with authority, "Loren, you gave your life to the King of Kings in your youth, but hatred and jealousy choked the Spirit of the Living God until only the seed remained, dormant in the soil of your sinful heart. Now you dare to rise up against His elect? Your mother's prayers still resound in My ears. Turn from wickedness before you share its defeat!"

Crissa turns her head to look at the old man and the other towering bodyguard. "Michael," Crissa pronounces, "You have spit in the face of your Creator. I will bear with you no longer."

The white-masked Pravdanian bodyguard, standing protectively close to the Director, wobbles and then topples down dead in front of us.

Muscular, statuesque Loren turns away from Tim to look down at his dead compatriot. Loren yelps like a little boy and tears the white plastic mask from his face. He stares at pregnant Crissa where she sits on the hospital bed. His young, splotchy, handsome face quivers with fear and awe before he turns abruptly and runs down the hall away from us. Helen and I exchange a wide-eyed glance. Crissa's gift of prophecy has me living with a constant covering of goose bumps today.

Tim lunges forward, his Taser in hand, to attack the old man who stands alone and unprotected.

"Wait," the Director holds up a white gloved hand and Tim hesitates.

The Director stares past Tim as though the threat of the Taser means nothing to him, "You belong to me, Ivy. Your child is *the one*. I know this."

I step backwards against Helen, afraid of the evil man and his penetrating stare.

His eyes lower to my stomach as he continues, "Should you leave this place today, I will hunt you down and bring you back. But not before killing everyone you love. All of them," he says gesturing at our group, "will die at my hand if you leave this building."

The Director steps forward, daring Tim. Allowing the Taser to rest against his silver-suited chest, but Tim doesn't press the button.

"Do not doubt me," the old man threatens icily. "You may speak of deities, but here," he waves his skinny arms, "I am God. I spoke the word and your pitiful town burned. I sent death to all of your people and I lit the match that burned them where they fell. Where was your God then?"

Helen grabs for me as I start towards the sick old man.

The Director smiles and then coughs a wet cough full of phlegm and spittle, "I know where your loved ones are hiding. Thomas and my wife? Your boyfriend may think he hid them well enough, but no one moves that I don't see it. They can't hide from me! This is my kingdom and I decide who lives or dies. Do you want to be responsible for Thomas being ripped limb from limb?"

Finally, Tim plunges his Taser into the wet, irritated skin of the old man's neck, and electricity sends the Director twitching to the ground. Tim pushes the Taser against the old man's heart and discharges the shock over and over again. Tim must have known the horrible man. It must have tortured Tim to work all this time for the man who killed his father. Tim continues to send bouts of current through the pudgy-chested man long after he has gone still. Crissa cries out suddenly in pain. Her labor pains are back in full-force.

Chapter Forty-Nine
Something's Cooking

Each step I take away from where we left Harmony filets another slice off of my wounded heart. We jog down another hallway, pushing Crissa's bed, looking like a team of doctors at first glance. A second glance might notice our peach spandex arms sticking out under the short papery green sleeves of our stolen nurse's uniforms. An inquisitive eye might notice the girl's SefIs under the gossamer thin hair nets. Thank God, we've yet to pass a living soul. We've moved out of the belly of Pravda and into the outer hallways that are lit with dazzling light from the late morning sunshine.

I haven't stepped into the sun since God's most recent judgment on mankind. Our Elder's theorized that the rest of the curses wouldn't affect us, as long as we stay close to the Savior's side. But they weren't completely sure about it.

The halls are empty because Pravda's employees are afraid of the sun. One of God's kindest gifts - the warm, life-giving light of day - is terrifying to His creation. There is so much symbolism in this curse, just like the other curses. God's holiness shines brighter than the sun, and anyone not covered by the blood of Jesus will burn in the presence of His holiness. He is trying to show them. Calling them to Himself for salvation. Pushing them; begging them to come.

Patrice slides herself against the wall, avoiding the sun's rays as we hurry down the hall. When Tim pushed her ahead of us into the light, the skin on her exposed arm sizzled and burned, making my hungry stomach gurgle. Tim, Helen and I walk through the beams of light unharmed. Crissa rides through the brilliant sunlight with painful contractions, but unaffected by the sun.

Perched on the edge of Crissa's bed, Chloe winces in the light - not burned like Patrice but not unaffected either. I wonder how long it will take for her to accept the blame for her own disease. It's driving me nuts to see how much Tim cares for her, despite her rotten attitude and her diseased state. I know I'm a hypocrite. Matt was odious to Tim, and I wished Tim would give him a chance. Somehow, Tim sees something of value in Chloe's backslidden heart. I can't keep myself from wondering if her curvy figure has something to do with his patience.

Tim shields Patrice when the shadows give way to too much sunlight. She leads us to an outer door and punches in a code. The door beeps and the lock disengages. Tim opens the door and pushes Patrice towards it.

"Please!" she begs, "I can't go out there!"

"I'm truly sorry," Tim apologizes, "but you have to."

Tim whips the sheet off of Crissa and drapes it over Patrice, "Stay under my arm and I'll shield you," he offers with a compassion I haven't seen from him since he assumed his new role.

He's been Dr. Shepherd for so long; I'm relieved to see Tim Markowitz resurfacing from beneath the zombie makeup.

Patrice grabs Tim's arm and begs, "I promise, I won't turn you in! Please let me stay here!"

"Don't make me use this," Chloe threatens.

I don't remember setting the button down, but I must have let go of it when we were in Harmony's room. Patrice's orange face is twisted in fear, but not because Chloe has a hold of the button. She's terrified of the sun. There are streaks where her makeup has worn off and left diseased skin exposed. I thought she was bad with the makeup. Without it, she's hideous.

"It doesn't have to be this way," Tim says. "You can still repent. Ask God to forgive you and be free from these curses. You could come with us."

"No!" Chloe and I shout in chorus.

"Yes," Crissa says through her teeth, grimacing. "Please, Patrice. Accept the wondrous gift He offers, His precious blood will cover all your sins and heal your disease."

Another contraction takes gracious Crissa - who of all people could hate Patrice the most. Seven times Patrice has used and stolen from Crissa, but Crissa would forgive seventy times.

"Her contractions are getting closer," Helen says, her Asian eyes slanted with worry.

"Nine minutes left," Chloe says flatly.

Tim stares at Patrice, his hands on her shoulders, "Either way you are walking through that door. You choose what kind of woman the sun will shine on."

*****

Patrice cries and her flesh sizzles as we make our way across a paved courtyard. Our destination is on the other side of the lot. We're pushing Crissa and Chloe over the bumpy pavement towards a rusty metal door in the side of a long, metal building. All around the lot, chain link fencing with razor wire encompasses us. Somewhere in that building, Matt and my dad and my aunt are waiting. Once we get them out, we'll have to cross back to the main building to make our escape.

Tim does his best to shield Patrice, but the thin sheet is no protection and her face and arms are cherry red by the time we reach the door. Another key pad waits and this time Tim punches in the numbers. Patrice shoves her way through the door, desperate to be out of the sun. Chloe hobbles in behind her, her own skin bright pink like she spent a June day at the beach.

Crissa's bed won't fit through the door. Tim and Helen lift her down to help her inside. As they cross the threshold, Crissa's water breaks. Little Leila won't wait much longer for us to find safety. She is coming soon. I step over the puddle of amniotic fluid and into the dark stairwell of the Tomb, pulling the heavy metal door shut behind me.

The instantaneous temperature drop is a relief. The cool darkness lights up as Tim flips on his flashlight. The power must be out all over the compound. Tim searches the room with the diluted beam of light. We are in a small hanger full of old helicopters. The hanger seems more like a graveyard and the copters look like they've seen better days.

The metallic room echoes back the sounds of our group - Crissa's labored moaning, Helen's whispered shushing, Patrice's whimpers, our shuffling footsteps. More sounds from far below us add to the cacophony. Somewhere in the distance a grown man is wailing and the sound of his broken spirit makes me want to run. Metal bangs against metal like the rattling of prison bars and the clangs echo around us.

Patrice directs us down a narrow hall to a green metal door. Helen, Crissa, and Chloe file into the small room as Tim shines his flashlight into each corner. Before I follow them, I lift my arm into the darkness to my left. A noticeable breeze is blowing out of the concentrated darkness beyond my finger tips. I take a step towards the breeze, curiosity calling me forward. A hand grabs my shoulder and I yelp, startled.

Tim shines his light into the breezy dark and I see a never ending staircase descending. I had almost stepped off the top edge. Another cry from below bounces up the echoey staircase and sends an involuntary shiver up my neck. Tim pulls me past the green metal door to join the others. It's an old break room. Coke and Chip machines with barren slots reflect Tim's light. A dirty table with one chair upturned on top fills up the rest of the small room.

Chloe runs her hands up and down against the Coke machine buttons and asks, "Anybody have fifty cents?"

Money hasn't been worth anything for years. Coke hasn't been made for years. To buy one these days would cost almost a whole pint of blood. I remember the taste of it. Bubbly, sharp, refreshing sweetness. It was less than a year ago that I had a cold Coke at Jesse's kitchen table. I catch a glimpse of Matt's eyes in my memory of him reaching over and popping the top for me. I'm about to see those eyes again.

"Patrice and I are going down alone. I'll knock three times when we come back up," Tim says, fiddling with a dusty lantern he found on the floor.

"I want to go with you!" I argue as the lantern's yellow light flickers on and fills the small room.

"There will be guards, Patrice and I won't draw their attention."

"What if something goes wrong? What if you can't find them! I can't leave them here, Tim!"

"Ivy, I'll do everything I can to find them." Tim leans close to me, his eyes so serious they look angry, "But I won't sacrifice this group for them. We are all leaving here in less than ten minutes if possible. The minute that power comes back on, the cameras will find us and there will be no getting out."

"We should leave now," Chloe whines. "Your security shift is up and they'll be looking for you! We're out of time."

Tim gives her a soft look and I want to punch them both in the face.

"I'm going with you. If you don't find them, I'll stay behind. You can leave without me!" I insist.

"Take her," Chloe snorts. "This is taking too long!"

“Stay here. Help Crissa,” Tim says as he turns to leave.

“Patrice can stay here and help. I can wear her clothes!” I argue frantically.

Crissa cries out from where she is squatting over the oil-stained floor, “Hurry!”

“Ivy is right. I have to stay here. We can’t lose this baby!” Patrice says, stripping her white lab coat.

Patrice isn’t concerned with the value of human life or Crissa’s ill-timed emergency. All she cares about is testing Leila in the do-or-die hope that she will be LS free.

“I’ve got this,” Chloe says confidently to Tim, holding up Patrice’s button and the gadget for blocking the Sef Is.

Tim stalks out of the room and I grab Patrice’s coat and hurry after him. Tim bounds down the stairs ahead of me. His flashlight bounces as he descends and makes my progress behind him dizzying. I pull Patrice’s coat on and finish buttoning it as we stomp lower and lower into the earth. A smell tickles my nose and I slow my steps. The odor matures with each downward step until the onerous stench of decay and human waste push against me like a living force. The Tomb, Tim called it. I feel claustrophobic in the putrid dark. I hold my sleeve over my nose as we plunge deeper.

I bump into Tim’s back when he finally stops. Our trip down has bathed my skin in clammy dampness. I breathe through my mouth to keep from smelling the wicked stink at the bottom. Knowing the kind of air I’m inhaling makes me nauseated. The stench is so thick I feel like I’m poisoning my lungs with the wet, germ-filled particles. It’s like we fell into an outhouse.

Chapter Fifty

I Bet You Didn't See That Coming

A dark hallway slinks before us and in the distance I see pricks of lantern light. As we hurry along the tunnel, a ravine with steel tracks stretches alongside us. I try to remember the word for the trains that ran underground when I was a kid. My legs are tired from the long trip down, but Tim jogs as though we have much farther to go. I'm glad I've kept up with my treadmilling. The wails of the crying man that I heard above originate somewhere down the long tunnel. Closer and louder, the sound of torment makes me want to cover my ears and scream.

My stomach turns and leaps around. Not from the baby, not from the smell, not from fear, but because I'm about to see Matt again. I'm thirty weeks pregnant. My belly is gigantic. My long, curly hair is gone. My ear is torn and bandaged. My peach spandex zombie suit clings to my misshapen body. Even as I know it's ridiculous to be concerned with my appearance at a time like this, I know that it will break my heart if Matt recoils at the sight of me.

When we last saw each other, anger and jealousy marred our last few minutes together. Will it still hang between us seven months later? I told him I didn't want anything to do with him. What if he gave up on me? Got over me like Tim did? I've grown closer to him, yearning for him through the lonely months. It may have all been in my head - imaginary moments we spent together in my dreams - but I've loved him more every day.

A lantern grows closer and brighter and Tim and I slow to walk. The lantern bobs along until the guard is only a few feet away. My muscles clench with anxiety and I fight to keep my head up and my eyes straight ahead. Will he notice my peach legs sticking out beneath Patrice's coat? Is the hair net completely covering my shaved head and bloody ear? The silver-suited guard is mask-less. Aside from Loren, who Crissa just scared the pants off of, I've never seen a guard's face.

"Dr. Shepherd," the trim, silver-suited young man nods, and Tim nods back - not slowing his brisk steps.

I glance sideways at Tim after we pass the guard, restraining myself from looking back. Another lantern lies just ahead. The tracks beside me aren't empty anymore. Metal cages sit still on the tracks below us, set back to back to back. The cages are labeled *100.* I peer down through the gray bars and see hopeless faces. Disease eaten faces. Men reduced to skeletal, rag covered zombies. Some of them watch us as we walk. Some of them lay still as though dead, but their eyes blink at me like spasms of electricity passing through a corpse.

"Where are they?" I whisper to Tim as we pass cages marked *300.*

"Further," he whispers back.

As the cages recede behind us, the entombed look more and more lifelike - evidence of less time in Pravda's prison. The cages stretch on ahead of us as far as I can see. If we aren't yet to my Dad and Aunty Betty's cage, Matt's cage must be far in the distance. Pravda's heinous cruelty is written on the faces of the prisoners we pass. What if Tim has no intention of finding my Matt? What if he says it's too far down? I can't leave without him! But can I see my father after all this time and not go with him?

Another lantern, another mask-less guard approaches. Tim slows and stops by "500".

"Can I help you doctor?" the ugly man with a piggish nose and bandaged ears asks Tim.

"I need 511 and 512," Tim says with calm authority.

The man stares at me with beady eyes and asks, "Why aren't we following protocol?"

"All personnel are on overtime with the carriers, this power outage is a pain in the ass," Tim cusses easily and my eyes widen unintentionally. "This is Dr. Mara, she's new," Tim says, nodding at me.

"Ma'am," the guard nods at me and I stare back. "What numbers you say again?"

"511 and 512."

Walking down the row ahead of us, the guard stops at a cage and punches in a long series of numbers. Before opening the door, the guard flicks his arm and a long stick, sizzling with electricity, unsheathes itself in his fist. An electric weapon to subdue defiant prisoners. I dig my fingers into Tim's arm, terrified that the man will use it on my family.

"511 and 512," the guard snarls.

A single figure stands up in the back corner of the cage. A hood of ragged cloth covers the prisoner's face and head. Is it my father? My aunt? Someone I love stands in the shadows unmoving. How have they survived this hellhole? Tears of anticipation and pity begin to gather in the corners of my eyes and I put all of my effort into holding the tears back.

"512's been dead for months. You come to take her body? Nothing left to take," an old man's raspy voice mutters.

It comes over me slowly that this is my father. He doesn't sound like my father, but how could anyone sound the same after so many years in this place? I won't recognize him and he won't recognize me. If he is 511 then Aunty Betty must have been 512.

She's gone.

I fight back the tears, but one of them escapes me and slides down my dry cheek.

"512 was taken out of the system when it expired," the guard says accusingly. "Excuse me Dr. Shepherd, but I'm supposed to flag non-protocol transactions and this doesn't sit."

I loathe the guard who called my Aunty Betty an it.

"Go ahead and flag away, Porter," Tim says as though bored. "I have another specimen to collect. Let me know how that flag goes for you. They've got nothing but time for your important problems with the sun burning everyone's skin off and carriers dying and the power outage. I'm sure they'll jump right on your protocol flag. Patrice loves to be bothered with minutia," Tim spits.

"Yes, sir," the guard says with much less confidence. "511!" the guard barks and the man in the shadows steps out of the cage and into the dim lantern light.

I force myself to stare at my emaciated father. He stares down at the floor, broken by years of slavery. His clothes are shredded and greasy with black mildew. A full beard of gray hair covers his face and more gray hair hangs long and shaggy beneath the hood he wears. He is taller than me and from where I stand I can see his eyes though they are downcast. He looks sideways at me and I see intelligence not lunacy. His eyes are bright and clear and his face is healthy beneath streaks of black grime. He Lives.

Tim turns to continue down the long stretch of decay filled cages and I snap into place beside him. There will be time for reunions later - if we can make it out of here.

"Sir!" the pig-nosed guard shouts after us and my stomach lurches.

Tim pauses and then turns - cool, calm and collected.

"Don't forget the stick," the guard warns and tosses Tim a narrow cylinder.

"Thanks," Tim says, catching the twisting cylinder out of the air with a steady hand.

Tim flicks his wrist and a long electric rod extends, sparking at the end. Tim motions with the rod and my father takes his place in front of us, leading the way down the never ending darkness of death row.

*****

After we've walked a good distance from the guard and his lantern, Tim steps quickly towards my dad. "Sir, I need to know if you are well. He is risen."

My dad stumbles and trips, falling forward on his hands. I yelp and reach for him, but Tim grabs my arm roughly and holds me back, shaking his head silently at me. Tim doesn't want my dad to know who I am. I know he's right. I know it won't get us out of here quickly and we desperately need quickly. I submit to his wisdom and take a step back.

"Sir? He is risen?"

"He is risen indeed," my dad whispers.

"Are you able to run? We might need to run soon. Not yet, but soon."

"I can do all things through Christ who strengthens me," my dad rumbles quietly.

He's so old. When I last saw him, I was eleven and he was forty-seven. He's only fifty-three now but The Tomb has leached his life away and stolen the years from him. He looks like a seventy year old man. And he sounds like he's ninety.

"My daughter is here," my dad gravels and I clamp my hand over my mouth to hold in a sob.

Matt must have gotten word to him that I'm here. I want so much to hold him and tell him I'm ok.

"Right up here," my dad says, his feet shuffling faster into a limping jog.

Tim looks at me with concern. We're both worried that dad might not be as lucid as we had hoped, as we need him to be.

"Hazel!" my father whispers.

"Hazel!" my dad says with quiet desperation and my world spins.

"Hazel!" I hear before I feel my body falling towards the floor.

Chapter Fifty-One

I Impersonate The Devil

"Ivy!" my name comes with a sharp sting on my cheek.

I blink into Tim's flashlight and see the old man staring down at me, dirty tears streaking down his weathered face.

"Ivy, we have to move! Please tell me you can walk!" Tim urges desperately and I nod.

Tim pulls me up to my feet. The bearded old man stares at me and I stare back at him. I smile at the stranger who is my dad and he lifts his dirty wet beard in a smile too.

"Let's go!" Tim urges and we hurry after him.

I know our time was up a while ago. Every second we're down here puts everyone in our group in greater danger. The world is spinning too fast and the seconds are flying by in fast forward. Hazel is here! My father and my sister and Matt! Please God, I beg silently. Please, you must get us out of here! Miracle Maker, make a way for us!

"Hazel?" Tim whispers.

"Hazel?" my father and I whisper.

"Hazel!" a crazed man nearby takes up our chant. "Hazel!" the disembodied voice shouts and then giggles maniacally.

"Here," A man's whisper travels towards us from farther down.

We sprint towards the saner voice.

"Here!" he says again as we pass his cage and we stop hard and turn towards the voice. "She's out. She's not well."

Tim cusses again and though I hate to hear curses come from him, I understand.

"Let's pray for her, Ivy," my daddy prompts and my heart swells like a little girl.

My dad and I kneel down and reach our hands through the bars. The man inside lifts a lifeless form and lays her against our hands. A mild shock reverberates through my body when I bump against the metal bars. I jump and move my arm away from the bars. With my sister in our arms - avoiding the metal bars - my dad prays.

In this dungeon, the cold cement beneath my knees, the rank smells of waste and death in my nostrils, my long lost sister near death in my arms, I am overcome with peace. My dad's gravelly voice speaks with authority and camaraderie to our God. I feel a peace and safety next to my dad, who abandoned me years ago, and I know it's Heaven sent.

"Father, this moment is worth all the gold and silver in the world. To hold my children before I die -" my dad trails off, consumed by emotion.

"Jesus," I continue, "Please touch Hazel with your Healing Hand. We need you God, revive her like only You can. Give her wings like eagles and lead us safely through this valley of the shadow of death. We beg you, God -" my voice is stolen from me, too; and my dad and I hold Hazel together and pray a wordless prayer of desperation and thanksgiving.

Then it happens again. The same way He came when He brought Harmony back to life, the Holy Spirit burns in me. His power flows over my skin like icy water blanketing me in goose bumps and chills. A peace that I couldn't describe to someone this side of Heaven swaddles me like an infant and enraptures my soul. Hazel gasps and comes to life in our arms.

"Hazel, Hazel," my dad whispers and she lifts a dirty face to look back at him in the weak light of Tim's flashlight.

"What's your number?" Tim whispers to her with urgent desperation.

"832," my sister answers weakly and my father and I weep at the sound of her voice.

"Get up!" Tim insists and then yells, "Ho!" to a lantern in the distance.

I pull myself up, bumping the metal bar again and jumping again at the small shock.

"Hazel, we're getting out. Don't look at us, look down. We're getting out," my dad whispers to her.

He stands back up and slouches subserviently as the guard's lantern light washes over us.

The lantern belongs to the pig-faced guard.

"832." Tim says with anger in his voice.

"Yes sir."

"832!" the guard calls out as he opens Hazel's cage, the electric stick snapping and popping in his gloved hand.

Hazel steps forward. She is wearing a dirty, peach bodysuit. Hazel was a carrier? The carriers are Pravda's precious hope. What did she do to deserve her time in the Tomb? One look at her and I know that she's been here for years. Her long hair hangs greasy and jagged around her head. Her face is gaunt and her legs are so skinny that her torn spandex suit hangs loosely around them. Her feet are bare and covered in red bumps and oozing sores. Her hands are welted too. She looks up and stares directly at me and I see emptiness in her eyes and LS all over her face.

"A girl?" the guard asks with skepticism all over his hoggish face. "The doctors only take men."

"What is your name?" I step forward and command in my most powerful voice.

Channeling Patrice, I glare the guard down and step close enough to smell his lunch on his breath.

"How dare you accuse the doctors who fight day and night to prolong your miserable life? I will speak to Patrice personally and see that you are refused blood treatment for the next year if you delay us a moment longer."

My voice is full of loathing and hatred and none of it is fake.

Whirling to face Tim, I ask incredulous, "Is this how things are run here? Because I will report to the Director about the insubordination I've witnessed and He will *gut* this place!"

Tim stares wide eyed at me and opens his mouth to speak and then closes it.

"We require one more prisoner. You will go and get him for us while we wait here," I spit at the ugly guard.

I turn back to Tim expectantly and lift my eyebrows at him.

"1,245," Tim says quietly.

"You have five minutes," I bark, "Or you'll find yourself living in this cage!" I point to the hole we just pulled Hazel out of.

"The 1,000 block is more than five minutes walk!" the man sputters.

"Then you had better run," I answer.

*****

Five minutes have passed and Tim and I pace in front of the cage that held Hazel. I've bitten my nails to the quick and begun to chew on the skin around them. The man might have called up to Patrice. He might have gathered more guards to take us down. He might have gone to Matt's cell and found him dead. A hundred scenarios play out in my head and none of them are positive.

My dad and Hazel are huddled together whispering. Hazel being here, being a carrier, being diseased, has been too many new things to process. I don't know how we'll get everyone out. Tim better have a plan after we leave the Tomb. No one up top is gonna fall for me being in charge.

A point of light appears down the line and grows rapidly. Tim and I share a worried glance and wait as the lantern bounces closer. Two forms take shape around the lantern and instead of relief I feel overwhelming anxiety. This is it. Matt is here. Seeing him is all I want and at the same time my biggest fear. I'm so different. I've changed. The Tomb will have changed him, too.

The sound of slapping feet grows closer and the light grows brighter. An electric stick crackles with blue light and one of the runners yelps. The runner in front stumbles towards us and falls to his hands and knees directly in front of me. The guard behind him closes the last few feet, panting, the electric stick still crackling dangerously in his hand.

"Let's go." Tim says annoyed.

Tim waves his stick at my dad and dad nudges Hazel towards us. The man on the ground is still on his hands and knees, trying to catch his breath. What if it isn't Matt? Make that a hundred and one terrible what if scenarios: the guard could've brought us the wrong prisoner. *Please be Matt! Please be Matt!*

"I said move!" Tim commands, brandishing his electric stick at the man on the ground.

The prisoner at my feet lifts his head up to look at me and I stare down at his eyes. Eyes so green they mesmerize me and loosen the ligaments in my knees. Matt's eyes. I smile at him and he smiles at me. Then he arches his back in pain and screams as Tim electrocutes him with his stick. I swivel to scream at Tim. Only God, Himself stops me. I can see the pig nosed guard's face and it is clouded with suspicion. If I defend Matt, I'll damn all of us.

I direct my cold fury at the guard, "You have been insubordinate and obstructive. I don't believe you are qualified to continue in this job. You are forthwith suspended. You will work out the remainder of your shift and then report to Patrice for a disciplinary hearing."

Turning to Tim, my glare intensifies, "I am not impressed."

I can't do anything now, but Tim is going to pay for that later. This may be all an act for the sake of one guard, but my anger is palpable. I have to force my jaw to move naturally. Matt is lying at my feet twitching and I want to claw Tim's face off. My teeth chatter against each other and I feel the restrained power of pent up fury in my limbs.

"I said move it!" Tim barks again with less conviction.

Matt stands slowly, drawing himself up to face Tim. Matt squares his thin shoulders - strong and proud and Tim stares back at him with thinly veiled disdain. Matt's rags look like they've been down here much longer than he has. His dirty hair hangs long around his chiseled face. Despite his filth, he is radiant. Alive. He stares into my eyes and winks at me, his characteristic half-smile playing at his lips. The angry energy I had harnessed a second ago fizzles and I bite my lip to keep from smiling. He's okay. And he's still him. And I love him so much. Subserviently, Matt slouches his shoulders and shuffles ahead of us. Tim and I follow behind our three "prisoners".

"Sir?" the guard asks as we walk away.

"Curing humanity," Tim says over his shoulder.

"Serving the world," the pigman returns, dissolving into the darkness behind us.

Chapter Fifty-Two

The Best Medicine

Each step up the dark staircase puts the tomb behind us. Each step brings fresher air. Matt and I lead the way up, our hands intertwined in a fierce grip that feels like neither of us will ever let go. Tim is behind us, helping my dad with Hazel. The stairs are too narrow for them to pick her up and carry her, which would be faster. She stumbles, despite their supportive arms around her. I wonder how long she's been here. Once we're safe, I'll ask them all the questions that are buzzing in my adrenaline amped brain.

I want to know about my mom. Is she alive? Did she find Life? Maybe now we can all go find her. As we climb, I envision our future together. We'll nurse Hazel back to health and tell her about God's amazing grace. She'll find Life too, and we'll all be a family again. I can't believe God has given me back my family. I don't deserve this superfluous blessing. He's too good to me.

And I have Matt, too. All of my worries were for nothing. I can tell he still cares for me as much as I do for him. My father will marry us. The baby will come and he'll have parents, grandparents and an aunt! I have to ask Matt where Thomas is. The Director said he was hidden somewhere with Jessie. Does she believe now too? We'll go get them and our baby will have an uncle too. Matt and I haven't been able to speak much yet and there is so much to talk about. I look over at him and catch him looking back at me. I smile at him.

Matt's face is smudged with dirt and his hair hangs stiff around his jaw, caked with grossness. His muscled arms show through a torn jacket. He has only a thin undershirt on underneath. I look down and see his bare feet are covered in bloody scabs, his ruined toes that healed but didn't regenerate look worse than I remembered. And still, he is the most handsome guy I've ever known. A heavy layer of stubble covers his face and it makes him look rugged and mysterious. His emerald eyes flash at me and I think that all of his essence is caught up in them.

"I love you!" I blurt as we climb.

"I know," he winks at me.

"I'm sorry," I admit about the past that is long behind us, but still so recent.

"I know," he says quietly.

"I'm pregnant," I confess.

"I can see that," he says with his crooked smile.

"Hurry!" Tim says, right behind us.

"Stick me with that pole again and I'll use your mustache to clean my armpits," Matt says good-naturedly.

I laugh.

I can't remember the last time I laughed. It feels strange and wonderful and I smile at the sound as it echoes around us.

At the top of the stairs, a baby is crying. Tim knocks three times on the green metal door and the door swings open to reveal Crissa holding little Leila. Patrice sits nearby, spotted in blood from the birth, her streaky face unreadable in the yellow lantern light. Chloe and Helen stand over Crissa, smiling down at the squawking baby in Crissa's arms. Something happened in the small room while we were gone, something stranger than a baby being born in the break room of an old airplane hangar.

It's Chloe's face. Her radiant skin glows bright in the dimly lit room. While we were gone, Chloe made things right with God. I imagine it's hard to watch life come into the world and not be awed by it. Chloe smiles up at Tim with teary eyes. I watch Patrice where she sits on the floor with her back against the wall. She witnessed both miracles, the baby and Chloe's transformation. She has searched for years for a baby that would be the cure and, in a way, this baby was. Did it touch her heart? Is God still calling for her or did she harden her heart beyond His touch?

"Chloe," Tim says, crossing the small room in a step and wrapping her in his arms.

Chloe's rejuvenation should make me happy, I know it should.

Tim and Chloe hold each other and I look away. I shrug when Matt finds my eyes and his unruly eyebrows lift in curiosity. If God grants us a miracle and we manage to escape this place together, Tim moving on is the least important thing we have to talk about.

I look around at the faces crammed close to me in the small room. My dad is holding Hazel who looks barely with it. She hasn't looked me in the eyes yet. She looks so much like mom. I wonder if she realizes who I am or if she just doesn't care. I've always blamed myself for her leaving. After all, I was born. That's why she left. Maybe she still regrets my existence. A long line is forming for folks who feel that way. She'll have to find a spot near the back. Still, God has given her back to me. That's something.

"Uncle Tim, this is Leila," Chloe says, holding the tiny pink baby wrapped in green nurse's scrubs out to Tim.

Tim smiles, the truest smile I've seen from him in as long as I can remember. He accepts his mother's namesake into his arms and croons quietly at her. Leila goes calm and quiet in his arms and Crissa smiles proudly.

"We are going to find your daddy," Tim whispers close to Leila's soft forehead. Looking up at Crissa, Tim promises, "We will find him, Crissa. I promise."

As relieved as I am that everyone is okay, a baby is only going to make this harder. There are nine of us not including Patrice. Six Sef Is and only one transmission blocker. Three people who can barely walk. We need a "Walk through the Red Sea" kind of miracle. Chloe leans against Tim and stares down at baby Leila. Tim kisses Chloe's forehead and beams at her. He's a proud uncle and his girlfriend's heart is right with God again. It's a good moment for him.

"Now what?" I ask brusquely, interrupting their nauseating moment.

"I have people waiting for us not far from here. We just have to get to them," Tim says, looking around the room and realizing what I've already been thinking: too many people, too little time. "We have to move, can you walk?" Tim asks Crissa.

Tim hands Leila to Chloe while Helen helps Crissa down from the old table. Crissa stands on her own, albeit unsteadily. The single bulb hanging from the ceiling suddenly blinks on, bathing the small room in bright, white light. Tim, Chloe and I blink up at it in horror.

"I'm guessing that's bad?" Matt asks.

"Hurry!" Tim barks.

Matt finds my hand again as the ten of us file out of the small room and into the well lit hallway. Lights fill the stairway down to the tomb and I hear shouting in the distance. Tim pushes Patrice ahead of us into the hanger. I look back at the rows of deceased helicopters and wish God could restore one of them the way He brought life back to Chloe's heart.

Patrice's docile behavior vanishes as we walk towards the door to outside. Terrified of being burned by the sun, she tries to run. Tim grabs her by the arm with a vice like grip.

"Wait!" she begs.

"We have to go and you're coming!" Tim roars.

"No, there's another way!" she insists, hysterical.

Tim opens the door, ignoring her.

"There's a helicopter!" she screams, completely unraveled.

I've never seen Patrice lose her composure. She stands in the doorway, both arms out, clutching the door frame, with tears on her cheeks. Tim shoves hard against her chest and she stumbles out into the sun, screaming. I drop Matt's hand and push past Tim, grabbing Patrice's gloved hand and pulling her back inside the hangar. She falls to the floor in a heap.

"What are you doing?" Tim yells at me, "We have to go now!"

"Whoa," Matt cautions, stepping between Tim and I.

"Didn't you hear her?" I yell around Matt. "She said they have a working helicopter!"

"What are we going to do with a helicopter?" Tim screams.

Matt, still in between us, takes another step towards Tim, "The Lord is going to take care of us, there's no reason to panic."

Tim and I pause mid-scream and stare at him, neither of us used to a Spirit-filled Matt.

"I've been in a helicopter a few times. I think I could fly one," Matt says almost cheerfully.

"Where?" Tim growls at Patrice.

Patrice looks up from the floor. Her face is blistered and blackened by the sun and she is crying.

"Where?" Tim says again, lifting her by her shoulders and shaking her.

She looks remorsefully into his eyes and then trains her gaze at the far corner of the hangar. Tim stares hard in the direction Patrice is looking and then reaches out his hand.

"Chloe, the button."

Chloe lays Patrice's button in Tim's hand and whispers something into his ear.

His face and shoulders soften slightly.

Holding up the button, Tim threatens, "If you are lying..."

Chapter Fifty-Three

Every Time A Bell Rings

Tim pushes Patrice ahead of us towards the corner and we follow silently after her. Matt finds my hand again and squeezes. I look up at his calm, pleasant face and feel slightly disappointed in myself. He's faithful. He's Alive. He's certain that nothing can harm us unless God allows it. I'm a little ashamed of my doubt. Then, the alarm begins to sound and every thought but panic is pushed from my mind.

At the alarm's first blast, Tim swivels with lightning speed and knocks me down on his way to Chloe. He wraps his arms around Chloe, Helen and Crissa, protecting them from Pravda's signal with the device he brought. In that same moment, Patrice, Hazel, Matt, and my dad fall to their knees in agony.

I drop to my knees, not in pain but desperation. Matt is moaning in my arms, arching his back and twitching from the signal that is sending excruciating sound waves through his brain. Ten feet away, my father and Hazel are spasming and groaning on the cement floor. I pull Matt with all my might towards Tim and the girls. Towards the device that will block the signal.

Tim, with his arms around the girls, maneuvers towards me. When Tim is close enough to reach out and touch my shoulder, Matt's struggling subsides. The circumference of Tim's device only provides about four feet of shelter from Pravda's signal. Matt lies panting on the ground as he recovers from the pain. I look up to see my father and Hazel still writhing. I start towards them but Tim grabs me.

"Get in the center and hold this!" Tim barks, handing me the small device.

Trusting Tim to help Dad and Hazel, I plunge into the middle of the peach spandex suited bunch. In the nucleus of space between Helen, Chloe and Crissa, I find myself pressed against the crying newborn in Crissa's arms. I push hard against the panicking girls, forcing them away from little Leila. Tim appears on the edge of our circle with Hazel. Her eyes are closed and she is unconscious. Matt stands slowly and Tim transfers Hazel into

Matt's arms. Patrice shrieks in pain nearby. Tim darts towards her.

From inside the circle, I can't see my dad. I don't know if Tim has already helped him or if he is still twitching in agony on the floor. The bodies pressing against me are making it hard to breathe and the baby won't stop crying. Crissa bounces the little one in her arms, crooning at her. The siren outside is still blaring and the baby's crying intensifies, echoing around us in the metal walled hanger. Bleating in between the rhythmic lulls of the siren. Unending noise pollution.

Siren

Crying

Siren

Wailing

Siren

Screaming

Patrice's campfire face appears on the other side of Chloe and Helen. Patrice's orange makeup and red and black burns look like a mask of embers that are still smoldering. She is weeping and leaning against Tim. I spin inside the circle, looking for my dad. I don't see him anywhere.

"Where is my dad?" I shout at Tim as he pushes the moving mass of peach arms and legs towards the corner Patrice had been leading us to.

Tim looks straight ahead, ignoring me. Confirming the dread that's been building like a volcanic eruption inside of my chest. I fight to free myself from the center of the huddle. Tim grabs at the collar of the white coat I'm still wearing, holding me back.

"Let me go!" I scream at everyone around me.

"The signal disrupter, Ivy!" Tim exclaims, ripping the device from my hand.

I push against the current of the moving group, breaking free as they wash over me. My dad lies still on the floor across the room near the open door. The alarm is still sounding outside. Matt is calling my name. Newborn Leila is still bleating. But none of the sounds matter. My daddy is lying still on the floor. I stumble towards him.

How?

How can I live through another loss? How can God take him away from me? What was the point of freeing him only to lose him moments later?

I drop to my knees next to the gray bearded man I barely knew. Loss clogs my throat and the weight of it is unbearable. I feel smashed down, shattered into meaningless pieces. I lean closer to the wrinkled face that smiled at me in the Tomb and the weight of grief on my back tips against me and drives me downward. I lie against my father's filthy clothes and grind my cheek against his shoulder. I'll never know now.

Never know how he came to be here.

Never know when he found Life.

Never know if my mother found Life.

Never know if she died or is alive somewhere waiting for my dad to return to her.

I'll never know and it was all for nothing. I came here for Dad and Aunty Betty. They are both gone. I can't leave without them. I'll stay here and die next to my father. I scream into my father's unmoving shoulder. Pravda's alarm screams with me.

*****

"Ivy."

I lay unmoving against the wrinkled clothes of my wrinkled daddy.

"Ivy, everyone is waiting on the chopper. We have to go now," Tim says over the sound of the alarm.

I open my eyes where I lay on my father's chest and look out the open door at the building Pravda has kept me in for the last six months.

As though all of Heaven was against us not for us, a troupe of Pravdanian masked guards appears at the door on the other side of the sunlit parking lot.

Tim crosses to the open door and slams it shut. I watch silently as he flicks his arm, igniting the electric rod in his hand, and plunges the blue sparkling stick into the electronic lock box next to the door.

Kneeling back down next to me, Tim says, "Ivy, I'm so sorry. We're out of time. We have to go now!"

I don't answer him.

I don't move.

"Matt needs you, Ivy!" Tim begs.

I hear another sound. A helicopter spinning to life. It's a distinct sound - the blades rotating and beating at the air. Outside, Pravda's guards have reached the door. They are banging against it and screaming as the sun burns them. A few feet away from me a window breaks and a hand reaches through. All the windows are barred from the inside but more panes of glass shatter in succession along the wall. More hands reach through and screams come through with them.

Tim tries to pick me up. I struggle. He scoots me against himself and slides his arms beneath me. I slap him hard across the face and all my grief and fury goes into the motion. Tim falls back in shock and the look he gives me - he horror and hurt on his face - it's everything I feel in my soul. He stares at me as I crawl away from him and drape myself back over my dad. I've decided to die here.

I AM DONE.

Tim shoves me off of my father and I roll over against the cold cement. Tim picks my dad up and cradles dad's dirty, limp body in his arms. I look up at him from my grave on the floor. He leaves me there. I turn my head to watch as he hurries across the room with my father in his arms and disappears around a long dead airplane.

I lay beaten.

I lay lost.

I lay ruined.

I lay empty.

I am incapable.

My feelings are burying me like dirt over my open grave.

But -

I am suddenly not the only thing I feel. I feel Him there. He seeps in through a crack I left uncovered. He is there and He aches with me. He is there and He mourns with me. He is there and He pleads: *live.* He fills me up with ice and fire like when I prayed for Harmony. Like when I prayed for Hazel. But this healing is for me. For my broken heart. He helps me lift my head and then my arms. He pulls me to my knees and then I lean against Him as I climb to my feet. He whispers: *run.*

I run.

Glass shatters around me as more windows break and gloved hands appear along my path. I veer away from the windows and sprint towards the sound of the helicopter somewhere on the other side of the wall. A door at the very back of the room hangs open for me and I dart through it.

Outside, the helicopter shimmers in the sunlight. The blades spin where it sits inside a paddock; fenced all around by tall chain link fence with razor wire. Peach suited arms are outstretched, waving me towards the chopper's open door. I duck my head and run as the wind from the blades buffets against me. Patrice cowers in the shade of the white and silver helicopter, her burnt arms ready to help me in.

As I reach the open side door, I look up to see Helen pointing behind me with a warning on her face. Before I can turn, my limbs lock in sudden excruciating pain. Electricity zips through my muscles and bones like lightning through my body. The pain is emanating from my leg. As I fall, my legs twist and crumple beneath me. I fall on my hands, protecting my pregnant belly from the ground, and my hands light up with pain. I look up to see the pig-nosed guard from the Tomb standing over me with an electric shock rod. His mask-less face is twisted with malice.

The pig-faced Pravdanian raises his rod to swing it at my face and then he freezes with his arm above him. His mouth opens in a scream I can't hear over the roar of the helicopter's blades, and he drops the electric rod. Patrice appears behind him as he falls to his knees. Patrice, with blood on her white gloves.

The silver-suited man falls forward onto his face next to me, a long sharp piece of metal protruding from his back. Patrice saved me. Tim pulls me up into the chopper as Patrice and I stare at each other. The sun has burned her face beyond recognition but she stands still and stoic as I stare back at her. I hold out a hand to her. Asking her to come with us. She shakes her head, *no.*

Behind me, Tim screams to Matt who is in the pilot's seat, "Go!"

Matt cranes his head around the seat and his eyes find mine. He looks sad for me and relieved. He turns back around, and I stare out the open door at Patrice. Her skin is smoking. She lifts her bloody, gloved hand in a farewell wave as the helicopter lurches forward along the ground. I lean towards the open door to watch Patrice fall to her knees alone as we move away from her, leaving her susceptible to the signal once more. She lies on the cement, crumpled in a small ball as the sun burns down on her and the Sef I in her ear incapacitates her.

The helicopter skips across the short yard. Up a few feet then back down and then up again. The girls and I hold on to each other. None of us are buckled in and the door is still hanging open. Crissa clutches Leila and wraps her hands around the baby's ears. The noise of the helicopter is deafening and the baby's new ears are so fragile.

Helen stands up, stepping over Hazel who is still unconscious, and leans over to close the door. The chopper tips at the wrong moment. Helen falls forward, and I grab for her just in time. Helen's shoulders and head hang out of the open door for a moment before I snatch her back in. We pull the heavy door closed and cling to each other.

Tim yells at Matt over the noise of the blades, "Can you do this?"

The fence around the paddock is dangerously close to the spinning blades of our wobbly helicopter. Pravdanian guards are pouring through the door from the hangar, running after us. Matt shouts triumphantly as the helicopter lifts suddenly into the air. My stomach lurches with it. We move jerkily up into the air and out of Pravda's clutches. Tim points off into the distance and the helicopter tips to the right. We leave Pravda behind us. I leave Harmony there alone. My father's empty body lies still and peaceful next to me as we fly on angels wings away from his killers.

*****

IMMANENt Coming Soon!

*****

Elizabeth Forkey

Elizabeth Forkey is a Christian blogger, novelist, and an award-winning creative writing teacher (she has a keychain to prove it!). Her debut novel INFEC†IOUS is a Christian Post-apocalyptic Zombie Love Story and is the first book in The INFEC†IOUS Series.

The next book in the series, IMMACULA†E is available now; and, the final installment, IMMANEN†, is expected to hit the shelves Spring of 2016. Elizabeth is also an award-winning sugar artist and cake sculptor and the mother of two very adorable, outspoken daughters.

www.ingramcontent.com/pod-product-compliance
Lightning Source LLC
Chambersburg PA
CBHW060540180626
46817CB00002B/650